THE
CUNNINGHAMS

THE
CUNNINGHAMS

A Legacy of Memphis

J.M. HOPKINS

ARCHWAY
PUBLISHING

Archway Publishing books may be ordered through booksellers or by contacting:

Archway Publishing
1663 Liberty Drive
Bloomington, IN 47403
www.archwaypublishing.com
844-669-3957

ISBN: 978-1-6657-2562-0 (sc)
ISBN: 978-1-6657-2560-6 (hc)
ISBN: 978-1-6657-2561-3 (e)

Library of Congress Control Number: 2022911481

Print information available on the last page.

Archway Publishing rev. date: 01/09/2023

Dedications
For my darling bride Carol –
"No man ever had a finer help-mate!"

For my stalwart son Michael-
Thanks for listening patiently to all sorts of excerpts!

For my faithful brother Steve -
Thanks for your merry band of readers, providing so much insight!

PREFACE

In order to understand this story a little better, you perhaps would want to know a bit about me. I am, indeed, a product of the city I describe. I populate the story with characters *often* derived from and inspired by individuals I met, knew, and worked with. Fictional though they are, they are, nonetheless, believable.

The story of a frontiersman's quest to establish roots and a family legacy on a wind-swept Texas prairie settlement merely *begins* the tale of a clan for whom redemption is a way of life.

Along the way, meandering in much the same way as the mighty Mississippi does as it passes by Memphis, nearly one hundred years of the Cunningham family passes and, thus, its interaction with the city. This yields tales of love and loss; tragedy and redemption; and the story of good, strong men and the remarkable women who love them.

Having said these things, I say plainly here at the beginning that this is a work of fiction! It is.

Now indeed, some of the names represent actual Memphians and other Americans of historical, social, or other noteworthy interest, and I have portrayed them and their actions as accurately as I can. Other characters mentioned in this tale are completely fictional, and any resemblance to actual living (or deceased, for that matter) persons is entirely coincidental.

I sincerely hope you steep yourself in this tale of a lasting family and the beautiful and vibrant city that they, through their generations, helped shape.

With these things said, I now invite you to sit back, relax, and most especially:

Enjoy!

Chapter 1

THE CROCKETT PARTY GETS TO MEMPHIS

As a crossroads, Memphis has always had its share of less-than-savory characters passing through. As a meeting place, it has frequently had a significant role in American history by bringing together diverse individuals for interaction and events with significant impact. Nonetheless, Memphis could always manage to spawn home-grown characters of its own. From river rats and pirates in its earliest days, to Machine Gun Kelly in the 1930s and from early musicians like W. C. Handy and Memphis Minnie to Elvis Presley and his worldwide acclaim, Memphis has produced movie stars, authors, singers, comedians, scientists, and leaders in almost every field of human endeavor. It only seems right that Memphis would also produce some scoundrels, too!

1827

Val Dimand stood resolutely on the bluff overlooking the busy landing area. The place where he stood was along Front Street (and Front Street it is to this day), and it gave him a bird's-eye view of the doings below. He had become quite adept at scampering down to the water's edge rapidly in order to quell impending trouble or to help someone unfamiliar with the rules and etiquette of putting ashore along the Mississippi at Memphis. Val had, earlier in the year, become one of the newly established town's first peace officers (a total of eight volunteers in all) and was assigned to watch the waterfront. The flatboaters and keelboaters who came up from the water's edge were, by and large, a rough-and-ready bunch. Frequently armed to the teeth, they did not instantly convert from the skills and attributes that kept them alive on the sometimes treacherous waters easily into civility. Add to them, a generous helping of wide-eyed farmers on rafts or in wagons, along with every kind of con agent, grifter, pickpocket and ne'er-do-well known to man, and you had what Val considered an interesting cross section of humanity. Much like the smells along the waterfront, it changed almost daily.

Also very interesting to him was the sight of Angie MacFee skipping lightly across the walkways separating the boat moorings as she made her way, presumably, back to Levi Gold's dry goods and sundry store with an order for supplies such as flour or meal, eggs, or the like. Many of the boaters along the river needed fresh supplies to continue their journey downriver, and Gold's was happy to supply them. If the order was small enough that Angie could carry it to the river's edge in a couple of canvas bags, she would collect payment first and then go to Gold's and pick up the order, returning with the completed list in good time.

If an order was too large or heavy for Angie to deliver by hand, Mr. Gold had a light wagon built, which was perfectly-sized to navigate between the moorings. He employed a middle-aged fellow as a clerk who could double as a deliveryman on such occasions. Henry Speck, honest as the day was long, was ideal for this duty. He could write, do sums, and knew how to measure out partial quantities to give the customers exactly what they wanted. Henry was assiduous with the monetary transactions, as was Angie herself. Mr. Gold's delivery system worked well for those customers who did not want to make the climb up the bluffs to Front Street and then the quarter-mile walk up it to visit the store itself. For those who did choose to make the trek, afoot or ahorse, a dazzling and growing array of wares awaited.

Val cared very little about how well Gold's marketing and delivery system was working for him; he cared quite a bit about the trim set of legs, pert bosom, and mop of honey (almost orange) blond hair prancing his way. He had hopes of making their casual, "once-in-a-while" couplings much more permanent.

She, for her part, really liked Val and his physique and used it for her pleasure as it suited her. But she enjoyed the company of other men as well, so the current situation suited her just fine.

Val glanced at the sun and reckoned it was about three in the afternoon. He had been at his post since just after daylight at about seven that morning, and it had been a mild but interesting day so far. Several trips down to the water's edge had been necessary. There, he'd assisted the "landing fees" collector in making some of those unfamiliar with putting ashore at the Memphis municipal landing aware that using these facilities now carried a cost. The fees were clearly posted on two large, hand-painted signs near the water's edge for those few who could read. These charges were based on the size of vessel, the length of stay, and the mooring services needed. He had even passed by Angie on her way with an order, and she'd treated him to an affectionate hug, a light peck on the cheek, and a promise to meet up later that evening at Wilson's Tavern for a light supper and drinks. The afternoon sun had positively lit her orange-blonde hair to radiance.

Although everyone assumed Angie was Val's girl, nothing was really set in stone. She was attracted strongly to him, and he to her. Angie enjoyed the implied protection that her closeness to Val generated, and he would easily have that job at the drop of her hat or hankie. Though they did get mutual benefit from each other, they weren't yet exclusive.

Probably since the first people navigating the wide Mississippi, putting ashore at this conveniently wide section of riverbank had been free as could be. However, now, this was a part of the Town of Memphis and subject to legally mandated charges as outlined by the fees collector. The hard men who navigated the river for a living frequently didn't take well to being told what to do, much less parting with cash money, and sometimes disturbances erupted. Val was used to wading in vocally on an impending altercation but, these days, seldom had to assert himself physically. Above the normal noise and clangor of the waterfront, his voice carried, and his presence backed it up.

Val Dimand was an imposing specimen of a man. At just a shade over six feet, he was easily taller than most men of his time. At 220 pounds of lean-muscled power, he was agile and amazingly swift for his size and honed by life on the frontier for action. No one who saw him took him for granted as an easy mark. Women, for their part, saw him as highly desirable and a prime catch.

Besides being imposing in his own right, Val wasn't alone at the landing. Just as Val was stationed up on the Front Street bluffs to over-look the landing area, his partner, Ben Davis, was stationed down among the people bustling in the landings themselves. By talking to them di-rectly, as well as sidling up to them and just listening, Ben was able to keep tabs on the general mood on the landing area and spot potential trouble before it became such. By going down periodically and consult-ing with the older and less-mobile officer, Val could keep up with the day's undercurrents in something close to real time. Ben's significant contribution to this partnership lay in his lack of physical intimidation. To just look at him, he seemed like the neighbor you'd known for years and could tell anything, or maybe a man you'd just met but liked right away. So, even though Ben wore the same badge and uniform elements as Val, he got to hear much of what the bigger officer might not.

Just this morning, Ben had heard that Jim Bowie and a fair-sized group of his Arkansas toughs would be in Memphis that very day to meet up with and travel together with Davy Crockett and his companions. Ben's informant couldn't be specific about the purpose of the meeting or even the veracity of the rumor. Word had also come from the officers assigned to patrol the two roads leading south out of the young city and heading toward Mississippi's farms and plantations that Barry Raider's old gang had been making a stir down in Natchez over the previous weekend and was seen heading north toward Memphis. When Ben re-layed this tidbit to Val, they both recognized it as potentially troubling news. Just a few years before, Raider and Davy Crockett had had a vicious two- hour fight on the river, and there might still be bad blood about that.

Both Val and Ben recognized that the potential for trouble from three armed groups of hard men (used to getting their own way) colliding in Memphis, was too great to ignore. They devised a plan to have Ben speak to Bowie, since he was already familiar with him, while Val would seek out Crockett (if he did come through) and speak to him about the advisability of avoiding trouble.

———————◆———————

At dawn that morning, they had come. Ghostlike out of the mist at the woods' edge, six buckskin-clad riders who looked tough and capable rode with their rifles across their saddlebows. Aside from the parting of the mists, the sole additional clue that the riders were passing was the creaking of the leather of their saddles and sounds from their horses. A Crockett-led party was seldom less than six men, because Davy liked to have at least two men on watch at any time through the night, and with six men, the shifts could be rotated every three or four hours. Practicalities and preparations such as this ensured that Crockett was popular as a party leader. Certainly, trouble with warlike Indians was not as prevalent as it had been some years earlier, but a band of roving thieves or ruffians could make off with most of your supplies and leave members of your group shot or beaten in their wake. A war party from one of the supposedly-"tamed" tribes around could also be real trouble and, thus, should be avoided, if possible.

So it was that good scouts and guards were a hallmark of a Crockett band on the move. As they traveled through new territory, each member was taught by Davy to frequently look behind them at the area they had just passed through. Picking out landmarks would help guide them if they happened to come back that way, and sharing that information with the other members would help the group. Thus, a return trip was not made through "unfamiliar" territory.

Another hallmark of a Crockett party was its ability to shoot. Of course, each frontiersman was often quite a marksman in his own right, but Davy stressed fire discipline when faced with the need to shoot. Massed fire against a charging group of men and the use of a second, already-loaded rifle to fire again before adversaries could reload had often been a tactic thwarting an attack by a seemingly superior force. Davy Crockett himself was known as a crack shot and frequently proved it by providing fresh meat for the group as they went along their way. A couple of the other men were very nearly as good.

The six men in the Crockett party were an interesting assortment. Besides Davy himself, Loane and Slattery were a couple of Crockett's acquaintances from over near the town of Jonesboro, Tennessee. They had established a freight-hauling enterprise between there and Fort Nash (today known as Nashville) in order to supplement their meager farm earnings. But they were along on this particular journey because of their familiarity with the Caddo Indians of east Texas.

Crockett had gotten a letter from Steven Austin down in Texas asking if he would be interested in guiding potential settlers to the new lands Moses Austin, Steven's father, had received grants for from the government of Mexico. Crockett would be paid handsomely for the effort, Austin assured. Since Davy was already familiar with the route through Arkansas and down into Texas, he decided to go down through Mississippi and Louisiana and then westward into the eastern portions of Texas, where Austin was establishing some of his settlements, to see if that might be an easier route for families on the move. They'd pass right through the Caddo lands on the way.

Loane had assured Davy that this could be all right—if something came of it for the Indians in the way of trade or fees. As a boy, he had spent time among them and knew them to be a peaceful and industrious people. Living as they did in the swampy area of western Louisiana and eastern Texas, they were very familiar with the conditions there, and Loane thought they might easily hire out as guides through that part of the journey.

Norman Slattery agreed with his partner wholeheartedly about the Caddo and their suitability for this journey. He himself had had a Caddo woman for a time until she had been taken by the pox, and he looked forward to being among them again.

Another member of the party was Crockett's old friend and traveling companion, Billy Pickles. Though he steadfastly maintained it was his real given name, others were highly skeptical. Even Davy had his doubts, to a point. But he had been Billy Pickles through thick and thin, scrape after scrape, so how was Davy to say otherwise?

Billy was a crack shot, too. In fact, it was generally regarded they were "nip and tuck" when it came to that, though Billy would never say so. His high regard for his friend Davy bordered on worship, so many times had Davy pulled him out of a scrape. The fact that Billy had been there for Crockett just as many times mattered not at all.

The fifth member of the party was another longtime friend of Davy's, George Russel. He was an interesting character in his own right, to say the least. A completely competent frontiersman, especially as a ghostlike woodsman, Russel was the most educated. He also had the gift of being able to teach what he had learned, so many nights around a Crockett campfire were spent in discourse about politics on a national scale, civics, history, and even mathematics!

Well read (he had been educated in his youth in New Jersey) and urbane when it was appropriate, Russel was extremely useful when it came to making city officials comfortable with having this undeniably rough-and-ready, well-armed group passing through (much less stopping in!) their town. As glib-tongued as Davy was, if the mere mention of the Crockett name and the well-known coonskin cap wouldn't do it, George's habit of studying laws and regulations for immediate recall had pulled them out of plenty of tight spots when facing authorities.

Over the course of years, Russel's friendship with Crockett would help take Davy into the history books. But on this trip, he was needed to help make certain this was a sound business venture. Everyone enjoyed, and was enriched by, what George Russel brought to the group.

The final member was perhaps the most interesting, but certainly the most central to our tale.

Robert W. Cunningham certainly cut quite a figure in his buckskins with a New York State Militia "fore-and-aft" cap on his head as he rode at the end of the group. "Our compact Hercules" was how Russel liked to describe his new friend, and friend he was indeed. The young man from the woods of upstate New York already carried years of frontier experience before he joined the group outside Fort Nash and was worth his salt in almost any sort of scrape, the group had found.

Sturdy and impressively muscled, he was five feet nine inches of power with huge hands, and he wore buckskins like he was born to them. If he put his huge arms around something, it was going to move. If he got his massive legs churning behind the struggle, it was going to move in a hurry. Man, beast, nor obstacle of any kind could stand when Bobby Cunningham needed to get by.

At almost twenty-three years of age, Bobby could easily have been expected to be a "tenderfoot" when it came to the types of country and characters the group was expecting to pass through on this journey. Nothing could have been further from the truth. Davy himself had been fascinated by how much experience the younger man had already crammed into his life thus far. He spoke to him over supper for several evenings outside Fort Nash, and he admired the way Cunningham recounted his experiences quietly and without any trace of braggadocio.

Being in Bobby Cunningham's presence could be a refreshing change from the loud and boisterous company of many habitants of the rough-and-tumble frontier. He went about everything with a quiet assurance and never asserted himself forcefully into a conversation. If something needed doing, he did it quietly and promptly without attention being drawn to himself. If he did need to draw focus on something, he spoke during a natural pause in the conversation, showing respect for his elders and their experience. His questions were seldom interruptions and were always well-thought-out and relevant to the situation at hand.

In short, it was easy to be around Bobby Cunningham. But there wasn't a man in the group who doubted that, when it came to real trouble, Bobby would stand firm. Born in western New York in the territory of the Senecas, he had been in the woods practically since he could walk. He'd seen and been in his share of conflicts by the time he was a teenager. He'd spent time in the villages and lodges of the Senecas, Tuscaroras, Onondagas, and other of the Iroquois tribes of the Finger Lakes and western New York, trading with and escorting French Canadian trappers operating there during both peacetime and time of strife. Alone on many of these expeditions from the time he was seventeen, Cunningham always managed to return home to his beloved parents and siblings in one piece, although often by the skin of his teeth! He had even managed to enlist at eighteen in the regular New York State Militia, serving only a short time but falling in love with the order and discipline of military life, which would imbue his character for the rest of his days. The militia insignia he wore festooning his buckskins spoke of his fondness and regard for those times.

Later on, Bobby had had the opportunity to work for a group floating hardwood down the Ohio River from Indiana, on down the Mississippi to New Orleans on keelboats. It was during these trips that he developed his newly found but deep love for the water and working upon it. The monetary value of the wood being transported guaranteed his acceptance as one of the guards of its well-being, but he surprised everyone, including himself, by developing into a top hand on the boats as well.

The time he had spent in Louisiana had managed to introduce him to Barry Raider while on the river, and he described his impressions of the man as a "bully and a mean drunk," both of which Crockett thoroughly concurred with.

During his trips down the Mississippi, he had even put in at the new Town of Memphis. At that time, it was just a nice place to put ashore for a few hours of rest and resupply but not yet the trading destination it would become in just a surprisingly short time. So, as he and Davy had spoken at Fort Nash, it had become more and more obvious that Robert Cunningham might just be the right man to join their expedition through Memphis on down to Texas.

Plus, as a bonus, Bobby was a good trail cook! He could whip up flour, baking soda, butter, and water into a couple of pans of tasty campfire biscuits, and with just a few vegetables to chop and some fresh meat, he could make a tasty, rib-sticking stew. The delicious aromas of a campfire stew and biscuits had, more than once, drawn visitors to "set down and have vittles" with them.

Besides the prospect of not starving on this trip, the members of the party enjoyed the way Bobby had taken on the duties of quartermaster for the group, making sure each man had ample supply of clean, dry gunpowder and shot but also full canteens and other trail-necessary items before the start of each day's movement. He was a handy man to have around!

Shortly after they left the shelter of the woods, the group got on the southbound dirt road into town. Within just a few minutes, they rode into sight of the somewhat crowded and fairly bustling riverfront landing area. They caught their first view of Val Dimand at his post at the same time, and the quiet ride ceased its silence.

Val hailed the group with a friendly air and asked of them to hold up a few moments.

"Are you fellas by any chance the Crockett party that's supposed to pass through today?" he asked.

Billy Pickles replied, "Who's asking?"

Val was used to being challenged in this manner, so he didn't make anything of it but simply replied, "Val Dimand, sworn peace officer of the Town of Memphis, at your service, sirs."

At this, Davy spoke up. "I'm Davy Crockett, and these are my friends. We mean no trouble for the short time we're gonna be here. We intend to just pick up a few supplies to continue on our way, and then we'll be gone south through Mississippi down to Texas."

Val said, "Thanks, Mr. Crockett, but we got word earlier today that Barry Raider's old bunch were liquored up and heading up toward Memphis, and we'd like to avoid trouble if we can, in case they have hard feelings toward you still."

"Call me Davy," he replied. "What if we left one man to pick up supplies and follow in the morning, while myself and the rest of these 'trail rats' skedaddle on south of town and camp overnight off the main road? Would that work for you?"

Val's reply was immediate. "I believe that would be fine, Davy."

Davy called out, "Mind stayin' back and gettin' supplies, Bobby? You might have to find a place to stay overnight, and then find our camp in the mornin'."

Val piped up, "Mr. Gold's store is just a quarter of a mile straight up this road, and he'll probably have everything you'll want, so it won't take too long. But if you're still in town by dusk, come on down to Wilson's Tavern just a little farther down Front Street here, and I'll treat you to your supper!"

Bobby Cunningham spoke quietly. "I can handle it, Davy."

"Then that's what we'll do. Everybody tell Bobby what you'll need for the next week or two, so he can make a list. Got cash money enough, Bobby?"

Cunningham nodded and pulled out writing materials for a list as the other riders spoke of their needs. There was no haste or babble, just six seasoned men talking quietly.

Soon the other riders moved off while Val and Bobby spoke further, with Val pointing to direct the younger man where to head to begin his quest for supplies.

Meanwhile, Angie MacFee had been coming up the hill toward Front Street when she spotted the unmistakably dashing figure of Val Dimand talking and gesturing with another man, the sight of whom immediately made her knees weak and her crotch moisten. She had never seen a man like him. Young he was and with a physique that made her immediately want to run her hands all over him and her mouth, too, truth to be told!

Dressed in buckskins and high-topped moccasins, he presented a frontier appearance certainly. Adorning his tight-waisted, fringed buckskin jacket was an impressive amount of Indian beadwork along each side of his massive chest, with more beadwork as epaulets on each shoulder, topped off with what looked like some military insignia, and a military-style cap on his head. His longish black hair was pulled back into a ponytail, and his clean-shaven face was handsome, even from this distance! She immediately regretted her acrid sweat aroma.

But the thing that grabbed Angie's attention and just wouldn't let go was the breechclout he wore with such grace and ease. Far more common on the frontier in earlier days, this garment was something you just didn't see worn so much now, having given way primarily to full trousers of woven fabric. No one could deny its practicality for a man moving through rough, untamed country, but the exposed upper leg and hip that it left visible was more than a lot of men had the fortitude for. The stranger's breechclout, rather than buckskin, was a rather military-looking blue rectangle bordered in some sort of golden embroidery. Rather than hide the contours of his body in that area it covered, it seemed to accent them, particularly as he moved, which just drove Angie wilder with more visions of what she could touch and do if they were only closer!

As the strikingly handsome stranger began to ride on down Front Street, Angie realized she had been standing there gaping at him for far longer than was polite, so she gathered herself together to continue up the hill to Gold's with her last order for the day. Thankfully, that order was big enough that Henry Speck would need to deliver it in the wagon, and maybe she wouldn't have to go along to help.

Perhaps, when she got back, Mr. Gold would let her retire to her room in the back of the store, so she could lie down as she would tell him. What she wouldn't tell him was that it wasn't rest she needed but a chance to relieve the impossible throbbing in her loins. If her hands weren't enough, she had a specially carved wooden rod that would give her immense relief.

She strongly suspected she would go straight for the rod.

Chapter 2

LAST DAY, LAST THOUGHTS

Clean, clear and sweet, the tap water in Memphis has always been some of the best in the country, in my opinion. For cool refreshment, you couldn't beat a tall glass of it over ice on a hot summer day! Drawn from nine-hundred-foot-deep artesian wells, it was a treasure! Along with the tree-lined boulevards, imposing bluffs over the Mississippi, or the smells of any one of a myriad of barbeque restaurants, it was one of the thousand or more things that made Memphis the treasure it was and is, to this day!

1836

March 6 began as a dreary day; cold and still in the predawn morning; slowly it warmed as the time went on.

Of the original 232 defenders of the Alamo, only 81 men could "toe the line" that morning, and several of them required assistance to even do that. That they, as well as the "able-bodied" few who were left to fight, would do so was a testament in courage and fortitude.

Even more than this, the Alamo defenders were unique in their own right.

A more diverse group of men fighting for a single cause you were not likely to find anywhere. You had tall, lanky Tennesseans in buckskins fighting next to simple farmers in rough homespun clothing. Next to doctors, teachers, and other educated men were Tejanos of Mexican heritage, for whom the opportunity for freedom from the tyranny of Mexican rule seemed a worthy fight. They all fought next to men of many stripes who yearned for a life in this land called Texas.

They came for a variety of reasons; they stayed because they were trapped. Rescue wasn't coming; they were doomed to die, so they fought to the very end.

They came from just about every state in the United States; from Mexico itself; and even from places as far away as England, Ireland, Scotland, and Denmark!

They fought ferociously, bravely, and well to the end.

Thus far, it had been a busy day for Bobby Cunningham, beginning long before sunrise. Serving as he was with Dickinson's artillery units, much preparation of munitions and supplies was necessary before the day's strife began. Gunpowder loads were apportioned for each of the variety of artillery pieces still serviceable, along with carefully stacked single-shot and canister loads for each of the weapons still available. The chill night freshened the air and made the work go lighter, as well as making the air a bit nicer by morning. Though fainter now, gunsmoke still tainted the air. The desperately-close living conditions, coupled with the odors of the dead and the dying made the smell of the adobe mission unimaginably heavy. Defenders often retched at the aromas.

The two eight-pounder cannons mounted on field carriages with large wheels were Cunningham's favorite because of their ease in repositioning. They were able to fire against a new threat in the heat of battle quickly, as needed. Captain Dickinson, who commanded the artillery, was proud of the massive eighteen-pound gun they had managed to bring inside the Alamo's defenses before they were cut off. But Cunningham knew the smaller, lighter weapons would be deadly for the sort of close-in fighting he expected to occur. The bigger gun had been somewhat effective in counter-fire against General Santa Ana's massed artillery early in the battle. But with the arrival of fresh, more-experienced batteries, the Mexican artillery became much better positioned and harder to hit. Still, when the eighteen-pounder spoke, everyone listened.

Bobby's New York State Militia experience had included artillery service, and Captain Dickinson had been glad to have someone with that experience, since he had to teach his other batterymen literally everything.

Cunningham himself was assigned to lead a team responsible for keeping an ample supply of munitions, powder, slow matches for the touchholes of the cannons themselves, and full water buckets nearby to douse errant flames as they might occur. He and his team had done the prep work thus required before turning in for the night. They were ready for what turned out to be the last day.

Captain Dickinson had jostled his boot to awaken him with, "They seem to be stirring out beyond the north wall out there, so let's get ready!"

Bobby quietly replied, "It's already done, Captain."

"Good man! See to your personals then, Robert, and good luck!"

With a fatalistic grin, Bobby thought, *"I'm glad I got to know him."*

After filling up gunpowder horns for their long rifles and filling containers with fresh drinking water, Bobby Cunningham carried those items over to where his old friends, Davy Crockett and the Tennesseans, had bivouacked against the low east wall. They expected their early action would take place along it.

Deadly as a firing team, they had been used at Colonel Bowie's recommendation to pour accurate, long-range fire into groups of officers attending "officer's call" or cannoneers setting up artillery pieces and about to fire. The group proved lethal at this, depriving the often-inexperienced Mexican units (particularly cavalry) of leadership and making artillery service far more hazardous than it usually was.

Every man among the Tennesseans had several already-loaded rifles at his disposal. Each man fired his first shot and then dropped the spent weapon and repeated the process until all the rifles were empty. With a couple or three extra men serving as loaders to recharge the empty guns, the four (it had been five) core group of sharpshooters (out of the thirty

Tennessee volunteers who had come with Davy) could do an amazing amount of damage in a short time.

Davy had also taught them to establish individual "zones of fire" and the fire discipline of not moving the rifle around to find targets but, rather, allowing a target to enter their "zone of fire"—proving quite effective.

"Keep your aim and let 'em get right into it!" Davy said repeatedly.

Bobby had been delighted to see that his old friend still carried "Betsy" as his primary weapon, having regained it after trading it away for a horse, years before. Davy told him one night early in the siege that he had had the gun barrel melted down, re-cast, and re-forged by the same gunsmith who had made the original barrel in about 1795. "Worried about how weak the breech might be gettin' after all these years, so I went ahead and did it. I changed caliber at the same time, too. It had been .48, and I dropped it to .40. It seems to hit hard enough for anything but bear, and the bullet flies a might farther than you'd expect."

Davy continued, "Sometimes them fancy-coated officers with the big, plumed hats just move back a little where the .45s can't quite get to 'em, and I wait for the breeze to die down a bit, and I can pick 'em off with Betsy!" He chuckled. "The gunsmith, man he did me right! He even mounted the new barrel into the old stock, so the feel is the same as it ever was. Shoots maybe even a mite straighter than it used to, though."

Bobby said, "I see you converted it to cap lock, too"

Davy replied, "Yeah, it works better, and there's no time lag between pullin' the trigger and it firin'."

Billy Pickles sidled over at that point and joined the conversation. Cunningham was pleased to see his old trail companion again. It was the first time he had gotten to speak to his friend. He'd seen him, but with all else happening around them, there was just no time to speak to his old wilderness buddy.

"Hiya, Billy," he said delightedly.

"Hey, Bobby," Billy said with a wry grin on his face. "We sure got ourselves in a fix here, didn't we? Not much like the old days, is it?"

"Nah, but I'm still glad to see you! It's been a couple of years.

"I fixed up you boys some loads of powder and shot—all .45, I'm afraid," Bobby went on. "But I also made ya'll some biscuits, and I had a little stew left over from last night, so I thought maybe we could have a little breakfast for old times' sake before things start gettin' busy."

Davy's reply was quick. "That sets well by me! I could go for some vittles right about now. And, don't worry about the .45s, Bobby. I melted up some new lead, got out my bullet mold, and cast me three dozen new .40s last night, so I'll be able to send a goodly number of these so-an'-sos to Hades with brand-new, shiny bullets in their hearts!" Davy's next words were a quick, "Let's eat!"

The other two remaining Tennesseans, Henry Dillard and Jim Ewing, came over at Davy's behest and joined their light but very welcome breakfast and the pleasant conversation that ensued. They spent quiet moments reflecting on the paths each man had taken to lead him to this point. The gloom touched them all.

There was no false sense of hope among them. They each could see how their numbers had dwindled. Each one of them had said goodbye to others, not necessarily with words; sometimes a squeeze of a shoulder or a pat on the back had to replace words they simply could not muster.

For days, the Mexican buglers and other bandsmen had been playing the nonstop somber musical air "Degüello" (meaning "No Mercy") to let the defenders know they would suffer the ultimate fate. For men used to living on the frontier, this was a reflection of that life, where death could come quickly from a snakebite or an arrow, a fever or a falling rock, a bear or a bad man.

For those not so used to frontier life, it might have been different. But by now no man in this fight, seasoned or not, cowered in a corner. Regardless of their motivation for being there, they stood tall, proud of the battle they had put up so far, and determined to finish it with as big an honor guard of enemy dead as they could take with them to eternity.

So, the friends spoke of the original trip to Texas from Memphis, which had served as Bobby's "breaking in" and of subsequent treks together as a group of comrades, of his beloved Angie and their homestead here in Texas with their two wonderful little boys, and of how his memories of Memphis and meeting Angie there were cherished and dear to him. He told them of writing a letter to Angie and another one to his folks in Arkansas and how he hoped the letters had somehow made it through the Mexican lines. He regretted that Angie might not know what had happened to him, and he hoped beyond hope that she would not see him as having forsaken her.

◆

An hour later, after that final cavalry charge overran the crumbling defenses, Bobby lay mortally wounded. Pierced through the lower abdomen by a Mexican lance, with four additional sabre cuts to his legs and chest, he was trying to slowly and painfully crawl toward where Davy and his friends had made their final stand. They now lay in a ragged heap in the dust of the open plaza area between the main mission and the long, low barracks structure. The pall of smoke hanging over the crumbling mission signaled its fate for a long distance.

The first two attacks of the day were cavalry charges the Texans had repulsed. But with the third, the Mexicans had changed tactics. Attacking the higher north wall somewhat successfully, and getting some troops inside the plaza drew the attention of the defenders to that area, while a new cavalry thrust came over the low east wall. Instead of lancers to the fore, this time they had sabre-wielding riders come leaping over the low wall, hacking and slashing and then riding on through, followed by the lancers and their murderous, if unwieldy, weapons. This combination of forces was too much for the miserably few, thoroughly spent, and sadly depleted defenders to counter as they were literally torn apart by the heavy spears. The carnage was incredible, but it wasn't over.

While some of the desperate remaining defenders made it inside the barracks and the church, the ones trapped in the plaza became part of a scene that devolved into horror. For almost two weeks the Mexican forces had been halted; for this they took their revenge. Military discipline was totally lost in the furor.

Defenders who were missing huge chunks of their flesh and bleeding profusely writhed in agony in the dirt, while riders laughed and speared them again for sport. Other men, dazed and unsteady on their feet, even still trying to raise weapons or reach fallen comrades, were shot or ridden down and saber slashed to the amusement of the swirling Mexican troops, mad in their bloodlust. Most of the sounds were not cries from defenders, but yells and jeers from attackers.

No quarter had been promised. None was given.

Slowly, ultra-slowly through this horrible abattoir so full of gore and depravity, Robert Cunningham steadfastly made his way toward his fallen comrades, not through any false hope that they might be still alive, but rather, that he might be among his friends in death. Even through his intense pain, Bobby could still think clearly, and he knew his time was limited on this earth to just a few more minutes.

He wanted to reach his friends, not provide more sport.

As he had lain and crawled so slowly as to be unnoticed, Bobby had seen much of the atrocity around him, so he was careful to try not to provide another target for their blood sport. To this end, he had purposefully left the lance in his body, the massive iron tip protruding out of his back and the ten-foot-long shaft now a manageable two-foot stub, broken when the lancer's horse stumbled. The rider had toppled from the saddle at Robert's own killing blow with his axe.

By this point in the conflict, the defenders now fought with anything they could bring to hand. Ammunition gone and weapons broken, they still fought like wounded lions, using pitchforks and axes (as Robert had) or, as in the case of the remaining Tennesseans, swinging their now-useless rifles as clubs against their foes. Bobby had even heard the voice he recognized very well as that of Jim Bowie coming from the area of the infirmary, bellowing at the top of his lungs. After the Mexicans had broken through to his sickbed, Bowie had invited them to "taste my pepperbox pistols' flavor" and join him in hell! As they'd bayonetted the bedridden Bowie repeatedly, he'd cursed them in the little Spanish he knew and had flailed at them with his hallmark knife. All over the compound, defenders fought valiantly to the very end.

Robert had seen some of his friends' final moments with his own eyes, and his heart was filled with pride for their bravery and accomplishments. His journey toward them had perhaps covered ten or twelve feet when a new and impossibly-momentous eruption changed the complexion of the courtyard.

The Mexicans had charged the defenders' eighteen-pounder and pointed it toward the chapel door. The giant explosion and subsequent shattering focused all attention to the open maw thus created, as troops poured shot after shot into the opening. Through the thick fog of gunsmoke, dust and debris, Robert saw his chance, and he took it.

Since all attention was centered (even if only temporarily) on this new breach, Robert decided it was time to move out toward the Tennesseans more quickly. His previous tactic of avoiding attention by lying quietly face down with the lance head sticking out his back had worked well for having marauding Mexican troops dismiss him as "already dead."

Now, the need for more speed toward his friends made Bobby reach with his left arm around his back and grasp the bloody shaft of the lance just below the head. He drew it in one move out from his body. The pain wasn't what he might have expected, though it was intense, and the bleeding didn't seem to increase much. His hand came back bloody from gripping the lance shaft.

Robert felt as though he might well make it to his friends before he passed away, and it gave him renewed vigor for the effort. As he scooted along the ground lying on his side, he watched carefully for undue attention coming his way; seeing none, he picked up the pace.

When he touched Billy Pickles's fringed buckskin jacket he gave a small sigh of relief at having made it there. Davy's body lay just beyond. Bobby looked back along the way he had come and was pleased to see that the trail he'd left wasn't too obvious, so it might just be that no one would notice that he'd moved.

Nestling between Billy and Davy, Bobby felt a tremendous burden had been lifted from him; calm flooded his soul. As one last act of a true friend, he took Davy's coonskin cap and put it under his belly. This might help keep the Mexicans from easier identification of Crockett's body in case they would want to mutilate it later; it also helped compress and stanch the flow of blood from his own wound. By this time, Robert W. Cunningham was very near to the end of his mortal journey, but he was content.

As the clearing out of the barracks and church continued to rage into the morning, his thoughts drifted to memories far more pleasant than his present circumstances.

A final lift of his canteen and a welcome swallow of cool water down a parched throat and Bobby Cunningham was left with his memories.

His first thoughts were of Angie, little Bobby, and baby Oskar. He had a sharp mental picture of the three of them down at the stream running by the cabin. Oskar sat contentedly, laughing in the stream; Bobby happily, endlessly splashing him to his peals of delight; and Angie sitting peacefully under the elm, viewing it all over the edge of her book, her skirt hitched up above her knees, sunning her still-trim legs.

It was the thought of those legs that did it.

———————◆———————

As his body got colder from blood loss, delirium set in; warm memories began to flood his mind and so began to lift his spirits. Boyhood days with his brothers and sisters in upstate New York mixed in with images of his mom and dad swinging him by his arms among the tall trees near his home and suddenly gave way to images of his later teen years escorting French trappers through the Seneca lands toward Canada and of his adventures among the Indians and their lodges.

Sharp memories came of the time Waupee, chief of the particular band of people in that village, had been extremely pleased with the horse he'd purchased from Robert earlier that day. Afterward, he rode it clumsily but delightedly all through the village; then he invited the seventeen-year-old to stay the night in a lodge and have supper. The trappers had laughed heartily as they were leaving and made much sport of Bobby, though he had no idea why.

At dusk, when he was shown to the lodge, he began to find out.

———————◆———————

As he threw back the entrance flap to the lodge and stepped inside, his eyes took moments to adjust to the dark, flickering conditions within. A small fire was going underneath the vent hole at the top of the room, down at the end. A little smoky inside, the smell of the fire carried on it aromas of food cooking; in front of the fire were cooking pots with stew, venison chunks, and corn pones, all arrayed before him by three Indian women kneeling on the other side. Various animal skins were arrayed around the lodge, ostensibly to sit, lie, or sleep upon.

As he stepped more completely into the room, the lodge flap was closed behind him by someone on the outside, accompanied by a delighted laugh.

One of the women motioned him forward to sit on a bearskin as she said, "Eat now," in Seneca.

Robert, because of the part of New York he was from, was conversant with (though not necessarily fluent in) many of the Iroquois dialects. Seneca, Onondaga, and Tuscarora he could handle fairly well; for the others, he used common words and hand gestures to converse.

As he sat, the oldest of the three women pointed to the pots in turn, and Bobby nodded at each. At this, she put some of each dish into a generous wooden bowl and lifted it toward him. Familiar with using his hands to eat, Bobby began to satisfy his hunger eagerly. When he had pushed the bowl away from him, signifying he was finished, the woman, who he came to know later was called Bright Path, held out a gourd filled with water to quench his thirst. As he drank, she opened her robe to reveal her dark bosom. Bobby's surprise caused him to spill some of the water, but Bright Path just smiled a little smile and took Bobby's hand and placed it on her breast.

While he was feeling the warmth and softness of Bright Path, the middle woman (who Bobby came to know as Moon Flower) came around and sat behind Bobby, gently encircling him at the waist with her arms and, letting her long hair fall over his shoulder, smothering his neck and ear with delicate kisses.

Now, Bright Path stood up and walked over to another fur arrayed on the floor, where she was joined by the third woman. Bobby never found out her name, but he judged her to be the youngest. As this happened, Moon Flower's hand dropped to Bobby's leg and reached into the gap between his buckskin legging and his breechclout, bringing a sharp gasp from Bobby!

Moon Flower's giggle was like a brook babbling over pebbles.

Just as the third woman stepped behind her to catch it, Bright Path's robe fell completely away, revealing her form in the pale, flickering light. Standing before Bobby with her feet well apart, unabashedly but not quite brazenly revealing her entire front side to him, Bright Path presented herself. No longer young, she still was trim and honed by a life of work. She revealed shapely legs and a lean waist, flaring nicely into the chest that had, moments before, captivated Robert. Her husband had been killed two years before by a bear, and she had not had a man's touch since. Waupee was her brother-in-law and had known of her need. He had arranged this affair just for her benefit.

The tiny flecks of gray in Bright Path's hair were not visible as Bobby surveyed her form with newfound appreciation. He had seen glimpses of his sisters at bathing, even his mother (unbeknownst to her) from behind but had never seen anything like this!

As her last act in this appeal to Bobby, Bright Path got down on the fur on all fours—elbows and knees—with her trim but still-generous bottom pointed straight toward Bobby, and then looked back over her shoulder, straight at him!

By this time, Moon Flower's hand found the flesh inside Bobby's breechclout, and he had sprung to immediate attention, causing Moon Flower herself to gasp!

Third Woman had restoked the fire, meanwhile, and had positioned herself at Bright Path's side. In the newly increased light, Bobby watched with a mixture of excitement, lust, and not a little fear as Third Woman began to separate Bright Path's cheeks, thus exposing even more of the treasures found between. Then, she began to rub gently into the valley between them as Bright Path arched her back up and down, moaning all the while.

Moon Flower moved in front of the still-sitting Bobby and, dropping her head into his lap, began to undo his breechclout and belt. Freeing his rigid shaft, she dropped her head to the tip of it and sank her mouth on it as far as she could manage, while still stroking with her free hand.

Bobby's loud groan brought new laughter from outside the lodge. Though he was embarrassed, no thought was given to stopping.

Just then, Moon Flower stood up and gestured for Bobby to do the same. She quickly and quietly removed all the rest of Bobby's clothing, having him step forward out of the pile. After dropping to her knees and once again showering Bobby's shaft with exquisite caresses with her hands and unbelievable sensations with her mouth, Robert W. Cunningham knew with sudden clarity that the night he was about to experience would probably be a memory he would carry for the rest of his life!

As if on cue, Moon Flower stood again and, pulling him gently by his shaft, brought him over to Bright Path. Gently she got him to kneel behind the older woman, and then she began to rub the head of Bobby's manhood between the wet outer lips of Bright Path's exposed femaleness. Rubbing up and down her exposed valley in this way, Moon Flower made sure Bobby saw and touched each of the treasures nestled within before she finally brought Bobby's tip to Bright Path's hole and began to gently guide it in. Her lubricant was deliciously smooth.

Bright Path immediately arched her back and thrust backwards against Bobby's shaft, sinking it deeply into her. The feeling was impossibly exquisite for him! As she thrust back and forth against him, again and again, her moans became louder and wilder till Bobby finally had to grasp her hips, and holding his manhood as deeply and tightly into her as he could, Bobby exploded inside Bright Path. Their combined moans and grunts brought a new chorus of approval from outside the lodge. Grunts and jeers momentarily embarrassed him; he blushed.

As Bright Path fell back forward into the furs, her crotch glistening in the flickering light, Bobby was led by Third Woman back to his original place, where she lay side by side with him while he rested. In a little while, she gave him water and a bit more food (which Bobby needed), so he continued to rest and thought about what had just happened. In all of his times of glimpsing briefly the nude female form, he had never seen anything like what he had witnessed that night! And, in all his times of masturbating, he had never felt anything like what he had just felt, and he believed it might not be over yet. His inexperience really showed.

Third Woman had cupped his testicles with one hand and was manipulating the head and shaft of his rod with the other as she licked up and down the shaft itself. She moaned softly. Bobby rose steadfastly and rapidly to the occasion.

"I want some!" and, "It tastes good!" were the only words Bobby could make out clearly during Third Woman's occasional lapses from moans into actual speech. But Bright Path had not even paused in her moaning and, as Bobby looked toward her and caught her eyes looking back at him, he saw Moon Flower lift her head from Bright Path's crotch. Her face was thoroughly wet with Bobby's and Bright Path's juices as she smiled at Bobby.

The balance of the evening and on into the early morning consisted of frantic couplings between each of the women and Bobby, with every orifice explored, plus various groupings of the women and Bobby, servicing each other in every way possible.

Much of Bobby Cunningham's way with women was shaped that one night in Waupee's lodge.

———————◆———————

After his brief but wholly satisfying and incredibly valuable service in the New York State Militia, Bobby reflected he had done many things to lead him toward being a settler in Texas with a beautiful wife and two young sons.

Of the many things he had done, flatboating on the Mississippi had been one of the most rewarding, providing both interesting work and travel. The variety of people he'd met along the Ohio and Mississippi rivers had only added to a treasure trove of experience for the young Robert Cunningham. He hadn't had any expectation that he might be good at it, but it turned out he was. His tremendous physical strength served him in good stead when poling against the current or manning the steering tiller. When they occasionally hit a sandbar, floating debris, or other impediment, his gargantuan strength got them smoothly floating away downriver with the current. He grew to love the water and its flow.

Many times, Bobby had been the one to toss aside a floating log or entire tree trunk before it became trouble, and once he had single-handedly lifted the prow of the fully loaded keelboat they were navigating off the tip of a sandbar just above Memphis, making for a safe landing for all!

As they'd put ashore on the landing that time, Bobby had spent some time letting his tired, twitching muscles rest while lying up on the riverbank and enjoying the breeze coming over the water and ruffling the leaves with their gentle sounds, while he assessed the relatively new town of Memphis. He could easily see that its broad landing area could accommodate quite a bit of river traffic putting in for respite, trade, or both. He also saw the wide-open plains of what looked like good farmland stretching to the west over in Arkansas, as well as the plentiful stands of virgin forest on the Tennessee side, stretching right down to the bluffs overlooking the river. Yes, it seemed there was much here to draw a man of vision who had the industry to make that vision come to fruition.

Now, as a still-young man Bobby hadn't gotten all his wanderlust completely satisfied yet, but he could see the advantage of choosing a place to settle that promised plenty of opportunity for the future. Memphis, with all its potential as a transportation hub, industry center, and agrarian marketplace, certainly might be ready for him when he was ready for it.

Then, there was Angie. He'd been through the landings at Memphis by water several times before and hadn't seen her. But on his first trip overland to Texas through Memphis with Davy Crockett's party, he'd spotted her scampering among the tethered boats in the landing area and wondered immediately who this exciting creature might be and if she could stand to meet Robert W. Cunningham, frontiersman.

Throughout its history, Memphis had been a meeting place, and it was that day as well for the two young people.

For Angie had been stopped dead in her tracks by the sight of the handsome and robust young man in his unusual frontier garb, but he had ridden away down Front Street before she could accost him, disappointing her tremendously.

Thus, she could do nothing more than continue on toward Mr. Gold's general store and bring in the day's final order.

Angie MacFee pushed open the door, stepped in, and came face-to-face with Bobby Cunningham.

Their eyes locked instantly.

Chapter 3

ANGIE'S CHOICE: BACK TO MEMPHIS

Most people do not realize the depths of intrigue and depravity which imbued Memphis politics, giving it a sickness easily on a par with New York City or Chicago. From the days of E. H. "Boss" Crump forward to today, no dirty trick was unknown there; no foul deed was untried.

1836

Angie Cunningham absently noticed that the *clop-clop* of the horses' hooves seemed to be exactly in rhythm with the swish of their tails as the wagon made its impossibly slow journey toward Memphis. Sitting beside Val Dimand, she gazed at his profile for perhaps the thousandth time on this trip. She reflected that, if anything, he was even more handsome than when she had known him almost ten years before.

As the young Angie Macfee, back in Memphis she'd had an on-again, off-again relationship with the rugged French Magyar frontiers-man. She'd never even considering marriage or family as being applied to Valentine Dimand (pronounced Val-en-*teen* Dee-*mond*, as he would say, mimicking his grandmother's accent), enjoying rather the zest and liveliness of their times together.

All that changed the day she first saw and then met Bobby Cunningham.

To say Angie and Bobby's initial night together had been torrid would be a pale description.

Bobby had just completed his purchase of supplies needed for the rest of the Crockett party, and he had assembled them into a suitable pack for his horse. Asking if there was a space available to store them until he could load his horse for leaving, he'd accepted both Angie's invitation to join her for dinner and the place she offered to store his pack, which was in a corner of her room behind the store. Mr. Gold always thought it best to have someone on premises at night, and Angie was perfect, as she knew everything in and about the store. Val Dimand, the rugged peace officer, seemed to frequently be nearby or "checking in on her," so Levi Gold slept a little better at night knowing his place was fairly secure.

This night as they walked to Wilson's Lodge to eat, the beautiful young girl filled Bobby's ear with observations about Memphis and various people and places she thought he might find interesting. Of course, the thing Bobby found most interesting was Angie. This bright, bubbly girl had him captivated.

Angie tried to tell Bobby about her friend Val, but Bobby had already met the lawman and shared his own impressions of the tall, striking peace officer.

"He struck me as the kind of man you could count on, even in the worst kind of trouble, and that's a great friend to have," Bobby opined as they walked. "And when he came to us with his request to avoid trouble with Barry Raider's gang, he was very respectful of our group and the inconvenience that his asking might cause us."

Angie chimed in, "I hated Barry Raider! He was a drunk and an absolute boor, and when he came to town and was plastered, he was hard on any women around. I barely got away from him with my dignity intact once at Wilson's, and I had the bruises to prove it!"

She went on. "The next day, Val wanted to break him up into little pieces when he saw what he'd done to me and I'd told him about Raider's behavior, but I stopped him. To this day, Val can't stand the sight of the man."

"Are you and Val together?" Bobby asked in a quiet voice.

"No, not really. Nothing serious," Angie replied. "It's not as though he's asked me to marry him. And why would he? He has every woman in town—and any others who even just see him—lathering every time he walks by, so he has his choice!"

Angie didn't tell Bobby about the times, and there had been several, when she had come upon Val sitting at a more secluded table at Wilson's or Bell's Tavern farther up Front Street. Sitting down next to him on the bench for a few moments of light banter if there was time and scouting the room carefully, she would surreptitiously open his trouser fastenings and then reach in and massage his shaft until it was rock hard. This seldom took more than one or two tugs.

Then she would slip her specially made, ultrasoft lambskin sheath over his erection and straddle over him, settling into place while moving sensuously and slowly with him inside her until their mutual orgasms subsided, the noises muffled and stifled by their passionate embrace and the clatter of dishes and talk.

Angie's randy moments didn't occur every day, but when they did, she had to scratch that itch!

Before that, Val had simply enjoyed the secluded seating because it allowed him to survey the room, seeing who was in town and what trouble might come of it. But, after Angie snuck up on him and did that to him the first time, he regularly asked for "my table." Because having the lawman in the house added safety, he was obliged whenever possible.

Val Dimand was quite accustomed to women wanting him.

◆

Angie's midsection had a sort of "quivery" feeling as Bobby held the door for her and she stepped inside, followed almost immediately by the striking young frontiersman in buckskins. The racket of the eaters and the smell of food hit them at once, immersing them immediately into the atmosphere.

Wilson's, started as a frontier eatery, had grown and evolved with the town. It was a simple affair. Low ceilinged and longer than wide, its dark confines held a mishmash of furniture styles as far as tables, benches, and chairs went. Most were acquired from travelers passing through who could no longer put up with such burdens on their trek. A robust fire in a yawning fireplace at one end of the room provided light and heat, while each table was individually lit by its own lantern. The pattern of light thus created lent a shadowy aura to the place.

Memphis, a river town with more than its share of transients, was accustomed to all sorts of dress being worn by visitors. No assumptions about means were taken in frontier establishments in regard to manner of dress; a man might be dirty and unkempt simply because he was just in from hard work and merely wanted to make a purchase from his ample funds.

Wilson's was the higher-toned establishment of the two available; even so, it sported a variety of customers in various garb already seated.

Nonetheless, stepping in only shortly off the trail in his buckskins with the extensive Indian beadwork, the blue-with-gold-fringe military-looking breechclout exposing naked upper thighs, and the high-topped moccasins all topped by the military fore-and-aft cap with New York State Militia insignia, Robert W. Cunningham made quite an impression on the diners and drinkers at Wilson's from the moment he entered the room. Flickering light only enhanced this.

With his long, straight black hair pulled back into a ponytail for convenience away from his clean-shaven, strong young face, at first glance in the dim light, Bobby Cunningham might be mistaken for an Indian himself! His Herculean body, its contours barely hidden by the clothing he wore, moved with a woodsman-like grace through the assembled customers, followed in its every move by many pairs of eyes as he made his way toward Val Dimand's table, where Angie had already been seated by Val.

Standing, Val thrust out his hand toward Bobby and said, "Welcome, young man! Bobby, isn't it? Val Dimand, from earlier today on the road, at your service!"

The grace and effortless charm that Angie found so appealing in Val was on full display tonight.

"Please be seated, and join us as my guest for dinner," Val intoned, not loudly but firmly enough that many sets of heads (and the eyes in them) rapidly returned briskly to minding their own business.

After an exchange of pleasantries, dinner began in earnest. Their orders were taken by Belle Woods, the genial hostess for the evening at Wilson's. Meals were from a simple board of fare, primarily consisting of "breakfast," "lunch," and "dinner"—serving up whatever the cooks had prepared for each meal, with small embellishments and additions the only exceptions.

Belle was quite familiar with both Val and Angie, so she suggested small additions of steamed yams and fried potatoes to augment the evening's stew and corn dapples. The incredibly handsome, muscular young stranger seated with them accepted both with a smile that turned her insides to liquid immediately.

"My pleasure, folks! I'll tell the cooks right away," Belle said brightly before she made her way weaving through the tables toward the kitchen.

While they awaited supper's arrival, Bobby told Val of the overall plan for the Crockett party, starting the next day.

"Davy reckons we'll need about six weeks to travel to Texas, scout out the situation, see if we can even do what Mr. Austin is wanting, and get back to Tennessee.

"I have the supplies we needed and packed them for my horse, so I'll be on the road early tomorrow morning," Bobby continued. "Davy and the rest of us are camped south of town off the main road, so as to not run afoul of Barry Raider's old gang if they happen by, and we got word to Jim Bowie and his group to meet up with us on the South Road."

Val asked, "Are you familiar with Jim Bowie?"

"Yes, I flatboated on the Mississippi with him several times over the last few years, and I like him," Bobby intoned. "I know he has a reputation as being a tough customer, but he was always square with me. And I think that any bad idea about him is from people who don't really know him. I do guarantee you he is prepared for trouble if it comes, though."

"I've heard word he's sort of exchanged Arkansas for New Orleans as a home base, and he's trying to make something better of himself down there," Val put forth.

Bobby said, "That's interesting because my father came with me one time down the Ohio to the Mississippi, ferrying a load of hardwood to New Orleans. We got down here to Memphis, and he took one look across the river into Arkansas and said, if he ever got there, he didn't think he would ever leave."

"What's your father do?" Angie spoke up brightly. To this point, she'd been sitting back and enjoying the conversation between these two extremely desirable men, as well as the attention she had been getting by being in their company.

"Oh, he's a farmer in upstate New York," Bobby replied. "But he also raises horses—both saddle and draft."

"Arkansas's good country for both activities, so he'd probably easily succeed over there," Val put forth.

"I'm pretty sure he's going to really give it a try," answered Bobby.

At this point, conversation ceased. Dinner had arrived, accompanied by none other than "Chubs" Wilson himself. The rotund and jovial owner was delighted to see two of his favorite patrons, particularly accompanied as they were by the dashing young stranger in the unusual garb.

Chubs Wilson liked anyone who brought extra "color" to the place. People would talk. Talk was good for business.

Dinner was good. Very satisfying, it was filling as well.

Topping off this simple repast was fresh apple pie from locally grown apples, causing the diners to be sated and satisfied. They each sat back and enjoyed the atmosphere immensely.

Just then, Val had an idea.

He had seen Belle Woods's reaction to Bobby, and he thought he might take advantage of the situation. Val knew that often, when a woman is excited by a particular man but can't have him, she will lavish that excitement onto another, available man.

Val had had Belle a number of times, and he knew she could be exciting as hell.

She was pretty, quite slender, and a little older, but tight holed and ready to use any of them at any time. One of Val's favorites was multiple times in the back way, using his emissions to help lubricate for the next time. He had once managed three in a row, and by that last time he was completely submerged into her, to her delight. He'd awakened later to find his shaft being devoured by her ravenous mouth.

What also guided his thinking was the fact that she had a great place, secluded and remote, where she or he (or both) could make as much noise as was needed.

All these thoughts flashed through his mind before he spoke.

"Why don't you two young people go on ahead before it gets any later and get Angie home safely, and I'll stay here and take care of the bill," Val said with a wide smile. "Can you escort her back before you have to leave, Bobby?"

"Sure, Val, I'd be most happy to."

After quick good-byes, accompanied by a chaste peck on the cheek for Val from Angie, Bobby took Angie home.

Meanwhile, Val paid the bill and had an earnest talk with Belle.

———◆———

As it turned out, since it was a short walk down Front from Wilson's to Gold's store, Bobby had Angie home well before Val could make Belle wail for the first time.

There would be other wails and moans through the night—many others.

As the two young people reached the side door of Gold's that led directly into Angie's room, Angie spoke up boldly. "You don't really have to leave until morning, do you? It's quiet and warm here for you to stay the night, and I'd be pleased to have you here tonight."

With those few words fresh from her lips, she tiptoed up and kissed the handsome young man squarely on the lips.

Bobby's reply was somewhat breathless. "No, I can stay the night and leave very early in the morning. I'd be a fool not to stay, and I may be many things, but I hope I'm not that!"

With a very bright giggle, Angie turned to open the door. Bobby followed her inside, where she lit a lantern, latched the door, and closed the curtains. The room was pleasantly warm and dry. As she returned to Bobby, she undid the fastenings to the bodice of her dress before putting her arms up for his embrace.

As his massive arms encircled her in what she found to be an unexpectedly gentle yet firm embrace, their mouths met with a passion that surprised both of them. Swirling tongues found sensuous delight as they expressed their ardor without any words; no sound escaped at all, in fact, except the moans that were unavoidable.

At last, Bobby stepped back a little. With one fluid move he gathered her entire skirts into his massive hands and lifted her dress completely off her body and laid it gently and neatly over a nearby chair back. A similarly smooth move disposed of her full-length undergarment, leaving her naked before his rapturous view.

What a beauty! Bobby immediately thought. With her slim-tapered thighs, lovely calves, trim waist, and firmly projecting girlish breasts with their soft pink rosebud nipples, Angie was an absolute vision of female perfection.

After absorbing her with his eyes, Bobby immediately began to kiss not only her lips but also the nape of her neck as well, as he lifted her and carried her toward the bed. She responded by settling into his strong but surprisingly gentle arms with a sigh of content. So far, everything was going exactly as she would have wished, as if she had written it up as a story from her dreams.

Nothing in her life, not even from all the experience she had already had from men, could have prepared her for this! For Angie was a truly beautiful girl who had been pursued and won by males a number of times from the time she was thirteen. Her mom had told her one day,

"Aye, and you're gonna' to be one they can't leave alone. And, if you've got much of me in ya, you won't want to leave it alone, either!" Her mom had told her about having to outrun the shepherd boys back in Scotland in her youth and about what happened (in graphic detail, pointed out on her body!) when she no longer could. Angie's mom had explained that, though it might hurt a little at first, Angie was likely to enjoy sex so much that she'd seek it out herself.

She explained the troubles that that could bring—with pregnancy and bad marriage and, because of that, poverty and being tied to an unfulfilling life. She then gave Angie a newly made lambskin sheath with explicit instructions in its care and use.

Angie had been working on the waterfront for the better part of five years now and was familiar with (and even friends with) a number of the girls along the landing area who regularly sold their bodies for a living. She herself had been offered such compensation many times, but she refused, wanting sex to always be her choice, at her desire.

With all the preparation Angie had had in her life and the variety of men she had encountered, nothing but nothing had prepared her for this.

After Bobby had placed her on the bed, quite comfortably and with surprising gentleness, she was expecting him to perhaps continue kissing her on the lips, face, and neck and then seek some kind of approval from her before going further. Bobby did, indeed, kiss and caress her further in those areas, but then he moved immediately to her tight pink nipples. Pinching and pulling them gently, the word "beautiful" escaped his lips as he continued to generate waves of pleasure between her legs with the flickering of his fingertips over her mound and its now-moist divide. She wondered how in the world those huge but gentle hands could possibly be as light a touch as she was experiencing.

Just as she was beginning to moan uncontrollably at his ministrations, Bobby effortlessly flipped Angie over onto her stomach. With his left hand, he ultra-gently and sensuously brushed the orange-blonde curls of her hair off her shoulders. Her beautiful hair smelled faintly of shampoo and had a slight aroma of Wilson's Tavern's fare mixed in. His right hand returned to her crotch from the opposite side, plowing her slit with the work-hardened side of his palm, while rubbing her clitoris gently with his forefinger. Her bare shoulders now felt the touch of his tongue and lips, and as he moved inward toward her neck, Angie felt a new feeling down below, almost indescribably intense. By this time, she had become extremely wet between the lips of her mound, as her slot was being rubbed by the ridge of Bobby's hand.

As he had begun to caress her moist slot with his other fingers, his kisses and licks had started to move down her spine, causing a new tingling. The first shock had come when one of Bobby's moist fingers had brushed lightly across her other opening. Her slight gasp was followed by a soft mewling. She had already arched her back and brought her buttocks up into the air. Bobby was working his delight with her slot into a wanton expression of rut, and this widened the gap between her buttocks, exposing the little button of her anus.

Bobby's finger, and then fingers, circled the perimeter as he brought up more and more lubrication from her vaginal area, where it was beginning to drip onto the bed. The lube helped him to move faster and faster around the cavity while he continued to kiss along her spinal column, approaching her buttocks.

Bobby suddenly dipped his head down and began to fondle, nip, and kiss the delicious small areas of fat at the top of Angie's thighs. These soft little mounds would prove irresistible to him normally, but from behind, they were indescribable! As he kissed and gently caressed the backs of her legs, the view of her exposed valley between her gorgeous cheeks lay open fully to his view. As his tongue moved over her clitoris and up her slot, Angie flexed back toward Bobby to increase her clitoral pressure against Bobby's mouth, and her vigorous "*Yes!*" made even Bobby startle a tiny bit. He then used his tongue, stiffening it to repeatedly flick her clit with hard jabs, which made her gasp with each thrust. When he finally began to flick and suck the tiny bud as fast as he could manage, her orgasm almost lifted her off the bed.

As Bobby held her very tenderly afterward during post-orgasm, she realized he hadn't even gotten his clothes off; nor had he entered her in any way!

Robert W. Cunningham had seldom, if ever, met such a beauty, and he was going to take his time with her and make the most of it. What Angie had not been at all prepared for was how there was not one square inch of skin, one fold or fissure, or one opening on her body that Bobby had not caressed, kissed, or explored without pause. Moreover, she might easily have been shocked a day ago to even think she would let anyone do such things or touch her in such places, but, now that she had, she would do it again in a heartbeat.

In fact, Angie was weak and trembling with the idea that she might explore Bobby in the same way.

Her chance came in short order as Bobby stood and began to remove his clothes, starting with the high-topped moccasins. The short buckskin jacket he pulled off over his head, revealing his massive chest, tight abdomen, and lean waist. Unfastening his buckskin leggings from his tooled rawhide belt, he dropped them to the floor, exposing his massively chiseled legs.

As he turned from her and began to remove his belt and breechclout, Angie was treated to the view of this powerful young man bent over slightly, with many muscle groups shockingly exposed to her ravenous view and wanton imagination.

Angie thought she had never seen anything quite so magnificent and beautiful. She knew in those moments that she would do anything to please Bobby, dignity be damned.

She had never seen a man's penis hang down that far between his legs before, and when he turned to come to her, it was no longer hanging. That magnificent rod had become a spear projecting to the center of his flat belly as he reached the side of the bed, climbed in, and quietly lay down beside her.

Angie wasted no time on words as she smothered him with kisses and stroked his manhood with ardor. As she lay beside him doing these things, she realized she had changed in a subtle but important way.

Before, she had done these kind of things to a man when it pleased her. Now, her *only* desire was to please him, right now and for the rest of her life!

Her mouth was drawn like a magnet downward toward the head of Bobby's massive shaft; when her lips first tried to encompass its girth, she began to understand what a special prize this would be. Occasionally moving away from the head to smother the outside of his shaft with her lips, up and down, up and down, Angie got a taste of Bobby that, along with the smell and feel of him, had her quite intoxicated with him in short order. His earthy woodsman aroma did it.

As she continued with Bobby in and out of her mouth, he flexed deliciously one way and then another as he lay nude beside her. He began to try to touch and pleasure her as she was tending to him, but she pushed his hand away to let him know this was for him alone. Eventually though, her legs separated somewhat and her own hand inexorably found her slit and began its wild dance to bring her to heights of passion. Their moans and cries intertwined into the night.

Suddenly, his eruption filled her mouth with the liquid fire from his passion, a torrent that was huge yet dreamy in its flavor and texture. She had hardly swallowed the last of it before she was back at his rod again, caressing and kissing it as gently as a baby. Soon she was back to his face, playfully licking and kissing his neck, lips, and ears as she tried not to let him see the tears of joy welling up within her.

Angie could not explain it; it was somehow as if she was now suddenly happy.

Later, after she'd finally been able to work and accommodate his massive member fully inside her and she was rewarded with another gushing flood, she lay on top of him thinking thoughts that seemed to go in all directions. The one thing she knew clearly was, *I want this to be my future, with you, Bobby.*

Sometime later, while she was still kissing Bobby so softly it wouldn't have disturbed a butterfly, she felt him finally go completely soft and come out of her with a soft *plop*, letting his juices flow softly over both of them.

Angie fell asleep on top of Bobby, two gorgeous nudes floating on an afterglow that kept them motionlessly asleep till morning.

Bobby awoke first, while it was still predawn dark and began to do what he needed to do. He gently covered the still-nude and sleeping Angie, marveling all the while at his unbelievable fortune in coming to this point with her.

He then silently dressed and slipped out the side door with his pack of supplies, went down to the stable, paid his tab, and rode south down Front Street. Alone again in the pre-dawn still air of the silent town, Bobby remembered and smiled; he was coming back to claim his prize, oh how he was coming back!

Angie awoke with the first light leaking through the curtains, and the first thing her eyes focused on was the single red rose Bobby had found somewhere, plucked, and snuck back in to place lovingly on the pillow beside her. Even though she had a hollow feeling in the pit of her stomach at the very idea that he was gone, he had told her he would be gone about six weeks and would return after that, so she would give him the six weeks.

But, Angie MacFee wasn't going to be content for that six weeks! No sir, not until Robert W. Cunningham was firmly back in her arms was she about to be happy!

Oh, no indeed.

◆

With that emphatic thought, Angie Cunningham awoke on the sacks of provisions Val Dimand had arranged into a makeshift bed for her to nap on in the back of his dray wagon. The jostling back and forth along the uneven surface of the rough dirt road did nothing to brighten her mood upon awakening from such a dream.

For Bobby had indeed come back within the appointed six weeks, marching jauntily up Front Street, throwing open the door to Levi Gold's store, and announcing he was there to see Angie MacFee as soon as she was available.

They were married three days later by an itinerant Presbyterian minister who happened to be in town, with a beaming Levi Gold and an enigmatic Val Dimand in attendance as witnesses. A statement of marriage was filed with the city clerk for later transmittal to the state capital.

Two more days of taking care of sundry business, and they were on their way to Texas. Bobby spent quite a bit of that time, as Angie gathered and packed her things for the journey, conversing with Levi Gold about the masses of settlers about to pass through Memphis on their way to the settlements in Texas and their need for tools and supplies; Gold's might be able to fill such needs for them as they passed by. Mr. Gold was duly impressed with the budding business acumen Angie's new husband thus displayed, and he well intended to be prepared for this potential new stream of revenue.

Till the day she died, Angie never knew it was Val's lust for another woman that had sent her home with Bobby. She was simply happy it had happened that way.

For his part, Val always regretted that one night's rut had perhaps deprived him of this special woman's most beautiful and youthful years. For by the time he saw her again, Angie was no longer the spritely girl she had been. She was now a grown young mother of two, with lines etched in her face that had not been there before and a permanent depth to her eyes from losses she had suffered that he could not change.

But Val knew what a treasure Angie was, even yet, and he told her so. In fact, on the trip so far, Val had spoken more to Angie about his feelings for her than he ever had before. He told her that the intervening years they had been apart had shown him he had a love for Angie he just did not have for other women. Even though they might still be attracted to him, he no longer wanted their company; he wanted to marry Angie and settle down with her and the boys, for the family he hadn't had since he was a child. But would Angie still want him after all these years spent on the Texas frontier with Bobby and the boys?

These thoughts weighed on Val's mind as they clop-clopped toward Memphis.

Angie, after a break to feed and water the horses and let the boys run around for a few moments from being "cooped up" inside the wagon box, decided to come up onto the seat by Val again as they started off once more toward Memphis.

This had been a welcome break for the whole party, and the liveliness of the boys' play gave a fairly festive outlook, even to the road-weary adults. The sun proclaimed it to be midafternoon, which meant it was about three hours more before supper break and a stop for the night. The woods on this stretch came practically up to the roadway, making it still and hot - sleep-inducing.

Things had begun to settle into their "on-the-road norm" quite quickly, but the reverie was broken by Val's voice quietly but forcefully hissing, "Road agents ahead, I'm afraid.

"Let me do the talking. Keep quiet and in the wagon, and maybe we'll get through this all right." Val's voice had a rasp to it that Angie had never heard before. "Men like these are usually looking for travelers with more money or goods than we have, so they may give up and just leave us alone when they see what we don't possess."

The smaller of the two men in the middle of the road hailed them first.

"Hello, the wagon! Stop a while and take your rest!"

Val called back as he kept the wagon moving slowly ahead, "Thanks, friend. We've already done that, so we'll just be moving on ahead. Stand aside and let us pass."

The two did not move from the center of the road, but the smaller one called out again as he drew a pistol from beneath his jacket. "There's no reason for unpleasantness. We just want to share in your wealth and maybe your woman, too! So, you just step down real careful-like from that wagon seat and put your hands up in the air."

Val whispered to Angie as he handed her the reins and prepared to get down, "If they cut me down, get out of here as fast as you can and use my pistols to hold these scalawags off. Don't hesitate to shoot them; they'll rape and murder you *and* the boys if they can get to you."

Val kept his front facing toward the bandits as he got down from the wagon seat, and he smiled a friendly smile as he raised his hands upward and began to walk slowly toward the front of the draft team.

Angie was amazed at how coolly Val was reacting to these threats and prayed he wouldn't be hurt. She glanced down in the foot trough and saw four of Val's pistols lined up there for ready use: two single-shot dragoon or horse pistols and two of the fairly-new Colt Paterson five-shot revolving pistols. She knew they were all loaded and ready for action. And at Val's insistence, she had shot each one right at the start of their journey, just in case.

Val had thought two to one wasn't the worst of odds and had stopped at the right side of the road just as a hidden third man stepped out of the trees about ten or fifteen feet farther down the road. He was carrying a rifle of some kind, and really looked mean with a powder burn across the left half of his face.

Val spoke first in a voice he was sure Angie could hear; he wanted to make sure she was fully aware of what was going on each step of the way. "Well, it sure seems like you fellas have the drop on us, and we're at a real disadvantage here. What can we do for you to let us get on our way without harm to us?"

Ruined-face spoke up for the first time. "Oh, we'll take good care of your woman and the boys, no doubt. Just use 'em a little first, that's all.

Angie felt a little pat on her side as the tip of the barrel of one of the two Hawken carbines Val had kept in the back of the wagon began to slide forward. Little Bobby's quiet voice followed. "I loaded it, Mama. I used two balls and rammed them together. Just cock it, and you're ready to fire."

Angie slid the short rifle forward as far as she could without it being visible as Ruined-face continued to speak.

"But, as for you, Val Dimand, you're going nowhere—"

Action erupted without even the blink of an eye as Angie gripped the Hawken tight to her side as Val and Robert before him had taught her, cocked the hammer, and turned her body to face the sallow-faced road agent standing in the road with the pistol in his hand.

She pulled the trigger.

The explosion from the gun startled Ruined-face enough that he was slow in bringing his rifle to bear on Val, and the large, thick knife suddenly growing out of his chest made him stagger. He still managed to get off his shot, hitting Val in the upper left thigh. The horses began to whinny violently, and buck and rear.

Angie saw Val fall out of the corner of her eye, but she was busy controlling the frightened and plunging team. When she saw the bandit she had shot at trying to aim the pistol he was still holding, despite the growing bloodstains in his shoulder and chest, she grabbed one of the Paterson Colts, cocked it, and fired right into his ugly face as she plunged by. He fell to the dusty road, making a cloud of dust puff from the roadway.

She then saw Ruined-face trying to aim his rifle at Val lying on the ground and she cocked the Colt again and shot the outlaw in the side of his head, cocked again, and shot into his falling body. He too fell onto the smoky, dusty roadway.

As soon as she could get the panicky team under control, Angie stopped the wagon, set the brake, and looked back into the wagon at her frightened boys. Then she hopped down, running toward Val with the Colt revolver held in both hands before her.

With her main thoughts divided between the necessity of getting to Val's aid as well as protecting little Bobby and Oskar from these foul men, she ran with her heart in her mouth all the way to Val and dropped to her knees at his side.

A quick look around showed plainly that both robbers she had shot were down, still and silent, while the third fat man (who had seemed completely unarmed) was hurrying back down the road just as fast as his clumsy, stumbling gait would take him.

Just then, little Bobby's voice broke through the fog and confusion of her thoughts. "What are you gonna need from the wagon, Mama? I left Oskar to pat the horses' noses and keep them calm, and I'll go stay with them and him, too, so don't worry about us." He went on. "I just thought you might need some supplies for Val before I went back to seeing about Oskar."

"That's good thinking," said Angie. "Please try to find one of my clean white nightgowns to make bandages from, some scissors, a small knife, and the bottle Val keeps folded up in the oilskin in the wagon box."

"The whiskey?" Bobby asked.

Angie quickly replied, "Yes. That'll help clean the wound and ease his pain as well."

Bobby took off on his errand and was gone less than five minutes.

Angie had cradled Val's sweaty head to her bosom. After quickly removing her short outer jacket and wadding it roughly into a pillow of sorts, she gently lowered his head onto the more comfortable placement, straightened his un-wounded leg and unfastened the canteen fastened there.

Soaking her handkerchief in the water, she gently bathed the handsome face before her, cooing softly as she did. "Val, you wonderful man, if you hadn't had us so well prepared, the boys and I might have been seriously hurt right now. But we're all right, thanks to you. You know I love you." Angie spoke softly, almost a whisper. "Please get better. For us. For me. I need you."

Her tears may have been felt by Val on his face, for his eyelids fluttered at that point.

Angie kissed him gently. His eyes opened.

Just then, the boys arrived with Angie's supplies, and Val smiled weakly at them.

"Thanks, boys! Val's not hurt terribly badly, so back to the wagon with you two! Val's gonna be all right, but right now, I have to see to his wound. You boys see to the horses. Give them a little extra food and water and keep them calm. This will take a few minutes."

"Yes, Mama!" Little feet trudged up the road toward the wagon as Angie spoke.

The rest of the afternoon consisted of cleaning and examining Val's bullet wound and then bandaging it with clean white strips cut from Angie's nightshirt.

First, Angie let Val take a couple of mighty pulls on the bottle of whiskey while she cut up her nightshirt for bandages, and then she folded a leather strap into a compress that Val could bite down on so his outcries might not frighten the boys or the team. After kissing him gently and then putting the leather into his mouth, she told him how sorry she was that she was going to have to hurt him more. Angie then set about cutting away part of his pants leg and cleaning and dressing his wound.

The wound had both an entrance and exit point, so no bullet remained in Val's leg to poison him or cause the injury to fester from the gunpowder residue. The bleeding had been significant at the beginning, but had tapered off to a manageable level within a few minutes. Angie had made a couple of compress pads of several layers of the white cotton, fastened snugly into place by wrapping a band of the cotton around his thigh, tied off and held in place with a belt to put pressure on the wound.

Val's breathing steadied within a few minutes, and his hot and sweaty face cooled under Angie's damp cloth wiping.

In less than an hour, Val was sleeping peacefully.

She began preparing to camp there for the night.

Val was still lying pretty much where he had fallen, just to the side of the road. Angie called out to the boys to walk the team with the wagon back down to them. And when they got there, she gently guided the horses off onto the side of the roadbed. There, she unhitched the team with Bobby's help. At almost ten years of age, he was becoming quite a little man, she thought proudly. Oskar stayed close by and gathered up dry sticks to make a fire.

The sun was lower by this time and the shadows longer.

Angie walked over to the wagon seat and put the partially empty Colt revolver back into its holster on the backside of the seat box and got the other one out, checking to see that it was fully loaded before walking back toward Val. She would later reload the empty chambers in the first pistol, but for now she wanted a fully ready firearm by her side and on through the night.

No sooner than she had gotten a small fire going, than the sound of horses' hooves and wagon wheels penetrated the growing twilight.

Angie didn't exactly know what best to do, so she hid the boys along the road edge behind some bushes, sat down beside Val, and placed her hands holding the Colt into her lap, where the folds of her skirts hid them from view.

A loud but not totally unfriendly call erupted from the roadway as several figures drew into view.

"Hello! What's this then? Someone's had a bad time of it, it seems."

Angie found herself staring straight into the face of Pasquinel Benoit with three other riders, all unknown to her. His visage, scarred and marked as it was by years of a life harder than most, gave Angie no comfort after her recent exchange with the would-be robbers and murderers.

The boys were still hidden, silent as ghosts, and Angie still held the fully loaded Paterson Colt hidden in her skirts.

For some reason, she felt surprisingly calm.

Chapter 4

THE REST OF THE WAY BACK TO MEMPHIS

If you don't like the Memphis weather, just wait a minute; it'll change!

1836

Angie Cunningham did not know how she felt at that moment, staring into the somewhat-familiar face of Pasquinel Benoit, but at least he was known slightly to her. Her husband Bobby had called him friend, and Bobby had the most infallibly correct judgment in that area that she had ever seen, so she guessed she could extend Benoit a little trust.

That did not mean that her hands were abandoning the Colt pistol hidden in her skirts, however.

Because it was clear that Benoit was well known to and well-liked by Val, Angie did loosen her grip on the Colt pistol a little and invited Pasquinel and his companions down to sit by the fire and discuss the next moves in getting their party safely back to Memphis. Benoit and his regular traveling companion, Auguste Marno, had been joined on this trip by two companions, addressed only as Hughes and Glass, who had been tasked by Levi Gold himself to find Angie and Val and escort them safely to Memphis.

The reason Hughes and Glass had been added to the party, along with their wagon, soon became apparent. They had been sent out by Mr. Gold in the wake of Henry Speck's robbery and bludgeoning murder at the water's edge of the Memphis river-landing the prior week. Though Henry had been robbed of his cash receipts, the assailants had nevertheless seen fit to savagely beat the slightly older man. He'd died in horrible agony two days later at Dr. Bradford's office and had been laid to rest just two days ago.

Angie was horrified to hear of Henry's brutal death; she had been looking forward to renewing her friendship with the small, quiet man who she had come to enjoy very much. He hadn't been one to put himself forward at all, but Angie knew how bright, intelligent, and witty he could be and was secretly looking forward to him meeting little Bobby and Oskar. As an accomplished juggler (he had once been a circus performer as a youth), Angie knew he could probably keep both boys spellbound with that one talent.

Henry Speck's murderers were heard dismissing Val Dimand's potential for catching them and making them pay for their crimes, saying within earshot of several witnesses, "We'll take care of Val Dimand if he tries to come after us!"

Mr. Gold had then put together the expedition to find Val and Angie along the road and see them safely up the Natchez Trace back to Memphis.

Pasquinel Benoit had begun to describe the miscreants they sought by saying, "One of them has dark shaggy hair and powder burns on one side of his face, and the other has dirty blond hair with a pinched, kind of rat like look to his face."

Angie then knew why their assailants had done and said what they had. *"Rather than usual highwaymen, these goons lay in wait specifically to kill Val."*

She stood slowly, still gripping the pistol (clearly visible to all now), and went over to where Powder Burns still lay and pulled back the jacket she had thrown over his face.

"This one of them?" she hissed. She flung the jacket back disgustedly.

Benoit nodded.

She marched the intervening fifteen feet to Rat Face and similarly uncovered him.

"This the other?" Her voice was positively venomous. Her loathing was acid.

Again, Benoit nodded.

"I'm glad you gentlemen found us, but I wish you'd been a little sooner," Angie rued openly. "Val's hurt, the boys were frightened, and I was more than a little upset myself!" Her words were a bitter moan against the slight breeze.

Pasquinel said brightly, "Well, it certainly seems you and Val handled the situation well, Angie. So why don't we send Mr. Hughes and Mr. Glass on back to the sheriff in Memphis with those two varmints in their wagon to present to him. Then Mr. Marno and I will accompany you, Val, and the boys on back to the house Levi Gold has picked out for you. You can stay there for at least a little while, until you get a chance to choose something that suits you better."

"If Auguste and I handle the driving, loading and unloading, feeding the team, and the like, all you'll need to do is see to Val and the boys. And maybe we can help a little with them, too." The fire itself seemed to dance at the idea of this, and sparks flew upward. Angie's mood brightened, just a bit, at this sign.

Early the next morning, after a fairly restful night alongside the road, the enhanced party began their last leg of the journey on to Memphis in a much-improved humor, with Angie lavishing Val with all the attention she could muster, propriety be damned. Nestling as close as she could to her wounded hero, Angie kissed him incessantly. Val, for his part, maintained that the pain wasn't too great and that she, Angie, could attend to others as needed. He, of course, was deliriously happy to have her rich, plush body nestled so close to his and providing him with many comforts.

The boys found tremendous interest and humor in the way Auguste Marno could whistle a thousand tunes quite melodiously and sing silly songs he would make up right on the spot, while they drove the weary hours away. And there was even more.

Aside from being very exotic-looking, Pasquinel Benoit could play the concertina! With a lively and spirited air, he could fill the otherwise dull Mississippi backwoods with music, and his rich baritone voice meant zesty vocals, too! The boys were enthralled with their new companions, and the miles seemed to pass much more quickly than they had before.

Angie relished the newly minted atmosphere of hope their new companions brought out in everyone, as well as the lighter spirit that seemed to settle over the group.

The very moment Hughes and Glass had disappeared around the next bend in the road, with their wagonload of dead outlaws headed to a final reckoning in Memphis, everything had seemed to change. A pall over them seemed to lift a bit.

Angie knew in her heart that nothing actually had changed. She still had yet to come completely to grips with the specter of being a widow with two small boys to take care of alone and with the challenge of resuming some kind of a life in Memphis.

Benoit was some help here. He spoke of Mr. Gold's assurance that Angie would be welcomed back as an employee of the store, if she wished, and that he had secured a house for Angie, little Bobby, and Oskar. Pasquinel had also opined that the house could serve as a convalescent quarters for Val for as long as he needed to be under Angie's care.

"Levi Gold really cherished you, you know," Benoit said softly. "It wasn't just because of what you did for the store, though he said that was aplenty. I guess he sorta thought of you as a daughter he never had, and when you left with such little warning, it affected him more than he would have thought.

"He also had a great respect for Robert. Frontier garb or not, he said that your man was one of the most astute natural businessmen he'd ever run into, and Bobby's advice about stocking tools, work clothing, and supplies for settlers passing through was so on the spot that Mr. Gold ended up opening a new settlers' branch of the store a few years back, and it's been going great guns ever since." Breezes softly rustled the trees' leaves with a gentle chorus as he went on.

"He was also so sorry that you lost Robert at the Alamo, and he grieved so for you; he really did. He tore his clothes and everything!" Angie nodded slowly.

"When Val said he was going to see if you wanted to come back, rather than being stuck there on the frontier as a widow with two kids, Levi Gold was the first to say go.

"And while I'm at it, I might as well say a word about that man you have back there in the wagon. Valentine Dimand is one of the finest men I've ever known, and if you're sort of inclined toward him, you could do a great deal worse, believe you me. I know the wounds in your heart from Robert's passing have to be too fresh to make many decisions about your future right now, but that man really has something for you. When he determined to come and get you, nothing, and I mean nothing, could stand in his way!

"By the way, the treatment you're giving Val is terrific. I'm not talking about keeping his wounds clean and such, though you're doing great with those things. The way you're staying close to him, holding him and kissing him, there's just no better medicine.

"Would you listen to me go on? I haven't talked this much since I tried to out-argue Davy Crockett and George Russel! My jaws hurt."

With that, Pasquinel Benoit fell silent.

After a short while, Angie crawled back to Val and began her treatment of him again. She had much to think about.

That night, things changed.

Angie and Val were in the back of the wagon, with Val resting comfortably after a good supper. The boys, as they usually did, fell asleep in the front part of the wagon just behind the driver's seat, nestled in their bedding like little puppies, oblivious to all else around them. Benoit and Marno had talked late into the evening before settling into their bedrolls down on the ground below, and the fire diminished slowly down to just embers. A soft night breeze was the only movement in the camp, except for an occasional stirring from one horse or the other or a snore from one of the men on the ground. A light blanket over Val's nightshirt was all he seemed to need to keep him comfortable in the night air.

Lost in her thoughts, Angie idly ran her fingers ever so lightly over Val's sleeping form, careful to avoid his wounded thigh. In so doing, she could not help noticing there was a rise forming in the blanket over the area of Val's crotch.

A wry little grin creased the corners of Angie's mouth as her fingers crept under the blanket. Looking around her surroundings carefully and seeing nothing, she allowed her hand to slide under Val's nightshirt and begin to caress his rock-hard manhood, stroking softly with two fingertips right under the head in a circular motion while putting her face next to his, lest he should awaken suddenly, cry out, and startle the camp.

Her lips stifled his deep groan at his release, and her mouth remained on his until his spasms subsided. His silence thus obtained, Angie kissed him once more and whispered, "Go on back to sleep now and rest, my love."

Angie then took her fingers to her lips and savored deeply every drop she could scavenge from Val's sleeping belly. For hours it seemed, she was alone with her thoughts, the taste and texture of Val's effluent giving a wonderful highlight, and basking in the knowledge that she had finally made her decision.

Angie Cunningham was now at peace.

The next morning broke bright and cheerful around the camp.

Breakfast over, they made quick preparations to begin the journey again.

The next two days' ride was uneventful, and they made the South Road into Memphis itself by midafternoon. Val's wounded thigh had been suppurating nicely, and Angie was able to clean and wipe away the discharge without any sign of infection. She had been boiling the water she used during the cleaning and bandaging, washing the nightshirts she had been cutting up for bandages in the boiled water with strong soap, and changing the bandages often.

Val's pain had gradually lessened (although Angie had seen him wince and knew he was being at least somewhat stoic). But now he was even handling short times outside the wagon on his feet with a tree limb for a crutch, as well as sitting by the evening fire on a camp stool for supper.

Angie was cherishing these times, not just for Val's company but for what it did for Bobby and Oskar. The boys had really taken to Val, and were delighted with all the company he could provide them. The chimes of their laughter as the three men joked with them and told them stories, real and imagined, warmed her heart as it had not been for months. She began to have a glimmer of hope in her soul that the life she could have with the rugged lawman, woodsman, and waggoneer could be happy and full. Tree-dappled sunshine lit their path forward.

Still, Angie could not help, as they rolled into town, feeling a little out of place. So much had changed in the nine years she had been gone that she was no longer the center of everything or even *at* the center of anything!

Memphis was growing by leaps and bounds, with no end in sight. The settlement in Texas where she had lived so happily with Robert had just reached a lofty fourteen houses total; here in Memphis, some blocks on the streets they went down had fourteen or more houses on that single block!

Auguste Marno led them down a street called Adams up to an attractive clapboard house, stopping the wagon along the front of the house and cheerily calling out, "We're here!" before hopping down.

Benoit stayed with them there at the house while Marno took one of the horses in toward the riverfront, less than a half mile away according to him, to let Mr. Gold know they had arrived. Meanwhile, Benoit looked to getting Val Dimand into the house and resting comfortably on a settee in the front room and then helped Angie bring in the few precious possessions she couldn't leave Texas without.

While all this was going on, of course, the boys went exploring—first the house room by room and then the yard. Val could see that the new experiences: the sights, sounds, and smells of city life would easily occupy more than one day's exploration; there was much to keep Bobby and Oskar occupied for days on end.

Half an hour or so later, Mr. Gold's light carriage came driving up, stopped, and discharged Levi Gold and Dr. Bradford, a studious-looking younger man. The two men exchanged brief pleasantries with those outside before continuing into the house. There, Levi ran headlong into Angie with a huge hug of delight as Dr. Bradford knelt by the settee saying, "Mr. Dimand, I'm Dr. Hiram Bradford, and I'm going to examine your wounds quickly, if that's all right with you. I'll try not to hurt you any more than is absolutely necessary."

Val nodded, and Dr. Bradford bent to his work, first cutting away the bandages on Val Dimand's thigh.

"My goodness' sakes!" he exclaimed. "Who's been doing this marvelous wound treatment? Is this your work young lady?"

Angie nodded sheepishly, as a blush beautified her even more than usual.

"Well, let me tell you, this is first-rate work! This bullet hole is absolutely free of apparent infection, is assiduously clean, and is suppurated and healing nicely. Fine work, indeed! Would you like to come to work for me as a nurse?"

Levi Gold spoke up quickly from the small table where he had been conversing with Angie during Dr. Bradford's exam. "Oh, no you don't, Hiram! Angie has a job with me at the store for as long as she wants it and on any terms she needs, so hands off."

Hiram Bradford already knew how Levi Gold felt about Angie, and the smile on Gold's face as he said those words just served to underscore that love. The long-lost daughter had come home.

Dr. Bradford turned to addressing Val. "Mr. Dimand, the bullet went completely through your thigh without tearing any major blood vessels. There may be some tendon damage or loss, which will possibly necessitate the use of a cane by you, at least temporarily. Perhaps it'll be permanently, but probably nothing more serious than that."

Val spoke up quickly. "Will I still be able to ride a horse?"

Bradford's reply was equally quick. "Yes. I'd heard you were a fine horseman. Riding is fine; in fact, it'll be good for your healing and the strengthening of your leg. Just easy at the beginning. You'll want to learn to dismount with your good leg first, is all."

Angie asked, "Is it all right for Val to stay here?"

Dr. Bradford smiled as he said, "I don't think he'll get better care anywhere in town, even at my office!"

Night found the entire group, Angie, Bobby, Oskar, and Val, comfortably nestled in the handsome little clapboard house awaiting a new dawn in Memphis.

A light breeze through the open windows brought comfort and hope.

Chapter 5

THE LITTLE HOUSE ON ADAMS

Just about any year, the Memphis phone book would show you that there were truly more churches than gas stations in the city.

1836–1840

The next morning did dawn bright and fairly cool, as fall was approaching. The family woke in good humor across the age and gender strata, and all were in fine spirits, with a solid roof over their heads for the first time in what seemed like forever.

A Mrs. McGevney from farther down the street showed up at their door professing to be a good friend of Dr. Bradford and carrying a basket full of warm breakfast goodies, along with a pot of fresh coffee and some cool milk for the boys. Staying just long enough to serve up the breakfast, she left discreetly with a standing invitation for Angie, Val, and the boys to visit her and her husband down the block—oh, just anytime it was convenient.

The boys had barely gobbled down their breakfasts before they begged to be excused from the table to begin their explorations of their new home afresh. Angie warned them about staying back from the road, being quiet and polite for any of their neighbors, and generally being well-behaved through their excitement. The serious looks on their faces as they listened was almost overwhelmed by their desire to be off on their adventures.

Bobby was nine by this point, and Oskar was six. They listened carefully when Angie stopped them at the door and said, "I'm going to need to get Val back to bed so he can rest, so you play quietly when you're outside the window. We all want Val's leg to heal just as soon as it can, so let him rest and sleep, if he can."

She was met by two serious, "Yes, Mama" replies, almost in chorus.

Angie and Val sat at the table a while longer, discussing as much of the seemingly endless list of things needing to be done to "settle in" as they could call to mind. Then Angie helped Val hobble back to the bed and stretch out as comfortably as she could make him. She left a pitcher of water and a glass on the bedside table and bent to her dressing for the outside as Val looked on.

"I could die today, and no man would have ever seen so rich a treasure," he intoned. "I'm glad you and the boys are safe!"

Whatever his next words were or might have been, they were smothered beneath Angie's passionate kiss, fringed as it was with uncontrollable tears of joy and relief. When she finally allowed herself to breathe, Angie said in a mockingly stern voice, "There'll be no more talk of dying from you, Valentine Dimand! I want you to live, and me with you, for years and years and years, together. I want to grow old with you and sit happily by the fire, enjoying our memories, together. Together, do you understand?"

The knock on the front door broke the moment and sent Angie flying to complete her dressing.

She was of breath when she opened the front door, and Auguste Marno rescued the moment by speaking first. "Good morning, Miss Angie! Mr. Gold sent me to see if you needed to go anywhere or get anything to help you get situated in the house. He also suggested perhaps a buggy ride for the boys to let them see some of the sights." Marno quickly added in a voice that was almost a whisper, "He also said that, if you needed money for anything, just ask. He said to please ask; he thinks of you as the daughter he never had, and he wants you to have whatever you need."

All Angie could say was, "Mr. Marno, how nice! Yes, there are a couple of things we could pick up that would help quite a bit, and I have money for now. Tell our lovely Levi Gold ..." Angie stopped midsentence, thought for a moment, and continued, "If it wouldn't be too much trouble, could we stop by the store as we go about? I'd like to thank Mr. Gold in person for all his kindnesses."

"I think that would be just fine, Miss Angie! I know he'd love to see you, anytime."

Angie went to tell Val of her good fortune and let the boys know she was leaving for a short while. Bobby was put in charge; and, if they'd been good in her absence, they might have a surprise treat coming this afternoon.

All these things completed, Angie and Auguste drove away in the buggy.

Adams Street at that time was simply a dirt roadway where the trees had been felled, stumps pulled and filled in, and the whole thing graded off by dragging heavy timber blades behind horse-drawn wagons. But it led directly to Front Street. There, a simple left turn, and about another quarter of a mile down Front, led directly to Gold's store.

Angie was interested to see that Wilson's was still in business, just beyond, although the exterior looks of the place seemed to have changed somewhat over the intervening years.

As Mr. Marno held the door to Gold's Mercantile open for Angie to enter, she couldn't help noticing that changes had occurred there as well.

Midmorning it was by this time, and the studious younger man behind the counter looked up when the strikingly gorgeous young woman, accompanied as she was by Auguste Marno, graced Gold's. The look on his face let Angie know that this fellow was thoroughly male, highly interested, and about to be deflated.

"Good morning, young man, I'm Angie Cunningham. Is Mr. Gold available to speak to me at this time?"

"I'm so sorry, Mrs. Cunningham. Mr. Gold is out just now. He's down at the waterfront overseeing a large delivery which just came in, but he should be back soon. Would you care to wait?" The young man continued after Angie's brief nod, "I'm Louis Ottenheimer, Mr. Gold's assistant, and I'm pleased beyond measure to meet you; I've heard so much about you! He left word that I might see you today and to extend to you every courtesy."

Angie said brightly, "I have a list of items we'll need to set up household. Could we see to filling that as we wait? Mr. Marno, would that be all right?"

Marno nodded, and young Ottenheimer suggested, "Why don't you simply give me your list, and I'll see to getting it filled. If you'd like, you and Mr. Marno could have a seat over on the settee and relax while I'm attending to your order."

Angie and Auguste did just that and chatted while the industrious young man went about filling Angie's list. It included staples like flour, baking soda, corn, potatoes, and the like. Added to those, pots and pans, knives, forks, spoons and kitchen utensils supplemented what had survived the trip back from Texas.

After a few minutes, Louis called out from the back, "There at the front counter, you'll find some of the latest New York and London newspapers. If they're of interest to you, please feel free to glance at them as you wish!"

"Oh my goodness," exclaimed Angie, "I haven't had any fresh news of the world in I don't know when! Thank you."

As she picked one up, she exclaimed again, "These are less than a month old! How do you do that?"

She sat down with a New York paper and began to devour it greedily. Auguste Marno began to take cloth bags of supplies back out to the carriage, installing them gently and securely into the back cargo area. After he had placed the last bag securely, he turned around to go back in; just then, Levi Gold's personal buggy drove up, and the storekeeper immediately hopped out with a quick, "Is she here?" before scurrying to the door to see for himself.

A veritable explosion of hugs later, Levi Gold and Angie Cunningham were in converse, quietly and intensely, as Angie prepared to leave again with Mr. Marno.

"Mr. Gold, I just want you to know that I intend for us to make our living by earning it. Your generosity, and that of others, has been incredible! I'll never be able to repay anything close to the kindnesses you have all shown me. But I do insist on being able to make my own way." Angie was almost in tears, but she kept her composure as she continued. "I truly loved those years I worked for you, and if the opportunity exists for me to return, I'd be more than grateful and happy to do so at any salary you deem fair. I will need to make arrangements for my children's schooling, however."

Mr. Gold's reply was quick. "You have a position here anytime you want it; we'll see to the boys' schooling and come up with a plan. Goodbye for now, and I'll see you again soon."

After Marno helped Angie back into the buggy, Levi Gold motioned him over for a final word. "She wants for nothing, understand?"

Marno nodded emphatically. He climbed into the buggy and loosed the brake, and they drove away.

It was almost eleven by the time Angie got back, so she decided to fix an early lunch. Val was sitting up in the front room on the settee, and the boys were playing a sort of bowling game on the front porch as Angie and Auguste carried the bags of supplies into the small but tidy kitchen.

Angie immediately invited Mr. Marno to have lunch with them and set about preparing freshly sliced cheese and soft rolls and a lettuce, tomato, and cucumber salad with olive oil and vinegar dressing. A light meal in the middle of the day was probably best for now, with a fuller supper for later tonight.

Val had said as she was putting groceries and supplies away that the boys had been "good as gold all morning." That had allowed him to get a little more sleep. Therefore, the stiffness in his upper thigh that he had felt on arising that morning was completely gone.

The front window to the porch was open, and the peals of laughter coming in told a tale of a clever game that was growing to a conclusion.

"Look, Oskar! You've only got three pins left to knock down, and you'll beat me again! How did you get so good at this?" Bobby's encouragement for Oskar came through the open window.

Angie called out to the boys, "Finish up your game, boys, and then come in and wash up for lunch. While we eat, I'll tell you about your surprise for this afternoon with Mr. Marno!"

Bobby and Oskar came trooping in just as Angie finished setting the table, and all were seated shortly afterward. As the food was passed around, Angie's heart began to take on a warm glow of contentment that had not been there in quite a while. Her boys were safe and happy; her man was as well and content as she could seem to make him; and she would be able, it seemed, to have a job that would help to pay the costs of the household.

And yet, all was not yet perfect for Angie Cunningham. She hoped to become Angie Dimand someday fairly soon, just as she and Val had spoken of along the trail up from Texas. There was a problem with that, however.

Angie didn't know why, but Val just had not taken her to him.

She knew he was healing, of course, and she suspected his leg hurt him a lot more than he let on. Because of these things, she'd never expected that he would come dancing up to her and plow her like a furrow. But still, she had made sure he saw her as naked as she was able, as often as she could manage. She enticingly touched him whenever she could and slept as close as he seemed comfortable with.

Still, nothing!

With a giant mental heave-ho, Angie set these thoughts aside for another time and concentrated on the present. Val was explaining to Bobby and Oskar that their afternoon would consist of a buggy ride around town to see the sights of Memphis with Mr. Marno and that they both needed to be on their best behavior. Solemn nods in the affirmative could not completely mask their excitement as Val explained to Auguste that he thought the waterfront would be something for both the boys to see and then the sawmill that had opened out on Third Street. That could be a special treat for Oskar, Val said.

Angie chimed in, "When Oskar was just a toddler, he was fascinated with boards. Actual finished boards were very rare on the Texas frontier, so naturally he wanted to know where they came from. Everyone told him they came from trees, but he couldn't see how you could open up the tree and get them out! So, perhaps he might be quite interested in seeing them come out from trees, after all!"

"I'd sort of like to see that, too," said Bobby.

Auguste Marno was quick with his reply. "Well, all right then. It's the waterfront and then on to the sawmill and who knows where else on this afternoon adventure! Let's go, boys."

As the buggy pulled away with its three excited occupants, Angie's heart began to glow again.

For his part, Val was indeed having more pain than he sometimes admitted. He tried to remain stoic around Angie and the boys, but he still was worried about what the final disposition of his leg would be. Every time he'd tried to put his full weight on it, the leg had buckled immediately and spasms of pain had practically paralyzed him.

He remembered Dr. Bradford had said he'd probably need to use a cane to walk, perhaps for the rest of his life, but that was small comfort when trying to pick himself up from the floor, wracked with pain.

Beyond these concerns, Val had been away from his freighting business for far longer than he was comfortable. He had left the day-to-day operations to his good friend Pasquinel Benoit, so he was relatively confident the business was probably going well. But he worried anyway. Pasquinel was an old hand at wagoneering and was as trail savvy as anyone Val had ever known, as well as being assiduously honest in his monetary transactions. So, what did Val really have to worry about? Precious little, it would seem.

Still, Valentine Dimand chafed at having to lie up inactive.

Dr. Bradford had said he would come by the next day, which was a Thursday, to have another look at Val's leg. He'd also spoken of bringing a selection of canes with him for Val to try out. Val looked forward to this because he had questions for Doc Bradford.

It turned out, Angie had questions of her own.

The boys came rushing in with Mr. Marno in tow later that

afternoon, full of tales of the city and what they'd seen and just generally bubbling with excitement. This brightened the mood considerably and brought both Val and Angie out of their pensive moods.

When he could get a word in edgewise, Auguste tried to fill in the afternoon's events, starting with the waterfront, which had indeed caught the boys' fancy, particularly Bobby. He had been fascinated by the variety of people there, from settlers to riverboat men to dockworkers and what he called "fancy ladies." The bustle at the water's edge could easily have kept him spellbound all day, if Marno had left him there. While Oskar had liked the waterfront too, the part he was most drawn to was the steamboats putting ashore there and the operations that serviced them. But just as Val had predicted, it was the sawmill that lit up his eyes as he spoke.

He tried to describe the big circular saw blade and the sound it made as it cut through the logs; it was almost like he was still there in his mind as he spoke. He then talked about something he called "wood dirt" that was everywhere. He described a great big pile of it that he would love to play in, if he ever got to go back there.

Val leaned over to Angie with a smile and said, "Sawdust!"

Oskar had gotten sawdust in his blood.

It would last a lifetime.

The thing Bobby talked about, besides all that they had seen, was the cherry sodas they had gotten to drink there by the river as they watched everything going on. "We sat on these little benches and drank them and watched, and it was so great!" Bobby intoned. "We had almost enough money for the cherry sodas from the money you gave us this morning, Mom. Mr. Marno gave us the two extra pennies we needed, and we didn't even have to ask! We did say, 'Thank you very much,' though."

"Well that's good," Angie said in mock seriousness. "But I'm not so sure about you and Oskar spending more than you have! That can cause a lifetime of troubles, young man.

"Mr. Marno, is there some task these two young men can perform for you to help repay your kind advance?" Angie asked wryly.

Auguste stroked and pulled on his already impressively long chin while saying, "Hmm, now let me see, just let me see!" By the time his little comedy bit was over, you would have thought his chin was two feet long and that he was pondering the fate of the world.

The boys rolled with laughter, and Angie and Val were holding in their reactions through sheer effort.

"Boys," Marno at last sagely intoned, "your mother wants you to repay a kindness I showed you. But I think a kindness that has not yet been repaid needs to be done. There are two kind and patient horses out there who hauled you two all around all morning without complaining a bit, and I'll bet they're a mite thirsty. How about going to the well and drawing two buckets of water—one for each penny—and watering those good animals. How does that sound?"

"Yes, sir!" came the chorus, followed by scampering feet.

"They're such good boys," Marno said after they had left. "I'm sorry I never got to know their father."

Auguste continued before Angie or Val could reply, "Do either of you need me to take you anywhere else this afternoon? If not, I'll be getting on back to Gold's. I do work for him, after all."

Angie and Val both shook their heads.

While they watched the boys have a wetter time than was absolutely necessary watering the horses, yet still getting enough water actually in the animals, the adults lightly planned for the next day or two's needs.

Marno left, and Angie began to prepare supper, after seeing to Val's comfort on the settee.

That night, the supper conversation ran long after the food was finished, and the flickering from the fireplace embers danced over the sleepy eyes of the boys, desperately trying to keep awake to recount all of the day's sights and experiences. Angie bundled each one lovingly up into her arms and carried them off to their beds, where the shroud of sleep enveloped them almost instantly.

Returning to Val, she gently guided him to their bedroom, where she undressed him and checked his wounds, putting a fresh bandage and dressings on before putting on his nightshirt and helping him into the bed, which he could almost now do completely by himself. From her casual observation, his strength and muscle tone seemed to be improving, almost daily. She longed fervently for his libido to take a similar compass swing, pointing due north rigidly and firmly. All she could currently do was care for him and hope for the best, and that she would continue to do faithfully.

Perhaps Dr. Bradford would have answers to help her in the morning; tonight, they would rest together, and she would make sure Val knew that Angie's very all, each fiber of her being, was pledged to this rugged, handsome, pinnacle of a man.

The morning broke with Bobby and Oskar on some kind of yard adventure when the doctor arrived in his buggy.

As Dr. Bradford was about to rap on the front door, it opened with Angie standing there.

"Doctor, since Val isn't quite out yet, could I ask you a delicate question while we're waiting for Val to be completely ready?" Angie said in a quiet voice.

The studious young man smiled a bit and said, "If it's the one I think you're going to ask, the answer is, it's far more common than you might think and tends to take care of itself by just giving it time. If you aren't having your romantic couplings, and there seems to be no real reason for it, don't worry.

"Is that what's been bothering you?" he asked.

Angie just blushed a sharp crimson and nodded briskly.

The doctor went on. "Often, when a man has undergone a trauma such as Val has, he doesn't respond to cues you might give him that you want him. The shock to a man's body from a bullet wound can be significant on a man's mind as well as his body, and let me tell you, Val's was. If that bullet had gone in an inch closer to his groin, he might have bled out completely before you could have done anything to help him. And, if the bullet had gone in any higher, all the tendons in his leg might have been severed, instead of the single one that I believe is severed or nicked, leaving that leg useless for the rest of his life. As it is, he'll need a cane or a walking stick for months, or perhaps even the rest of his days, but he'll be able to get around just fine."

Dr. Bradford finished with, "As soon as he begins to feel like a whole man again, something will trigger the urge in his mind, and everything will be right as rain, you'll see! Val is quite a man, and I'm glad he's my friend."

No sooner had the doctor finished than Val appeared in the doorway between the bedroom and the parlor. He then one-leg hopped over to the settee and sat with surprising grace.

"Hello, Val! Let me examine you briefly and change your dressing, and then we'll try out some of the walking sticks I've brought for you to sample."

"OK, Doc! You're the boss, as well as my friend," Val said.

"Thanks, Val. That means a lot to me, coming from you."

The next few minutes were in relative silence, punctuated only by sharp breath intakes and small grunts as Val reacted to the inevitable pain.

When he was finished, Dr. Bradford closed his bag, sat back, and smiled. "Your progress has been exceptional, Val, due in no small amount to the care you've been receiving from Angie and the boys."

The doctor went on, "Now, let me show you a selection of canes and walking sticks I brought with me. First, I do want you to use this crutch for the next two weeks while your wounds close completely. Am I correct that, any time you put weight on your leg, it collapses on you with a great deal of pain and puts you almost helpless on the floor?"

At Val's curt nod, Dr. Bradford continued. "You *must* not ruin the healing that has already been accomplished by trying too much, too soon. Use the crutch for support and gradually return weight to your leg. When you are able to stand alone for ten minutes, you can begin to think about using a cane or a walking stick. Two weeks! No less!"

Then the doctor unrolled a carrier with several canes of thigh height inside, along with several shorter walking sticks with smaller knob handles, rather than the familiar crook handles of the full-height canes. Val and Dr. Bradford spent a number of minutes discussing the various merits and limitations of each type before deciding that Val should probably carry one of each. A full-height cane for indoors use seemed advisable, and a walking stick for when he was on horseback was least likely to be in the way. Dr. Bradford showed Val the ordering materials, suggesting he might get them through Gold's, and then repacked his samples and prepared to leave.

"Angie, I believe you met Mary McGevney, didn't you?" the Dr. asked as he was headed for the door.

"Yes, I did!" exclaimed Angie. "She brought us a lovely breakfast a couple of days ago and was just the sweetest person."

"Well, she and her husband, Eugene, are teachers. They've established a school on or near Court Square and are currently enrolling pupils. Bobby and Oskar are perfect candidates for this, and you'd walk right by there on your way to Gold's store in the mornings and could drop them right off. Mention it to Levi when next you see him, and he'll help you get set up, if you'd like. And that other thing we talked about, let me know if it doesn't resolve itself within a week or two." And with that, Dr. Bradford was off to his carriage and gone a few moments later.

Angie and Val spent the rest of the morning talking pleasantly about the future in a thousand different ways, in the way that newly coupled people often do. As the morning warmth melted into muggy afternoon, Val's eyes drooped, and his participation got less sharp, so Angie gently helped him to bed for an afternoon rest and healing nap.

Val was drifting off on a cloud of impending sleep when he spotted Angie standing in front of the window with sunlight streaming in, turning the plain white cotton fabric of her nightshirt almost transparent. She was leaning forward, both hands on the inner windowsill, and her pendant breasts were clearly defined for his eyes to feast upon. Val knew she wasn't the maidenly girl of more than nine years ago; two children birthed, and married life on the frontier of Texas, had changed her body in important, if not necessarily detrimental ways. She had left a girl; she had come back a woman. And what a woman she was! Her nipples were no longer pert little rosebuds; they were now satisfying, chewable morsels of beautiful deep red pleasure. Her face, though etched slightly with the lines of having seen too much loneliness, was still an absolute vision, and when she smiled (which was almost constantly), she was radiant.

It was when she turned slightly to face into the sun that it actually hit Val.

It was, always and forever, those legs.

No longer the fascinating maidenly legs that used to flash before him as Angie skipped from mooring to mooring along the Memphis waterfront, these legs had picked up a little weight without becoming overly fleshy. They now were the beautiful, but sturdy underpinnings of a woman who could handle her own load and yet still back up to her man to provide him with a satisfying place to expend his ardor into her, no matter how vigorous.

Then, when Angie turned full toward the window while looking for the boys, she put the last facet of the jewel into view. As she stood there, bent over a little with her legs slightly apart, Val could see the whole of her mound and, in addition to the beauty of her large lips, he saw little sections of her smaller lips hanging out between, which began to drive him absolutely mad with desire to explore the situation further. Val Dimand had been between the legs of many women and had seen many things but never, never with such a desire as this!

He just had to spend the rest of his life with her, starting right now and beginning right there.

———————◆———————

By the time supper was over, the evening family gathering happily completed, and the boys tucked into bed, Val was thoroughly ready for Angie to join him in their bed.

Getting Val into bed had been requiring Angie to help lift his legs and swing them around until Val was fully and securely lying prone in the bed, at which time Angie would cover him with the quilts they were using; she would then climb in beside him and nestle close. On this night, however, Val managed to get fully into bed and cover himself completely unassisted and was there waiting for her when she came into the room.

"Well, my my! I see you've been busy practicing. Are you having any pain from getting into the bed?" she asked. "Dr. Bradford said not to rush things so as not to reopen your wound, remember?"

Val replied huskily, "Very little pain, my dear, but you might want to look at my leg to make sure I haven't torn anything open."

As Angie peeled back the covers, she gasped.

Val was naked underneath, and as she peeled the covers further, she found he had a raging erection hard enough to bend steel.

Angie looked carefully into Val's eyes and whispered softly, "Are you sure?"

Val's smile and nod were all Angie needed to strip her nightshirt with one smooth move and climb into bed with her man.

While one might expect a vigorous and passionate coupling between the two, that wasn't what happened at all, only partly out of concern for Val's wounded leg.

As she entered the bed, Angie let Val guide her into the position he wanted for her, which was facing away from him. Then, as she began to nestle her soft, warm bottom against his crotch, Val used a free hand to guide the tip of his manhood between her cheeks, stroking it back and forth in her valley and releasing copious amounts of lubricating moisture before finally gently inserting it into her.

Val slid all the way into Angie, which made her gasp. As Angie naturally began to try to thrust against Val's deep incursion, he held her shoulders very gently and whispered, "Let's just hold each other like this for a while, all right?"

Angie's, "Yes!" came out almost as a moan as she felt the pressure increasing inside her.

The two lovers would have appeared motionless to a casual observer, yet tiny, unavoidable movements from either of them sent shockwaves through the other.

Angie discovered her own delight in pushing down onto Val's erection with her legs and suddenly releasing the extra pressure. Val's response each time seemed to be to fill the void thus created, which gave a sense of urgency to the coupling that the lack of overall motion would seem to belie.

Just when the pressure was mounting to an almost intolerable level,

Val's hands found her nipples. Taking a hard projection between each set of fingers, he began to pull firmly out and down with each one, causing Angie to gasp from the new sensations her nipples created in her crotch.

Val's gentle kisses on her back and neck, which he had been lavishing her with from the beginning, suddenly paused. A very soft, deep groan began to come from his throat and gradually increased in power until his, "Oh!" punctuated the massive release that erupted from his shaft into the very core of her being.

Angie herself had her release almost simultaneously. Her nipples had set up a group of waves, which swept over her body and carried her orgasm to every corner of her being. Her stifled scream she buried in the covers as best she could; thankfully, the boys slept through the brief outburst.

They remained motionlessly coupled for many moments afterward. For her part, Angie was trying to place the experience she had just had into the overall panoply of love encounters that she had had in her life thus far, and she could not.

It was like nothing she had ever had before!

As her mind wrestled with how to properly categorize what had just happened with all her wonderful memories of her nine years with Robert Cunningham, she began to slowly realize she was going to have to separate her life into two separate lives. The beautiful life she'd had with Bobby had tragically ended too soon, and she needed to cherish and preserve those memories without comparing them to anything else. Her new life with Val Dimand, just beginning, would build up its own treasury of memories, distinct and separate from her first life.

Angie's decision would serve her in good stead for the next forty-five years.

Val, likewise, was consumed in thought. He pondered how to uplift, protect, and demonstrate to Angie how much a part of him she would be.

His thoughts for their upcoming life touched on money, education for the boys, resculpting his business so he could spend as much of his time at home as he could manage, and a thousand other things to help shape their lives together. For Val not only intended for his new family to have a future together; he intended for it to be bright, indeed.

Chapter 6

ANGELINA AND THE BIG HOUSE

All women are beautiful. Some, it just takes a little longer to notice.

—Lazarus Long

1840–1841

Angelina Marie Dimand was born in the Adams house at two o'clock in the morning on June 15, 1837. Squalling and kicking her way into the world, she was loved at first sight. She, of course, became the immediate center of attention in the household, and a surprising amount of that was from the boys themselves.

Bobby, in particular, was fascinated with her. He could spend hours on end beside her crib, just watching her, smiling at her, and talking to her, telling her a thousand and one things about how life was going to be as she grew.

Oskar, also thoroughly besotted, wanted to play with baby Angelina from the start. Her lying there, just a blob, was not satisfactory at all! But Mom patiently explained that babies take time to grow. She reminded Oskar that he too had been a blob, at one time, with an older brother who wanted to play immediately, and look how that had all worked out.

Angie's pregnancy had not been overly difficult for her; Angelina had been a smaller baby than either one of the boys. Were it not for the oppressive Memphis heat and humidity already in full swing by June, you might have said it was actually an easy pregnancy.

Nestled back as it was among the shade trees, the Adams house was airy and cool by comparison to others. The well was deep and a good source of cool, fresh water.

Day-to-day life in the Adams house was as ideal as they all could make it; busy as it might be on any given day, there was always time for family and fun. Bobby and Oskar grew like weeds with plenty of exploring their new environment, while Angie did indeed return to Mr. Gold's employ at the store, walking there and back on her assigned days.

Mary and Eugene McGevney had gladly enrolled Bobby and Oskar into their school. Val and Angie paid cash up front, unlike many parents, for whom cash was scarce and who often paid with in-kind bartering, instead; the boys were absolutely thriving. Every Monday through Friday, they would walk with Angie and sometimes even Mrs. McGevney herself (since she lived right up the street from their house) to the school to begin their school day. Their mother walked on to Gold's if she was scheduled to be there or back home if she wasn't.

Bobby and Oskar, aside from being three years apart in age, were so similar to each other in many respects they didn't always seem their respective ages to those who first met them. Bobby, the elder, showed an enthusiasm for new things and experiences, which, coupled with a tremendous curiosity, could make him seem younger than he was. Angie hoped he would never lose those traits. Oskar, though younger, seemed as though he might be destined for a life of study and deep intellectual pursuits.

The boys had grown up fairly self-sufficient on the Texas prairie, able to prepare a light meal for themselves if needed, fetch water and firewood for the household, wash dishes, and do other household tasks, just like most other frontier kids could do.

However, Angie had always feared that the isolation of their small settlement would limit the boys' educational opportunities. Memphis opened up a whole new world to Bobby and Oskar, and they were drinking it all in.

Angie was also grateful for the relative safety the town afforded them. She no longer had to scan the horizon for Kiowa raiding parties or grass fires, and if one of the family was sick or injured, a real doctor could be summoned. Sleeping peacefully through the night was now an expectation, rather than a hope.

She understood clearly that not everyone was suited for frontier life. Her nine years' experience with the rigors and deprivations of being in the small settlement with Robert and the boys had shown her that the rich memories she treasured from those times were not something she could bear repeating.

Angie understood that it was Robert who had lent her strength to bear up under the hardships of daily life on the prairie, out of his inexhaustible storehouse of such strength.

Robert Cunningham had been born on the frontier and lived his whole life on it; Angie had not. Her family had been in the towns of North Carolina and Tennessee for decades, gradually moving westward. Her paternal great-grandfather (for whom Oskar was named, complete with the Danish spelling) had been killed in a fight with some Creek Indians years back, but the frontier was not in her blood.

So, even as Angie cherished her memories of Robert and her Texas frontier days, she was nevertheless supremely grateful to Valentine Dimand for making the trek to Texas and shepherding the three of them back to her familiar Memphis. She felt like Memphis was destined to grow tremendously, and her new family could grow right along with it.

Dr. Bradford's advice about Val had been perfect. The two of them had been like giddy teenagers for weeks after that first glorious night, unable to keep themselves from each other, day and night. Angie calculated that Angelina had been born exactly nine months to the day (practically to the minute) after that first incomparable coupling.

The marriage vows between Angie MacFee Cunningham and Valentine Dimand took place in a small but lovely ceremony before friends right there in the backyard of the Adams house among the spreading trees on October 8, 1836. It was warm for the time of year (Indian summer), and the trees had not yet dropped many leaves.

Angie had somehow found a simple, but beautiful creamy white dress, which several of the ladies in attendance had adorned with some pastel ribbons and freshly cut flowers. Angie had made her own veil from a piece of French lace, held in place by a garland woven of deep-green ivy perched on top of her orange-blond hair.

Val's handsome figure had been accentuated by his trim black trousers tucked into shiny, knee-high riding boots and all topped off with a handsome deep gray tails jacket with a frilly white shirt.

The boys attended to the guests under the watchful tutelage of Auguste Marno and were perfect little knights in so doing.

Val had been able to stand through the entire (mercifully short) wedding ceremony, using his new black-lacquered, silver-ornamented gentleman's cane for occasional support.

When Angie looked back on the wedding and the ensuing several months since, a sense of peace and satisfaction began to flood her. Just then, Angelina began to make bubbles between her lips and gurgle with delight. Angelina was, overall, what could be described as a happy baby; the boys were creatively absorbed both at school and at home; and Val's physical recovery was proceeding nicely, along with a very healthy upswing in Val's freight-hauling business.

Returning to freighting on a daily basis had been a concern for Val. He had immensely enjoyed all the time he'd had available to spend with Angie since he'd first driven up to her cabin door that soft, gray day in Texas....

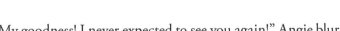

My goodness! I never expected to see you again!" Angie blurted aloud as Val climbed down from the wagon seat. "Come in, come in, Valentine Dimand! Even after all this time apart, I recognized you instantly!"

"Hello, gorgeous!" replied Val as though it had been only yesterday since he had last seen her, rather than nine years. "It's wonderful to see you! You know we get freight wagons down here fairly often, and Pasquinel Benoit told me he'd run into you and Robert a couple of times on his runs into east Louisiana. After I heard about Robert at the Alamo, I was so sorry for you, and I wanted to see if I could help. Levi Gold sends his best wishes and promises for help as well."

"Well, what are we still doing outside? The boys are down at the creek, so we'll be able to talk in peace for a while before they get back with all their rambunctiousness."

Once inside her cabin, after looks of wonder, expressions of delight, and impossibly close hugs were at least briefly complete, Angie herself was the first to break the moment with the obvious question. "Well, Val, why have you come all the way to Texas to see me?"

"Actually, I've come to take you and your boys back to Memphis, if you'd like to go."

"My word, Val, I don't know. My friends and my life are here now; what would I do?" Angie moaned, but Val could see she was already considering the move.

Angie took a while to warm to the idea of returning to the familiarity of Memphis and her friends and former coworkers there. It wasn't the move itself but the looming difficulties that stood in the way.

Before any clear decision could be made, disposition of the property and goods she had held with Robert Cunningham had to be dealt with, and the only likely pool of interested buyers would be the other settlers themselves.

The biggest item for consideration would be the homestead (land, house, and improvements) itself. But in this, Angie already had a serious potential buyer of means on the hook. For more than a couple of years Anson McDonald, a neighbor in the same settlement, had been making cash offers to buy Robert and Angie out.

Their spot had been transformed into the jewel of the settlement by its natural features and water supply, as well as the many desirable additions Robert and Angie had made over the years.

The cabin they'd constructed (with the help of some of the neighbors) had, from the beginning, been designed as the initial portion of a much larger home. This would accommodate their family, which was sure to grow in the future. Along with Robert's many innovations in its design, a rudimentary pumping system sat on the back porch to get water from the creek (perhaps later a well) and up to the house easily. The smokehouse, as well as the cool cellar (dug into the side of the hill for storage of home-canned and dried foodstuffs) and the small but quite serviceable blacksmith forge (which Robert had had plans to grow into a brick kiln) all helped make the value of their place quite estimable.

In fact, over the last three years, the family had grown very little of the food they ate, instead trading blacksmith-made hinges, horseshoes, wheels and the like for settlement-grown corn and vegetables. Since Robert had been on the frontier from the time he was a boy and was also an excellent shot, there was almost always plenty of meat, fresh and smoked, for the family. The surplus was often traded for food items, cloth or other settlement-produced items, or sometimes even just labor to help out around the homestead.

Robert had even gotten some clear plate glass, painstakingly cut it himself, and carefully fitted it into window frames he'd made, giving their home the only clear glass windows in the settlement.

With the two good bedrooms separated by the closable breezeway, which opened right into the storage cellar, the house itself was the envy of all the neighbors.

Angie, while not overly anxious to divest before this because of all the work she herself had put into their home's building, now had a stronger motivation to sell. McDonald had a standing offer of $500, plus considerations for the place, livestock, and improvements.

Angie knew it was a fair offer, considering.

It was fair for the time and place; cash was drying up all over, leading to a huge recession or even depression. It was also fair because Anson McDonald's family had been generous about helping the newcomers get settled in and begin building their new home. His two sturdy sons had been much help with preparing and laying the heavy timbers for the foundation, floors, and walls. Pregnant with little Bobby at the time, she'd greatly appreciated the help of her good Scottish-descent neighbors.

Angie was Scottish on her mother's side and Danish on her father's. The McDonalds had put forth much effort to help make the Cunninghams' new home the best it could be.

The considerations McDonald offered in addition to the $500 were also quite estimable. He offered half up front, an almost astounding offer; the rest was to be paid within a year. This would mean that Angie would have quite a tidy nest egg of cash to draw on to finance her start-up needs in Memphis, plus more coming in over the next year. Plus, she would be repaying the kindnesses shown by a friend. McDonald, being Scottish, knew he was getting quite a value for his money at that price, but Angie was willing to let the place go to a friend for considerations.

The final consideration in the package offered by McDonald was to throw in the painting of Robert done a couple of years after their arrival in Texas by an itinerant portrait artist, perhaps from New York, touring Texas and seeking commissions to finance his excursion.

The striking portrait depicted Robert Cunningham in his beadwork-decorated buckskins, standing in a grove of what appeared to be red gum trees. Standing with his Kentucky long rifle at ease in his left hand and a tomahawk in his right, Robert wore his fore-and-aft New York State Militia cap at a jaunty angle. His Indian-beadwork epaulets also sported some type of military insignia. The blue breechclout he wore was fringed in gold piping.

The deep black ponytail of hair extending from Robert's neck helped to frame the strong young face of this obviously capable young frontiers-man, caught in a quiet moment in the woods.

Many years later, examination by art experts of the painting while it hung in the state museum in New York (as part of a "heroes of New York" exhibition during the centennial of New York's statehood) brought speculation that brushstroke similarities to an artist named Grentilz who later moved permanently to Texas might attribute it to him.

All Angie knew was she didn't want to leave such a memorial to Bobby behind in Texas. Anson McDonald agreed wholeheart-edly; he only owned the painting because the artist had rendered a less-than-satisfactory portrait of the McDonald family. The artist had thrown Anson's good friend Robert's portrait in on the deal to get McDonald to pay the full price for the disliked family portrait. Angie had admired and cherished the painting every time she visited the McDonald home.

Anson McDonald's words were simple to Angie. "Sure, girl, and I canna let you leave here without taking your bonnie Bobby with you to your new home!"

Fortunately, all their household goods, implements, and clothing were easily going to fit inside Val's generous freight wagon's bed, even with a specially-prepared bed and play area for Oskar and Bobby.

So, along with kitchen utensils, bedding, clothing, and the rest of the myriad of items making the trip to Memphis was a heavily padded rectangular bundle, securely placed so as not to jostle about on the long wagon ride.

◆

After they finally arrived in Memphis, Val and Angie placed the portrait lovingly up on the fireplace mantle in the sitting room, where it was a constant tribute to the man and his principles. It had arrived in perfect shape and was thus displayed the entire time the family was in the Adams house.

Angie initially worried that Val might be somewhat put out by having the portrait of her tragically dead husband on display as a constant reminder.

He attempted to set her straight in short order about that. "Sweetheart, I met him before you did; I respected the young man tremendously!" Val began. "It's a real tragedy that your time together was cut short, but your nine years in the Texas settlement seemed to have been a happy time for you. I just hope I can give you many years of happiness here in Memphis as we begin this new chapter of your life."

That new chapter seemed to be beginning auspiciously as Angie, Val, and the boys settled into the new routines that now included baby Angelina. As the boys, both Bobby and Oskar, delved deeply into their studies at school, amazing new vistas of knowledge opened themselves up, from mathematics to language in all its forms, from great literature and stories as fresh today as they were hundreds of years before, and from the burning Sahara sands to the mysteries of the Orient. It seemed each day brought a new slice of the big, wide world to be digested.

"It's story time!" Mary McGevney would call out once a day, and then she had the rapt attention of Oskar and Bobby, as well as most of the rest of the class. "Where shall we go today?" Then, real or imaginary, she would read or tell a tale of a far-off place and its inhabitants, whether people or animals or both.

When she could do so, she would often show the students where the places she was describing were on one or more of the generous number (for that area and time) of maps the McGevneys had managed to gather for their classroom.

Maps were a huge part of showing the world and its makeup to the boys, and both of them showed a keen interest in the maps they could occasionally bring home from school. Add to this Val's interest and willingness to show Bobby and Oskar the places he'd personally been on the maps, and it made for fascinating, downright educational evenings for the male side of the family, while Angie had time to herself to bond with Angelina, nurturing her as a mother should.

Thus, in the evenings, the Adams house became a child-oriented, educationally centered enclave of growth for all in the household, bringing warmth and deep enjoyment, along with discovery.

As the months and years passed, the dining room table often had one or two school friends of Bobby and/or Oskar in attendance for supper. Often Mr. Marno, Mr. Benoit, or Mr. Gold himself might grace their supper table. And sometimes even Mr. or Mrs. McGevney, or even both, would take supper with them after school.

They were in the Adams house for a little more than four years, and in each of those years, it became a more bustling, active place. As the boys got bigger, the house got smaller. Coupled with the increased activity on their part and that of their friends, Angelina began rapidly to grow into the tomboy she was going to become—until boys came into her notice and changed her world again.

Another set of shouts and shrieks had been added to the general Dimand house tumult.

Active, physical games from morning till dark and loud, boisterous friends tramping through the house, eating everything in sight or not well concealed, all made the Adams house the place for the Cunningham boys and Angelina Dimand to grow up in an atmosphere of love and protection, and so they did.

Val and Angie had been married well before Angelina was born, so after her birth, they had decided right away to make some decisions about the children and their names.

It started late one night in pillow talk.

"Val, sweetheart? Have you given any thought to what last name the kids, including the baby, are going to have now that we're married?" Angie had whispered softly into Val's ear while caressing one of his "special" spots.

After a short discussion, followed by a longer time of passionate handiwork for each, agreement was reached.

The boys would keep the surname Cunningham, out of respect for Robert's memory, while Angelina would carry the Dimand name to recognize the new union that had produced her. Both Val and Angie thought this was an equitable situation.

In order to help keep Robert's legacy and memory alive, all three kids would be taught thoroughly Robert Cunningham's history, from the Indian Territories on the frontiers of New York to his final days at the Alamo. That way, when friends or guests in their home asked questions about the portrait over the mantle, they could each give answer and help keep Bobby Cunningham's spirit alive.

Something else significant was happening during these busy, active days. Val's business was flourishing and beginning to grow exponentially.

When he went to pick up Angie down in Texas in one of his freight wagons, he'd had ten wagons total, six freight and four lighter delivery wagons. Now he had forty. Twenty were of the largest overland freight size for long-haul trips between states, and the other twenty were more or less equally divided between smaller, narrower wagons used for in-town deliveries, and specially fitted units for service picking up and delivering goods at the waterfront. These wagons were sized and equipped to run between the docking slips at the water's edge. They also had special drop sides so cargo could be loaded or unloaded from the edge, as was often necessary.

Add to this array of rolling stock the requisite livestock needed to keep it moving, along with the tack, harness, and hardware needed for such a bustling enterprise, and you needed a place of considerable size just to house and run such an operation. Val had been fortunate enough to buy a small livery stable and corral a couple of years back from a man really needing to sell. Although he really didn't need the livery aspects of his purchase, it made a most suitable base of operations for his expanding shipping business.

Now, however, his business had radically outgrown its present location and Val was faced with quite a dilemma. He could: either open another operation and run his business from more than one locale, with all the attendant communications problems that would bring, or he could build a new place, with room to expand and adapt built right in.

Val's decision didn't turn out to be all that difficult for him. He couldn't see having employees traveling between various locations all day long, carrying messages back and forth and using up valuable time and money. He started scouting locations almost immediately.

At that point, residential development in Memphis was being most heavily emphasized to the south and east of town, while to the north was still open for business and industrial development.

Val chose an available site along what was then called the North Road or North Trail. This road headed north toward Kentucky, nowadays through modern towns such as Covington and Dyersburg, along what has become US Highway 51 North. The lot he chose was ten acres, giving ample room for all his present needs with plenty of room for the growth he rather expected to accompany his burgeoning enterprises.

Val was going to need to construct a set of corrals and feeding facilities for his hitch teams to pull the wagons, along with hitching facility areas for connecting the horse teams efficiently to the wagons. Since coupling areas were needed to be constructed, they might as well be part of the long, low buildings housing the sheltered stable facilities for keeping as many of the horses as possible out of inclement weather.

Once again, caressing pillow talk managed to come to fruition in the Dimand household.

Shortly after Val and Angie moved into the Adams house, Val had assumed the responsibility for the rent, and he (instead of Levi Gold) had been paying it ever since. He gave Angie a household allowance each month for supplies and expenses to run the home. Angie was free to use the money she earned on her own in any way she saw fit, and Val encouraged her to save any capital she could, including the Texas homestead monies, in a savings account in her name.

For the first time in her life, Angie was a woman of some means.

Val's business property search would also allow him to view prospective sites for a new family home of their very own. Four lots he viewed with Angie were prime candidates for a home setting to replace the Adams house.

The lovebirds finally picked out a nicely wooded lot over on Bethel Avenue for a home site on which to build a more commodious abode than the Adams house. The Bethel site was just under one acre, with a magnificent spreading oak right in front of where he envisioned the house to be constructed. It had ample room for a nice yard on each side, along with a four or five stall stables, a carriage house, another outbuilding, and a quarter-acre (or larger) garden in the back. Best of all, at the rear the property sloped downhill to a point less than an eighth of a mile from the new freight yard location.

As fortune would have it, both properties were offered by the Greenlaw brothers.

Val's cash position with the business was such that he was able to pay in full for both sites outright.

Wonderful times ensued at the Adams house, with evenings spent around the cleared-away dinner table making sketches of what each person would want in a new house. They were discussing such things as porches, windows, and outbuildings that might be needed and where they would go.

Everyone got an equal say, and as the rough drawings began to take shape, Val was able to predict something he could take to an architect or a builder.

The overall design would include spacious rooms with twelve-foot ceilings, a central fireplace with smaller fireplaces in each bedroom, a spacious attic with a high-peaked ceiling itself and dormered windows at each end, and a full basement with complete walls and flooring.

While Val wasn't looking to build anything ostentatious, he *did* want to provide Angie and the children with a home they wouldn't have to be grumbling about shortly after moving in. He wanted some of the latest in modern conveniences without extravagant expense, and commodious comfort at a reasonable price.

One special feature designed into the home from the outset came about after Val himself had had a particularly difficult time going to the privy at the Adams house one icy winter day. Val came staggering in, clothes torn and lip bleeding, after making the short trip to and from the little outbuilding.

"Oh, honey!" Angie shrieked in dismay as soon as she saw him. "Whatever happened to you?"

Before Val could answer, Bobby and Oskar came into the dining area where Val had collapsed into a chair and asked, almost in unison, "What happened?" Bobby added, "We heard a noise outside a moment ago. Was that you?"

"Yes," said Val. "I fell pretty badly coming in from the outhouse when my leg gave in, and I scratched up my face on the walkway paving stones. It really looks worse than it is."

After a chorus of "I'm sorry" from everyone, Val said finally, "It did give me a good idea for the new house, though. How about an indoor bathroom and privy inside the house, at least for the winter months when it's so cold and slippery?"

The boys thought it was great from the outset, but Angie was concerned about controlling the odors indoors and said so.

Val answered, "I'll see what the architect has to say."

Angie's reply made a lot of sense to Val when she said, "If we build it in now but can't use it right away, at least we'll have it already built for when we can."

"Great idea!" said Val and punctuated his approval with a big, noisy kiss for Angie on her cheek, much to the amusement of Bobby and Oskar, both of whom absolutely rolled with laughter. With a great deal more sketch drawing and lively conversation by the family members about the house over the course of the rest of the winter, everything was ready to take to the architects in early spring to generate the drawings to use to build the house.

As the drawings were being produced, workers began to work on clearing overgrown brush from the lot, trimming trees and starting to dig a foundation pit for the massive timbers on brick structures that would support the new house. The messy job of digging the foundation pit consumed the efforts of more than a dozen men for over a week's time, much to the fascination of Val and Angie's kids. Even little Angelina would come home many nights from the job site looking like a little mud ball, despite everyone's efforts to keep her clean. The boys got dirty, sure, but Angelina came home covered head to toe – and stinky, too.

The little girl just loved dirt and mud!

The beautiful spreading oak tree in front of the home site received a handsome trim for symmetry and shape, while the areas set aside for lawns were cleared and reseeded with grass. Behind the house, set back from it by about fifty feet, the five-stall stable began to take shape. It included not only quarters for riding stock, tack, and equipment such as buggies and carriages but also a stableman's quarters and residence.

The final bit of grounds work involved fencing off a permanent garden plot of just under half an acre, flanked on its western edge by a good-sized orchard, initially planted in apples, pears, and figs.

An early spring rain, unusually intense for the time, caused a brief work stoppage, but otherwise work proceeded apace.

First, the foundation needed to be built in the pit that was dug into the small hill. Rather than a series of stone, brick, or wooden pilings as was usually done, a brick wall two layers thick was constructed all the way around the perimeter of the house, upon which the floor joists would be laid. The two layers were separated by a layer of oilcloth for waterproofing. Places that needed additional support for load bearing got pilings or interior walls. After the initial tile and stone floor was laid, the interior walls of the basement were built in, and then the huge job of setting the massive floor joists into place began. Each of the eight-inch-thick, twelve-inch-wide cypress beams could be as much as fifty feet long, requiring as many as eight men at a time to set each beam in place to a precise measurement accurate down to the nearest one-eighth of an inch.

Overseeing all this labor was construction foreman Leslie M. Hammond from Nashville. He could be either quite jovial or downright surly, whichever mood seemed to accomplish his needs of the moment.

After all the floor joists were laid in, Les Hammond had his installers go and intentionally try to disrupt what they had done, looking for weak points and flaws. Very few such aberrations were found and corrected, and so the work of raising the walls with their doorways and windows began.

Each of the children found something fascinating to watch during the construction process. Mr. Hammond was quite patient and accommodating in allowing them each to safely (and out of the workers' way) watch things as they happened.

Angelina was especially rapt while watching the plasterers apply their wet mixture to the thin wooden lath slats between the walls' upright studs. What she was most delighted with though, was the way that the fresh plaster squeezed through the narrow openings between slats and formed an almost abstract pattern on the backside of the lath. She would giggle merrily as the long swaths of goo appeared on the backside of the lath, and when parts of some swaths broke off and fell to the floor, she was enraptured. As long as there was someone to hold her, her natural tendency to want to play in the fresh goo was thwarted.

A couple of times, she got by. What a mess!

Bobby seemed to be most interested when certain tasks seemed to require teamwork between two or more employees. Thus, when the floor joists were being laid by teams of up to eight men at a time, Bobby sat or lay motionless under the oak tree while absorbing it all as though he were to be tested upon it later. And when a wall section was completed and about to be raised into position, Bobby was first in line to observe. After all the first-floor wall sections were up and fastened in place, floor joists for the attic floor needed to be installed. Teams of men climbed and walked high up in the structure of the house.

Oskar loved to join him in watching the interior structure going up, with men clambering all over it.

But the thing Oskar enjoyed most seemed to be the endless supply of sawdust that was available for him to share with Angelina, endlessly piling it up, swishing it around, and sweeping it back up again into a small bucket with an old whisk broom they had found. Hours of fun play was right there, and when Mr. Hammond saw the kids sharing the old whisk broom, he got three brand-new ones so each child could have his or her own.

One day in late spring, since the attic floor was fully installed and the main attic stairway had just been completed, Val himself paid a rare visit to the job site. He was inclined, overall, to not "joggle the elbows" of Hammond and his crews while they were working, particularly with potential changes to the overall design and fabrication. But on this day, he wanted to see one thing for himself, and ask a question about a potential design change that had recently occurred to him.

When he asked Leslie Hammond for a few moments toward the end of the workday to discuss two things, Mr. Hammond was only too glad to accommodate his genteel customer. At his request, Hammond led Val up to the rear-facing dormer window, still just framing at that point. Val hauled out a medium-sized spyglass and a set of binoculars at that point and placed them on a nearby drawings table.

Stepping to roughly the center of the window area and looking out over the edge into the backyard, Val said, "That's quite a view!" Then reaching for and looking through the spyglass and the binoculars in turn, Val turned to Hammond.

"Just what I had hoped for," said Val as he handed Hammond the binoculars for a look. "You can see most of the freight yard out the window without help, and binoculars get you a lot of detail. That's all actually a little better than I had hoped for."

Leslie Hammond replied, "Yes, I can see the construction going on with your buildings in nice detail from here. That'll be nice to be able to see your entire operation without having to leave home."

Val countered with, "Which leads me to my next question, and I realize it may cost extra. Is it possible to extend the back porch ten or twelve feet more into the backyard and then roof it over to provide a place for the family to sit up there in the cool of the evening? And, if so, could we provide steps down from the attic to get to it for privacy?"

Hammond thought for a few moments before replying. His response was positive and thorough. "Yes, we could do that even at this stage of the construction without having to rip up anything we've already done, I believe. We might need to cantilever in a couple to four beams to hold the additional weight plus people, but we can prepare for that now but do it later if you decide to proceed. Since the additional back porch space will lie outside the original foundation perimeter, doing it this way will mean we don't have to lay a robust foundation just for the back porch. That'll save you plenty."

Val had a wry grin on his face when he said to Leslie Hammond, "I'm running into cost overruns everywhere I turn over there. I sure hope I can keep it this side of bankruptcy over here!"

Hammond's arm went around Val's burly shoulders. "Don't worry! You are still well within your initial outlay on this project, and I don't see missing the mark by more than a couple of hundred dollars—if that. If we do the back porch expansion, you'll know how much it'll be well in advance."

With that, the two men shook hands, bid each other good afternoon, and went home.

After the framing for the walls for the attic, siding went on the outside of the house, and cedar shake shingles went on to complete the roof. Once the doors and windows were built and installed, the place became rather impervious to the weather, so interior finish could begin in earnest.

They had only missed the deadline for exterior completion by one week, and the fall weather was mild and conducive for painting, papering, and all the thousand and one finishing details. Those would turn what was now the shell of a house into a home.

As work proceeded apace, Angie was in her element with paint colors, paper patterns, furniture choices, and the like. The kids were all having great fun changing the big, empty space into a home. Bobby and Oskar each got to design their own sleeping space, while Angelina got to pick everything that went into her new room.

Angie had wanted only two things special for her and Val's bedroom. One was a deeply upholstered chaise lounge. The other was a tilting full-length dressing mirror. A nice upholstered chair for sitting was also added to the mix. All these items were ordered through Levi Gold's store, along with most of the other furniture and fittings for the house.

Gradually, the furnishings and other supplies came in, and the items were safely stored in the kitchen area until the rest of the house was finished to the point of installing them. Angie was delighted when the time came to move the furniture into the various rooms and set it up, put on bedding and such, hang curtains and generally begin dressing the house to be a home.

After rugs went down on the floors, dishes into the cabinets, and pictures on the walls, the house was ready for the final touch, with every family member gathered around. The final, yet vital piece of furnishing was about to be installed.

Val lifted the portrait of Robert W. Cunningham into a specially-prepared spot on the new mantle and fixed the anti-slip stops so it was completely immobilized and secure.

Val spoke next in his best "Sunday go to meeting" voice. "Well, Bobby, I hope you are pleased with how everything is going and that you'll help look out for us as we go forward. I know you treasured these precious people, as I do, and I promise to take the best care of them that I can as we go forward as a family." Val reached forward with one hand and gently touched the corner of the frame for emphasis. "You'll always be with us."

A round of applause followed, and Angie slipped her hand into Val's and said quietly, "Thank you, for everything."

Chapter 7

VAL IN THE NEW HOUSE

It's just a Memphis thang!

1842–1847

Aside from being a remarkably handsome man, Valentine Dimand also cut quite a wide swath through early Memphis society along several other fronts. He could just as easily have been a thoroughly bad man, an outlaw, so to speak. There were indeed rumors and whispered tales to the effect that he had once actually been such, though no definitive proof was ever offered. But there was that pesky newspaper story in the *Memphis Appeal* from years back that labeled him as "Sudden Death … with Either Hand!" He had dispatched both the Boswell brothers to their final reward, even after they had the drop on him with their pistols already drawn and pointed at him. After coolly shooting each one of them between the eyes (one left-handed, the other right), he'd then stared down their companions, daring them to make another move. He'd only had two more of the single-shot pistols, and there were three targets left, but no one wanted to be one of the two who definitely would die.

For those not easily inclined to pay credence to the moniker in the paper, it wasn't the reporter who actually described him in such colorful terms. It had been said by local lawman Bill Deene, a thoroughly bad man in his own right, who had witnessed the whole encounter.

But Val Dimand also knew the Scriptures thoroughly enough to lead church service as a lay minister, which he did from time to time. When he really got going on how the Lord God empowered and equipped Nehemiah to rebuild the walls of Jerusalem, you would come out of that service knowing that, with the Lord's help and blessing, anything was possible.

Quiet encouragement was one of Val's strong suits.

Steadfast discouragement of things he didn't approve of was, also. Listening to him describe Paul's dilemma in the Book of Philemon only began to provide a glimpse into Val's abhorrence of slavery in all its forms.

Now, Val wasn't a street-corner antislavery Bible thumper, but he would have nothing to do with it. If a slaveholder came in to the freight yard with one of his chattel, Val made sure to speak to that man as respectfully as he did his master, giving the slave every courtesy any man deserved.

A crew of highly skilled slaves working in the freight yard would have saved tremendously over having to pay the help Val hired instead. This had been suggested many times to him, to which his response was always, "I'd rather cut off my own arm!" That he usually said so with one hand on a pistol butt lent extra credence to his words.

Valentine Dimand was a crack rifle shot, along with being a deadly pistoleer. But, as many of his wranglers, drovers, and waggoneers could attest, he was also deadly accurate at throwing knives or tomahawks. It was also rumored, but without any recent evidence, that he was a fine fencer, swordsman, and duelist as well.

No one really seemed anxious to find out.

Another thing Val was very good with was women. That he had already had most of the available women in Memphis had been bandied about and snickered over by busybodies and bluenoses throughout the town.

His friendly, easygoing manner, coupled with his dashing good looks and brilliant smile and enhanced by his trim, muscular physique only served to make him an absolute magnet for the fairer sex.

But things had changed for Val Dimand lately. Though there was really no way he could have been as prodigious at coupling with women as was often described (without parts falling off the man), for the past few years, Val had been completely a one-woman man.

The stunningly beautiful woman who had married Val and changed his life was the former Angie MacFee of Memphis, whose first husband, Robert W. Cunningham, had died in defense of the Alamo. She provided Val with an opportunity to not only be a husband to her but also a father to her two young sons. The story of how Val had made the long trek to Texas to retrieve Angie and the boys, and bring them back from the frontier to the relative safety of Memphis was often told.

The allusions to the book of Hosea were obvious.

Stock in Val as a man went up.

This was especially true when one heard about Val losing the full use of a leg for the rest of his life. He was wounded while confronting road agents who lay in wait for him and the young family. All this spoke of a man who could be depended upon as a provider and protector for a woman and her offspring, not just a bauble for a hot afternoon dalliance who would be gone with the breeze.

Val had also always striven to be assiduously honest and fair in his business dealings. Because of this, people were comfortable paying him and his agents, frequently in cash. Their shipments received were always correct, and their outgoing parcels and freight were always treated with the utmost care and expedience.

Thus, much of the daily monetary intake of the freightyard was cash receipts, while the commercial or business shipping was usually handled by check or bank draft. Either way, bank deposits were handled on a daily basis, initially only by Val himself at the recently established Union Bank of Tennessee but later, as the business had inevitably grown, by the cashier from documents prepared by the overseeing bookkeeper.

Daily management of the money coming through the Dimand S hipping and Express Company soon became just too large for one man to handle. You might think increasing the number of hands the money passed through on its way to the bank could lead to more chances for robbery, and you'd be right. Stealing from Val Dimand had been tried several times, with a singular lack of success.

Payroll for the workers was paid on the first Monday of the month, done as "cash on the barrelhead," giving each worker his entire monthly earnings all at once to manage as each one saw fit. This always happened on a Monday. That way, a worker could have a chance to pay some bills before the lure and temptations of the saloons and gambling houses over a weekend became too great for a man with cash money "burning a hole in his pocket." If he wanted, a man could leave some or all of his payroll "on deposit" with the company and draw against it as needed. Val charged nothing for this service (although it cost him in labor and salary to keep up with it), and many of the older or married wranglers, stockmen, and drivers took advantage of it as a way to have banking services convenient to work.

Val fully believed, as the Scriptures said, that "the worker is due his wages." Therefore, a full month's salary was paid to each worker, regardless of any time missed. Adjustments for illness, family needs, and other absences were made up in time, not money. An equitable system it was deemed to be, by workers and management alike.

So it really wasn't hard to see why Valentine Dimand was viewed with great favor by many segments of Memphis society, high and low.

Even if you didn't know him at all, you could almost immediately recognize him if you saw him coming, particularly on horseback.

Years before, Val had ridden with Auguste Marno and Pasquinel Benoit out of western Louisiana, all the way to Santa Fe to avoid a trumped-up charge of assault and homicide centering upon Benoit's explosive temper. Nine months was required to clear the charges for a safe return.

Their time in Santa Fe made an indelible mark on Val, as the flashy but hardworking Mexican vaqueros showed Val a level of horsemanship he had never seen. Their silver-adorned and highly tooled saddlery was something he immediately wanted to emulate, along with the absolute élan and abandon of their riding. By the time the three riders (no longer wanted as outlaws) rode back east to their home territories of Louisiana, Mississippi, and Tennessee, Val habitually wore a short-waisted, tight vaquero's jacket and a flat-brimmed, short-crowned black hat with a silver band.

Such garb made him instantly recognizable on the streets of Memphis, setting him apart from the myriad other horseback riders found on the city streets on any given day. If the day was to hold much in the way of manual labor, the jacket and ruffled shirt worn for meeting clients and other business affairs was substituted by a loose, drawstring-necked sleeveless shirt, which served to accentuate his impressive muscular arms. With his lean waist, long legs, and impressive chest, Val Dimand presented a fine figure of a man.

Every morning that Val was to go out, Angie Dimand would help him get dressed and groomed for the day. Obviously, Val could do these things for himself, but it gave Angie great pleasure to sit in Val's lap and brush his long dark wavy hair, trim his flowing mustache, and sundry other things that made her man appear his best out on the street.

Sometimes, things went a little bit further than that.

"Ooooh!" whispered Angie as she brushed Val's lustrous locks. "That's going to make you late if you keep it up." Val's left hand had gently cupped her right breast, and he was gently kneading her erect nipple between his thumb and forefinger.

"How so?" he asked, continuing his nipple play a little faster. "I have some important matters to see to today, and I must be about my business in short order."

"Well, have you considered this?" Angie cooed as her robe spread open revealing her naked crotch, spread open and moist from her continuous handiwork. As Val watched in fascination, two fingers inside her furiously burrowing in and out became three without missing a beat and then all four were inside her and slowing down to a sensuous crawl compared to the previous torrent. As her fingers buried themselves deeply into her and then were withdrawn so tantalizingly slowly, Val could see the creamy, rich juices they were absolutely coated with as she brought them out.

As Angie brought her dripping fingers out for the final time, she began to ever so slowly and gently rub the beautiful tulip lips hidden inside her outer lips, making sure she was thoroughly moist everywhere. She had slid back on the bed and opened her knees wide so Val had a totally unobstructed view of her tantalizing crotch and the exhibition she had just given.

"Now, if you can spare just a few moments from your busy schedule for me, here's what I need." With that Angie flung her robe up over her waist, bent over the end of the bed, spread her legs wide and squatted a little, looked back at Val, and said, "Take me now, as hard as you need to, and then go on your way. I'll try to keep myself wet for you all day till you come home, and then you can take me again tonight."

Val stepped up behind her beautiful backside and thrust his entire considerable length into her moist chasm, but instead of beginning to thrust immediately, he stood there motionlessly for a few moments, savoring what he had just witnessed. As he stood there, he rubbed and caressed various parts of Angie. And then an overwhelming force came up from deep within him, and he thrust twice, as deeply as he could and sent his entire load of emission deep inside Angie.

Angie moaned and fell forward onto the bed and rolled over onto her back. While Val fixed his trousers, she lay there, rubbing absently at her crotch. But when Val's seed began to stream forth from her plundered hole, she began to rub it in every fold and fissure, completely coating the outside of that whole area with milky juice.

Sticking fingers inside herself she said, "Have a nice day, honey, and I'll see you tonight!"

Val walked out to a long and lusty, "Oooh."

He had a certain grin upon his face as he went through the day's efforts, with an extra bounce to his step. He had had an unruly team that just didn't want to be hitched, and even though he got slammed in the shoulder pretty hard by the yoke before they were finally harnessed, in the end, the wagon rolled out of the freight yard. The drivers were fully in control of the wagon, its freight, and its team. Even this morning mishap did little to dampen Val's mood, and he was positively cheery all the rest of the day.

When work was over for the day, Val rode his horse home to the new house, where he spent a few moments with Anton, the new stableman and groundskeeper for the house. He, along with Carmella, the new housekeeper and cook, represented the entirety of the hired household staff for the new home. Not one to put on appearances of affluence or position, Valentine Dimand nevertheless wanted to have Angie's daily burden lightened from drudgery so she might devote the bulk of her attentions to being wife and mother.

Anton had the duty of unsaddling whichever horse Val had ridden for the day, feeding and watering him, and grooming him before bedding him down for the evening. Anton, himself a Basque Frenchman from the border area between France and Portugal, was an accomplished horseman and trainer. He had been around horses all his life and was delighted to come to work for Val, who he had known for years.

A sturdily built six-footer, Anton was larger than the average Basque. He had first become acquainted with Val Dimand when they were about twenty years younger. Val had helped save his young daughter's life when she had been injured on the farm by a wild boar. Val had immediately swept her up on his horse and raced her the fifteen miles to the doctor's office in town. She'd made a complete recovery, and Anton was Val's friend for life.

Of the three horses Val chose to stable at the house, Vindicator, a large black with flowing mane and tail and more than a little of the Spanish Barb in him, was easily Val's favorite. He had bought him while in Santa Fe and had ridden him since. Horse and rider had, therefore, become one unit, inseparable. Anton walked Vindicator, cooling him down slowly and then fed him his supper of high-quality hay, followed by half a bucket of oats. A rub down and a generous session with curry comb and brush followed, and then it was into his spacious stall for the night. Val would typically let Anton know the evening before which horse he chose to ride the next morning, so Anton could have the horse ready when Val was ready to leave, usually about seven.

After Anton was finished with his evening duties with the horses and their tack, he could retire to his quarters in the carriage house for a comfortable night's rest. At least once or twice a week, he took his supper with the family at the dining table; other nights, when he might not be fresh enough for the dinner table, he could take his meal on the lattice-screened back porch, often with Carmella.

Sometimes, Carmella would inform Angie or Val that Anton was taking his supper later in his quarters with her, so she'd be away from the house for a while, after her post-supper cleanup was done.

Once, when Angie wanted to ask Carmella a quick question, she went out to the carriage house, stepped in, and turned toward Anton's doorway. The normally-quiet building still held muffled noises; she approached anyway.

She stopped in her tracks when she spotted him thrusting violently into the housekeeper sprawled on his bed. Carmella was moaning in extreme pleasure with her legs firmly around Anton's hips, and they both had their eyes tightly shut.

Angie backed out silently and turned back toward the house, a crooked smile on her lips and the question forgotten.

Carmella was, like Val, a French Magyar descendant from the part of southern Mississippi bordering Louisiana. They had not known each other before, but their families were known to each other. It was Val's mother who had told him years before what a good cook and household help a girl from the DeMarco family would be, and Val remembered all these years later. When Angie brought up meeting her at Gold's, Val immediately suggested she ask Carmella if she'd be interested in the position. In addition to a nice salary, she would also have her own living quarters right there in the house, as well as board.

Val paid higher than the going rate for both positions, so with the good salaries and living quarters provided, both Anton and Carmella were happy to be there.

Carmella was almost to her forties, slight of stature with a very fine complexion the color of light caramel, and Angelina took to her immediately. The boys gravitated more toward Anton and followed him about whenever they could. But they were all crazy about Carmella's cooking. She would often treat the kids to freshly squeezed lemonade with some spice (she would never say what it was) dashed in, and they were over the moon.

Since it was only a few months after they had moved in, everyone was still exploring their new abode. But now that it was spring outside, exploring the wilderness that surrounded the new home site was a priority for the kids. Bobby was more or less the de facto leader by being the eldest, so it fell to him to make sure Oskar and Angelina stayed in sight and relatively out of trouble.

The house was less than an eighth mile off the North Road and surrounded by lush growth, so it made a handsome estate. Its proximity to the freight yard meant Val had a short ride there in the morning, and he could arrive fairly fresh. Many days, Val would need to ride through the city to speak to existing or potential customers, so he was often on horseback for much of the day. When he could, he would try to set up personal visit appointments in advance so he could just leave from home, but often he needed to get the yard started to begin the day. Days spent mainly at the freight yard, he was dressed more appropriately for the manual labor of such, whereas meeting customers called for a higher level of attire and appointments. As he rode through town on those days, he presented a more professional look.

On this particular day, he'd had to spend more time at the yard than he had expected, so by the time he got home, he was hot, tired, and dirty.

As he came in the kitchen door from having spoken to Anton, Angie wrapped an arm around his waist, drew him into a close kiss, and spoke quickly. "My, you're fragrant tonight! Why don't you head for the bathroom, undress, and I'll draw you a nice bath. That way, by the time Carmella has supper on the table, you'll be fit to join us."

Val replied, "I guess I do need a little freshening up, at that."

"More than a little, I'm afraid," she replied saucily. "I'll have Carmella heat a pot or two of water so your bath won't be totally cold."

Moments later, while Val was still removing his shirt, Angie came in with a pot of hot water. She bent over and made sure the drain plug for the tub was securely stoppered and poured the hot water in. She then began pumping the handle to the water pump, and a satisfying stream of cool water flowed into the pot. Val watched as her breasts swung back and forth with the effort. That potful and two more gave Val a start to his bath, and he got into the shallow water and just let out a long, "Aahh," as he relaxed. Angie continued to fill the porcelain tub while Val watched her delicious bottom move beneath her robe.

With a light peck, she handed Val a bar of scented soap and a wash-cloth before saying, "Let me go to the kitchen and get another pot of hot water, and I'll see how long before Carmella has supper."

With that, she was gone.

After a few more moments of simple luxuriating, Val began the process of soaping and scrubbing himself. Hardly had he begun, however, when Angie returned with fresh hot water. She added it to the bath to a lusty, "Aahh!" from Val. Standing up, she began to pump water into the pot and pour it into the tub.

"Got anywhere you need me to wash, handsome?" Angie cooed.

Val stood up, even on his wounded leg, and presented his manhood to her. "Here would be great. Sometimes I have some difficulty reaching it." He grinned.

Angie gave him a full in-the-mouth kiss on the tip of the aforementioned area and then looked up at him and smiled herself.

"I'm expecting bigger things out of you later, so be ready for me. All nice and clean and fed up properly and ready to go!"

Before she made it out the door, she opened her robe so Val could see her naked body beneath. "I guess I need to dress for dinner." She added a kiss.

Then she added, "You have fresh clothes laid out on the bed, and Carmella said dinner in fifteen minutes, so I'll gather the kids to the table and see you there, darling."

Val came to the table with a jaunty air about him, and the dinner conversation was lively. Val and Angie kept little undertones going between them, and the kids were oblivious to it all, merely enjoying the mood thus created. They had been exploring the areas surrounding the new house, traipsing through brush and bramble all day long. So, after supper, Val read to the boys about explorations in Africa, comparing them to explorations in early North America and mentioning Spanish conquistadores, French trappers, and early mountain men. He told the boys how their home on the Texas frontier had been part of the opening up of that part of the West and how big a part in all that their father, Robert Cunningham, had played. He even told them stories of the riverboat men on the Mississippi coming through Memphis and how Robert himself had been one of them.

Meanwhile, Angie and Angelina paired off over a project of arranging ribbon pieces onto old doilies to brighten them up for use in the new house. Angelina was delighted, as each piece of ribbon she selected was sewed onto a doily's backside, adding a splash of color showing through.

Soon enough, though, all three children were rubbing their eyes and nodding. Carmella had long before come in from taking her supper with Anton on the back porch and had cleared away and washed the dinner dishes. Anton had gone to his quarters perhaps an hour before, and Carmella soon retired quietly to hers. Val picked up Bobby from the settee and carried him to his bed, tucking him in afterward. He went back into the parlor and did the same with Oskar, who was so completely somnolent he took no notice at all. Meanwhile, Angie had carried Angelina to her bed, and then she came in to look at the boys and give them a kiss. Val went to Angelina's room and did the same. She did not stir.

Meeting back in the hallway, Val and Angie's eyes met as she crooked her finger at him in a come-hither gesture, with Val's hand fondling and caressing her delicious rear as they walked the short way to their bedroom.

As Angie quietly closed the bedroom door into the hallway and turned the locking latch, Val went over to the other door, which led to the bathroom and on past Carmella's room to the kitchen, and latched it quietly as well. Turning to face his bride, he found her with her arms folded across her chest and an inscrutable look on her face.

"Do you remember how you left me this morning? I was in a fix all day, trying to keep myself wet and ready for you when you returned. Carmella must have thought I had a case of something, because every twenty minutes or so, I was coming in here, shutting the door, and rubbing myself into a frenzy. A couple of times I had to go into the bathroom, just to keep from coming in here so often." Angie's face blushed bright red as she said the next part. "She must have even heard me cry out a little, because when I came out, she said my face was flushed and was I feeling all right?"

Val asked quietly, "Is there something I can do for you now?"

"Yes, you can. You can start by removing every stitch of clothing on your body and then lying down on your back on the chaise and letting me see you naked." She continued in a fierce whisper, "Then you can start to massage and rub that spear you have between your legs until it is full grown; I want all of you tonight. I had a time today, and I tried something new, and I want to do it again with you."

As Val was complying with her wishes, Angie moved the tilting, full-length dressing mirror to just beyond the end of the chaise, tilting it just a little, stepping back next to Val and examining the results and then repeating the whole process until she was satisfied.

She then sat down on the bed and waited for Val to finish his getting ready. She always enjoyed watching him undress, seeing his rippling abdomen, muscular chest, and ropelike arms as each part appeared to her gaze. But when his pants came off, her eyes were glued to his lower half, front and back. A finely-proportioned man by birth, Val Dimand's work and regimen kept him in tip-top physical shape, and his lean rider's waist, tapered legs, and small but firm buttocks only served to provide Angie with a visual feast. When he turned to face her, his manhood kept up pace with the rest of his body in kindling her desire.

Once again, Angie saw the bullet entrance scar, now not nearly so visible, on the front of Val's thigh. The dimple in the rear of his leg was larger, more pronounced, and probably there for the rest of his life. Those marks on that beautiful body only served as a visual reminder of Val's love for her, and she said so often.

"Go ahead and lie down now, sweetheart, and start rubbing that beautiful thing for me. I want to watch for a while," she said quietly.

In the several years that had passed since the encounter with the bushwhackers, Val had improved greatly at being able to stand and even move about without the assistance of a cane. But by this time, he was ready to lie down and did so. "Is this what you want?" he asked in a husky voice as he began to stroke himself.

"Oh, yes! That's nice, but put your knees up in the air and spread your legs. I want to see the whole thing!" Angie was beginning to sound a little breathless, but she had a fairly inscrutable look on her face.

"This better?" Val put his knees up and spread his legs while concentrating on the tip of his now fully-erect shaft. The tip was very moist, and a slight squishing sound could be heard as he moved his hand.

Angie smiled as she said, "I'd better get started myself before you get too far along. Can you see yourself OK?"

"Yeah, it's great; what made you think of the mirror?" he asked.

Angie was quick with a reply. "Oh, I caught a glimpse of myself fingering in the mirror, and it looked so sexy it made me wonder what we would look like together there and that made me convulse until I didn't think I could stop. When I finally did, I had to go into the bathroom and take a bath myself."

"Well, you certainly had an exciting day!"

"I hope tonight is even better," Angie cooed as she dropped her robe and bent down and put her mouth where Val's hand had been. "Can you see this?"

"I sure can!" Val groaned. "Even more than that, I can feel it! You look beautiful down there."

As her lips pooched out over Val's shaft, Angie slid them up and down, with a slowing and concentration at the tip. Val groaned and Angie lifted her head off him and put a finger to her lips.

"Not too loud, darling. We don't want to attract attention and wake anyone." She smiled while she spoke and then returned to his shaft with gusto.

Then Angie stood, dropped her robe and stepped over to Val.

Swinging a beautiful leg across him, she settled her crotch onto him, sinking his manhood as deeply into her as she could.

"How's that?" she groaned softly.

"Great," whispered Val. "And it looks wonderful in the mirror," he added as he continued to slide in and out of Angie.

She turned her head to look. "Oohh, that's nice," she purred. "But I want to watch without straining my neck, so in a moment I'm going to turn over and face the ceiling."

Val's reply was immediate and simple. "Yes, dear!"

So, after a couple more minutes of exquisite pleasure coupled together in that way, Angie pulled herself off if Val and stepped down to the floor. Gripping his now-reddened shaft in her hand as she turned toward the mirror, she straddled the chaise, lifting her leg over him and giving Val an exquisite view between her cheeks of all the treasures there, particularly as she sat back upon him. They had done this position many times before, but the view in the mirror gave it a new zest, as both of them could see their crotches, moistened, engorged, and slamming together in an impossibly exciting display of raw sex between lovers.

Make no mistake about it, they were, indeed, lovers.

Married and with children, they still found the time for each other and, indeed, thought of each other at many points in every day. Their love had a firm foundation, and Val intended to keep it that way. All his past dalliances with other women were a thing of the past, and his heart was set true for Angie.

As their impassioned lovemaking proceeded to the point where they were having to stifle themselves from loud exclamations of pleasure, Val finally had to have his release. Just as he came, his shaft popped out of Angie's beautiful tulip-lipped opening and began spraying his white emission over her lips and folds, covering them completely before it began to run down between her cheeks and over her anus.

Angie moaned softly and reached down to her crotch and began to smear the creamy liquid all over her outer and inner lips and then began with the other hand to rub some over and then into her anus.

"I know you're probably quite tired and ready for sleep, but could we just lie like this for a little while?" Angie finished her question with a soft kiss.

"Sure, sweetheart, as long as you want. Just wake me if I nod off."

"I just love to lie naked with you."

After a while Angie got up, and after a quick washup by the night-stand, she brought soap, a wet towel, and a dry towel over and did the same for Val. Then she helped him into bed. She scooted the chaise over to its normal position, rolled the dressing mirror to its place, put on a nightshirt in case one of the kids might need something in the night, and went to bed, drawing the covers up over both of them.

A beautiful, soft, and peaceful night ensued.

Val's mount the next morning was Sidewinder, a sturdy short-coupled buckskin cutting horse, often called a quarter horse by Westerners. Val liked to say that Sidewinder could "turn on a dime and give nine cents change!"

But just like his rattlesnake namesake, the horse sometimes needed to get his bucking done at the beginning of a morning, just to show his rider who was boss. Val was used to this, so when Sidewinder began his conniptions in the stable yard at the house, Val was ready and rode through every twist, buck, and turn until Sidewinder was ready to be controlled, usually for the rest of the day.

Val had purchased him from a fellow just up from west Texas on his way back to Pennsylvania to care for aging and ailing parents. At Val's earlier freight yard, which had been a livery stable before, the man asked Val if he knew someone who could use such a horse. When the man described Sidewinder's characteristics, Val soon realized such a horse might be extremely useful in handling the stock of his expanded operations. Before the man stepped onto the stage out of Memphis toward Pittsburgh, Val owned Sidewinder.

In his flat-brimmed, flat-topped black hat with the silver hat band and his shirtless, black leather-vested torso with his bulging, sculpted chest and muscular, knotted arms, Val himself could be, and often was, mistaken for a Westerner riding the streets of Memphis. With trim-fitting black trousers tucked into highly polished black riding boots completing his workaday look for the freightyard, he did cut the image of a no-nonsense Western rider.

That he had actually been such, years before, was known only to a few people. Only Auguste Marno and Pasquinel Benoit, out of all the people living in Memphis, knew what it was to have seen a grinning Val Dimand, reins in his teeth and bent over sideways on his saddle, firing a Hawken carbine under a galloping horse's belly to unseat another rider or throwing a spinning tomahawk right into a Comanche warrior's chest at a full gallop. Armed habitually with the Hawken, two (or sometimes, even four!) Colt single-shot horse pistols, a tomahawk kept razor-sharp, and a huge drop-pointed knife he claimed had come from Jim Bowie himself, Val was a foe to be reckoned with, indeed.

Angie loved the leather-vested look with its black loop-and-pawl fasteners, fringe, and the exposure of her lover's extreme manliness. She knew what other women would probably think as they looked at Val, but she didn't care, knowing he was hers alone. When Val was in his short-waisted vaquero's jacket with a ruffled white shirt and puffy sleeves, she could see how any woman on earth would be attracted to this dark, exotic man.

But every night he came home to her and made her feel like she was the only woman in the world.

Over the next several years, life was good there at the Bethel Avenue house. Everyone seemed to flourish; the kids did well in school. While schooling for girls was not a common thing in those days, the McGevneys were willing to enroll Angelina as she reached six years of age, along with a limited number of other female students, and teach the girls separately for the younger grades, eventually combining everyone at sixth grade and above. Angelina would be happy to stay with Mom and Carmella in the kitchen at home all day, but the prospect of reading about something new was the elixir that drew her to the classroom instead.

Bobby and Oskar were fascinated by how various things worked and were excited to learn all they could. Bobby seemed most interested in the various jobs that had to be done to, step by step, build a bridge, cross an open mountain range, or build a steamship. Oskar was similarly interested in such things, but it seemed more from the calculation aspects of what it would take in materials amounts, strengths, or types. Oskar had discovered a love for mathematics, Bobby, not so much. Both boys were solid in their English studies and well spoken. Oskar, however, was the glibber of the two, often amazing Angie and Val with his dinner table rhetoric about current events, so much so Val once asked Eugene McGevney what he thought of Oskar's future prospects as a lawyer.

The headmaster's reply was quick. "I've often thought of it myself, so much so I'd like to see how he takes to tutoring in Latin for next school year, if it's all right with you."

"Fine," said Val. "Let's see how far he can go!"

Eugene McGevney added, "I think he'll go very far; I think he's brilliant."

Angie aged gracefully into a trim, rare beauty. Val became a pillar of the community, as his unswerving principles, kindness, and generosity became known throughout the city. Their kids were popular companions for other young people, so the house was often abuzz with young voices in merriment. Anton and Carmella became such fixtures of the household that they became like family.

Certainly, there were ups and downs, uncertainties, and mishaps along the way. From a strong foundation of love and togetherness, though, they were handled as they arose.

Through it all, the portrait of Bobby Cunningham presided over this happy, blossoming home.

The Dimands did not do a great deal of entertaining socially. This was primarily due to Val's hesitance to seemingly flaunt their good fortune or position. They were also very busy and absorbed with each other. They had no hint of a reputation for "standoffishness," and they accepted the social invitations they could. When they could attend an event, they were widely known as charming and engaging guests.

Another reason they did not over-socialize was to help hold expenses down.

Val had a "rule of thumb" to live on no more than half of what he made each month, and as far as possible, he stuck to it. His net profits from month to month might vary somewhat but seldom widely.

By spending only half of what he made and banking the rest, Val Dimand was quietly becoming quite wealthy. Angie was growing as a woman of means as well.

Val's next step would be to begin providing for the future of his children. By thoroughly enjoying the present within his means and actively planning for a bright future for his family, it was no wonder Val's stature within Memphis society at all levels grew remarkably.

He had risen quite a bit from his early days serving as a volunteer "sworn peace officer" standing watch over the river landing at the top of the bluffs along Front Street.

Chapter 8

THE KIDS BECOME TEENS

Many an outlaw headed out from Memphis, across the Mississippi onto the plains of Arkansas and into oblivion, never to be heard from again.

—*Bill Deene*

1845–1858

"Mom, I'm home!" A solid baritone came ringing out to break into Angie's midafternoon reverie. She still couldn't believe those manly voices she now heard came from the two little boys who'd splashed and played in the prairie creek not so long ago down in Texas.

The years since they moved into the Bethel Avenue house had been quite kind to Angie's appearance; her skin remained firm and milky; her figure was trim and shapely still, if perhaps only slightly more lushly padded; and the few silver strands in her orange-blond hair were almost unnoticeable.

"Val sent me home early so I could get ready for tonight. I'm taking Bernice to the Palace tonight, and he wanted me to have plenty of time to get ready, so he could clean up when he got home." Bobby continued, "They've got this new variety show down there, and it's supposed to be a real hoot, so I want to be able to get Bernice in plenty of time to catch the opening curtain. It was tough to get tickets, and these are really good ones. I don't want us to miss a thing! Could we use the buggy?"

"If your dad says it's all right, I don't think we'll need the buggy tonight. But be sure if you are to use it you let Anton know in advance so he can have it ready." Angie changed the subject. "Did Val say if he wants me to draw him a nice, warm bath for when he comes home? I'll need some time between your finishing and getting it ready for Val if he does want that."

Bobby chuckled, which came out as a low rumble. "No, he didn't say specifically. But I'm sure he would appreciate it, and when you get a whiff of him, you'll know that you will appreciate it too!"

Now, it was Angie's turn to laugh. "I already had that idea—if you're any indication! Off to the bathroom with you."

As Bobby clumped on down the hallway toward the bathroom, Angie thought about her firstborn and sank into a new reverie. As her first, little Bobby had been some trouble for her to deliver. Robert, her first husband, had been trying to help as much as he could, but when Julie MacDonald, her neighbor who had five kids of her own, came over to help, she really saved the day.

Bobby was born healthy, with a healthy set of lungs, and his inclination to use them at the top of his voice didn't abate all the way through his childhood. You could always hear where Bobby was, and by association, you knew where Oskar was because he followed his big brother around like a puppy.

By the time of their return to Memphis, Bobby had been leader of, and responsible for, Oskar for long enough that some of the better parts of those character traits had begun to sink in for Bobby as a way to live life. His capacity for thinking ahead and accepting responsibility began to show through at an earlier age than for most boys. His actions along the road to Memphis, particularly when they'd been ambushed by the road agents, had shown this clearly.

Val had begun to test these traits in Bobby by giving him small tasks that, if completed satisfactorily, would lead to more and greater responsibilities. As Bobby grew in stature, he also grew as a young man.

School also played a large part in Bobby's development in character. In addition to the fact that Bobby loved school, he also loved the McGevneys and the way they exposed him to the broad panoply of learning that could be his.

School also taught him some difficult lessons. Not everyone felt the same as he did about school—or anything else. Fighting was not encouraged at school or at home. And if he came home in trouble at school, he would surely have trouble at home! When other boys wanted him to join in their hijinks, at the interruption of his studies, his initial reaction was to yell at them or punch them in the gut if they wouldn't stop that behavior. Gradually, this gave way to a more conversational, if not conciliatory, approach.

Those who already knew that the punch in the gut could be next, stopped at talking. Those who took it too far found out the hard way.

Thus, Bobby's school days were marked with excellent progress in most subjects; average was the best he could achieve in several others. Val brought home newspapers and magazines frequently, so current events were always on Bobby's mind. One day an article in the *Memphis Appeal* said a move was afoot to start a high school for those who had successfully completed elementary studies and were wishing to go further. Bobby brought the article to Val and Angie one night after supper.

———————◆———————

"Could I try?" he asked.

It was Angie who spoke first. "You want to keep on learning?"

Bobby answered, "I know there's more I can learn, and I'd like to at least try, if I could."

Now it was Val's turn. "I think it's a good idea. But how are you going to look out after Oskar? He still has two or three years to go."

"I really don't know. Perhaps I could walk him to school on my way," was Bobby's rejoinder. "But I really don't know where it will be. Could we all attend the meeting and find out and then make plans?"

The entire family agreed this was a good idea, and that plan was adopted.

Angie felt this had been the beginning of a new chapter in her life (as well as that of the entire family). Bobby (and gradually the other two kids would follow) was beginning to show the independence that would allow him to break away from her eventually and stand totally on his own.

A slight tinge of sadness crossed Angie's heart.

Again, Bobby's natural leadership and abilities shone forth, as did those of Oskar, who followed his brother just two years later. Eugene McGevney, as head master of the elementary school, had recognized Oskar's academic prowess and was more than pleased and confident to pass him into high school early to join his older brother, himself a solid student who could serve to guide young Oskar through the high school years.

Both boys had proven fluent in their English studies and were well-spoken. Bobby seemed to enjoy quoting literature and passages from plays, which surprised many people. But it was his passion for and uncanny ability to quote poetry that was the greatest surprise of all! Several times during his high school days, he had demonstrated these talents during school assemblies, parents' nights, and the like, often to great wonderment.

Oskar had been studying Latin under Mr. McGevney; he wasn't given to quoting it or other oratory, although he could, but his Latin really assisted his understanding of English. Eugene McGevney's motivation for introducing Oskar to Latin had been with an eye toward an eventual path for him in law or medicine.

Every educator who had come into contact with Oskar fully agreed with this assessment. So, Oskar's high school years were crammed with as much math, science, language, civics, and history as he could get.

One more thing occupied both boys' high school years—quite heavily. Both boys went head over heels for girls! Oskar had been following Bobby's lead since he was a baby, but he needed no urging in this.

Angie thought for the thousandth time that the two boys probably couldn't look less like brothers. Bobby wasn't particularly tall, but he was muscular and robust, like his dad had been. He'd taken to wearing his thick black hair longish, like Val and Robert W. before him. His usual garb consisted of rider's wear, again like Val. With trim pants tucked into high-topped boots, topped by a flowing white shirt, he often wore a dressy vest and a narrow colorful bandana at his neck, which could easily be pulled up over his face against the dust, if need be. Unlike Val, however, he didn't yet wear a hat on a daily basis, preferring instead to opt for one when he worked at the freight yard with Val, which he did more and more frequently these days.

Oskar, on the other hand, taller and thinner than his big brother, dressed fairly nattily every day, unless he was staying home or going to the freight yard. He had several business suits of good (but not extravagant) quality, all selected to be able to compliment his pale blonde good looks, and to mix and match pieces in order to create many different combinations. Added to these were a variety of dressy shirts, both solid and striped. These, coupled with an amazing array of ties, both string and bow, gave him an enormous selection of looks for any given day. He had begun to pay such attention to his mode of dress at the beginning of high school, when he'd discovered girls noticed such things, and he had kept it up ever since, although in truth, his beaming smile alone would have done the trick.

When Val had the boys down at the freight yard working, he never took advantage of the "free labor" but always paid the boys a fair wage for the time they worked. They were free to save or spend the money as they saw fit.

Bobby primarily used his money to enhance his social life with the girls, who were always hovering about him like moths to a flame. Cherry sodas were always a popular way to end a buggy ride after school. The touching and smooching that went on before he got a girl home kept Bobby at the forefront of afternoon dates.

Angie reflected somewhat ruefully that Bobby's savings habits were rather stunted by his spendthrift ways, but the boy *was* popular.

Of course, there was the time she caught him up in the attic with not one, but both of the Irwin sisters. Sarah was nineteen, and Alice was seventeen. They were both slender, pretty girls who were lively and active at school and around town.

Several times in the afternoon she thought she had heard noises coming from the attic. Finally, thinking it might be a rat or a squirrel rooting around up there, Angie had crept up the side stairs to take a look. What she saw was completely different from what she might have expected and stopped her in her tracks.

Bobby, with his shirt thrown open and his pants around his knees, had Alice with her hand pumping up and down slowly on his engorged manhood while kissing him passionately open-mouthed. Sarah, meanwhile, had the tip of his shaft in her mouth and was moving her head up and down much of its considerable length in almost complete unison with Alice's hand!

Angie's momentary dilemma about whether to say anything right then was solved by Bobby's sudden explosion into Sarah's mouth, out onto her face, and down the front of her neck and chest. As Sarah began to hastily wipe herself with the bottom hem of her dress, Alice bent down and took Bobby's still-hard rod into her own mouth, lavishing it thoroughly.

Still unseen and unnoticed, Angie crept silently down the stairs to the kitchen below, where Carmella sat at the table with a quizzical look.

Angie put a finger to her lips, calling for silence. She then put a finger in the air signaling Carmella to wait before speaking. After a few moments, sounds could be heard from the attic, and Angie said in a voice slightly loud, "Carmella, I'm glad you're here! We can start to get supper ready."

"Yes, Mrs. Angie. How many places should I set tonight?"

Angie was lost in thought about what she would say to Bobby. "What? Oh all five, I guess. I believe we don't have any company tonight, and I think everyone's going to be home."

As Bobby and the girls came down a few moments later, Angie feigned surprise. "Bobby, I didn't know you all were up there! Who are your friends?"

"Yeah, Mom, the view's great from up there, and I thought Sarah and Alice might enjoy seeing it!" Bobby went on, "Mom, meet the Irwin sisters, friends of mine from school."

"Hello, girls. Will you be staying for dinner?" Angie asked sweetly. "We can easily set two more places."

Sarah spoke right up in reply. "Thank you, ma'am, but no. We gave our folks no notice we might be doing that, so we'd best cause them no worry and get on home."

Alice joined in with, "Supper another time would be very nice, if we could see that view again."

Angie's reply was equally gracious. "Anytime you can arrange it, you'll be most welcome. The view will always be waiting for you."

She added, "Bobby, next time, please let us know you have company. That way you won't be disturbed."

"I'm sorry about this time, Mom. I looked for you and Carmella but couldn't find either of you.

"That's all right, son," Angie went on. "But we do need to have a little talk about house rules for bringing girls over."

"Sure thing, Mom. Just let me get the girls home, and I'll be right back."

"All right, but don't dawdle! Supper will be ready by then, and you know how your dad likes to have everyone gathered around for blessing."

Angie finished with, "Come back anytime, girls!"

Bobby and the girls trooped out the front door.

Despite a certain inevitable amount of necessary dawdling, Bobby was back in time to sit for supper in a timely fashion with the rest of the family, which Angie greatly appreciated. Around the dinner table that evening, the mood was light. Oskar had a sort of a smug grin on his face, and Angie wondered why.

After dinner, the entire family stayed around the table at Angie's request. Carmella cleared the table and then slipped quietly from the room.

Angie broke the ensuing silence. "Val and Oskar, Bobby had a couple of very nice young ladies, sisters in fact, over this afternoon without my knowledge. Both Carmella and I happened to be away at the time, so the fault for not letting us know is hard to lay on Bobby." Angie continued, "It was quite a surprise when they came down into the kitchen from seeing the view up in the attic! Neither Carmella nor I knew there was anyone up there, although I did think I heard noises earlier.

"So I think we should have some house rules about bringing over company, particularly of the opposite sex." Angie looked across the table at Val. "What do you think, darling?"

Val absently fiddled with his neckerchief as he spoke. "I really suppose we do need that, although we do trust you boys to exercise good judgment in social matters."

He continued almost immediately. "Having said that, like always, if you are unclear on the right course of action in any given situation, all you have to do is ask Mom or me. It's very likely we'll each give you almost exactly the same advice, or close to it."

Angie said brightly, "Let's make that rule number one. Ask. And rule number two could be part and parcel with it. Don't invite anyone until you've gotten approval from one of us, particularly if there is a chance they might stay for lunch or dinner."

Val spoke up and said, "I think we need one more rule to guarantee you young men the privacy that you and your guests deserve, and that is rule number three. We need to know where you and your guests are, and if you are in the house, no closed doors. That sound about right, honey?"

Angie answered, "I think those three rules will do until it's shown we need more. What do you young men think?"

Bobby said quickly, "I think I can live with three simple rules, right, Oskar?"

Oskar merely nodded.

"Then I guess we're finished." Angie resolved to speak to each of the boys individually.

From that time forward, Bobby and Oskar had a veritable procession of fine young ladies through the house, following (more or less) the established house rules.

Meanwhile, over the course of the next few years, Anton and Carmella became friends and mentors to all the children and, indeed, became like members of the family themselves. Bobby enjoyed helping Anton with the horses, and Oskar learned much about using tools from him and, indeed, even set up a small shop to experiment and build inventions that his fertile mind brought forth. Even Bobby used the shop from time to time in working with his budding interest in firearms. Both the boys and Angelina loved Carmella, and not just for her cooking, although she certainly had that in spades. But Carmella also seemed to intuitively know when something was wrong and was always good for a quick word of encouragement, along with a cup of spiced coffee.

Angelina also was quite fond of both Anton and Carmella. As she grew into a young lady, she began to notice certain differences in the way people treated each other depending on whether they were family or not.

Angelina loved Anton for teaching her to ride horseback Western style, instead of the sidesaddle way most Memphis women rode, if they rode at all. Daddy had told Anton to let her choose how and if she wanted to ride and teach her that way. Most of the city boys couldn't even ride at all, and Angelina was quite safe up on Ranger, the third saddle horse stabled at the house. A medium-sized roan gelding, Ranger was gentle and very controllable (unlike Vindicator or Sidewinder), so both Angie and Val felt comfortable when Angelina rode alone. Angelina loved the feelings she got when she rode, especially lately.

She used to camp out most of the day in the kitchen or wherever in the house Carmella might be, peppering her with a thousand and one questions about whatever she might be doing as she worked or trying to see if she might give things a try herself. Carmella was always gracious and very patient with her as she grew from a little girl to a schoolchild and then to a teenager. But there were certain questions from Angelina that were answered with, "I think you'll need to speak to your mother about that."

That was the case when she tried to find out more about the feelings she got between her legs as she rode now.

Angie, as mom, had already had frank talks with both Bobby and Oskar as they approached the threshold of sexuality, explaining the changes they were experiencing in their bodies, as well as the rules and customs of dealings with the fairer sex. She was not at all surprised when Angelina, fairly shortly after her breasts began to bud, came to her about sensations she was having in her groin area as she rode.

Angelina had already reached menarche and they had had the mother-daughter conversations about sex and pregnancy. But now it was time to talk about her own bodily sensations and how to manage (but not thwart) them.

Angie told Angelina softly and carefully to cherish these feelings as a vital part of being a woman, which she was quickly growing up to be, and to prepare for the love of a good man. Angie explained that she had been fortunate enough to experience the love of two amazingly special men, Robert Cunningham and Val Dimand, more than most women would ever have.

Angelina came out of these conversations comforted and encouraged. Angie cautioned that her feelings were entirely normal and would grow and become an important part of her everyday life, particularly if she met a nice young man to share her life. She also explained, as her own mother had many years before, the life choices and hardships an unwanted pregnancy could bring about and that it was her choice, and her responsibility, if she wanted to begin having sex.

"Your breasts are just beginning now, but as you grow up, they will get larger, perhaps as big as mine or even more. In fact, you look so much like I did when I was your age, I know all the boys in town will be after you very soon!" Angie huddled closer to Angelina and continued, "Sex will become a very important part of your life, and if you ever have questions or doubts, you can always come to me or your father with them."

Angelina pulled back a little and looked at her mom quizzically. "You mean actually talk to Daddy about this stuff? I don't think I ever could! I would be so embarrassed."

"Well, if you let embarrassment get in your way of getting good advice, that's your fault and yours alone," Angie replied. "Your father knows more about women and how they should be treated than any man I've ever met, and I've met plenty! He told me once that he learned from his mother, who had had a hard life from all the discriminations and persecutions of her people back in Europe and that the day-to-day niceties a man could do for a woman added up to more than all the gold he could bring to her."

Angie continued fervently, "Look around you at what I have, and what you have. Val Dimand has built this life up with his bare hands, his grit, and his determination. But at the end of the day when he gets into the bed beside me and puts his arms around me, it wouldn't matter if it was in this fine house or a little cabin on the Texas prairie like I had with Robert Cunningham, because I would be happy!"

Angie gave Angelina a soft kiss on the cheek as she got up and said, "Just remember to seek your happiness not with things but with someone, and you'll do fine. You come to me or your father for advice anytime. I promise you won't be turned away."

As Angelina went out, her mind was a whirlwind of thoughts. The best way she knew to clear her head besides riding was to go up in the attic and sit on the old settee from the Adams house. Her mom and dad had placed it up there to provide a nice place to sit while enjoying the view, which Angelina did frequently.

Angelina, ever the quiet one when moving about, had crept up the stairs so silently no one knew she was there. After she had sat for about a half hour, she began to hear noises at the base of the stairs, as though someone was about to come up. Not wanting to be discovered at that moment, she silently slipped over to an area behind some canvas bags of excess bedding stored until winter.

As she peeked out carefully between two of the bags, she saw her brother Oskar come up the top of the stairs and motion for someone else to come on up. In a moment, she saw a head of honey-blond hair followed by a voluptuous body in a gingham dress. It was Becky Thornhill, who Angelina had met several times at school and who she liked very much. Becky always had a kind word for her and had an ear for her when she questioned why the older girls did things a certain way. You couldn't really call her a confidante, but at least she did not ignore or tease the younger girl for her naiveté.

Ordinarily, Angelina would have greeted Becky cheerily, but

something told her to hold back and remain hidden. Her reluctance was rewarded with the sight of Oskar and Becky sharing a deep open-mouthed kiss with tongues flicking back and forth, while Oskar undid the back of Becky's dress and let it fall to her waist.

Free from her bodice's constraints, her ample breasts exposed their edges around the edges of the slip she wore underneath, and Oskar made short work of that by slipping the slender shoulder straps holding it up over her arms and letting the whole thing fall to her waist. Her first sight of Becky's generous attainments made Angelina acutely aware of the miniscule size of her own breasts. Yet when she touched them just then the pleasure was undeniable. She had seen her mother's beautiful breasts with their large, meaty nipples, and her mom had said her own might be as large someday.

Naked to the waist, Becky stood there while Oskar bent to her and placed one of her large round nipples between his teeth as he placed a hand on her other breast, kneading it as he chewed on his original target.

Angelina heard the sharp intake of breath from Becky as she said, "Ooh that feels so good! Don't stop!"

Angelina noticed she was getting a little short of breath herself and, not wanting to be heard for any sharp intakes of her own, slowly and silently she let out her breath and took in a new breath the same way.

When she looked back at the pair of lovers, Oskar now had his other hand between Becky's legs and was moving it in some kind of rhythmic pattern. Angelina couldn't see exactly what Oskar was doing to Becky and exactly where he was touching her, but the reactions she was giving him were undeniable and hard to miss.

With her head thrown back and her knees bent as she leaned back against the settee, she was letting out low moans steadily. Her skirt was hanging down except where her brother's hand had it bunched up at her crotch and was making slow back and forth motions, along with going in and out occasionally, which made Becky gasp little cries of pleasure.

"Sshh!" whispered Oskar. "I'm pretty sure we're completely alone, but there's no reason to draw attention, if we can help it."

After a couple more minutes of Oskar's handiwork, Becky suddenly convulsed rather violently with a long, low moan and grabbed Oskar's hand at her crotch and held it still while she shuddered and held herself tightly to him.

Angelina had been feeling some of the same feelings in her crotch that she felt horseback riding, and she slid a hand down to her dress hem and pulled it and her slip upward to where she could feel the mound at the apex of her legs beneath the thin fabric of her undergarment. Curling her legs back silently, she rubbed the mound lightly, enjoying tremendously the sensations thus created.

When she could finally open her eyes and look again at the scene before her, Becky was on her knees, still naked to the waist, and Oskar's pants were down at his ankles exposing his glaringly white legs but also exposing the long, slender shaft protruding from his hairy crotch. Becky had it in both her hands, pulling back and forth on it while occasionally taking the engorged tip into her mouth as she tugged.

Now it was Oskar's turn to throw back his head and moan softly. As she watched, Angelina's pressure on her mound gradually increased until she could tell something might happen, even though she didn't know what. She could tell from Becky's earlier reaction that it was likely to be very pleasurable, but she did not want such a reaction to lead to her discovery, so she eased up a little to prolong the end. She detected a growing bit of moisture at her crotch and wondered if she should stop to investigate, but the sensations she was feeling wouldn't let her stop for even a second!

Besides, Becky had stopped using her hands so much and now was continually running her mouth up and down Oskar's shaft while her hands were fondling his testicles and occasionally reaching around to caress his exposed buttocks. Angelina felt herself about to cry out with the overwhelming intensity of it all and stopped her rubbing of her crotch. She began to pinch her nipples and bit her lip and then clamped a hand across her mouth to keep from crying out. The pleasure mixed with a little bit of pain caused sensations all the way down to her toes, and it was all she could do to lie silently; and truth to be told, she wasn't sure how much longer she could even do that.

Her problem was fairly short-lived, however. After a couple of more moments of Becky's oral ministrations to his crotch, Oskar put his hands to both sides of her face as he suddenly stiffened his stance and gave out with a soft "Oohh!" Whitish fluid appeared at the corners of Becky's mouth, followed by a torrent of the same stuff down her chin, neck, and over her naked breasts as she moved her chest from side to side to catch some of the flow on each breast.

Becky grinned up at Oskar while he was putting himself back into his pants. She remained on her knees rubbing Oskar's juice into her nipples, spending time between circling them with her fingertips and pinching them between those same fingers, until she stood and offered her nipples one at a time to his greedy mouth.

Oskar buried himself into this task, sucking and biting each one as it was given to him, while Becky stood there with a look of extreme satisfaction on her face.

Then, after her clothing was set right anew, the two lovers shared more passionate kissing before disappearing down the stairs.

Angelina lay there long enough to confirm that the sensations in her crotch came on whether there was visual stimulation or not. And then giving herself enough time to hear Oskar and Becky leave out through the front door, she straightened her own clothes and crept silently down the stairs into the kitchen. From there, she stepped into the hall and saw it was not yet three o'clock in the afternoon. Since Mom and Carmella were due back from the market soon, and since she had decided to ride over to the freight yard to see Daddy, she left a note for her mother explaining what she was doing and then went out the back door toward the stables.

Anton was just at the stable doors when she got there, and she asked him if he could saddle Ranger for her afternoon ride over to see Daddy.

"Of course, I'd be happy to!" was his cheery reply. "But, are you all right? You seem pretty flushed. You aren't coming down with something, are you?"

"No, I'm fine, Anton. I'm just excited to go over and see Daddy." Angelina went on, "I was looking out the attic window, and I saw him ride up on Vindicator, so I know he's there. And I thought it would be nice to surprise him."

"Yes, I think it will be a nice surprise. But you just be careful around all those wranglers and hands over there," Anton warned. "You're getting to be of an age to become a temptation, and while I don't think any of them are liable to cross your father by taking advantage of you, you just be careful."

"I will and thank you very much!" Angelina replied as she swung up into the saddle. A few paces across the yard to the gate, and she swung it open and passed through, closed it, and proceeded on down Bethel. She had Ranger at a slight canter as she turned into the North Road, and the action of his shoulders at work was transmitted through the saddle directly to Angelina's crotch, producing those wonderful feelings she had come to crave.

By the time she had gotten to the freight yard, her long blond hair was wonderfully tousled from the ride, and her complexion carried a nice flush. Many sets of admiring male eyes followed her as she rode through the yard and dismounted in front of the office.

Inside, Angelina found not her father, but Pasquinel Benoit sitting behind the counter, mired in what seemed to be a sea of paperwork.

Upon looking up and seeing her standing before him, his mood instantly brightened and concentration lines on his face gave way instantly to what, for him, passed as a smile.

"Well, hello there, young missy! What brings you here this afternoon?" Benoit rasped in that voice that could not be imitated.

"I came to see my father, just to surprise him a little," replied Angelina. "I saw him ride in just a little while ago. Is he still here?"

"He sure is," barked Benoit. "I think he's down by the wash trough still, so let me get someone to go get him while you wait here."

Pasquinel spoke authoritatively to the only other person in the room, a nicely dressed, middle-aged man also behind the counter. "Sam, how about going and rustling up one of the hands, maybe Billy, to go and fetch the boss and let him know Angelina's here?"

"Sure thing," said Sam as he went out the front door of the office.

Angelina knew her father and Pasquinel Benoit had been friends for many years, and though no one had said as much, she suspected some of those years had been marked by troubles and strife. Her father's friend certainly looked as though he could handle trouble with his mixed Indian and French face marked with scars and wrinkles from hard times, but she was somehow comforted and felt protected in his presence.

As they chatted while waiting for her dad, she felt Val was right to trust the day-to-day operations of the freight yard to Benoit and that he was a true-blue, faithful friend to him.

Bobby and Oskar both came to the freight yard frequently to work, earning money for themselves, as well as helping Val out and learning about the business. Angelina didn't get to see her father frequently at work, so this afternoon was special for her, and she hoped it was for him.

Any doubts she might have had were instantly erased as soon as he came through the office door. "Sweetheart!" he boomed. "This is great! I was just thinking of knocking off a little early this afternoon, and nothing would please me more than to ride home side by side with you.

"Can we make that work, Pasquinel? I don't want to leave you with extra work, but I'd love to spend time with my only daughter," Val added, turning to his friend.

"Sure thing, Boss! I have some invoices and other things that need your signature, and that shouldn't take more than a few minutes. Then you could be on your way; I can handle everything else."

Benoit went on, "If I had a daughter like her, I'd take every chance I could get to ride with her, believe you me!"

"I've told you a thousand times, if you'd married that Spanish girl in Santa Fe that wanted you so badly, you'd have kids of your own by now." Val smiled at his old friend. "But you left her crying. She must have seen something very special in you!"

Angelina smiled at the two of them. "I'm just going to wait outside and look around, if that's all right, Daddy."

"OK, sweetie, but stay pretty close to the office. The wagons will be starting to come in soon, and I don't want you run over by a driver not seeing you."

"I don't think there's much chance of that!" quipped Benoit as she went out the door. "In case you haven't noticed, she's growing up to be a beauty, just like her mom."

"Oh, indeed I've noticed and I suspect a number of the wranglers will if I leave her out there too long. So, let's get to those invoices and such, so I can get out of here with her before there's a commotion started."

Ten minutes later, father and daughter rode side by side along the North Road toward Bethel Avenue, both chatting amiably and smiling. Several times people along the way who were quite familiar with the tall, handsome Val Dimand riding his impressive black horse Vindicator smiled and waved as usual. A number of them called out to ask Val who the young girl who rode with him.

Beaming with delight, the proud father would call out, "This is my daughter, Angelina!"

It was the best ride she'd ever had, and she promised herself there'd be many more.

Chapter 9

KIDS BECOMING ADULTS

Memphis grew tremendously in size and importance in the years between 1840 and 1860. The advent of steam-powered vessels plying the Mississippi meant that people could now travel upstream as well as down, thus connecting Memphis to St. Louis as well as New Orleans. Paddle wheelers loaded to the maximum with bales of cotton, along with travelers aplenty, made Memphis the cotton-trading capital of the world, and a major travel crossroads and destination.

1858–1861

The letter from Bobby arrived a couple of days before New Year's Day, 1861 from Fort Smith, Arkansas. It had been mailed just before Christmas, so delivery had been rather quick. In it, he had told of his strong desire to come home for a visit in the early part of the incoming year, so Mom and Dad were excitedly hopeful.

Bobby had been at Fort Smith for about a year, making regular excursions down into Texas to repair and "tune up" the Walker and 1851 Navy-model Colt revolvers the Texas Rangers carried as their main sidearms. The durability and reliability of the relatively new revolving-cylinder pistols from Colt had improved markedly from the original Paterson Colts which the state of Texas had purchased back in 1837, but still they needed repair and adjustment after hard use on the dusty plains of Texas. Replacing worn pawl springs, adjusting cylinder locator pins, and cleaning built-up gunk from the cap nipples for reliable firing was not at all what you could call exciting work, but the Rangers whose pistols Bobby returned to proper operation were truly grateful, and it was a good living. Each trip was to a different troop, and Bobby stayed at their headquarters until every Ranger in the troop had a correctly functioning weapon.

Bobby wrote that, when his contract with the Rangers was finished, he had plans to open his own gunsmith shop, perhaps right there in Fort Smith.

Angie had missed mightily having Bobby present for Christmas, but she knew her oldest child was a man now, responsible for his own plans and actions, and she could only hope the family could be complete again someday, perhaps with Bobby sporting a wife and child. She didn't know how she felt about perhaps being a grandma (after all, she was not yet quite fifty!). But she felt like she could handle it. She could easily have passed for no more than thirty-five, but some days she felt the full weight of her years, especially when she thought of Bobby being out on his own, almost five hundred miles away. He hadn't yet written of meeting anyone in particular, but Angie felt it was probably just a matter of time.

She instantly recalled, not without a tinge of pride, the time just a couple of years before she had come up the stairs to the attic and found Bobby with not one but two partially clad young women, both of whom were busily engaged in seeing to Bobby's desires—as evidenced by his significantly wet and gleaming erection plunging steadily in and out of one girl while he had one hand up in the other girl, who was leaning back against the settee as he kissed and chewed on her dark brown fleshy nipples. Not wanting to be noticed but still unable to look away from her firstborn performing in such obvious pleasure, Angie remained silent at the top of the attic stairs with only her eyes and the top of her head visible. The scene continued unabated with Bobby smoothly switching partners. Now plunging himself energetically into the second girl, the first girl stood up, turned around to face Bobby with her legs spread and, leaning against the settee, received the ministrations from Bobby's left hand up her crotch and the attentions of his mouth and tongue on hers and her breasts.

Angie, fortunate to be at an angle which made her not easily visible, silently crept back down the stairs and sat quietly at the kitchen table until she felt she was able to move again, at which time she went rather noisily out into the backyard to the clothesline and began to gather in the wash.

Now, years later, even though she could wish for a wife and baby for Bobby, her strongest desire was to have them home together permanently. Angie was glad indeed that he had found a useful and productive line of work, but she did not see as how he had to be so far away to do it!

Oskar had finished high school and had enrolled in Montgomery Masonic College in Clarkesville and had begun a prelaw course of study. Two hundred miles away, her youngest boy had seemed gone forever, as he could only come home for long holidays or the summer. The infrequent times she could have him home were punctuated with the delight at his arrivals, the treasure of his company for the days or weeks he could manage, and the anguish at his departures to return to his studies. Angie knew in her heart this was something he needed. She herself had, in fact, moved the three of them back to Memphis so Oskar and Bobby could have such opportunities. Closer than East Tennessee College over in Knoxville, the school in Clarkesville was a perfect alternative, close to the state capitol in Fort Nash (or Nashville as it was now commonly called) and an opening to all manner of potential job opportunities after Oskar passed the bar exam.

Oskar excelled at college and finished the four-year course of study laid out for him as a prospective attorney in only three years. He'd then made his way back to Memphis (to Angie's delight), moved back into the Bethel house, and began to "read for the law" at the Metcalf law office uptown. Mr. Metcalf, himself a fairly new lawyer and new to town, saw no difficulties sharing his office with a bright young man studying to pass the Tennessee bar. If nothing else, an extra pair of hands and set of legs could periodically come in handy.

Oskar's earnings were practically nonexistent until he got his legal certificate, so living at home was a big plus to the whole arrangement. He could occasionally work a day or two for Val at the freight yard, and the savings he had amassed before he left for college had not been ravaged by his frugal living while there, so he was able to live on his meager income.

Oskar had come back from college even taller and thinner. Carmella constantly threatened to "fatten him up" with a smile on her face, and Oskar loved the attention; she was someone he adored.

Working for Val, Oskar had noticed that the level of equipment needed and obtained to run the freighting business was significant indeed. One day, he asked Val if he'd ever done an inventory of the business's assets, including the property and livestock.

Val had seen personally what a mess it could be to close down a business after someone left or died, and he knew, therefore, the value of an accurate inventory.

After Levi Gold had died, Jacob Ottenheimer had had to shepherd the store through the seemingly unending morass of paperwork, accounting, past-due accounts (Levi Gold had been most generous and accommodating), and the thousand and one other things that seemed to crop up. Angie had been helping the store for several years before Levi's death, advising him on merchandise suitable to a number of different buying groups, such as settlers passing through Memphis on their way to their new homes and workers seeking sturdy work clothes and tools, but perhaps more importantly, Memphians seeking home furnishings and ladies' fashions.

Levi's principal objection whenever she would suggest something new was, "Where will we put it? There's no room!"

She would most frequently reply, "We'll find room."

Eventually, they did run completely out of room. The store was absolutely filled with merchandise, and a customer could walk through the shop and eventually find what they were seeking. But it was Angie who convinced both Gold and Ottenheimer to separate the wares into different areas or "departments" so a customer could be directed to more easily find his or her desired item. One innovation she championed was a dressmaking and sewing department that carried patterns and sewing supplies to make clothes for the entire family. This brought ladies into the store who might never have shopped there otherwise.

These days, though, she was seldom in the store except as a customer.

Her children were practically grown, except for Angelina who, as a teenager, had a mind of her own and seldom came to her mom—or even Carmella, for that matter—for advice. These days, she seemed completely wrapped up in a never-ending stream of boys.

Angelina had been at Gold's store one day to pick up her mom and had seen overalls for sale in the work clothes, and they quickly became part of her new standard of dress, along with gingham shirts and high-topped riding boots. Since she was riding Ranger practically daily, a broad-brimmed western hat was a necessity to complete her ensemble.

Thus, Angelina became very recognizable walking or riding through the streets of Memphis. What was also recognizable was that she was growing up to be the image of her mother as a raving beauty; she was filling out in all the womanly places and began to make the overalls bulge in areas the designers probably never envisioned.

Angie had had the same talk with Angelina that she herself had had so many years before with her own mother, complete with the bestowing of a lambskin sheath for protection and the cautions about what an unplanned pregnancy could do to the rest of her life.

Carmella was still with the family after more than ten years, as was Anton. She was still slim and lively, though she might not get around as much (or as rapidly) anymore. Her cooking was still a pleasure for the entire family, and she could pretty much be counted on to know where the kids were at most times and when they'd be home. In fact, there wasn't much that went on in the Dimand household that Carmella wasn't aware of, though she kept a tight seal on her lips as far as others were concerned.

Angie grinned wryly and slightly ruefully, thinking about the first time she'd really needed that trait from Carmella. For years, she had helped Angie to prepare herself for going out by laying out the clothes she wanted, helping her dress, and helping her undress upon returning to don one of her beautiful housedresses and robes.

Carmella never failed to comment on how beautiful Angie was, whether she was wearing clothes or not, and in all those times, Angie thought nothing of it.

All that began to change one afternoon as Angie was taking a nice bath in the bathroom tub.

———————◆———————

Lying back and luxuriating over thoughts of the morning lovemaking she had shared with Val, Angie unconsciously began to pull her nipples till they stretched out so much there was a little pain. Then she would twist and rub them to ease them, before beginning the whole process again. As she moaned softly thinking of the creamy mess Val had left between her thighs that morning, Carmella came softly through the door with a washcloth and the new scented soap Angie had gotten.

"Excuse me, Miss Angie," she said very softly. "Would you like me to wash you with this new soap?"

All Angie could do among the growing blush of her face was to nod yes!

So Carmella dropped to her knees beside the tub, soaped up the washcloth, and then began to gently lather her, starting with one leg at a time. From her feet to her calves, past her knees, and on to her upper thighs, the washing continued at a languishing pace, punctuated by an occasional whisper of, "Wonderful!" or "Beautiful!" from Carmella.

At Angie's crotch, Carmella stopped and looked Angie in the eyes and said, "Do you want me to wash you here?"

Again, all Angie could do was nod yes.

Carmella proceeded at an even slower pace and Angie's moans grew stronger as washing subtly combined with caressing to bring Angie to a violent convulsing, at which point Carmella gave Angie a fierce kiss to stifle the sound as the pressure of her hand gradually eased on Angie's tender lips and folds. She then proceeded up to Angie's belly and then to those marvelous breasts with their sumptuously full nipples. Dropping the washcloth entirely, Carmella at first pulled and twisted Angie's nipples while watching her eyes for signs to go further.

When Angie's eyes closed and her head leaned back, Carmella immediately began to kiss, nibble, and thoroughly suck those meaty orbs of dark red, which brought another shudder and groan from Angie.

At this, Carmella stood and opened a bath towel wide for Angie to be enveloped and then held out her bathrobe open for her to step in, which Angie did.

As they walked together into the bedroom, Angie said, "I think I'll just lie here a little while like this, and I'll call you later when we're ready to start supper."

"Yes, Miss."

As soon as Carmella had snapped the door shut, the swirl of thoughts in Angie's mind took over. It wasn't that she was in any way dissatisfied with her relations with Val Dimand—far from it, she was happy and content. But what she had just experienced was powerful enough to want more.

As she lay there lost in her thoughts, one hand drifted down to the wet split at her crotch, while her other hand found an already throbbing nipple and began to pull it downward toward the floor.

◆

Now, even as a teenager, Angelina was highly aware that there was sex happening all the time around their house, and she had often been an undiscovered spectator to much of it. She had seen both of her brothers in naked congress with young ladies by accidentally catching them up in the attic "enjoying the view" as they enjoyed each other. Because she was silent, she went undiscovered. For her, the attic was a wonderland of hidden or forgotten treasures.

Angelina had been a toddler when the house was first being built, but just as she'd loved exploring it then, the desire to find new passageways and places to hide had not waned over the years. She'd discovered that, on the shelves in her closet, she could climb up to the ceiling, and by removing a covering piece of board above an opening in the ceiling, she could climb up into the attic through her bedroom closet. Moving some bags and satchels out of the way enabled her to get above her parents' room, directly over their bed and the chaise lounge beside it.

If she was silent, she could see what Val and Angie did at night without the risk of being found out. This had happened several times, with the first time showing Val taking Angie from behind on the chaise lounge. As Angie crawled up on the chaise, Angelina could see the splendid swell of her mother's cheeks and the solid, but generous, measure of her round, firm thighs which were just beginning to dimple a tiny amount. But what held Angelina's attention most was the darkish split between Angie's gluteal mounds which was punctuated with a dark hole and a divided bulge showing little pieces of flesh peeking through the split.

When Val got on the chaise behind Angie's glorious body, Angelina was again taken aback. Jutting out from Val's hairy crotch was a long, somewhat slender shaft, now completely rigid. As he began to rub his erect manhood up and down in her slot, Angie responded with a series of moaning, "Oohs", which grew into low-pitched groans after he sank his shaft into her and began to thrust slowly in and out, in and out.

The beauty of their bodies and the obvious pleasure of their physical contact made Angelina reach down to the hem of her nightshirt, pull it up, and begin to rub her own mound, which she had only discovered recently while riding could be the source of exquisite pleasure.

As her parents' lovemaking got faster and more frantic, Angelina's hand practically flew over her own mound until a great whiteness passed over her eyes, and she clamped her mouth tightly shut against her own cries, threatening to burst forth along with Angie's, and a series of dynamic shudders coursed through her body.

When she could finally look back again, she could see that Val's manhood, outside of her Mom but still proudly erect, was now glisteningly shiny—as was most of Angie's slot and mound. But when Val began to rub the tip of his hardened spike around the rim of Angie's other hole, Angelina saw and heard her mom look back at him with curiosity.

"There, too?" moaned Angie. "Do you think you can?"

Val was silent and just began to ease his shaft into her nether hole as she helped him get it in. As soon as he began to thrust in and out, Angelina could hear her mother's cries of profound pleasure grow in intensity until they were joined by Val's deep groan as he suddenly went still while he was buried deep within her. As he stopped moving and became completely caught up in his discharge, Angie moaned passionately, "Oh, Val, that feels so wonderful! I love you!"

As Val's now-limp member slid from Angie's behind, a flood of white went down her slot and moistened the inside of her leg as she rolled over onto the towel covering the chaise and put her arms out to encircle her husband. As the two lay there, neither spoke.

No words were needed.

From up in the attic, Angelina watched her parents lie there silently, embracing and caressing in post-coital bliss, and she made a decision for her life right then and there. She knew she wanted a man who would cherish her.

Her mother had told her how her own marriage to Robert W. Cunningham, which had begun with such a torrid night of passion, was warm and sexually fulfilling for all the time they'd had together, and she could see that Val and Angie's marriage was just the same. Her dad, besides being so good-looking, was desirable because he obviously knew how to treat and keep a woman.

For the past couple of years, Angelina had been riding Ranger frequently to the freight yard in the late afternoon to meet with her father and ride back home alongside him. She loved these times together, but lately she had been uncomfortable with the length of time some of the men stared at her and how some of the catcalls that came from them did not seem directed at the livestock. Nevertheless, she felt safe when she was with her father.

She realized then that she needed any man who could earn her love to be a protector of her and a provider for her. Val Dimand had certainly been a shining example of a husband in those two areas, and Angelina decided right then and there she wouldn't settle for less.

While Bobby and Oskar met many girls at school and courted lots of them, Angelina had found very few schoolboys who she felt could come close to her father at being a woman's man. Most of the young men she saw as she went about didn't really measure up either. The wranglers and stockmen down at the freight yard could certainly be masculine enough to give an impression of eligibility, but as far as civility went, they were rough as cobs. None of them that she'd seen so far had measured up.

All that changed one sweltering afternoon while she was up in the attic, enjoying what little breeze came through the flung-open dormer window as she sat there on the settee in a light cotton housedress. She was looking through her daddy's binoculars toward the freight yard when her eyes drifted toward the wash trough, where several of the handlers who had been working in the upper barn were currently heading. Dusty beyond imagination, the first one to reach the trough pulled a long lever attached to a cistern above. As the water tumbled in to fill the trough, much to Angelina's surprise, the dusty young man stripped off and shook out his clothing, laid it across a rail (and just as naked as he could be) climbed into the trough.

Angelina was treated to an almost obscenely frank view of the young man's body (both fore and aft) with the binoculars' magnification, exposing the interplay of his lithely sculpted musculature as well as the unrestrained swinging of his male appendage. She grabbed herself hard when he stepped over into the trough, exposing his crack and a different view of his manhood.

A veritable parade of five young (one was not so young) men followed the first; as one finished and began to redress, another took his place in the water. Sometimes the new occupant drained and refilled the tub, sometimes not. With each succeeding bather, Angelina wasn't sure whether it was more exciting to watch them undress or put their clothes back on.

All she really knew was that the fire in her crotch was getting to a fever pitch, and the wetness down there was unmistakable.

And then, he came out.

A little taller than most of the others and already stripped to the waist, his lean and well-developed musculature was glistening with sweat and rippled as he moved. When he stripped completely naked, Angelina watched in amazement as he walked to the tub. His leg muscles literally popped as he walked, and his penis actually bounced from thigh to thigh with each step. Transfixed as she was, she could not look away as he climbed into the trough and exposed the most intimate areas of his backside to her feverish gaze.

Her orgasm was so surprising it was accompanied by a sharp outcry.

"Are you all right, honey?" a voice called from the kitchen below the stairs.

"Yes, Carmella. I just slipped up here, and I thought for a moment I might fall, but I'm all right. Thanks."

"Do you need me to come up there and help you?"

"No need now, and I'll be down in a moment," Angelina called back, hoping her legs would stop quivering soon so she could walk steadily down the stairs. The air had a heavy female musk to it, which she hoped did not follow her down into the kitchen.

"That's good, because I could use a little help with getting the rolls ready for dinner," Carmella called back.

"I'll be down in moments!"

When she got down to the kitchen and stepped in, Carmella immediately said, "Maybe you ought to go wash and change before you spend time in here. Something or another that you got into up there was pretty smelly. You'll need to wash your hands before you come back."

"Thanks, Carmella. I will." Angelina hoped her face had not revealed her embarrassment as she scurried to her cleanup in the bathroom and fresh clothes in her room.

Returning to the kitchen in unsoiled clothes and smelling faintly of lilac rather than rut, Angelina cheerfully helped Carmella with that evening's dinner preparations.

Later that night, she lay awake unable to sleep for the thoughts that kept flooding her brain. Angelina gave in to the inevitable and began to touch herself as she called forth the image of the Adonis she had spotted. The image was burned into her brain so deeply she had no trouble seeing the beauty of his face as he smiled and laughed—or the magnificence of his slender but muscular body as it shone in the sunlight. His long, curly blond hair had been encircled by a red bandana at his forehead, giving him a slightly piratical look. She imagined him taking her and doing things to her she had seen her own brothers do to other girls; she imagined him leaving her breathless with a stream of white effluent cascading down somewhere on her body as he backed away spent and breathless himself from the effort, his rigid member now soft once again.

She imagined the two of them collapsing into each other's arms, there to hold each other and smother each other with kisses, wordlessly denying the existence of anything else, even the world itself, in the sating of their passion. All the things she had seen her brothers do and even her father perform with her mother, she wanted for herself.

By this time, her nightshirt was bunched up around her shoulders, her covers kicked off, and her legs spread wide, while she fanatically rubbed her slot. If someone had come in at that moment, her embarrassment would have been terminal. Little did she know that either one of her parents, but especially her mother, would have understood completely.

Whatever thoughts were to come next were totally eradicated by the earthshaking orgasm that caused her to grab a mouthful of pillow to stifle her screams.

As she tried to calm her shuddering out-of-control body, Angelina suddenly realized she did not know how to make any of this happen. She didn't know how to make a man's penis stiffen into hardness, where to touch him on his body to bring him pleasure, or even how to get him to hold her and kiss her in the first place.

Angelina resolved then and there to research the subject further, and she knew already that she needed to go no farther than her own house to do it!

Chapter 10

ANGELINA GETS HITCHED

Most people heading west out of Memphis, whether bound for the California goldfields or settling somewhere on the prairies, traveled on horseback or in wagons drawn by horses, mules, or oxen. But once across the Mississippi River, the plains of Arkansas lay before them, all the way to the Ozark Mountains. This gave many travelers their first taste of travel into the West, and many found it necessary or expedient to drop off from their intended destinations and settle somewhere in Arkansas.

1861

By the fall of 1872, Bobby Cunningham had been living in Fort Smith, Arkansas, for more than ten years. He'd made trips back home to Memphis fairly regularly and had managed to stay a while each time.

Val and Angie found the visits over too soon, and Angie especially yearned for his company when he was absent. Val, on the other hand, knew that, when a man grew to a certain age and began to make his own way, the ties to his home and family could grow tenuous for a number of years until he settled into his retirement and leisure years, if he got any. Val knew that he, Angie, and the kids were always in Bobby's heart and that he would come home to see them as often as he could.

Life in the West could be hard.

Fort Smith was the very edge of civilization at the beginning of the Indian Territory and, as such, was the pathway for an amazing assortment of robbers, pickpockets, murderers, rapists, and general ne'er-do-wells to pass through on their way to the relative safety from the law that the territory afforded.

Bobby was plunked right in the middle of all of it. He had initially had a number of qualms about doing firearms repairs for men he could sense or see would perhaps put them to use nefariously. It bothered him to think a gun he'd repaired might be used in a robbery or a murder.

Val had put his mind at ease about that on one of his first visits back home. "Son, a gun is just a tool. Most times out West, it just remains on your hip." Val paused. "But if a rattlesnake rears up or a Comanche buck with fresh, bloody hair on his lance aiming to add yours to it charges or if your horse steps in a hole, breaking a leg, and you have to put it down, you'll be glad you have that tool with you and that it works properly.

"You'd have to be able to see into the heart of a man to know what he's going to do with a gun at all times. And so far, the Lord hasn't blessed us with that gift." Val added gently, "So, just fix them and pray to God your work never brings someone to undeserved harm."

"Thanks, Val! I got it." Bobby was grateful for advice that came from such a well-seasoned source. Val had never told him too much about the times before he went down and picked their mom and them up in Texas and brought them back up to Memphis, but he strongly suspected Val's good advice stemmed from experience gained the hard way. He'd overheard various wranglers, drivers, and the like when they were discussing Val's possible exploits out West, and if any of it was true, Val Dimand had been someone to reckon with. Bobby knew his stepfather had been a peace officer in his early days in Memphis and that he'd served on posses sent out to capture wanted criminals. But even Pasquinel Benoit would only say, "Ask your dad!" whenever Bobby began to question him about things he and Val (and even Auguste Marno) might have done together.

Bobby knew his father always spoke highly of his time in Santa Fe with a gleam in his eye, as though he might want to return someday. Fort

Smith, along with other Arkansas and Texas towns (particularly those with a Texas Ranger troop) were the farthest away from Memphis he'd been.

Most of his trips to Texas had been as a representative of the Colt Firearms Company to repair and adjust the pistols the Texas Rangers carried. But he'd been to Amarillo with Val, back in 1864, when they'd had to go and liberate Angelina from the predicament she'd found herself in.

Angelina and Billy Estes had been married at the Gayoso House Hotel downtown on the river in late fall 1861 in front of a host of people, including her radiant mom and absolutely beaming father. The guest list had included a veritable soupçon of every type and level of Memphis society, from freight yard wranglers to school chums to well-heeled "hoi polloi." Even Mayor John Park himself was there. Also in attendance was Billy's father, himself beaming with immeasurable pride.

The freight hands who were in attendance were universally jealous of the dashingly handsome Billy, who had captured the heart of the boss's striking young daughter. Everyone commented profusely on the beautiful bride and handsome groom ad nauseum, but it was still true that the young pair could have graced the pages of any fairy-tale wedding book.

Spending their first night together in the hotel, Angelina had luxuriated in a marvelous tub bath, while Billy overlooked the mighty river from their balcony. After a wonderful night of passion mixed with promises, he and Angelina took a short river cruise up the Mississippi to St. Louis, which allowed her to meet his invalid mother, and then back again to Memphis the following week. Their honeymoon was everything Angelina had dreamed it could be from the first time she had contemplated marriage to the handsome young man.

Angelina had spotted the youthful Billy while enjoying the view from the attic dormer window at her house. Sitting on the settee placed up there for that very activity, through her father's binoculars, she'd spotted the young man among a group of them getting cleaned up at the end of their workday, and she'd set her cap for him almost immediately.

There had been many hurdles to clear before their romance could even begin to bud. First, she had to turn eighteen before her mother and father would let her go out in the company of a young man. Second, she had to show her parents she was independent and responsible enough to return home at an appointed hour. Third, she had to conduct herself properly while she was out. Fourth, she had to be properly introduced to the young man. Fifth, she had to let her parents meet and approve of any young man she was to go out with, as well as where they were going.

The first hurdle was bad enough because nothing but waiting could solve it. She figured she was solving the second and third by the way she lived her daily life. Family chores and errands she took care of without a fuss and as directly as she could manage; Carmella could count on her for help in the kitchen when she needed it.

Pasquinel Benoit had helped her with the introduction. She had taken to riding over to the freight yard several days a week to meet her father and ride home with him. Thus, she had brought significant attention to herself among the drovers, wranglers, and drivers.

Billy Estes had certainly taken notice of the willowy strawberry blonde who rode home with the boss several times a week. He asked Mr. Benoit who exactly she was one day, and Benoit replied to Billy, "Now, don't go gettin' your sights set too high there, Billy, my lad. She's his only daughter and a real treasure, so he's gonna have high expectations for anyone wanting to get next to her!"

But when, less than a week later, Angelina asked much the same question of Benoit about who the blond-haired handsome wrangler was, his reply was subtly different. "Well, Miss Angelina, that there is Billy Estes. He is a fine, hardworking young man with good habits. His parents are upstanding citizens in St. Louis, and he had a fine upbringing, and it shows. He has good prospects for his future."

Benoit went on, "I could introduce you to him, if you'd like."

Angelina's heart leaped a little as she said, "Yes, please, Uncle Bennie!" She had used a name for the gruff-faced man she hadn't spoken since she was a little girl.

His face immediately softened to that of a doting uncle, rather than a beat-up old saddle tramp pal of her father's, and he proudly said, "It would be my pleasure, Miss Angelina!" He immediately sent a runner to find the young man.

As it turned out, Billy was not in the yard that afternoon. Angelina rode home with her father, frustrated at having to wait another day. It had been more than two years since she'd first spotted the handsome young man in her daddy's binoculars, and another day or two was a bitter pill.

Pasquinel Benoit waylaid Billy upon his return to the yard and stressed to him that he would want his best appearance manageable for the following afternoon at the end of the workday, in order to be introduced to Miss Angelina Dimand. Obviously, after a day of hard work, he could be a little dusty on his clothes, but with his face washed and most of the dust shaken off and his hair reasonably combed, he might just pass muster.

The next day about four o'clock, the introduction was accomplished in an informal fashion by Mr. Benoit. The two young people had been chatting amiably for a few minutes when Val Dimand rode up on Vindicator. Angelina piped up brightly with, "Uncle Bennie just introduced me to Billy here! Could we have him over to supper sometime? Please, Daddy?"

"I'll need to talk to your mother, but I don't think it will be a problem." Val spoke softly to his daughter. He next spoke to Billy. "I'm thinking Friday night about seven. Do you think that would give you enough time to go home, bathe, and get changed and still get to our house in time?"

"Yes, sir, it would. Could I bring anything?"

"Just yourself, son. You know where we live?"

"Yes, sir. I don't live too far away, just off of Adams near Fifth, so I can make it easily."

Val finished with, "I'll speak to Angelina's mother and make sure Friday's all right and let you know tomorrow."

With that, goodbyes were said, and Val rode home with Angelina. Thoughts swirled in his head the whole ride.

Val had seen the way the two youngsters looked at each other, and he could immediately see the attraction was definitely mutual.

He had known this day would come someday, just not so dad-blamed soon!

As he spoke to Angie about it that night, she allowed as how the two young people ought to have a chance to develop a life for themselves. Having the young man over for supper and questioning him a little about his future plans for himself and the two of them was about as much as she thought they should meddle.

"I've already had the talk about pregnancy with her; she's a responsible young woman, and she deserves a chance at happiness. We can't keep her locked up forever," Angie finished breathlessly.

Val replied, "You know, if there was one of my employees I thought was fit for Angelina, it *would* be Billy." He went on, "Oh, I know he's just a hired hand right now, but he wants to own and operate his own cattle ranch someday. And I think he can do it. Of all my employees, he's the only one I'd pick."

Val was glad Angie had had "the talk" with Angelina already, because he could remember how randy Angie had been with him (and he supposed others) when she wasn't much older than Angelina was now. He thoroughly suspected that Angelina, for all her ladylike qualities, would turn out to be much the same.

That first supper at the Bethel house with Billy was an unqualified success, at least with Angie. Billy's nice smile, handsome wavy blond hair, and his refined manners, so unexpected in a freight yard stock wrangler, won Angie over almost from the moment he stepped into the front parlor.

◆

Billy's first words, almost as soon as he stepped into the house, were, "Well, this must be the portrait of your ancestor!" The large, framed painting over the fireplace mantel was definitely an attention grabber, and Val gave Billy a quick synopsis of the artwork's importance to their family.

"You see, Billy, that's Robert W. Cunningham, Angie's first husband and the father of our boys, Bobby and Oskar. He was one of the defenders at the Alamo back in 1836, and he died in its defeat." Val gleamed with pride as he spoke. "I had known Angie for several years before she and her new husband, Bobby, left for a little Texas settlement of just a few families. And after he died (with Levi Gold's help and blessings), I went down to see if Angie wanted to come back to Memphis to try to make a new life for herself and the boys. Turns out she did, and after a little trouble on the road up to here, Angie and I fell in love and then got married, and then along came little Angelina.

"So, as you can plainly see, heritage goes a long way in our family!"

"Yes, sir, I can plainly see that!" Billy proceeded with a question. "But did you just mention Levi Gold? Was he by any chance the proprietor of a general mercantile store near the riverfront?"

Angie spoke up just then. "Why do you ask, Billy?"

"My father, Robert, owns Estes Brand Hardware in St. Louis, and he mentioned many times about doing business with Levi Gold. I wondered if it might be the same man." Billy looked earnestly from Angie to Val and then back again. "My father held him in high regard."

Angie answered Billy's questions simply, "Levi Gold held your father in high regard as well Billy. Had you and your folks heard of his passing?"

"Not in time, ma'am, to make it for his funeral service. You see, my mother is an invalid and cannot easily travel such a distance. But my father wanted to do something to honor Levi Gold's years of service, so he sent a donation to the temple Levi attended." Billy concluded with, "I'd love to see his store sometime."

"The new store is very different these days from when I worked for Mr. Gold," Angie said. "It's in a new spot on Main Street, and Jacob Ottenheimer is running it and even owns it, I believe. Jacob used to work for Mr. Gold, went over to Arkansas for a while to open a store of his own, and then came back a little before Mr. Gold retired. The last I heard, Jacob had brought his two nephews, the Goldschmidt brothers to Memphis to help him. Mr. Gold was a dear friend to our family and treated me as his own daughter from the moment he took me in off the streets when I was a young girl. He then helped me take care of my sick mother until she passed on and then even gave me a place to live.

"He helped with Val's care after he was wounded in the leg bringing me back from Texas and even provided a nice little house for me and the boys to live in." Angie went on extolling Levi's virtues. "He even sent Dr. Bradford to treat Val's wound and help him get healthy enough to return to the freight yard again."

Billy had stood quietly as Angie lovingly spoke of her former employer and mentor. "It seems he was quite a man."

Val now spoke up. "That he was indeed! He may have been small in size, but he had the heart of a giant. We could never repay all the kindness that man bestowed upon our family."

Carmella appeared at the door just then, waited for Val to finish speaking, and then made her announcement. "Dinner is ready!"

As the prandial portion of the evening progressed, the conversation was lively and punctuated with acceptance of second helpings from both Val and Billy. Oskar had arrived just in time to be seated before dinner was actually being brought in but had eaten very little as he listened intently to the dinner conversation. He was highly interested in what a prospective beau for his baby sister might be like, and he intended to compare notes with Val later.

Oskar had become practically indispensable to Val at the freight yard over the last few years and had come to know Billy fairly well as a wrangler. Now was his chance to begin to know him as a man.

Oskar had always been fairly protective of Angelina. Just a little boy of not quite seven when she was born, Oskar could spend hours just watching the baby grow it seemed. Later, he became her constant playmate when she wanted one. So now, if anyone was going to take her away from the family, Oskar was bound and determined to at least have a good judgment of whoever that was.

Just before Billy turned down his second dessert, pleading that he was as full as a tick already, Oskar asked the fifty-dollar question. "So, you think you can go into cattle ranching? I've heard that's not an easy way to make a living." Oskar was often not subtle.

Angelina piped in with a defense of Billy. "I think Billy will work as hard as he needs to in order to succeed, Oscar!"

"No one doubts Billy will put forth every effort needed to succeed." Val's words were gently spoken, primarily to Angelina, but his next words would help shape their lives as a married couple. "You see, if hard work was all it took to become a successful farmer or rancher, then more folks would make a go of it than actually do. But the unknown factors, like the weather or the health of the stock, loss from thievery or rustling, and maybe even just plain bad luck have to come into play. And you have to be able to weather or overcome them all. And then there's the time it takes to learn a business."

Val was almost in his "Sunday go to meeting" preacher mode now, and Angie's eyes were bright as she watched and heard her beautiful man dispense wisdom so tortuously learned over many years of hard work and deliver it to her beloved daughter and her young man.

Val continued, "Then there's the money. A cattle ranch requires the capital to purchase an already functioning outfit or at least the land for it. Then there's the livestock, and you have to spend at least three years from the time they're born feeding, watering, guarding (protecting from predators or rustlers), and seeing to their health—all before a single one is ready to sell. And then you have to get them to market.

"A cattle drive, to take the cattle you own that are matured enough to market, is a whole different proposition," Val went on. "Now, you'll probably need to hire extra wranglers and drovers to help out your regular ranch hands. You'll need probably half again as many hands as you employ for everyday operations, and all the money that's required for that and the thousand and one extra expenses that go with it will come out of your profits at the end.

"So you see, if it takes you three years to raise cattle to where they can be marketed and extra time, trouble, and money to get them to where they're sold, then you'd better make enough profit to last you till the time the next herd is ready to go for sale.

"Some successful ranchers do a herd a year to market by staggering the age of their stock, but I personally wouldn't want to be on the trail that much.

"It took me over twenty years to build my business from one wagon to over fifty. I now have almost a hundred people on the payroll, and we're still growing." Val finished with, "It didn't happen overnight, and it didn't happen without a lot of work and a lot of money. A whole bunch of luck and even a little bit of fighting, when it was absolutely necessary, were needed as well.

"Now, I'll shut up and let you talk, Billy. Thanks for listening!"

"How did you learn so much about cattle ranching anyway, Boss?" Billy was leaning forward looking intently at Val. "Now, the financials will work themselves out with my father's help. He has an old friend with a working ranch outside Amarillo, and his friend is getting older, with no one to leave the ranch to. He doesn't want to put it up for open sale, but he and my father came to an agreement that my dad would buy it—if Mr. Lowell would stay on and teach me the business. He agreed, and I'm supposed to head out there in the fall to start.

"So, I guess I'll be leaving your employ in a couple of months, Boss, to start on my own. I hope that doesn't upset you too much; I've really enjoyed working for you, Boss." Billy looked intently at Val as he spoke.

"Well, Billy, I'll hate to lose you because you've been a good employee, but I understand you have quite an opportunity lying in front of you." Val continued, "I know that, if you have a good teacher, you'll have no trouble learning the cattle business. To answer your earlier question, I learned many years ago from one of the very best ranchers out around Santa Fe."

Angelina spoke quickly. "Daddy, you've never told us about that, so please do."

"OK, OK, I will! But you'll have to understand that this happened back in the 1830s while your mom was down in Texas with Bobby Cunningham." Val shifted in his seat and looked upward, as if calling the story from deep memories. "Now, the first thing to understand is that I was a pretty wild youngster. I regularly rode with Pasquinel Benoit and Auguste Marno.

"Pasquinel got in trouble in Jefferson Parish down in Louisiana. He got in a fight with a man who later died. Now, by all accounts, it was a fair fight. But the man was a brother of the local sheriff, who swore out

a warrant for assault against Benoit and later upgraded it to murder!"
Val paused to gather his breath and continued. "Pasquinel immediately
got out of Louisiana and into lower Mississippi, where he met up with
Mr. Marno and hatched a plan to go out West where they weren't
known. Meanwhile, Auguste set his brother, an attorney, on the case in
Pasquinel's defense.

"Marno and Benoit came through Memphis on their way out
West, and I joined them because it sounded like fun. I was footloose
and fancy-free in those days, and this sounded like an adventure I just
couldn't pass up! So, we rode out of Memphis, ferried across to Arkansas,
rode across there, and dropped down into Texas around Amarillo. Then
we headed west to Santa Fe.

"In those days, not long after Mexico won its independence from
Spain, the Mexican Territory of Santa Fe was doing a brisk trade with
several places in the United States, particularly in Missouri. Trade in
agricultural goods and mules really flourished."

Angie watched Val as her husband told the story of the three friends
and their ride. Never had he shared this story before, and she was
fascinated.

Val went on, "Only a few years before, the Spanish were trying
to keep Santa Fe isolated and unknown. But then, after trade broke
through and Mexico gained its independence, we were as welcome as
could be. We all three found work on Senor Arturo Vega's estancia,
which is what they called their ranches. His family had held it as a
Spanish land grant ever since the 1760s. Together with his riders, or
'vaqueros' as they called them, Vega and his family had held the land
against rustlers, bandits, raiding Indians, and every other foe who could
come against them.

"We rode with the best when we rode with the Spanish vaqueros.
Along with ones from New Mexico and also from California, who
would sometimes make it over to Senor Vega's, well they were just the
best riders and hardest workers I ever saw. I learned a great deal about
ranching when I was there."

Oskar piped up with, "Why didn't you stay, Val?"

"Oh, I could have, very easily. I loved the riding and the fighting, truth to be told. Senor Vega was a fine boss, and I could have stayed for years, probably. All of us had great friends among the vaqueros. But after almost a year, the word came that Benoit had been cleared of all charges, and he wanted to go back home to Louisiana. Marno and I went with him, just to keep the three of us together, I suppose.

"Pasquinel had to leave a Spanish girl (very pretty and consumed with him) behind when he left. But I really think all of us expected to return to Santa Fe someday. After Auguste and I got Benoit back to Louisiana and made sure he was going to be all right, the two of us stopped briefly in Mississippi at his folks' and then headed to Memphis. And the rest is as you already know it.

"I've never since gone back West, but I think I'd like to someday!

"Does all that answer your question, Billy?"

"Yes, sir, it most certainly does. It was fascinating! I had no idea Mr. Marno or Mr. Benoit had ever done anything like that."

Val came back forcefully. "Don't ever sell those two short, son. They're two of the toughest and most resourceful men I've ever seen. And when you look at Pasquinel's face and see all those scars, just realize he's earned every one of them."

Val pushed back from the table, pulled his flowing (but now gray-ing) hair back from his face, and put a mighty arm around Angie's waist. Drawing her close to him and planting a kiss on her cheek, he spoke to her and the whole table. "Well, I think it is high time we let these two youngsters have time to themselves to get acquainted. Have you thought of showing Billy the view from the dormer, Angelina? It should be lovely tonight."

"Thanks, Daddy. I will!"

Oskar glanced through the door at the hallway clock and said, "I have just time to make my assistants' meeting, if I leave right now. So I'll say goodbye to all. It will probably be late when I return. We have an important court briefing coming up, and I'm to present it. So don't wait up for me, and I'll be as quiet as I can when I come in. See you around, Billy!"

Val and Angie walked together toward the hallway door, and Angie said as she passed, "Not too late, Angelina. Remember Billy's got to be at work early tomorrow morning!"

"Yes, Mama. I understand."

"I'll see you in the morning, Boss. And thanks to you and Mrs. Dimand for the fine meal," Billy said quickly as Val and Angie made it through the hallway door.

Val made sure they were out of view before he let his hand drop from Angie's waist to her left butt cheek and gave it a gentle squeeze

Carmella saw Val's fondling of Angie as she was coming out the hallway door from the kitchen but went on her way silently and unnoticed.

———————◆———————

As Angelina led Billy up the stairs to the attic and then threw open the dormer window shutters, her midsection was on fire and quivering.

"This is truly magnificent," Billy gasped. But his next words were stifled by Angelina's mouth desperately on his and smashing his lips. Her hands were running up and down his body as her midsection pressed close to his.

Billy tried hard to control his gallant reflex but to no avail. By the time he and Angelina had clumsily become seated on the settee, his trousers had a magnificent protrusion.

Angelina spoke very softly into his ear. "I know this is very forward of me and not very ladylike at all, but I've had my eyes on you for years now, and I just can't wait anymore to show you how much I want you!"

The astonished Billy couldn't speak; words would not come.

Words were not what Angelina wanted. She fumbled with the buttons to his trouser fly and, getting three of them undone, she searched diligently through the layers of cloth below until she finally brought forth his fiercely erect manhood into the cool night air. Placing the tip of Billy's shaft into her mouth as she had seen done to Bobby, Oskar, and Val, she began to run her mouth up and down, up and down along its length.

All the time, Angelina was thinking, *At last, it's my turn, and it's with the one I really want!*

Meanwhile, Billy's thoughts were consumed with alternations between *Oh, no! The boss is going to kill me*, and *don't stop. Please don't stop!*

With some help from Billy, the last of the buttons were overcome, and his pants were slid down enough to see the entire, considerable shaft that Billy sported.

The slurping sounds Angelina was making were punctuated by the soft moans and groans from Billy; soft as they were, each of the two young lovers feared discovery.

When Billy could contain himself no more, his inevitable emission went all over Angelina's face and neck. Sitting there glistening in the moonlight, Angelina undid the bodice to her dress and brought forth a small but delightful breast, tipped with a soft, pink, girlish nipple and offered it up to Billy's greedy yet surprisingly gentle mouth.

As she sat there luxuriating in what she had accomplished and the warmth of Billy's ministrations on her breast, Angelina hoped against hope that she would not have frightened him away. Hopefully, they had begun a relationship that would be able to grow into what Angie and Val had. As she gently pushed Billy's head back, she looked into his eyes and told him, "I hope you can see how interested I am in you. The thought of you leaving for Texas without me is almost more than I can bear. Please come back over as often as you can, Billy!"

After straightening her clothes and wiping her face, Angelina led Billy back down the attic stairs into the kitchen, and seeing no one there, she initiated a passionate open-mouthed kiss, which Billy returned with equal fervor.

When the two finally broke apart, Angelina whispered softly, "Oh my!" and then led him out into the hallway, down it, and out through the front door. A tiny peck on the cheek, and Billy was gone into the night.

When she was back inside and the front door closed quietly behind her, Angelina leaned back against it for a moment, her soul clouded in a swirl of nebulous visions.

In her bed, she alternated between soft, slow rubbings of her crotch and wild, unrestrained, almost violent tugging at her mound and the slit in between. She had, many months before, discovered her clitoris and was, by now, practiced in the art of bringing herself to orgasm in peaceful waves or thundering explosions.

By the time her exhausted body finally demanded sleep, she had lost track in her mind of how many orgasms she'd endured.

Billy's handsome face and wonderful body were prominent in all of them.

———————◆———————

The whole family seemed to take to Billy. Over the coming weeks, his presence at the Bethel house became more and more common.

Angie shared her daughter's assessment of the young man. She found his manners and breeding belied what he did for a living, although Val told her Billy's skills at riding and stock handling were top notch, and he fit right in with the other wranglers, most of whom were older and "rough as cobs," according to Val.

"There're a lot of those men I like and respect, but Billy's one of the very few I'd want near Angelina. I was so relieved when she set her sights on him, let me tell you. I was always afraid when she started coming around the freight yard that she would go for one of the others, and then I'd have had trouble. I've had to shut a couple of them up after they made comments about her as it is!"

Angie's reply was quick. "Oh, you know she was just looking for someone like her daddy—handsome and kind, who would know how to treat her right and would absolutely live to do so, like you with me!"

"I got so lucky when I found you, my love. How could I not treasure my every moment with you?"

"Let's both hope he's the one for her and they get married and give us grandbabies, and soon! I want to hold babies again."

"You're too young and beautiful to be a grandma."

"Well if you think so, you shaggy old man, just sit over there and let me trim you up and we'll see who's too young."

Val knew what was coming next, and he loved it. Since she was a girl, Angie had had a penchant for straddling Val's lap and trimming his hair, beard, and moustache while slowly grinding her crotch into his and producing an absolutely magnificent erection.

This particular morning was different. Angie surprised Val while she was trimming and kissing him by opening her robe to him while she was still in his lap, thereby exposing her not-quite-so-youthful body to him as she worked. Val's fingers pulled and stretched her meaty nipples until she almost screamed with pleasure, and she buried her head in his neck to stifle any outcry. When his fingers reached downward between her spread legs, he found her already amply moist to begin rubbing her slit and, finding his target, begin inserting his long, slender fingers into her.

"If you keep that up, old man, you're liable to have to go out with lopsided hair and half a moustache! Let me finish first."

Angie finished grooming Val, and they went from the chaise to the bed, where Angie took Val in her mouth briefly before she turned her smooth and still-supple backside to him.

Faced with such a sight, and his choice of receptacles for his tumescent shaft, Val chose her still-glistening opening as his entrance. And then sinking himself as deeply into her as he could manage, with a groan longer and louder than he wanted, he deposited a healthy load into her as she dug her face into the pillows to muffle her screams.

As the two lovers lay there in the afterglow, Carmella crept silently down the hall toward the kitchen.

———————◆———————

About three weeks later, Billy popped the question, receiving an instant and unqualified, "Yes!"

He had already laid the groundwork by seeking permission from Val. The trepidation he felt in approaching his boss with such a question, after such a short time, was only overmatched by his determination to see the process through and make Val know that Angelina was the one for him and he would have no other.

Before Val gave his permission for Billy to ask Angelina for her hand in marriage, much conversation ensued between the two men about what thought and preparation he'd put into life with Angelina, protecting her from all dangers and cherishing her so she would always know she was loved.

Val made it clear that these two things were essential for his permission to be given and, satisfied that Billy's intentions and capabilities were good, it was.

It was a whirlwind between the proposal and the wedding.

The house and all its occupants were constantly astir.

A meeting between the two fathers brought forth the plan that they would travel to Texas and on to the ranch with the newlyweds. Robert Estes went to handle the financials when they got there, and Val Dimand went for his experience with the route they were to take and to provide an extra measure of protection along the way. An exchange of telegrams between Val and Bobby brought his aid to the party for the short stretch between Ft. Smith and Amarillo. Since he was very familiar with the Rangers at the troop there, Bobby even wired the troop commander about their impending arrival and received Captain Rook's assurance that the Rangers would be on the lookout for them. Since fighting between Federal and Confederate forces had begun only a few months before, this only seemed wise, given the heightened tensions abounding.

As a wedding gift, Val had given Ranger to Angelina and the sure-footed, tranquil gelding would be an asset to her on the long ride to Texas. It also turned out that Robert Estes had been Captain Estes of the United States Cavalry during and after the Mexican War out in California. Therefore, he was familiar with what the ride might be and what precautions might be necessary.

Taking the southern route out of Memphis would have put them right into the crazed fervor for war that seemed to be seething in Mississippi, so the entire party (loaded horses and all) boarded the ferry across the river just north of Memphis, rode across Arkansas to Little Rock, and boarded the Little Rock and Ft. Smith railway before dropping down south from there into Texas and heading for Amarillo. Although anti-union sentiment had been growing at a slower pace in Arkansas (less dependence on slaves and western isolation were probably the cause), the ranch-bound party was careful to avoid any sort of engagement as they passed through.

Crossing through the Indian Territory would have been the most direct route to Amarillo out of Ft. Smith, but the two fathers felt the better course would be to drop down into Texas, go across, and then back up the short distance to the ranch, just north of Amarillo.

After all these preparations, the journey went off relatively "hitch-free," save for a horse that went lame and had to be replaced and a broken strap on a pack on another horse. They camped where and when they had to and stayed indoors at hotels or rooming houses when they could.

Along the way, Val sent telegraph messages to Oskar and Angie informing them of their progress at each stop. His last message to Angie was a crisp one:

Lovebirds installed in nest.

Stop.

All business concluded.

Stop.

Home about 18 October. Love.

Stop.

Chapter 11

ANGELINA COMES HOME

Native Memphians often leave the city for many reasons—employment opportunities elsewhere, marriage, caring for others, and many other things. But always, there is the call to return to the tree-lined streets, the friendly neighborhoods, the fine food, and that delicious water, and well, the pull to return is strong. Many can make a homecoming, but some just toil away their remaining lives, yearning in their hearts for their beloved home.

1864

Brush popping was one of the harder and more dangerous tasks any cowboy could do. Billy Estes had been down by the creek bed all morning, moving steers (who didn't want to go) up and away from the creek bank. He was hot and tired when he came upon several cows and two bulls near a cottonwood along the creek. He got two of the cows and one bull up and away and was returning when, suddenly, the other bull charged, and his horse veered to avoid the longhorn's wide, tearing reach. As Billy fell from his saddle, one of the bull's horns caught Billy in the abdomen and ripped him wide open. Billy's injury was so severe some of his intestines hit the ground before his feet touched.

In absolute agony, he futilely tried to gather his spilled internals back into his body. Seeing the futility of these actions and rapidly succumbing to the blood loss he was experiencing, Billy drew his six-shooter and fired three shots into the air before his arm no longer had the strength to hold it up.

Before the light went out in his now wide-open eyes, Billy's last thoughts were of Angelina, his wife, and his young daughter Valentina. He hadn't seen or touched them in a week. He and the hands were out gathering the herd they were sending to market, and this required them to be out on the range day and night, keeping the herd together and guarding against predators and rustlers.

The memory of the sweet love he and Angelina had made that last night....

———————◆———————

Tobias Warner was the first one of the ranch hands on the gruesome scene after the sound of Billy's shots from his Colt had faded away. As he wiped the vomit from his mouth, he stared into the lifeless eyes of his boss, Billy Estes.

Toby had never seen anything like this; he had seen men, women and children after the savages had gotten through with them, and it had not prepared him for what lay before him now.

As other riders galloped up, Toby covered Billy's lifeless form with a ground sheet he'd pulled from his own horse. Billy's mount grazed nervously some distance away, prancing some occasionally and whinnying nervously at the scene, as though it could tell something was dreadfully wrong.

The stench was overwhelming; several of the others also vomited.

Buck Jackson, the ranch foreman, took Toby aside and put an arm across his shoulders in an effort to calm the obviously shaken rider.

"What happened here, Toby?" Buck began. "Did you see any of it?"

"No, Boss," Toby answered shakily. "And I've never seen anything like that!" He pointed at the sheet with Billy's lifeless body under it. "The nearest I can figure he was gored by a steer. It ripped his guts wide open and spilled them onto the ground. And by the time I got here, three minutes maybe, Billy was already gone."

Buck hesitated a moment before saying, "Somebody's gonna need to go up to the house and be with Angelina and the baby while the doctor and others come from town. Can you do that, Toby, or should I send somebody else?"

"Not me, Boss, please. I don't think I could face her or give her any comfort myself."

"Burt!" barked Buck. "Over here! Quick!"

As Burt was speeding over, Buck said to Toby, "OK son, you be the one to go into town and get Doc to come out here with whoever he needs to take care of Billy's body. I figure Miss Angelina is going to need help to calm her and maybe someone for the baby, so several folks may need to come out to the ranch." He went on, "Tell Doc what you saw and that he's dead, in case he wants to send old Simpkins for the body and come straight to the ranch himself to care for Miss Angelina right away. And, Toby—don't go blabbin' it about town; nobody else needs to know right now.

"Burt, you ride back to the ranch house and find Miss Angelina. And get her inside before you tell her if you can."

Buck knew from experience that her first reaction would be to want to rush to his side, and he wanted to spare the young wife the horror of seeing such grue, if he could help it. Buck had one more thought.

"Toby, you'd better let Sheriff Dawkins know, too. But ask him to keep it quiet for now. I have to send a couple of telegrams to their parents, so tell him I'll be back into town later.

"Off you two go, now, and good luck." After Buck had dismissed the two riders on their difficult but vital errands, he turned to the other ten cowboys standing in a circle at a respectful distance.

"All right, you guys, it's a tough day. But we still have a herd to get to market, and Billy'd want us to get right back to work. You all know Billy would be right in there with us if he could, so just do your job just like he was ridin' next to you, and we'll come out fine!"

◆

Burt made it back to the ranch house less than half an hour before
Toby hit town, and he went up the steps to the front door and knocked.
Angelina, who had been in the kitchen with little Tina, came to the door
moments later with the child in her arms and said as she swung the door
open and smiled, "Burt, how nice to see you! But what are you doing
here at this time of the day?"

It must have been the anguished look on Burt's face that did it, for
just then all the color drained from Angelina's face, and she began to
crumple to the floor.

Burt reached forward and deftly caught Tina just as her mother's
grip loosened. And he continued the motion by stepping through the
door and placing the sleeping baby on the stuffed chair in the front
room. He then turned back to her mother and, gathering up her skirts
under her, gently picked Angelina up and placed her onto the settee next
to the chair that was holding baby Tina.

Burt then went into the kitchen and soaked a folded dish towel in
clear well water and brought it back to the settee. Placing the wet compress on Angelina's forehead caused her eyes to flutter.

"Where's my baby?"

"I caught her before she could hit the floor, Miss Angelina. Baby
Tina's here. And she's just fine."

Angelina sat bolt upright on the settee and looked at the drover with
an intensity he hoped he'd never see again.

"Don't you dare sugarcoat it, Burt! Just tell me the news, whatever it
is, straight out, do you hear?" Deep in her soul, Angelina was practically
begging Burt not to tell her what she already knew in her heart must
be the truth.

"I'm so sorry! It's Billy, ma'am," Burt began sorrowfully. "He was
gored by a steer late this morning. Ripped him wide open. It didn't take
more than three minutes for any of us to get there, but he was already
gone by then."

By the time Burt had finished speaking, Angelina's face looked as
though she had aged ten years in that brief expanse.

Quietly and plaintively she whispered, "What am I going to do, Burt? Whatever am I going to do?"

———————————◆———————————

Within moments of Angelina's plaintive question, Toby rode into town. His lathered horse was a living testament to his having wasted no time in doing so. Therefore, many sets of eyes figured something urgent was up when Toby went first to the doc's place and then on to the sheriff's.

When they saw the doc ride out of town moments later with Mrs. Malvern beside him in the buggy, followed closely by Mr. Simpkins in his wagon, they knew that, whatever it was, the news couldn't be good.

———————————◆———————————

A little before dark, Buck Jackson came riding into town after the herd was gathered and the night riders were riding patrol around them.

He had brought with him the text of two telegrams to be sent, one to a Mr. Robert Estes in St. Louis and the other to a Mr. Val Dimand in Memphis.

The telegraph operator looked up at Buck after he had read the address of the second recipient. "If this is who I think it is, we'd better get everything as close to right as we can, or there could be hell to pay!"

"You're exactly right, it is, and we will, indeed," Buck replied and then continued, "It's a downright shame about Billy, 'cause he woulda made it, I believe. Poor Angelina's holding it together, but I don't know how."

After a moment's reflection, Buck waxed philosophical. "You know, they were a pair you could draw to, Billy and Angelina. I would have bet my entire stake on it, but now this. That girl's got steel in her, though. Probably gets it from her father."

"And her mother, too, I'd say." The telegrapher spoke knowingly. "You ever hear the story of Val and Angelina's mom coming back to Memphis from Texas?"

Buck shook his head. "No."

"Then, let me get these sent right away. I have a break coming up, and you look like you could use a beer right about now or maybe something even stronger."

"Sounds good. I *could* use one!"

Ten minutes later, as they were seated at a round table over half-drunk beers, Sam, the telegrapher, told Buck the story of Val and Angie in Mississippi.

"Like I said, these road agents had them dead to rights because they had been layin' for them. Well, old Val gets down from the wagon box and faces off two of them with his hands in the air, and one of them has a rifle pointed at Val.

"Now, there's a third man in the road holdin' Angie in the wagon with a pistol in his hand. But, unseen by anybody, Angie's son Bobby (who's less than ten) slides a fully loaded Hawken forward to his mom, who proceeds to shoot from the hip into the road agent in front of the wagon and then get the wagon team back under control and then shoot the guy again with a Paterson Colt she pulled from the wagon box holster during the melee.

"Meanwhile, the man in the road with the rifle is fixing to shoot Val and does! Only his aim is spoiled by Val's big knife suddenly stickin' outa his chest, and his shot hits Val in the leg instead. Then Angie comes roarin' by and shoots this guy in the face with the Colt."

Buck had to ask, "How do you know all this?"

"Pasquinel Benoit was the first on the scene after it was all done, and he saw the bodies and Miss Angie tending to Val's leg. He told me about it years ago," Sam concluded.

"You knew Benoit?" said Buck in amazement.

"Yep, toughest man I ever saw! You know, I chewed some trail dust and stuff before I got this cushy job," Sam replied.

Buck was quick with his next comment. "I really see what you mean about Angelina gettin' grit from both her mom and her dad. She may indeed be able to tough this out because of it." Buck added, "You ever see Val Dimand shoot?"

"No, you?" Sam's face was a mask of curiosity.

"Yeah, when I was just a kid on our homestead up near the Canadian River. Val and Pasquinel came through with another friend of theirs just as a bunch of five or six out-of-range savages were raiding our place! Well, they all jumped down off their horses and started shootin' back. Val had four fully loaded single- shot Dragoon Colts, two on his horse and two on his hips. He pulled the horse pistols first and emptied them into those Pimas or Utes or whatever they were, and he didn't miss! Two shots and two renegades dead on the ground—two of 'em, with one bullet each.

"Then he dropped those two pistols, and while he was grinnin' from ear to ear and cussin' them in some sort of native tongue, he proceeds to pull the other two Walkers and tells them to come ahead." Buck had a look of almost reverence on his face by now. "So, this one buck who's been whoopin' it up something fierce and must have been their ringleader, says something to Val, and he charges. From at least a hundred feet away, Val coolly shoots him between the eyes. Then he says something more to the ones who were left, and they begin to come calmly and pick up their fallen men and put them on horseback. And within five minutes, the raiders were gone. Val and his buddies rode off later that afternoon, and I never saw him again, until he helped bring Billy and Angelina out to the ranch."

They finished their beers and went their separate ways—Sam back to the telegraph office and Buck back to the ranch, to see in what pitifully insufficient way he might be of help.

———————◆———————

Val and Bobby arrived the following Tuesday, too late to attend Billy's small, quiet funeral and burial. Mr. Simpkins had done an amazing job in readying Billy's torn body for burial, and they'd laid him peacefully to rest under a cottonwood near the house. Billy's father later provided a carved stone marker (which was still standing when new owners bought the property in 1918).

It turned out Billy's father was also friends with the family of Charles Goodnight, who was beginning to develop ranching and cattle-driving operations for larger, long-distance cattle drives to markets farther away. Robert Estes and Charlie Goodnight reached an agreement for him to buy the ranch over time, thus ensuring Angelina an income for at least ten years. If the ranch stayed profitable or was folded into a larger holding, then she might have an income that could last for decades.

Val and Bobby were there to take Angelina and little Tina home to Memphis, period. However, Val's scrupulous honesty would not let him take Angelina away while ranch hands needed to get paid for work they had performed or would in the near future. Bills for supplies were owed in town, and other obligations existed that were also as yet unmet.

Meeting outstanding responsibilities would have placed a huge load on the young widowed Angelina, so Val and Bobby shouldered that burden for themselves.

Val had been spending his own funds at first. All the hands were thus fully paid. Val stayed out at the ranch to see a smooth operation, based on his own payroll procedure in Memphis. Meanwhile, Bobby Cunningham became a very popular man in town, paying the ranch's running accounts in cold hard cash—something that was very scarce in those times.

A final stroke of (good, for a change) fortune came in the person of a cattle buyer from the state of Texas, who was interested in a rapid sale of the assembled herd for cash in silver, which offer was quickly accepted and the transaction completed.

The caveat to the deal was that the herd had to be delivered to a Confederate Army (Third Texas Infantry) supply depot outside Dallas, which the ranch's personnel did in good order with little trouble, right after Billy's interment.

Thus, with the ranch transferred to Goodnight, all the bills paid and the hands paid as well, and the final payment from the cattle in hand, Angelina and her kin could leave Texas with their heads held high, all the way back to Memphis.

To all effects, the tragically ended saga of the Lazy Moon Ranch was complete.

Bobby could have gone directly back to Ft. Smith, but he decided to accompany his "little sister" and her baby all the way to Memphis and then return home from there.

It almost cost him his life.

———————◆———————

Stagecoach service by the Overland Stage Company through Texas had not survived the beginnings of the Civil War because of Texas' secession from the Union. Thus, a mixture of private and small commercial operators filled the void with spotty service, which could leave passengers stranded at any time. To counteract this, Val telegraphed the Dimand Freight Company in Memphis.

They were asked to provide a wagon outfitted for the transport of the family and their baggage and an escort team of seasoned riders to help bring the family safely back to Memphis. They were to meet the wagon and riders at Shreveport, Louisiana, just over the Texas border. From there, they would travel across to the regular route between New Orleans and Memphis, which was used by the Dimand Freight Company at least once a week. The family would ride as a group on the stage to Shreveport after spending a couple of nights in a hotel in Dallas and meet the escort from Memphis.

Dallas, it turned out, was still rebuilding from the ravages of the fire of 1860, which had destroyed much of the downtown, including the only hotel. Thus, the best Val could find for Angelina and the baby was at a rooming house run by a kindly older lady named Mrs. Millicent Smithers, while he and Bobby took a room above the Imperial, one of the town's several bustling saloons. The accommodations were relatively clean but certainly not quiet.

It seemed that every night almost all of the thousand or so people who lived in Dallas at that time were out carousing. Sleep was in short supply, leading to irritability on the part of both the weary traveling men.

Neither man was usually given to strong drink, but a couple of whiskeys with a beer chaser helped them to sleep in that turbulent environment. Their second night there, since they were supposed to board the stage for Shreveport late the next morning, they drank slowly and quietly at a corner of the bar, hoping to slip off unnoticed and unbothered when sleepiness finally arrested them.

Alas, it was not to be.

Bob Dugan, one of the Texas Rangers who had been transferred to the Dallas Troop, recognized Bobby Cunningham and came over for a chat. He had known Bobby for years through his gunsmithing work for the Rangers and was more than pleased to meet his stepfather, the legendary Val Dimand.

The three men chatted amicably for a while about Dallas's growth potential, the state of the Rangers during this time of conflict, and the potential for trouble along the way back to Memphis. Dugan had advice for the two men on how to handle Confederate patrols if they ran into any.

"Lots of 'em are only a little better than renegades these days, so be careful and keep your valuables hid. They might try to take your horses, though. So, it's probably best that you give 'em up, rather than having to fight to keep your lives, what with your daughter and her baby along."

Val thanked Bob for his advice, and Bobby walked his old acquaintance toward the front door of the barroom. But as he did, trouble burst forth.

A group of three young toughs, fully liquored up and spoiling for a fight, came crashing through the swinging doors of the bar just as Bobby and the Ranger were about to exit. Their leader and Bobby crashed to the floor, while the other two took one look at Bob's Ranger badge, lifted their hands away from their belts, and backed out the door slowly, walking swiftly back down the street.

Bobby Cunningham, however, upon arising, found himself staring into the muzzle of a Confederate Griswold revolver. While that model was known to have reliability problems, Bobby was not anxious to find out if this particular one did, so he lifted his hands slowly. The barroom had fallen deathly silent as people watched to see which way they should move, if needed.

"I'm sure sorry, friend; I meant no offense. I'm not armed."

"You knocked me to the floor. If you're gonna go around doin' that, you ought to arm yourself," the young tough sneered.

Bob Dugan spoke up. "Johnny, you'd better haul those horses back in, before they drag you into trouble you can't get out of!"

"You think I'm scared of you, Ranger Bob? I already got the drop on him. I figure I could take you too before you could get that Navy Colt into action." Johnny's sneer was becoming louder and more vicious by the moment.

A new voice broke through the turmoil. "Son, how about I buy you a drink before things get too out of hand? The man said he was sorry, and from where I sat, the fault was as much yours as his, maybe more." Val's voice was loud enough to cut through the room but calm and assured. "Let's have no more trouble. Come get that drink."

Johnny couldn't miss the tall old man who looked like he could still bend a horseshoe straight with his bare hands, standing there facing him with his arms by his slender waist and his hands poised over the butts of two massive Walker Colts.

"Yeah, and who are you?" came the sneering reply.

"Well, son, I'm Val Dimand. That fella at the end of your pistol is my stepson, Bobby Cunningham. Now, can't you just put your gun away and come have that drink?"

Johnny's face had blanched at the name Val Dimand, and his arm got just a little unsteady from pointing the Griswold for so long at Bobby. A shadow crossed his mind with the thought that the pistol might misfire, or worse, he might not be able to get into action fast enough.

Completely happy to have been offered a way to get out of this situation with his head still up, Johnny carefully put his gun away and said simply, "A drink sounds fine, Mr. Dimand. And please allow me to apologize for my drunken behavior; I'm sorry!"

"Step right up to the bar, son. Mr. Travers, please serve this young man anything he'd like to have, on my tab."

Travers, the barkeep, poured Johnny a drink into a glass and then backed away from the bar with his hands out to reach the liquor shelf behind him. Then he settled back against it, leaning on his hands, while watching for further developments.

They weren't long in coming.

As Johnny set his glass back down on the bar after taking his first sip, something whistled past his ear and became embedded at least a half-inch deep in the mahogany top to the bar, less than a quarter of an inch from his fingers on his gun hand.

It was of all things, a real, honest-to-God tomahawk.

Val had, with blinding speed, pulled it from its belt loop, tossed it into the air and caught it, and brought it crashing down, all with no apparent effort at all.

With the axe head still in the bar, Val began to speak firmly to Johnny. "Son, you have a chance here. Go home and sober up, and tomorrow can dawn bright for you. You can live out your days being at peace with other men as the Apostle Paul said in Romans, or you can repeat this little episode as often as you'd like. But someday you'll run into someone who's not as patient as I am.

"Rest assured, son, that before I'd let you harm a hair on my stepson's head and make me have to bring the news back to his mother, my wife who I dearly love"—Val got downright harsh here—"I'd be wearing your eyeballs around my neck on a piece of rawhide!"

Johnny Jackson backed away from the bar, slunk across the barroom, and slipped out the doors, where Bob Dugan met him on the boardwalk outside.

"Well, Johnny, you made it out of that alive, thank the good Lord!"

"Yes, sir, I did. I let the drink cloud my judgment." Johnny's voice was weak but completely sober as he spoke. "I'll never do that again."

"Some people shouldn't drink, and I think you're one of 'em, son. Lucky for you that that man don't seem to have a mean or vindictive bone in his body." Dugan's voice was calm and quiet. "Isn't your dad still foreman on that ranch start-up out near Amarillo? The Lazy Moon or some such?"

"Yes, sir. He is. Why do you ask?"

Dugan replied, "When I was stationed with the Ranger troop out there, Buck and I were pals, and he told me a story about Val Dimand from when your dad was a boy. You ever hear that story?"

"Yes, sir. He told me a long time ago, in fact. But I never expected to meet him, at least not like that!" Johnny's voice was almost reverent in its intensity. "He could have chopped off all the fingers on my gun hand, but he missed me by a hair, on purpose! That man is something."

Dugan replied, "Now you see why they call him 'Sudden Death with Either Hand,' don't you?"

"Yes, sir!"

Dugan continued, "Well, my lad, you'll find enough trouble in your life without going out and lookin' for it. Sometimes you'll run into someone who's so good he doesn't have to fight, understand?"

"Yes, sir!"

"Then do yourself a favor, young Jackson, my lad, and never touch anything stronger than a beer again—and damned little of that!"

As young Johnny Jackson walked off into the night, he did so straight upright, with a new resolve and a new purpose in his life.

After a pretty good night's sleep, Val and Bobby rode the next morning to Mrs. Smithers's rooming house to pick up Angelina and Tina. They brought with them the unfortunate news that the stage to Shreveport had been cancelled without notice.

As Val was paying the kindly innkeeper for the lodging, he inquired whether there was a wagon and driver he might hire to use for transport to Shreveport instead of the stage.

Mrs. Smithers allowed, "I have a suitable wagon and a fella you can use for a driver available."

"What would you want for such an arrangement?" Val asked.

"Well, you could leave that handsome young man Bobby behind to keep me company," was her startling reply. "My own dear Joseph, my husband of fifteen years, took off for California some time ago to make his fortune, and I haven't heard from him since!"

"Well ma'am, we need to keep the family together for the rest of the trip, but could I offer you an extra ten-dollar silver piece for their use?" Val's reply was made with a knowing grin.

"All right, if that's all I can do for you." She practically whispered the final part. "But if either one of you ever get back by here and need a place to stay, I'll make you most comfortable, believe you me."

"Well, thank you, ma'am, but just the wagon and driver for now. Thanks!"

◆

An hour later, they were loaded into the wagon with Val and Bobby following behind on horseback, headed for Shreveport.

Along the way, they only ran into one impediment. A Confederate roadblock and checkpoint had been established a couple of miles south of the town proper, and there the troops were stopping and questioning all who passed their way.

Ostensibly looking for runaway slaves, their real purpose was to relieve travelers of any desirable horses or other valuable assets and to look for deserters.

Val and his family passed through the roadblock without too much trouble; the grizzled Confederate captain commanding the detachment pictured himself atop Vindicator or Sidewinder, Val and Bobby's mounts, but they were not to be had without a fight, and such was not justified.

Angelina spoke up to Val. "Papa, I don't think I could ever ride again anyway, so if giving them Ranger gets us through, I won't really mind. I just want to get home to Mama!"

And so it was that, after negotiations at the checkpoint were completed, the family rode into Shreveport with most of their belongings and treasures intact but minus one good horse and two spare rifles.

Early that afternoon, they met up with the contingent from Dimand Freight, led by Pasquinel Benoit himself. Getting on in years and sicker than he would let on, Benoit nevertheless came when his old friend needed.

Angelina introduced Tina to "Uncle Benny" to his (and her!) great delight.

The rest of the way across Louisiana, and much of the way up through Mississippi, he held Tina, making faces at her to her peals of amusement. His pockmarked and scarred face (which normally could frighten even the toughest ape) was softened and surprisingly gentle with the little girl. Angelina rode sometimes on the wagon seat beside them but sometimes in the back of the wagon on the cushions Benoit had brought along. Seeing her young child comforted by Uncle Benny was pleasant, and the thought of soon being home in Memphis brought a warm glow to her heart. But as she watched her long-haired (even if now gray), dashingly handsome father riding his magnificent horse behind them, a new and strange emotion crept into her soul.

For the first time, Angelina understood clearly what her parents had shared together for all these years, and she was jealous!

Her mind told her there would be plenty of suitors for a young and pretty mother, even with a little girl child, so she didn't have to be alone. Since her Mom had been through a similar tragedy, Angelina decided her mother might just be able to give her some meaningful advice on the subject.

Her father had been strong for her in her loss, and he genuinely grieved for Billy and her loss of him. But Val knew how tenuous life could be in the West, or on any frontier, and that mortal hazard could appear out of nowhere and made no distinction over whose life it might claim.

Bobby had told her of his trouble at the bar in Dallas, and how close he'd come to losing his life. When he'd gotten to the part about Val at the bar, Benoit exclaimed, "That's the Val Dimand I know! Not only one of my oldest friends, but someone you always want to have at your back."

Bobby chimed in, "He sure had mine."

"That young man's lucky he has any fingers on his gun hand. Val don't miss with a tomahawk, 'less he wants to," Benoit went on. "In the old days, Val would stand up to any kind of a fight, and if it went deadly, your dad was in the thick of it, pilin' up bodies till there weren't any more left to kill or until the other side called it quits!"

"He taught me to shoot, and I've stayed in practice. But I've never killed anybody. I don't even know if I could." Bobby spoke quietly. "I was on a posse once, and I got off a few shots at the fugitives, but I don't think I even hit anybody."

"I bet you found that shootin' from a running horse at somebody on another horse is a lot harder than hittin' a target nailed up on a post," Benoit intoned.

"I sure did!"

"Well, Val was the best I ever saw at it, and that's a fact." Pasquinel quipped. "He could, and I've seen it, hang off the side of and shoot from underneath a running horse at full gallop and hit a moving target, be it man or beast!"

"Why would he need to do that?" Angelina wanted to know. "That sounds dangerous!"

"It is, missy. But when you're in a running fight with a bunch of redskins out for hair, you'll either learn or die." Benoit wasn't quite finished. "He wasn't doing it for show, you understand, but for protection. He'd seen the Indians do it, and he admired them, so he learned to do it too."

"That's the thing about your dad. He can learn to do just about anything he puts his mind to. Did you know he actually learned to fence, and by all accounts he was deadly good at it?" Benoit finished up with, "I've never seen him with a sword, but I wouldn't want to go up against that man whether he had a rapier, a cutlass, a Bowie knife, a tomahawk, a pistol, or even just his bare hands—he's just that good."

"I've seen him with a Walker Colt, as heavy as they are, put all six shots into a three-inch circle at a hundred feet, and I just saw what he could do with a tomahawk." Bobby spoke up. "He was faster than you could believe and deadly accurate, too!"

Angelina chimed in with, "It was just a few miles up the road here where Mom and Dad had to fight off the men who were waiting to waylay them. Mom always said that, if Daddy hadn't thrown his knife into the chest of the one with the rifle pointed at him, he probably would have been killed right there.

"And she always says, even to this day, that it was so fast she really didn't see him throw it; it just appeared in the man's chest."

The group fell quiet as little Tina awoke from her slumber and began to clamor for attention. Angelina had Benoit stop the wagon momentarily so she could put the little girl and herself into the back of the wagon, where she could feed and play with Tina.

Bobby took that opportunity to change as outrider with Val, mounting Sidewinder to ride behind the wagon while Val took a break riding in the seat alongside Benoit.

With Vindicator hitched to the back, the wagon and its occupants headed northward again, through Mississippi on to Memphis.

After a few exchanges about the trip thus far, Val and Benoit launched into conversation about work.

"How are things at the freight yard?"

"Had a few more boys run off to join up and a couple of horses taken with one wagon but, otherwise, nothing exceptional. Could use a little more business, though." Pasquinel intoned seriously. "We could make more money if we carried some loads for Jack Tarry and his crew smuggling supplies south to the rebels. Belle Edmondsen herself came in and vouched for Jack and the fact that we would receive our money up front."

Val looked at his old friend with a hard glint in his eyes. "You didn't take any money from them, did you?"

"No, Boss. I knew you didn't want anything to do with that business, so I told them flat-out no."

"Good man! I know several in Memphis who are making quite a bit on smuggling, but I'll have no truck with it. The Federals could confiscate our entire business—lock, stock, and barrel—and my family's future is too important to jeopardize it by doing something like that." Val dropped into a contemplative posture. "Besides all that, you know I don't believe in what they're fighting for, and I just won't do it."

Pasquinel said, "I know, Boss, but we've all had to make hard choices as far as this war's been concerned."

"Yeah, and Angie's been one of them. When the war broke out, she thought of asking Billy and Angelina to wait about going to Texas until the thing played out and things got back to normal. Nobody expected it to last this long."

Val's last words were almost a curse. "If she'd asked and they'd waited, then I might not be dragging a widow with a young child back home to her mama."

Benoit's reply was terse. "You can't know that for sure, Val. You, of all people, know how quick death can come in the West."

"Of course, you're right, but this war has added an extra level of concern for Angie," Val explained. "She had to deal with Bobby being so far away when it started and then Oskar thinking of maybe joining up when it all began and then Angelina moving off to Texas. When the thought hit her that all three of her children might be out of the house and perhaps in harm's way by the war, she went through a really rough patch. I did all I could to help her deal with it, and when I finally was able to talk Oskar into at least waiting to join up, she got a little better. It's still pretty dicey, though."

"Oskar still thinking of joining?"

"No, I don't think he is. He never had strong feelings about the 'Southern Cause,' and he decided to concentrate on taking the bar as soon as he can in case lawyers are needed after the conflict is over, to maybe help sort things out in the aftermath."

Val continued speaking quietly. "I told him I thought that was a good plan and an excellent use of his time. Leave the uniforms, no matter how dashing he might look for the ladies, to those whose ardor for a fight would not let them stay out of it. Meanwhile, he could do something positive for his future and help make his mother more secure at the same time."

Angelina broke the momentary silence with, "I never knew that about Mama being upset! Neither you nor she ever told me."

"Well, sweetie, I had talked Oskar out of enlisting before you got married and left, and your mom was calmer by then. So there was really no reason for you to have to take that disquiet to Texas with you. You had a new life to start with its many concerns and opportunities, no reason to bring Memphis troubles with you."

Val added quickly, "How long have you been awake? Uncle Benny and I have been trying not to disturb you or Tina with our talk."

"Oh, just a couple of minutes, Papa. But I did hear that last part about Mama," she said. "I'm coming home now, and if I need to spend the rest of my days at Mama's side, I'll be happy to do so! Maybe I can give her some peace for her soul."

"I'm sure you can, my dear, and I'm sure little Tina can bring a spark and a joy that Angie hasn't had in the house since you were a little girl. Don't you think so too, Uncle Benny?"

"Yep, I sure do! That little darlin' would make anybody fall in love with her."

As he spoke, Pasquinel Benoit's face, which had been contemplative during most of the conversation, now took on almost a glow—as if some inner magic had warmed him enough to soften visibly the gruff and craggy exterior and reveal the beneficence that lay beneath.

They camped in a little grove of trees by the roadside later that afternoon, and the conversation turned inevitably to their relief at reaching Memphis.

Two days later, they did exactly that.

Chapter 12

BLUE, GRAY, AND YELLOW

Captured early on in the conflict, after the First Battle of Memphis, between Federal gunboats and Confederate gunboats on the river a little south of the city itself, Memphis did not suffer the ravages and destructions that befell other Southern cities during the Civil War. It existed under garrison by the Union forces till the end of the conflict. The Second Battle of Memphis was an ill-fated raid by Confederate General Nathan Bedford Forrest's depleted cavalry division in August 1864, which accomplished none of its goals, except for perhaps causing confusion and causing Union forces to have to chase after his highly elusive force. Real ravage and disaster waited for the yellow fever epidemics.

1861–1866

As the Dimand Freight wagon pulled up the carriage drive at the Bethel House, Bobby and Val rode up behind. They were just in time to be met at the top of the drive by Anton, who immediately greeted the whole party warmly and began to see to the animals. Val climbed down from Vindicator, gave him to Anton, and turned to address the others. "I'm going on inside to let Angie know we're here, and then I'll bring her out."

With those words spoken, he trotted up the four broad steps to the wide front porch and went through the front door into the house, where he met Carmella coming up the hallway. She looked somewhat flushed, as though she had just been exerting herself.

"Hello, Carmella! It's nice to see you! Can you tell me where Angie is?"

"Yes, sir. She's probably just finishing her bath."

Val nodded and headed on down the hallway toward the bathroom.

Opening the door, he was treated to the sight of his naked wife just wrapping herself in a towel.

"Oh, Val!" she screamed and flung herself into his arms. Her mouth found his, exploring it with a passion that belied her years, while her towel gapped open to reveal her ample breasts topped with fully erect, deep-red nipples, which leaped to her husband's touch.

Only moments before, they had been subject to Carmella's touch with her lips and teeth, while her slender hand had been most of the way up into Angie's crotch.

Angie had just barely had time to have those sensations begin to subside (and her shaking stop), when in came her beloved man to excite her all over again! "Do we have time to finish this, sweetheart?"

"Unfortunately, it'll have to wait till later tonight. Angelina and the baby are coming in now, so I'll let you get dressed. But later for sure!"

"Good! I want you deep inside me *tonight*!"

Val kissed her again with the passion born of years of marriage to a truly beautiful woman, stepped out of the bathroom doorway, and closed it behind him so she could dress. Then he was off to get the others into the house after their long journey.

◆

Over the next several weeks, life at the Bethel house took on a new normal. Angelina was an uplifting presence for her mother, and little Tina was a joy to everyone. Just beginning to walk well enough to get from room to room by herself, she loved exploring the big old house.

She could frequently be found in the front parlor. There she would sit cross-legged on the floor, staring raptly up at the old portrait of Robert W. Cunningham.

One time, her mama found her thus and asked, "What're you looking at Tina?"

"Man!" was Tina's emphatic reply, pointing a tiny little finger up at the painting.

Angelina said gently, "Someday, I'll tell you his story, and the story of your daddy too. They were both really good men, and your grandma and I loved them dearly."

"Story!" Tina said insistently.

"I tell you what, let's go to the kitchen and see if we can find Grandma, and we'll tell you a story, together. Maybe Carmella can find a cookie for you."

"Cookie! Story! Grammie! Kissen!" Tina began to pull her mama's hand toward the kitchen.

In the kitchen as she ate one of Carmella's delicious sugar cookies, Tina heard a wonderful story of the time a mama bear and two baby cubs had paid their family a visit at the homestead in Texas. Angie told the story very brightly and sweetly, even though it had actually been quite frightening at the time. She told Tina how Robert, the man in the picture, had come home and helped the bears to find their way back to their own place.

After the story was over and Tina was down for a nap, Angelina asked her mother, "How long was it before you stopped missing him, Mama?"

"Oh, honey, I still miss him every day. I recall a treasured memory of him, and I'm transported instantly back to those hard but wonderful days on the prairie with my beautiful Bobby. We had such times there, together!" Angie spoke intently to her daughter. "Don't ever try to get Billy out of your mind. You had a wonderful set of years with him, so keep those in your heart as the treasure that they were. But keep your heart open to love again, if the opportunity and the right man come along."

"Oh, Mama, I don't think I'll ever want another man! I don't think anyone could ever take Billy's place in my heart." Angelina was almost in tears.

"Certainly, dear one," Angie replied. "No man will ever take Billy's place, nor should he! But I think you'll find that, with time, your heart will have room for another man."

"Is that the way it was when you met my daddy? Did you make room in your heart for him?"

"Yes, dear. I made the conscious choice to treat my nine years with Robert as a separate chapter in my life and start a new chapter with Val. We've had more than twenty years together now, and they've been wonderful!" Angie's voice choked a little bit when she said the next part. "I knew your daddy was the man for me when he risked his life to save me. And when he was wounded and I had to consider what my life might be without him, well, that was a bleak prospect, indeed. So, I pursued him even more than he did me, and I was successful, and you're alive because of it!

"Bobby and Oskar live today because of Robert's chapter in my life. And you, my sweet, live because of my chapter with Val."

"So, Tina's a reflection of my chapter with Billy, and there might be another chapter to come? Is that what you're saying?"

"Yes, Angelina," her mother said. "I had already known your father, even before I met Robert, so I knew something of his character. He'd had a reputation as a ladies' man, and I knew it to be true. But when he showed in a thousand different ways that I was the one and the only one he wanted, well, my next chapter started right then and there on that road through Mississippi."

"We probably passed by that same spot on our way to town!" Angelina exclaimed.

"You probably did, my love, and that spot is burned into my memory. Though I'll probably never get to go back there, I'll have it forever in my heart and mind." Angie's voice choked again on the next part. "You see, Angelina, that spot in Mississippi is where I almost lost Val Dimand but where I made up my mind to let him into my heart instead. And

I have the living proof, right here in this kitchen with me today, that I made the right choice."

"Oh, Mama! I hope that happens for me too!"

"It can, my dear, but don't try to rush it. Give your heart a chance to heal; you're still too raw inside. After that, any man who interests you, study him and get to know how he treats people, and women in particular.

"Anytime you want advice, you know you can come to me."

This conversation, and the many others that followed, became a sort of catharsis for both mother and daughter. Angie needed relief from facing her advancing age and the trials of the war, while Angelina needed support to restart her life and be the mother Tina needed, even without a husband.

The two women, once just mother and daughter, had become much more to each other.

◆

The war years had been hard on Angie, probably harder than on any other member of the family. Aside from the deprivations, there were other worries that plagued her.

She had good reason for her concerns. First, her old friend and benefactor Levi Gold had passed away from illness several years before the war came, and with his passing, it had seemed like a piece of her had been ripped from her very being.

Afterward, the city was in a turmoil to get the state of Tennessee to secede from the union. Val and Oskar had been dead set against the notion and said so, which caused some hotheads to make noises about retribution. This seemed to worry Angie far more than it did Val or Oskar.

Oskar had even talked about going north to try to join the Union forces, but Val had gotten him to wait and see how things went before he made such a commitment to take himself away from his mother, Memphis, and his promising law career. Val pointed out that he was so close to finishing it would be a shame for him to have to wait out the duration. Who knew what the situation might be after the conflict was over? It was his mom's fragile state that ultimately won out and kept him from leaving.

In fall 1861, she'd sent Angelina and her new husband, Billy, off to Texas to start a new life together on a cattle ranch. Her daughter had just come back to her a widow with a young daughter of her own, less than three years later.

Meanwhile, she'd gotten word that the family's good friend, Dr. Hiram Bradford, had been killed while tending to the wounded from both sides after Shiloh. He'd been working at a field hospital that was overrun in a cavalry attack.

Val's wonderful friend, Auguste Marno, who had really become a friend to the entire family, had died in a collision between the buggy he was driving and a runaway stage team. His shattered body was so badly torn the service for him had the casket closed, with no viewing at all. Angie sat with Ruby Marno and tried her best to be a comfort for the sudden loss of her husband.

The "Battle of Memphis," as the papers called it, was fought on the Mississippi by Federal gunboats against Confederate gunboats in June 1862. By all accounts, the Union flotilla made short work of completely destroying the Rebel force, and Memphis went under occupation by Union forces shortly thereafter.

The occupation forces brought some stability to Memphis, and this brought a calmer overall tenor to the city in fairly short order. Underground, it was a different story. Rebel sentiment seethed, and smuggling of weapons and supplies (particularly medical supplies) flour-ished. Brothels sprang up and were rousingly successful, particularly after the *Memphis Appeal* packed up its presses and fled to other cities in the South to continue publishing. No longer the constant witness and gadfly to those who would corrupt its home city, the paper left in its absence a freer hand without such oversight for those who turned a blind eye to such corruption.

All this caused General Ulysses S. Grant to refer to Memphis as the "Gomorrah of the South," an appellation it earned in spades.

The Union occupiers brought with them at least two things that helped see to the continuation of Memphis as a viable city and to its long-term growth—cash money and hospitals. The garrisoned troops stationed in and around Memphis spent a large part of their meager earnings in the saloons, brothels, and shops around town. Since they were paid in desirable US currency (most often silver or gold coin), rather than the almost worthless Confederate scrip other customers were forced to use, their trade was welcome everywhere in town—even by the most ardent but cash-strapped rebel sympathizers.

Going from the home of only one hospital in prewar times to fifteen by conflict's end, the city became a center of wartime medicine, surgery, and convalescence, and this continued long after the struggle was over.

The spillover advantage to the citizens of Memphis was the better availability of doctors, nurses, and medical supplies. Though these were not always readily available to civilian residents of the city, exceptions were made in times of great emergency.

Medical supplies, stolen by profiteering staff or civilian employees, became a crucial part of the rampant smuggling that persisted throughout the conflict, along with stolen armaments, gunpowder, and other war matériel.

The Federal troops occupying Memphis did not waste time constructing new medical facilities; the Union commanders merely commandeered hotels and cotton warehouse buildings to convert into hospitals. The Gayoso House Hotel, where Angelina and Billy's wedding and first night together as man and wife had been, was one such casualty of the war's occupation. The newly constructed but not-yet-opened Overton Hotel was another.

With all the changes that had occurred over the first couple of years of occupation, Angie was having a difficult time acclimating to the new requirements for citizens to go about their daily routines. Angie tried to make sure someone, either Val, Oskar, or Anton, was physically in the house so it would not be empty if she or Carmella had to go out to the market or some such errand. She and Carmella had taken to only going out as a pair and only when they had to; the jeering and heckling by disorderly groups of soldiers loitering (ostensibly on guard) at many street corners was offensive to the two ladies, and they said so—both to the soldiers themselves and to Val.

The level of military discipline and order varied widely, both before General Grant (and, later, General Sherman) was present in Memphis to supervise, as well as after.

Oskar himself, early on, had been detained several times on his way to the law offices downtown. This caused Val to go see the garrison officer of the guard, to see if some sort of permanent pass might be issued for his stepson. As a leading citizen and staunch Union supporter, Oskar was issued such in good order and promptly.

Commerce continued, even under the Federal overwatch, but the level of business done by many entrepreneurs paled in comparison to prewar levels. Dimand Freight was no exception. Val's in-town hauling for stores to their purchasers' homes had become almost nonexistent, since retail trade, particularly for larger items requiring delivery (such as furniture), had almost dried up completely.

Over-the-road freighting was down as well. Many of Val's cotton bale hauling contracts were now situated in Rebel-held territories. His business carrying cotton from plantations and farms to Memphis, for shipment to Northern textile mills at the outset of occupation, was curtailed. The need for cotton at those mills to support the war effort, and the capture of more Southern lands as the war went on, enabled that portion of Val's business to return to more normal levels closer to war's end.

His contracts for hauling cut lumber from the Memphis-based sawmills suffered the least and even increased slightly for a while.

Val's well-developed routes and contracts with New Orleans shippers would put his drivers, wagons, and livestock at risk from roving, almost-lawless bands of Confederates (particularly cavalry) if he'd tried to use them, so he abandoned those till war's end.

Val was not willing for a wagon or some horses lost by such trade, much less a man! Although not trying to burden Angie with extra worries about money, still he told her about the current state of the business and its prospects at each step along the way, as a good husband and provider would.

Angie worried anyway. Her worries often centered on what the war would do to their financial status, which had been so healthy before the strife began. Both the Union Bank and the Branch Planters Bank, financial institutions healthy before the war, had been run out of business by having their assets seized shortly after the war came to Memphis.

Valentine Dimand, ever the astute businessman, had withdrawn the vast bulk of his holdings in each institution, in gold and silver, before the banks were destroyed. He had done likewise for Angie's holdings. Thus, the family's monetary accumulation was secretly held in a safe place known only to Val. Val assured Angie they were completely solvent—unless the war lasted twenty years or more.

Oskar had done important and exhaustive study in business finance; he and Val had done a thorough inventory and evaluation of the freighting business. Val's wealth as owner of Dimand Freight was estimable, to say the least. He owned his house and its grounds outright, and he also owned the freight yard, wagons, livestock, and tack fully. Therefore, if he needed to part with any part of his holdings, the proceeds thus derived from such a divestiture would not be reduced by any repayment needed for any mortgage or business loan.

Angie still worried.

Having two of her children close at hand was definitely a comfort to Angie. Bobby had stayed at the house with them for about two weeks after they brought Angelina and Tina back before he (pleading the need to return to his business) had gone back to Fort Smith. Going a little north from Memphis before he caught a ferry across the river, Bobby avoided military patrols and any other entanglements and made it back with little trouble. His telegram home that he'd made it OK was a welcome message to his parents indeed.

By this time, Bobby was as handsome as Robert W., his father, had been. He was getting to an age where he should be married and settled down, but such was not the case. And Angie fretted over this, too.

Little Tina had allowed Angie to slip into the role of grandma, and it turned out she was good at it, and it brought her much joy. Therefore, her heart held the desire that her sons should marry and present her with grandbabies to keep her company in her advancing age.

Oskar seemed to be on his way. He had developed a steady relationship with a very personable yet proper young lady. All the indicators were pointing toward marriage in the future after Oskar received his law certification, allowing him to practice.

But Bobby, now past thirty, showed no signs of being any closer to married. In fact, he showed no signs of even wanting such a thing. He had all the female companionship he wanted; he made a good steady living. His reputation among the ladies as a man of significant size and duration (attributes inherited directly from his father) meant he could enjoy female companionship for years to come.

Still, Angie wanted more little ones livening up the house, and she wanted her boys to get busy and provide her some!

Lately, Angie had been taking stock critically of herself in the full-length dressing mirror in the bedroom. Of a morning, she would sometimes open her robe to reveal her nakedness; sometimes, she would drop the robe entirely and unabashedly examine her reflection. What she saw was a woman of advancing years, beginning to sag in some places and bulge in others.

Angie didn't know exactly how old she was; record-keeping around the time she was born, particularly for immigrant families on the frontier, was spotty at best. According to what she could remember of what her mother had said, she had probably been born between 1803 and 1805, which would make her sixty or very close to it.

The tight, perky breasts topped with their light pink tips of her girlish years were now full and ample orbs with dark red, meaty nipples, which were now beginning to point toward the floor, instead of outward. Her magnificent orange-blond hair was now faded and shot through with silver.

Her frontal view was still pleasing, even with the slight bulge and roll at her waist, though her hair down there at her crotch was thick and solidly gray. The front sides of her thighs were remarkably free of dimpling;

alas, the same could not be said for the back sides. The once-smooth cheeks of her derriere were still attractive but now were beginning to sag.

Thus, Angie's melancholy was brought on and exacerbated by many different issues, none of which could be easily solved by Val, even if he'd known about all of them.

Angie had Angelina as a constant companion and little Tina to spark mirth and joy through the household, but still it wasn't enough.

What was still enough was Val and Angie's passion for each other in the bedroom.

Val had aged right along with Angie, and when she looked at it critically, the signs were there. His gloriously dark and lustrous hair, so long and thick, was now thinning (particularly on top) and shot through with plenty of gray. His neatly trimmed beard and moustache (how Angie still loved to sit on his lap and do that!) were now solid gray. His physique had not suffered the ravages of time; hard work and outdoor living had kept him trim and fetching.

Angie could always see the looks women gave him as they passed, and truly, she remembered the wanton brazenness of her youthful assignations with him. Sometimes back then, she was so randy for him she hadn't even worn undergarments!

Val was several years older than Angie (perhaps he was sixty three), and he had no right at all to still be so darned good-looking!

Several years before, Carmella had begun helping Angie to "bathe". As she explained it to Val, Angie had had difficulty in stepping over the high side of the bathtub as she had gotten into her fifties, so Carmella had made herself available to ensure Angie's safety when getting in and out of the tub, as well as assisting with drying off, dressing, and other necessities. What she didn't mention was that she also had fallen in love with Angie's still voluptuous body in the process. Thus, bath time became a sensual affair of washing and gently stimulating intimate areas of Angie's body, caressing, kissing and manipulating those marvelous nipples to peaks of erogenous pleasure and generally making sure that bath time was a time of pleasure that prepared Angie to receive whatever coupling Val had in store for her.

Recently, they had discovered while washing Angie's marvelous crotch that Carmella's slim hand fit almost all the way up in it, and this added another erotic element to bath time. Added to that was the time she accidentally came into the lovebirds' bedroom to clean one morning after Val had left for the freight yard. This was just after they had made love, and she saw Angie languidly lying back with Val's effluent all over her! Dropping immediately to her knees, Carmella whispered hoarsely, "Oh, Miss Angie! Let me clean that up for you!"

Burying her head in Angie's crotch, Carmella's tongue flicked over her mound and belly as she greedily lapped up the pearlescent drops and strings, ardently kissing and licking her way into the most private of areas. Angie's moans of pleasure could have threatened to attract attention, but no one else was there at the time.

Carmella's next whisper was, "Any time I can do this for you, it will make me very happy to do so."

Several more times, she did. Mornings were the best, and Val loved that Angie wanted to start their day this way more often than before!

Thus, over time, Carmella had come to know Angie's body quite well, and she fantasized about having Val in the bath room with them as she displayed for him the intimate parts of that marvelous body. Carmella wanted him to see what she did to her body in order to help prepare Angie to leap at Val's touch. Rubbing, caressing, and kissing those marvelous folds, valleys, and protrusions while in front of Val caused such strong images in her mind that she could hardly bear them without fainting away.

She had been working for Val and Angie for twenty years and had seen how Val treated his bride. The innate gentlemanliness of the dashing and beautiful man, coupled with the wonderful regard he showed Angie in all aspects of her life, well how could Carmella not be at least a little in love with him?

She had to suffer in silence, though, and take her fantasies off with her to her room at night and work them out on her own body, all alone.

———————◆———————

One already muggy August morning in 1864, Angelina and Angie sat together in the front porch swing watching Tina play a game she had devised with acorns and twigs from the massive oak in the front yard. The fog bank, which had rolled in that morning off the Mississippi (only about two miles away), had already burned off under the bright sun, and it threatened to be a scorcher of a day, which was quite typical for Memphis in mid-August.

The women heard the sound of thundering hooves before they saw anything. Then, in a cloud of dust, a double row of Confederate cavalry rapidly passed by the house, down Bethel toward the North Road. Oddly, each of the mounted riders was leading an extra unsaddled horse. Angie noticed the brand on some of the horses being led—it was the DF brand, for Dimand Freight! Just then, Angie heard several gunshots, not all together but punctuated by pauses interspersed with shouting.

Her first move was to quickly get Angelina and Tina inside the house. Then Angie went to their bedroom and got both of the Walker Colt revolvers from their holsters in the closet. Checking first to see that the front of the cylinders were well greased, she ran back to the front parlor, where Angelina stood at the front window watching the street and Tina sat on the floor wide-eyed. For once, she was not staring up at Robert W. Cunningham but, rather, was gazing intently at her mom.

"They've passed, thank God! But, I wonder where all that shooting and yelling was coming from! You don't think it could have been from the freight yard, do you?" Angelina's voice broke as she asked the question that Angie had dreaded.

Angie was looking out the side window of the front room, and she called out her reply without moving. "I'm sorry, darling, but I'm afraid it might have been. Anton's at the driveway gate, with two Hawkens and at least one horse pistol."

"What should we do, Mama?"

"Well, my dear, you stay here with Tina, and I'll leave you this pistol in case anyone tries to get in. You know how to use a Walker?"

"Yes, Mama, Billy showed me and made me practice with it. He carried Walkers because he'd seen Daddy carry them, and he always said, 'If Val carries it, then that's the gun for me.' But is it already loaded?"

"Cylinder greased, caps on the nipples, loaded and ready to fire, so you stay here with the baby and guard the front. I'm going up into the attic with the binoculars and see what I can of what's happening at the freight yard, after I talk to Carmella and Anton first."

Angie then hastened off to the kitchen, where she found a white-faced Carmella with a cleaver in one hand and an iron skillet in the other. "Carmella, I know this is frightening, but we have to protect the household. So just watch the back and let me know if you see anyone."

"They won't get past me, Miss Angie, not if I can help it!"

"You don't have to fight them Carmella, just let me know if you see anyone. I'm going up into the attic to see if all that commotion earlier came from the freight yard, so just call up the stairs, and I'll hear you."

"Miss Angie, I saw Anton headed toward the front gate with a couple of rifles and a pistol, and that old fool's too old to fight!"

"Well, don't worry. I'm going to have him come back and sit with you here in the kitchen to help keep watch out the back."

"Thank you, ma'am! You know I love that old man, and I just couldn't stand it if anything happened to him."

Angie went up the stairs from the kitchen into the attic and grabbed the binoculars to look out the dormer window over to the freight yard. She could see several of Val's wranglers moving about, one man lying covered up on the office porch, and several gray-clad Confederate figures lying in various places on the ground. The water tower was on the ground, its contents spilled, creating a huge mud puddle. Several sections of fence were broken to various degree, and one of the freight wagons was overturned. Angie's heart sank when Val was nowhere in sight. The haze of gun smoke that hung over the place was dissipating, but still her beloved was not to be seen.

Just when her despair was about to turn to anguish, Valentine Dimand came casually forth from the hitching barn, gesturing in one direction and then another as he barked orders to his men.

Angie's weak knees gave way as she fell back onto the settee and let the waves of relief roll over her.

He lived!

She went down, told Anton to go to the kitchen, and then returned to the front of the house to her daughter and granddaughter. All the way, step by step, elation filled her.

He lived!

———————◆———————

Though they did not know it at the time, the Dimand/Cunningham family had, once again, been touched by history.

Earlier in the day (as told to the family upon his return that afternoon), Val Dimand had, as usual, ridden to the freight yard expecting nothing more exciting than a broken hitch or a balky horse to interrupt a smooth, effortless day.

It started out that way.

After getting the day's wagons needed out onto their heavy-freight runs, the wranglers and loaders began on the in-town wagons for the lighter deliveries. As they were assembling the vehicles and teams for this, Confederate cavalry troops breached the holding corral, sent it into a turmoil of frightened whinnying animals, and began to make off with horses. Several of the Dimand Freight employees began to sprint toward the corral to try to stop the theft, but Val stopped them dead in their tracks instead and said, "Let 'em go, boys, and close up the corral after they leave! Nobody needs to get hurt here!"

As they stood there watching, Val had seen that each rider was capturing only one horse (it was really all they could control), fitting it with a hackamore, and leading it out of the corral. There seemed to be about twenty riders, so the theft would be capped at about that many animals. The five men who came running would stand little chance of stopping them anyway, particularly since only two of them had thought to arm themselves.

Val hated to lose the horses; he was not about to have his men risk their lives over them. Order was returning to the corral as the raiders finished.

"Wait till they've cleared out down the road and then close the corral, settle the stock down, and set guards with rifles and pistols to prevent another such raid. I'll go up to the main yard and send back more men to help. You are not to fire unless fired upon. Is that clear? If you do have to return fire, do so from cover, understood? This was a raid. Raids have to be fast, so they're not going to stay around for a prolonged gun battle—if they even come back at all."

They watched as the last of the Confederates left the corral and headed off down the Chelsea Trail.

"Close it up, men, and keep watch. I'll go get help!"

With that, Val was off toward the main yard.

He was almost there when he saw Pasquinel Benoit come striding out of the office onto the front porch and try to speak to the officer in charge of the new group of cavalry that had stormed in and were running amok around the yard. They had captured one of the in-town wagons, already hitched, and two of the troopers were seated up in the wagon box, trying to bring the frightened team under control. One of the two horses reared and bucked from the unfamiliar touch of the Rebel drivers. Another horse was down in the yard, screaming in pain from a broken leg. Yells from the Rebel raiders became a cacophony as the water tower crashed and spilled hundreds of gallons into the dirt of the yard.

Val could not hear what dialogue ensued between Benoit and the officer, but he did see the Rebel captain pull a horse pistol and shoot the unarmed and defenseless Benoit from about ten feet.

"AyeeAhh!" The enraged guttural cry erupted from Val's throat at the sight. Ignoring for the moment his old friend lying crumpled on the porch, his hand leaped to the Walker Colt at his belt. He drew and cocked it as he brought it up to firing position; the only indications the other cavalrymen had that anything else had happened besides the yell were the explosion of the Colt, the plume of smoke, and the .44 caliber hole between the eyes of the now-crumpled captain.

Another of the raiders close to the captain, a tough-looking sergeant by the stripes on his sleeve, brought his own pistol to bear on Val and squeezed off a shot, which grazed Val's left arm, causing blood to flow down. Val's return shot, calmly fired, unseated the Rebel backwards out of his saddle and sent him to the ground with a pistol ball between the eyes. His horse bolted, whinnying wildly.

By now several of the raiders, who had created havoc in the freight yard by toppling the water tower to a chorus of cheers and jeers, had now turned their attentions to the gunfire that had erupted and were charging in to eliminate this new and deadly threat. Shouting wildly, they charged forward on foot without any organization. The huge water spill from the tower made soggy going for many.

Valentine Dimand, in defense of what was his and of the people who worked for him, fired off the remaining four shots from the Walker and, as four dead Rebels hit the ground, calmly holstered that massive pistol, butt forward, back into its holster. Drawing cross-handed with his right hand (he didn't trust completely his wounded left), he brought the other Walker into play, firing into a sabre-wielding Confederate at full gallop. As the falling horseman went down, Val neatly caught the sabre as it fell from the rider's grip with his wounded left hand.

The gun smoke was thick now, but not so thick that the remaining Confederates could not see the enraged yet calm old man with the sabre in his bloody left hand and the deadly Walker Colt in his right! Nor could they miss the line of at least ten wranglers and drivers armed with both rifles and pistols who had assembled, weapons at the ready, behind their beloved boss to defend and protect him.

Totally unaware of the force at his back, Val's voice boomed forth. "The rest of you can leave now, peaceably with no harm. Or the next one of you that raises a weapon, I swear I'll kill all of you myself!"

A single Rebel rider, his arms calmly out beside him showing empty hands, kneed his horse into a gentle trot out of the freight yard onto the Chelsea Trace, followed by another and then another.

After the last had passed, Val spoke to the ones in the wagon. "You boys can keep the wagon, though I ought to make you walk for what you've done this day. But please take your dead with you, and if you can't get them all in on this trip, come back under a flag of truce by tomorrow, and you can get the rest, or I'll see that they get a Christian burial."

He sorrowfully walked over to the suffering horse; his last shot silenced it.

When the wagon was loaded with all seven of the Confederate dead and was out of the yard and trying to catch up to the rest of the raiders, only then did Val go through the relative silence of the yard over to the porch. As he sat, crumpled over in sorrow beside his old friend, a hand gripped his right shoulder affectionately.

"We know how much you cared for him, Boss. Take all the time you need with him. We're here for you. When you can, tell us what you need."

Val looked up into the caring eyes of Tommy Nichols, his yard foreman, with gratitude. "Thanks, Tommy. And tell the men thanks for backing my play there at the end. Ya'll didn't have to do that."

"Yes, Boss, we did. There's not a man here, I don't believe, who wouldn't have been with us if he could. By the way, you can thank Bobby Allen for getting that group together and armed so fast!"

Val spent the next while in quiet reflection with his old friend, stroking his thin, gray hair gently and gazing at the face he had known for almost forty years. Pockmarked and scarred as it was, it seemed to be softened, as if a lifetime of troubles had been lifted away.

A bit of calm had been returned to the yard, as Val's workers went about clearing debris and restoring order, quietly and calmly out of deference to their grief-stricken boss sitting with his fallen friend, a man they all had respected.

Val could not help but think how differently things could have turned out for his treasured friend if he'd only stayed back in Santa Fe with that senorita who was so sweet on him.

The whole fight had taken less than five minutes to complete from the time Pasquinel Benoit fell to the porch dead. But sitting there heartbroken beside his departed friend, Val felt like a whole chunk had been ripped from his life.

He was still sitting with Benoit when the Union cavalry thundered into the yard, with a new cloud of dust thrown up and a new envelope of sounds.

"We had reports of Rebel horsemen in this area, and some people reported hearing shots fired in this vicinity," the Union captain in charge called out to Val. "I see you've been wounded. What happened?"

"Evidently, they split their raiding party into two groups, Captain. I was dealing with the horse thieves down at the corral when another bunch rode into the yard, like you did."

"Go on."

"Well, sir, I was approaching the yard from the corral when I saw my old friend, Pasquinel Benoit, this man here, with his arms outstretched and his hands open, trying to talk with their captain. Then, deliberately, the Rebel officer pulled his pistol and shot my friend, while he was still trying to speak!"

"Yes, and then?"

"Well, sir, it was murder, most foul indeed, committed by a sworn officer in military uniform. And I just lost myself, may the good Lord forgive me! I took it upon myself to exact revenge, like the sinner I am, so I shot him out of his saddle, then and there."

Val fell silent, thinking about the enormity of taking a life in revenge.

"What happened then?"

"Yes, sir! I'm sorry for drifting off just then. After the captain fell, I had to fight off this one and then that one before they'd stop, but eventually they did. I let them gather up their dead and take them along, but I just wanted them gone."

"How big a force was it?"

"Well, there were eleven of them left when they went away, so I guess there must have been eighteen of them when they came bursting in and messing up my place of business. They had a similar number down at the corral, and they made off with about twenty horses, without harm or injury."

"So you let that group go without a fight?"

"Well, Captain, I wasn't willing to put my five men who were there in mortal danger over horses, and I could see that each Rebel rider was only taking one horse. I could stand the loss of them much better than I could the loss of a single man—only two of who were armed, by the way."

"So the only loss to the Confederates was here in the freight yard?"

"Yes, Captain, and I apologize for that! If I could have controlled my rage, there might have been no other loss than my friend. But after I shot the captain, a sergeant tried to shoot me and did wing me. I knew right then and there that my people were in real danger from those trigger-happy wolves, so I protected those around me who depend on me. And, I'd do that part again if I had to!"

"So you got seven of them? How many wounded? Dead?"

At this point, Bobby Allen, who had been leaning on the front porch hitching rail and listening, found he couldn't keep silent. "Captain, excuse me for butting in, but that was the damnedest thing I ever saw, and I saw it all!"

As Bobby recounted the story, shot by shot, his accuracy of recall was amazing. The Union captain, Hurlburt Graves by name, had called forth the surgeon of the troop, who attended to Val's wounded arm. Both men listened intently to Bobby Allen's account of the events of that morning.

"You read about things like this in the cheap novels, but I never thought I'd see it," Bobby exclaimed. "Mr. Dimand killed seven of them—five of them right between the eyes! And him standing out there in the open like he was on a parade ground, not moving an inch, it seemed like!"

"All by himself?" Captain Graves asked.

"Yes, sir. No help was out there until it was pretty much over. By the time we got out there with guns, the boss only had five shots left in his second Colt. But five more Johnny Rebs knew they might be the next to die, so I guess they just gave up. And I'm darned glad they did!"

"Bobby, you boys were more of a help than you know; you fellas probably made up their minds for them, I'll say." Val's voice took on a slightly stern yet sympathetic edge as he spoke his next words. "But, Bobby, we mustn't gloat in those men's deaths. There are wives and possibly children they'll never come home to. Think on that."

"Yes, sir, Boss! I'm sure sorry for not remembering their loved ones."

"Captain," Val continued. "The rebels are not more than twenty or thirty minutes ahead of you. They probably are joining together somewhere in town before they hit the South Road toward Mississippi. Both of the groups that hit us headed east on the Chelsea Trace, so they might be meeting up with a larger group."

"They most certainly are, Mr. Dimand. They're part of Bedford Forrest's cavalry division, and they hit us early this morning, after sneaking up on us out the fog that covered us down near the river. Evidently, he split up his forces to accomplish several missions, although at this time we're not clear on what they all were.

"One thing's for sure," Captain Graves went on. "The group that went riding into the Gayoso House downtown looking for General Washburn had him scurrying out in his nightshirt. He made it all the way to Fort Pillow with a guard detail, but he was still in his nightshirt when he got there!"

The surgeon had completed bandaging Val's arm and nodded to the captain that he was ready to leave.

Captain Graves assembled his men, who had been assisted by Val's men in watering their horses, and turned in his saddle to Val with a final set of remarks. "Mr. Dimand, I almost forgot! I bring you greetings from Robert Estes of Saint Louis, who I believe you know quite well. He said your daughter and his son were married in the Gayoso House Hotel, and I was to try to make your acquaintance if I ever got to Memphis. I have the pleasure to be quartered in the Gayoso, so may I invite you and your wife down for dinner some evening?"

Val's reply was prompt. "Please! Call me Val. It would be my great pleasure, Captain. Could I also bring my daughter, Angelina? As you probably know, tragically, she's Billy Estes's widow, and I think she'd enjoy meeting someone who knows their family."

"Surely, it would be my pleasure if she could join us."

Val had another curiosity and asked it. "Excuse me, Captain. But may I ask how you know Robert Estes?"

"Captain Robert Estes was my initial cavalry commander when I was first out of the Point and shipped off to serve in California. I learned everything I know about cavalry service because of that man!"

"A fine man, indeed," Val replied.

"Well, we must be about the chase." Captain Graves led his troop out of the freight yard and eastward on the Chelsea Trace in good military order at a quick trot in pursuit of the fleeing Rebels.

Val went to Vindicator, swung up, and rode off for home. The news about what Val had done left the freight yard even before the cavalry surgeon had finished bandaging his arm.

The story spread like wildfire.

Chapter 13

GAIN, YELLOW FEVER, AND LOSS

Creeping like the unseen killer it was, Yellow Fever attacked the city of Memphis several times after the Civil War—most notably in 1866, 1873, and 1878. Attempts to quarantine outsiders coming in from other afflicted areas got more stringent with each succeeding outbreak of the disease, but each time, it got worse. While the deaths started with only a modest number in 1866, they ballooned to over two thousand in 1873 and again to over five thousand in 1878. In response to the not-yet-understood disease's third trip of devastation through the Bluff City, more than seventeen thousand citizens fled to outlying areas, thus reducing Memphis's population by almost half. Many who stayed died. The city was so weakened its ability to govern and provide services for its remaining citizenry was abridged to the point it surrendered its city charter back to the state in 1879. It was governed by the state of Tennessee as a "taxing district" until 1893, when the full charter was restored.

1864–1873

To say that Val Dimand was welcomed home when he rode up and into the backyard of the Bethel house about noon on August 21, 1864, would be the understatement of the century. He was surrounded by every member of the household as he stepped down from his magnificent steed, Vindicator.

Giving the reins to Anton, he patted his old friend and stableman on the shoulder and then turned toward the rest gathered there in the backyard. Angie grabbed him around the waist and buried her face in his chest to keep him from seeing her cry, and cry she did.

When she was composed enough to speak, her words came out in a fervid torrent. "Oh Val, I'm so glad you made it home in one piece, but I'm so mad I could kill you myself! What in the world were you thinking?" Angie was practically blubbering by this point.

"Phil came over a little while ago and told us what had happened at the freight yard. What were you thinking, you old fool? Phil was practically bragging when he told us about you standing up to those Confederates all by yourself! He acted like it was the greatest thing he'd ever seen, you out there acting like you were forty years younger, just blasting away like you didn't have us back here at home depending on you!"

She reached out a gentle hand to Tina, stroking her hair softly and said, "Did you ever stop to think that you're not only a husband to me also but dad to Angelina and grandpa to this little one? And that we might want you to be around for many more years to come? Did you think about that? Well, did you, you big beautiful idiot?"

The sheepish look on Val's face and his lack of a response softened Angie's attack but for a moment, and then she was quick with more. "Now, don't you get me wrong, Valentine Dimand, I'm so proud of you, I could bust! But you've probably turned my entire head gray in this one day."

Angie pulled Val's face close and kissed him fervently and then whispered in his ear so no one else could hear, "Just wait until I get you in bed tonight. Let's see how young you feel then!"

Just then a small voice split the silence. "Grampa! Ride!"

Val rapidly hoisted Tina up on his shoulders and, gathering up Angelina and Angie in tow, strode purposefully toward the back porch and through the door into the house, where he collapsed into a chair at the kitchen table.

Carmella followed, her eyes filled with admiration.

"That's as far as I can go right now."

Val set Tina gently down onto the chair beside him and said, while looking at Carmella for support, "How about we each get a cookie for being so good?"

Carmella nodded with an enigmatic smile.

"Cookie! Cookie!" Tina clapped and laughed.

As Carmella brought them each a tasty sugar cookie, she glanced around. Then, seeing no one, she kissed Val on the forehead and went out of the kitchen.

Val and Tina sat there, eating cookies, only now Val had the enigmatic smile.

Angelina came in softly and sat across the table from Val and Tina. "Arm hurt much?"

Val simply shook his head. "Nah, it's not too bad, except when I flex it. Then it stings some. The surgeon said as he was bandaging it that it would be that way. He cleaned it and put some unguent on it before he bandaged it, and he said to change the dressing tomorrow, and every couple of days after that."

Angelina said, "I can help with that! I was all the time patching up broken-down cowhands and wranglers at the ranch …." Her voice broke off into quiet sobs. "But I couldn't patch up the one who meant the world to me! Oh, Daddy!"

As Tina looked on in curiosity, Angelina came around the table, sat in her father's lap, and nestled her head into his neck. Sobbing deeply (even though she was trying not to upset little Valentina), she exclaimed woefully over and over as though she might never recover. "Oh, Daddy! What am I to do? Oh, Daddy, Daddy! Whatever on earth am I to do? I miss him so!"

Val stroked the beautiful strawberry blonde hair of her precious head as though she were his little girl of old and tried to think of a reply to ease her pain. "Just give it some time, sweetheart. You'll never forget or stop loving your wonderful Billy Estes, but the hurting will stop with time."

"You sound just like Mama! She said almost exactly the same thing."

"Well, remember, your mother knows for sure. She dearly loved Robert Cunningham and had almost nine beautiful years sharing life with him, before he was horribly killed at the Alamo."

"But didn't those men want to be there? Didn't they all volunteer?"

"Yes, my dear, they did. But they didn't know when they volunteered that it was to be a death sentence. They expected to be relieved, but help never came. Then General Santa Ana ordered 'No Quarter' to be played by the buglers, to let the defenders know what was going to happen to them. And after they overran the fort, they killed every one of the few defenders left."

"How horrible, Daddy!"

"Yes, dear, but that's not the worst of it. Word came later that year that Santa Ana's men dismembered a lot of the bodies, burned them, and buried them in a mass grave."

"Oh, no!"

"Imagine what your mother must have felt, thinking her beautiful Bobby Cunningham had died and then been chopped into pieces and buried in an unmarked grave. Can you just imagine the anguish she must have felt?"

Val answered his own question. "Well, of course, you can! And you two women will always share that bond with each other. Lean on her and draw strength from her, and I promise you'll get through this."

"When, Daddy? How long will it take?"

"I don't have an answer for that, my dear. But I'll tell you this—when those Confederates attacked today, the first thing they did was shoot your Uncle Benny."

"Yes, Papa, I heard, and I'm so sad."

"I know you are, and I knew you would be. It was murder, and it made me so enraged I took revenge right there. I shouldn't have done it, but I did. But then, when the next man pulled his gun and shot me, well, from that point I was in a fight to save you, your Mama, Tina, Oskar, Anton, and Carmella, and really anybody else we cared about, because if they'd murder one soul, who knows where they'd stop?"

Val finished with one more thought. "So, it was my job to stop them from hurting my family, and I did my job."

With the loss of his old friend, and the change in the tenor and flavor of his business as the war ended and Reconstruction began, Val Dimand found less and less satisfaction in going to work each day. He had developed more desire to stay home and enjoy his family, watching Valentina grow, helping Angelina heal, and making as gentle as he could Angie's march into advancing age.

Oskar was instrumental in ushering Val into the next stage of his life.

For a while, the Overland (Butterfield) Stage Company had had one Eastern terminus very near Memphis and another close to Saint Louis. From these points stage service was offered all the way to California, thus connecting the East coast of the United States to the West. With the secession of Texas and the Civil War, the cross-country route was shifted northward to avoid seceded states. This put the Overland Stage right into the routes being run by the fairly new Wells Fargo passenger and express Stage Company, primarily operating to and from the California goldfields.

Perhaps as a reflection of the turbulence leading up to the Civil War (or perhaps due simply to political bungling), Congress did not pass a postal appropriation for Overland Stage in 1859, leaving the organization to have to try and deliver mail and passengers west without funds. More importantly, perhaps, the shipments of gold back from the western mines were now in limbo.

In stepped Henry Wells and William Fargo, two entrepreneurs who had been carrying passengers and freight and providing financial services since 1852. After 1860, Wells Fargo operated the Overland Stage as part of its operations until the war's end, and then consolidation of equipment, personnel, and routes began in earnest for Wells Fargo. The passenger stage operations would continue for about another ten years or so, but competition from local carriers, who could operate more nimbly in those distant markets, let them cease carrying travelers and concentrate on carrying freight (or "express," as it was commonly called), for a streamlining of operations and more profitability.

Thus, Henry Wells himself made the trip down by steamboat from St. Louis to New Orleans to investigate what oceangoing shippers were using to transport their cargoes in and out of port, and universally received glowing recommendations about a Memphis company, Dimand Freight. He'd heard similar reports from important shipping clients of his in St. Louis and Chicago.

Henry Wells sent a telegram to Val Dimand. He met with Valentine Dimand and Oskar Cunningham in the lobby of the Gayoso House Hotel in fall 1866.

To say that Mr. Wells met an unlikely-looking pair would be in his words "a tumultuous understatement"; when they walked through the front doors together and into the lobby, one was a slender (even slight) young man of about thirty, dressed as a businessman or lawyer would be in that day. But the other!

Instantly, Wells was taken aback by the appearance of the older man. Long formerly black hair, now almost solidly gray, descended from his black flat-crowned, wide-brimmed hat adorned with a silver band and cascaded almost to his shoulders as he freed it from the confines of that hat. His impeccably-trimmed beard and moustache, worn in the "Van Dyke" style, served to admirably frame his smile, which was wide and genuine. His black, tight-waisted short jacket was also adorned with silver embroidery, done in a Western Spanish motif. Trim, close-fitting black breeches were tucked into high-topped riding boots, polished to a glossy sheen.

Wells thought as the two advanced to greet him, *That man could be comfortable on any ranch or estancia in California!*

His first spoken words were in introduction though. "Hello, I'm Henry Wells from San Francisco, and I'm here in Memphis representing the Well Fargo Express Company."

"Hello, Mr. Wells! I'm Valentine Dimand, and this my attorney and stepson, Oskar Cunningham. It is a pleasure to meet you, sir. Would you please sit with us, and could I order a libation for you as we chat?"

"Thank you, sir. I will join you, and a whiskey, neat, would be fine!"

"Excellent, and spoken like a true Californian," Val said while waving a waiter over.

"Actually, I'm from Vermont and grew up back East, but I've been in California long enough to be thoroughly acclimated by now," Wells replied. "Excuse me for asking, but your mode of dress suggests you may yourself have spent some time in the West?"

Val's reply was quick. "Some of my most cherished memories! I spent time on the Estancia de la Vega outside Santa Fe. I and my friends spent many happy days there in our youth. Senor Vega was most accommodating, and his vaqueros taught me much about riding and ranching and, really, just about becoming a man."

Drinks came, and the conversation paused for a few minutes.

Wells broke the silence. "I've been to that very estancia myself, though I wasn't fortunate enough to make Senor Vega's acquaintance."

"Yes, he passed years ago."

"Well, Mr. Dimand—"

"Please, call me Val."

"Likewise, call me Henry."

"Well, Val, let's go and survey your operation."

The three men left together and mounted up for the fairly short ride to the freight yard, Val on Vindicator, Oskar on Sidewinder, and Henry Wells on a spare horse from the freight yard. They were at the freight yard in less than ten minutes, even after riding at a very leisurely pace, in conversation most of the way.

When they arrived, Wells was impressed with how accessible the operation was to the main roads of the area, opening directly onto the main eastward road, right at its intersection with the main north/south highway. Access into the vital waterfront landing on the Mississippi, that thoroughfare between Wells's desired terminuses of both St. Louis and New Orleans, was a simple right turn out of the freight yard's driveway and then straight ahead to the docks. Rail access, its development stunted by the recent conflict, was similarly within easy distance and connection. Wells knew that future expansion of the rail system, including a complete transcontinental railway was only a matter of time.

Oskar piqued Wells's interest even more with his news on the subject. "Before the war was very well along, we secured the right-of-way and set aside the land for a spur line from the Memphis and Arkansas Railway right to the freight yard. That agreement is in effect until 1872, though we should have it before then."

Oskar rode alongside Henry Wells as they toured the grounds. Oskar was in his element in highlighting the features of the Dimand Freight operations facilities and methods. He showed the stock holding corral, where the horses were penned at night; the team assembly barn with its feed loft overhead; the innovative water tower system; and the newly built and expansive loading/unloading barn, before bringing Wells back to the front office, itself brand new.

Val greeted them from the front porch. "Well, sir, did you get a good look?"

"That I did. Most remarkable!" Wells seemed truly impressed.

"Please, come inside and sit." Val was expansive in voice and gestures.

As the three men sat together inside, the ideas flowed freely. Henry Wells got a more complete picture of the company's maximum capabilities after assessing how many wagons and what type, how many horses, and the number of teamsters and other workers on payroll.

As Val outlined his payroll and holding procedures, Henry Wells couldn't help but admire the savings and other banking capabilities Val had made available to his employees right there on the premises and the acumen involved in keeping employees by treating them fairly. He saw strong parallels to the way he already ran his business, as well as new methods to improve his operations.

"Yes, Henry, we have men who have been with us since the beginning. We lost some during the war, enlisted and gone off. But I told each man who did so I was sorry to see him go and, upon his return, his job would be waiting for him. I had twenty-six hands leave, but nineteen of them came back to work at the war's end.

"I also have customers who have been with me from the beginning, and the vast majority of them are still with Dimand Freight. I lost a number of my cotton shippers during the war, because I wouldn't put my people in harm's way to maintain business in areas under combat, and I refused to participate in the cotton-smuggling enterprise that flourished here in Memphis all through the war. I lost thirteen accounts during the war, but so far, I've gotten eleven of them back, plus four more new accounts, one of them impressively large."

Val closed his remarks about the health of Dimand Freight fairly simply. "Henry, like everyone else, we experienced a big crimp in our trade with the war, but I didn't cut back on my payroll. I kept everyone on for the duration, because I knew I'd need them when the fracas was over. They needed their jobs. So, I kept them and put them to work making improvements in the place. That way, we could handle the business I hoped was coming after the war. So far, it has proved me right; our outfit is as solid as we were before the war. Actually, we're already back to prewar levels of trade in most areas of our business! You can see for yourself; I'll make our books open and available to you at any time."

Henry Wells absorbed these thoughts before he replied. "Your enterprise is very well positioned to capture an even more significant portion of the shipping business, once—and notice I didn't say *if*—the railroads become a national system, rather than a bunch of regional operators."

"For this reason," Wells continued, "I'd like to buy you out, if you're willing to sell!"

Val's reply came after a moment of bearded-chin stroking and obvious rumination. "Henry, I had not considered selling before, except to the railroad. They made a good offer before the war, and they said they were coming back when it was all over, but it might be a few years before the railways are consolidated and ready to expand." He offered up further, "I'm sixty-five right now, soon to be sixty-six. So, I believe, if we can come to agreeable terms, you'll be able to buy Dimand Freight Company—lock, stock, and barrel."

"Well that's terrific, Val!" Henry Wells practically shouted. "I'll fire off a telegram to my partner, William Fargo, and let him know the happy news."

Wells had another question for Val Dimand. "Once we agree on a price, will you want all cash or some sort of structured buyout?"

"Oskar can handle all those details as the time comes," Val intoned solemnly. "He has my complete confidence. We'll await your communication with Mr. Fargo, and then move ahead as expeditiously as possible."

———————◆———————

The buyout, when it was completed, made a Val an even *wealthier* man.

Oskar had spoken extensively to his stepfather about the structuring of the payout before the deal was consummated, about his wishes for the future, and about ways they might be realized without having to take a lump sum and pay taxes on it.

Val told Oskar that, first and foremost, he wanted Angie and Angelina (and Tina, as well) taken care of with monies just for them. He especially wanted for Angie to be able to retain her present standard of living after he was gone and to be able to employ any help she needed to do it as her age advanced and her ability to care for herself waned.

He also wanted Oskar to set up trusts for himself and his brother, Bobby Cunningham, funds to be available on the occasion of their fortieth birthday or fifth wedding anniversary, whichever came first.

The larger bulk of the purchase price was to consist of five equal payments over the next five succeeding years.

A problem with how to handle all these monetary transactions was that banking in Memphis, as within other secessionary states, was in a wartime shambles. Both the Union and the Branch Planters Banks had had their assets seized, and they were shut completely down right after Federal occupation of Memphis began in 1862. Therefore, by this soon after the end of conflict, no new banking establishments had come about to replace them.

Oskar decided to use Wells Fargo themselves as the holding bank for the Dimand Freight funds, as they had agents in St. Louis already and would soon be in Memphis.

Thus, the Dimand/Cunningham family, by the end of 1867, could, with a simple telegram, wire for access to more money than they'd ever dreamed.

Oskar's work in sculpting the terms of the sale was so impressive to Wells, and particularly to William Fargo, that they actually tendered an offer of employment to handle their legal affairs in Memphis as they established their operations there.

Having passed the bar the previous year, Oskar gladly accepted. He was happy to have found gainful employment so soon, particularly as it promised to be quite interesting.

Angie was thrilled at first to have her beloved husband around the house more. He too, cherished the mornings together that didn't require him to go riding off to work. Now, he was able to linger after breakfast over Carmella's delicious coffee and chat with his lovely wife or play with little Valentina until Angelina got up.

Tina was almost five now and curious about everything. She had a particular penchant for following Carmella around while she was doing her chores. Carmella seemed to enjoy the attention, but Tina could be a bit much when it came to constant jabbering and incessant questions.

The big old house didn't seem so big anymore.

Once again lively and filled with people, the house was often the scene of much joy but also some frustration for Val and Angie both.

Oskar, by nature neat and tidy, nonetheless had begun to outgrow his living quarters and really needed a place of his own. Bethel Avenue had sprouted more houses after the war, and they now had neighbors. Many of the building lots in what had been unofficially named "Greenlaw Acres" had been sold before the conflict broke out, but houses had never been started. Several had now been completed. A number of the available lots left were quite desirable, particularly down toward Woodlawn Street. Val asked Oskar if he'd like to look at some of them with an eye toward establishing himself as a property holder.

Oskar had a very interesting reply. "How about if you and Mom looked, and I took over this house? That way, the two of you could build the house of your dreams, one that could allow you to entertain the way this one couldn't."

"That's a very interesting thought, son. I'll ask your mom what she thinks," Val replied. "I don't know if she would be up to going through the building process again; we're quite a bit older than when we started the Bethel house."

Val went on very seriously. "The main reason we built our current house the way we did was because we didn't want to stand out or seem ostentatious. The lack of entertaining through the years was more for our lack of desire for that, rather than limitations of the house itself."

"I never thought about that, Dad. It does make a lot of sense, knowing how you are. But to me it makes sense for you to start a new house that takes into account the new family to live in the home," Oskar replied. "That way you could plan for any type of entertaining you'd like to do, plus have good separate living areas for Angelina and Tina as she grows up."

"Yes, we could, and we could plan for a carriage house and adequate servants' quarters." Val paused after voicing that thought and then went on. "I'm not really looking for more space for us or for more entertaining, but more help for your Mom and me as we age will probably be necessary, and we'll need to house them, so more room is what it will take."

"Yes, and the Bethel house is a perfect size for me, and Ruthie too, if we get married!"

"Is that likely, any time soon?" Val grinned widely as he spoke. "Not that I'm trying to rush you, but your mom wants more grandbabies, and it doesn't look like your brother is in any hurry to help out on that front!"

"Yeah, Dad, I know she wants more little ones." Oskar was grinning now, too. "Ever since Ruthie came over and spent all that time with Angelina and Valentina, she's sorta been dropping hints that she wants to get started developing a family, before I get too old."

The two men, one barely out of his twenties and the other more than twice his age, shared a hearty laugh together.

"Well, you've got a good job now, so you could afford it."

"Yeah, and you're as rich as Croesus now, so you could afford it, too."
They laughed again, almost spasming.
"Let's go talk to your mom."

———————◆———————

Angie had surprised Val at how much in favor of the idea of a new house for them she was. Lately, she had been feeling cramped by the lack of privacy she could find to couple with her beloved Val at any time other than bedtime—and little enough of that undisturbed, with little Valentina running about.

She also was missing her bath times with Carmella, what with Val about the house all hours of the day, but she couldn't tell him that. A few times since he'd retired, Val had gone riding after their morning lovemaking, and Carmella had been able to come in and do a thorough cleanup of the bedroom and Angie while he was away—to Angie's (and Carmella's!) great delight.

But, somehow, in all the newfound peacefulness about the household, those lingering, touching moments were missing for Angie.

She and Val were still enjoying a rich and rewarding sex life, if perhaps not as often as when they were younger. He had found a new enthusiasm for using his mouth, fingers, and tongue to make her as wet as he could and to bring her to the threshold of ecstasy and then standing up and suddenly plunging his erect protuberance marvelously deep into Angie and holding it there while he pressed his weight against her as she writhed against him and brought herself off to orgasm. The first time he did this to her, the screams that erupted from her, even muffled by the pillows, were loud and violent enough to bring a panicked Carmella running to the bedroom door.

"Are you all right, Miss Angie? Do you need me to come in to help you?"

Between heaves and convulsions, Angie managed to croak out a reply. "No, Carmella, I'm fine! Val is taking wonderful care of me tonight! I just had an incident, but I'm fine, now."

"All right, Miss Angie. I was just worried about you. I'll go on back to my room now."

"That will be fine, Carmella. I'll see you in the morning. Maybe a little extra cleanup will be needed then."

"OK and goodnight, ma'am."

As she walked down the hallway to her room, Carmella thought to herself, *"Yes, I'll just bet you've got that fine man in there taking wonderful care of you. I'll bet your 'incident' ended in a flood of creamy white, and you do need a cleanup. Well, I'd come in right now and give it to you, too, even if he was still in the room!"*

With that last thought having seared its way into Carmella's brain and her loins having suddenly turned into a flow of molten lava, the last few steps to the door she absolutely scurried, holding her hand under her crotch, lest she drip precipitously down onto the floor.

Alone in her room, the door now quietly but solidly closed, she grabbed her favorite curved-handle hairbrush. It wasn't her favorite because of any particular hairstyling quality. Rather, when turned just the right way and inserted into her at just the right depth, it touched the exact right spot to bring her to climax. Whether fast and furious or languid and luxurious, the choice was hers—the brush never failed!

Shrugging off her robe and hiking her nightdress up to her waist, Carmella dispensed with all preamble and began to insert the brush handle rapidly into her already moist cavern. As she fell back onto her bed, she held it in place, pressing against that delicious spot until the blinding light in her brain forced her to release the pressure momentarily.

As the first waves subsided, she began to move the brush handle in and out, in and out, while gradually modulating the pressure, soft and then harder. Even she was surprised at how little time it took before the next body-shaking orgasm erupted, seemingly up from her toes and all the way through her body before it exploded once again in her brain—causing her to convulse furiously.

When next she was calm and still, the images began to flood her mind. Carmella fantasized about being in the lovers' bedroom right then with her head between Angie's legs, lapping up every last bit of

Val's creamy leavings, while taking care to provide Angie with further pleasure, maybe even to another orgasm. Most of her "cleanup" sessions ended just that way.

The vision of having Val in the room, watching her do this, once again ignited a flame below.

Carmella was fifty-eight that year and still full of sexual desire. Her slim body was sheathed in beautiful skin the color of old ivory, and her once-brown hair was now shot through with gray. Her trim and shapely legs lacked a bit of meeting together at her crotch, leaving a small gap between her legs into which her small labia hung most charmingly, especially when she was bent over. Her very slim but quite shapely buttocks were firm, and her small breasts were capped with tight, pointy nipples of a rich milk chocolate color. Her French Magyar ancestry had produced a woman who had been exciting to both sexes since girlhood.

Never married and childless, she had, nonetheless, known love many times. Her years-long affair with Anton, the stableman in the Dimands' employ, had only recently ended.

It had done so tragically.

Early in the spring, Anton had been helping a neighbor move a horse to the small corral by the Bethel house's stables. Unfortunately in heat at the time, the mare attracted the attention of Sidewinder (always a more undisciplined horse than Vindicator, who stayed calmly in his stall), who kicked apart the slats of his paddock to get to her. Anton tried to stop Sidewinder and suffered a kick to his head. Val rushed his old friend to Dr. Barnett, who bandaged the wound and made Anton easier but to no real avail.

Anton died in his restless sleep two days later.

Val buried his old friend in front of family and a few friends and sold Sidewinder the same day.

◆

The start of the Woodlawn house began in spring 1868. Leslie Hammond, who had built the Bethel house, had died during the war and was no longer available. The job fell to his son, Armand, who had helped his father on the earlier project and had fallen in love with Memphis and moved to town with his family just before the war.

Armand Hammond was delighted to do the job. And after touring several other houses Armand had already designed and constructed there in Memphis, Val was delighted to have him do it.

It was an impressive project from the start. The winding drive up the slope from Woodlawn Street was flanked on either side by rows of newly planted oaks, and it curved on around the back of the house to the carriage house, corral, and stables. The house itself was a two-story affair, sheathed in white clapboard, with a wide front porch going most of the way across the front and featuring massive Greek Revival columns in the Corinthian style.

Inside the ornate entryway, dual curved staircases led upward to the second-story landing, which overlooked the entryway. The landing led off down the matching hallways to either side to bedrooms and baths upstairs, to the north and south.

Downstairs, through the space between the staircases, the entryway and smaller front room led to a large room that could serve as either an entertainment and gathering space, or a grand living room, depending on the need and furnishings.

The kitchen, pantry, and a bedroom and bath were to the south on the ground floor to one side of the grand room. The house also would have a dining room, another bath and bedroom, along with a study for Val and a sewing room for Angie (and probably Angelina as well) along the other side to the north. With a total of eight bedrooms (six upstairs and two down) and four bathrooms (two up and two down), all with running water and flush toilets already planned in ahead, the house was easily going to be the absolute centerpiece of the neighborhood.

As the house was going up, another momentous event occurred in the lives of the Dimand/Cunningham family. In the bountiful month of May, Memphis was, and still is to this day, an absolute vision of love-liness, with such things as azaleas, dogwoods, and magnolias bursting forth in bloom around the city. Oskar Cunningham, esquire, and Ruth

Anne (Ruthie) Simpson chose this time of renewal and rebirth from the winter to become man and wife, to the absolute delight of both sets of parents.

As a wedding present, Val and Angie gave the newlyweds the Bethel house, while they, Angelina, Tina, and Carmella, moved two doors down Bethel toward Woodlawn into a vacant house for rent. The new living spaces became sort of an adventure for everyone, most especially Tina.

The little girl would go from house to house, exploring and seeing what interesting items were being moved from one house to another and asking question after question about what was going on. When it got to be too much, as it sometimes did, Carmella could almost always be counted on for a sugar cookie and a glass of her spiced lemonade to slow down the little whirlwind.

With the newlyweds comfortably installed in their new abode, Val turned toward assessing the costs for the new house being built. Just as he'd done originally on Bethel, he bought the Woodlawn lot for cash, outright.

When he got the final estimate on the cost of the house, fully built and ready to move in, he found he could easily absorb those costs out of funds he already had on hand, without touching the Wells Fargo monies.

Val had, a couple of times, ridden Vindicator over to the freight lot, just to visit the old place and see how things were without him. Tommy Nichols and Bob Allen and most of the old crew were still at the freight yard, just now working for Wells Fargo rather than him, even though they continued to call the business Dimand Freight, temporarily.

All the remaining wranglers, drivers, and loaders greeted their old boss warmly. When told of his moving, a great number of them pledged their help in seeing that through. So, Val had all the sweat, muscle, and elbow grease he needed to help him make the short move down Bethel and then, later, the bigger move to Woodlawn. Tommy Nichols also pledged the use of as many wagons and teams as he needed for the larger move, when the time came.

The house on Woodlawn was finished in early autumn 1869, and the Dimand family began to move in soon after. For days running, wag-onloads of furniture and supplies made their way up the hill and around the back of the house, there to be unloaded by strong, somewhat rough and uncouth men and distributed throughout the house.

Oskar and Ruthie had presented Angie and Val their second grand-baby earlier that year, and the grandparents (including Ruthie's folks) were all over the moon with delight.

The housewarming was a spirited affair, with everyone there—from all the grandparents, plus Angelina, Tina, and little baby Robert Louis Cunningham (named for his grandfathers) to a dozen and half (or so) of freighters, plus their wives to friends from the neighborhood and, really, across Memphis. Even Val's old friend and former mayor, John Park, was in attendance, as well as the current mayor of Memphis, John Leftwich, joined by his and the boys' old friend and teacher, Eugene McGevney.

With a small orchestra playing on the balcony overlook and plenty of good food to be had, the air was festive. Plenty of tea and cider was available, and though a few of the attendees might have brought hard liquor to "liven things up," everyone knew Val Dimand did not hold to strong drink, and no one wanted to incur the wrath of Val "Between the Eyes" Dimand. So, although the housewarming was a lively and spirited affair, it didn't get out of hand.

Thus, when the last guest had gone home, Val and Angie could now seriously get down to making this new house a true home. The big house had enough room that family members could easily find a quiet place of solitude, whether inside the house itself or on the spacious, quiet grounds.

Indeed, Val could often be found napping out on the grounds in the back in his rope-and-canvas hammock, slung between two trees. Other times, he and his beloved Angie could be found sitting placidly on the front porch, rocking back and forth side by side in their matching rockers, watching Tina play.

Tranquil as the days were, the nights in the new house could be torrid with Angie and Val's lovemaking. At Angie's insistence, the chaise lounge and full-length dressing mirror were brought and installed in their new bedroom.

Now, however, they were not constantly having to watch how much noise they made or be vigilant for uninvited guests. The solitude their new bedroom arrangements allowed was very welcome indeed to the still-randy, although no-longer-young couple. As best he could, Val still made a valiant effort to give his beautiful bride an exciting time in bed. She certainly did that for him!

Their entertaining over the next couple of years was mostly hosting Oskar and Ruthie and then taking care of baby Robert afterward, while his parents enjoyed a little "time to themselves."

This technique must have worked, because, less than a year after they moved into the new house, Oskar and Ruthie presented them with the charming little Rose Ellen, a delightful little bundle of grins and bubbles.

Carmella's new kitchen was her domain, and she certainly made the most of it, abundantly feeding all the family well, with love. She also continued to help Angie with bathing, dressing, and other personal touches. Her personal touches were often a highlight of both women's days.

Angelina's "widow's wounds" gradually began to heal by spending time with her mom and heeding her counsel. In fact, mother and daughter were invaluable to each other. Angie helped Angelina heal and Angelina, in turn, provided an outlet for Angie's hard-won advice, thereby giving new purpose to a life advancing into its golden years.

By this time Valentina was an impossibly precocious eight-year-old.

◆

After the Civil War, banking in Memphis was a shambles for the next few years, since its two largest banks had been confiscated and shuttered for the duration. However, in 1869 financier William Farrington was granted a charter for a new bank, and he opened the new Union and Planters Bank in June of that year.

As an up-and-coming young attorney, the local legal representative for the Wells Fargo Company, and a close relative to one of Memphis's longtime leading (and wealthiest) citizens, Oskar Cunningham was asked to sit on the advisory board of the new institution.

Thus, one day as they were sitting over spiced tea in the living room, Val said to Oskar, "Son, I'm almost seventy years old now; who knows how much longer I might live? I think it's high time for you to draw me up a will to sign. You know better than anyone else what assets the family has and who needs to be taken care of. So, write me up your best effort at it, and I'll look it over. If I need anything changed, I'll let you know, and you can make those revisions.

"Oskar, I know it's a lot to ask, but can you do that for me? It doesn't need to be complicated, but it would put my mind at ease; it really would."

"Sure thing, Dad! I'll get right on it."

◆

One bright late summer afternoon in 1873, Val Dimand swatted absently at the *Aedes aegypti* mosquito that bit him on the forearm while he was lounging in his hammock, without a care in the world. Annoyance at the thing was his biggest reaction.

By the following afternoon, he was alternately burning up or shaking uncontrollably with the chills. No amount of drinking water—nor the supposed "fever balm" Dr. Barnett applied to his chest—offered any relief. A day later, his skin and the whites of his eyes had a decidedly yellowish cast.

When he began throwing up a horrible blackish paste two days later, he knew he was in trouble.

Chapter 14

BOBBY COMES HOME

"Thank you very much!" is a common Memphis expression, heard all over the city, and said by Memphians from all walks of life. Made famous by Elvis Presley, easily the most illustrious figure from Memphis ever, nevertheless it is part of the reputation for politeness that graces all Memphians!

1873–1880

Valentine Dimand went to be with his Lord on a sweltering afternoon in 1873 and was laid to rest three days later on August 19.

Angie moved in a fog throughout the entire process of laying her beloved to his interment, simply existing and going where led, doing what others told her to do.

Inside, she was completely hollow.

Her man, who she had adored almost all her entire adult life, the man who had literally stood up to blazing guns and laughed, was gone.

Even with all three of her children around her, along with all three of her grandchildren, she felt alone and adrift in the world. She could find no comfort anywhere.

Bobby had made it home to Memphis just two days before Val passed on; he and Oskar took on the responsibilities for the arrangements needed for the burial. Since Val was going to be the first to be laid to rest in the family cemetery right there on the grounds of the Woodlawn house, the arrangements mostly consisted of preparing the body, having a casket built, and having the grave dug. Bobby was even able to find a decorative stone mason to provide a granite tombstone, with a temporary wooden marker provided in time for the funeral, to be replaced by the granite one when it was finished.

No secret was or could be made of the fact that Valentine Dimand had died from yellow fever, once again making its way through Memphis. The source of this scourge was, as yet, unknown; the idea that it was perhaps highly contagious meant that not everyone Oskar or Bobby spoke to about helping with the funeral needs was very willing to participate.

Two undertakers turned the job of preparing the body down flat; a third undertaker took the risk only after Oskar doubled and then tripled his regular price. The grave diggers Bobby found who would even agree to come anywhere near the coffined body dug the hole in the relative cool of the morning on the eighteenth and agreed to return at a little before dusk on the nineteenth to fill it back in, all for more than double the normal rate for such a thing.

Brother Jack Tichenor of the Seventh Street Baptist Church was the one bright light to the whole somber process. Not only did he agree on first request to deliver the service, but he wanted no remuneration for doing so. Oskar made a very generous donation to the church to honor Brother Jack's unflinching service to his stepfather.

Because the whole rear portion of the lot on Woodlawn behind the house, carriage house, and stables was beautiful with flowers, shrubbery, and overhanging trees providing shade, this pastoral setting made the perfect place to let Val truly "rest in peace."

While the two stepsons were busy with the arrangements, Angelina stayed close to her mother, letting her talk and reminisce as she wanted, as well as just to hold her in silent bond when that was the most appropriate. Young Valentina also tried to be a comfort for her Grandma Angie. Though she did not understand death to any real degree, Tina knew the discomfort she felt knowing that Grandpa was never going to wake up again to play with her, and that Grandma was really hurting in her heart. Tina stayed close and let Angie absently stroke her hair as she told the young girl tales of when she, herself, had been young.

Much of the time during those days just before the funeral, Oskar had Ruthie bring the babies, Robert Louis and Rose Ellen, over to be able to provide their granny with at least some small measure of joy, which they indeed did. Almost as if they knew, they were cheerful and content almost the whole time.

The morning of the nineteenth dawned bright and clear, and Val made the trip from the undertaker's in his coffin to the Woodlawn house aboard the special wagon provided by that gentleman and was brought right to the graveside.

Bobby and Oskar Cunningham acted as lead pallbearers, along with four other gentlemen selected from the ranks of wranglers, drovers, and drivers from the freight yard. Terry Nicholls, Bob Allen, Phil Reesthaus, and Archie Baum were the ones who honored their old boss in this way, although there were a dozen or so more men from the freight company who were willing and who would gladly step in to serve if needed.

After the casket was placed on the lowering sling (itself on two sturdy slats laid across the grave opening), the family members and other guests gathered around and gave Brother Jack their attention. He opened in prayer and moved on to a brief message of secure hope through the resurrection of Jesus. He then asked if anyone, particularly Angie, wanted to say a few words before they lowered the casket.

Drawing on the strength that had stood her for almost forty years with Val, Angie drew herself erect and spoke in a strong, calm voice. "Val was my everything. I watched this man walk right into death's path to save me, just as calmly as you'd walk to the store. I can only hope my boys can turn out like this wonderful man. I'm going to miss him!"

Everyone else held back their remarks in brevity because the heat was quite oppressive. Soon enough, Brother Jack watched with the others as the four freight men lifted the canvas sling, raising up the casket, while Bobby and Oskar (quickly but with dignity) slid the slats from underneath.

The six men gently lowered the coffin into the ground. Brother Jack intoned a final prayer of thanks to God for this wonderful soul. Then, as each attendee passed by and looked downward, many were moved to drop a token onto the coffin or speak aloud a final farewell to Val.

As the entire group moved toward the back of the house, Bobby and Oskar held open the double French doors to let them come inside, where Angelina sat down on one side of Angie and Tina sat on the other.

Friends and neighbors passed by and offered a hand or a word to Angie before moving over to the table Ruthie stood behind. It held light snacks and small plates to hold them, as well as a punch bowl of Carmella's delightful spiced lemonade.

Miracle of miracles, floating in the bowl were chunks of actual ice, gotten from the ice house just that morning and chopped into pieces that would fit into the glasses at the table's end.

Ever watchful for a chance to serve, Carmella stood in the doorway to the kitchen, ready and able to replenish anything needed. Now and again, she ducked behind the doorway to dab at her eyes and her cheeks as the tears rolled down.

Somehow, after all the guests had left, the family sat in a sort of drained silence, just thankful for having made it through the day thus far.

Conversation would come later.

———————◆———————

When Bobby had seen the last guest out the front door, he returned to the living room where the rest of the family was sitting quietly, simply absorbing the events of the day.

Oskar had sent Ruthie back up the street to the Bethel house with the babies to get them fed and put down for naps. Carmella had gone with her to help and, Oskar suspected, have some relief from her grief.

Everyone else still sat, lost in his or her thoughts.

It was Bobby, who was staying there at the Woodlawn house for as long as was needed, who broke the silence at last. "Mom, I won't ask if you're going to be all right, because I know you will in time. But if there's anything you can think of while I'm here that I can do to make things better for you, please just ask me, and I'll be happy to give it my best try."

"Well, son, how about you try to settle down and get married so I can have more grandbabies?"

"Well, Mom, I have to tell you that, lately, I've been thinking of that very thing myself. I'm not as far away from it as I have been in the past; nothing immediate is on the horizon, but I'm closer than I have been for years." Bobby went on. "Oskar's done well for you in that regard, I must say! Little Bobby and Rose are two absolutely beautiful children."

"Along with Tina, they're a blessing to this old woman's heart."

Angelina chimed in next. "Oh, Mom, you know you're still a beauty!"

"Well, my dear, you have no idea how much you look like me when I was your age, but the years and the trials have taken their toll."

It was Oskar's turn now to add his thoughts. "Yes, Mother, all that is true. But all that living and the experience you gained, you have tried to pass on to us kids. You have *always* given us a 'leg up' in life. And I, for one, appreciate it more than you know."

"My old mother did the same for me when I was growing up, so how could I do less?"

The whole group fell for a while into a contemplative silence, once again broken by Bobby. "Mom, I'll take the carriage down and take Oskar home so he can help Ruthie with the babies, and I'll bring Carmella back with me so she can start supper and then get you ready for bed. Can I bring you back anything?"

"No, dear, just Carmella."

Her two sons went out to the drive in the back through the French doors and got into the family carriage. After Anton's tragic death, the family had hired a stableman and groundskeeper for the new house, so such things were routinely ready when necessary.

The brothers, no longer the competitors they had once been, drove to the Bethel house in conversation all the way.

"How are things in Fort Smith, Bobby?"

"Well, Oskar, I haven't been there all that much lately."

"Really? Why not?"

"Well, for the last six months or so, I've been deputized and pursuing fugitives for Judge Story there in Fort Smith. That means following them into the Indian Territory if they go there to avoid pursuit, but I have even had to follow a couple of characters all the way to California."

"You caught any?"

"Yeah, several. Judge Story puts out a warrant on each one, and my job ends when they're brought back to justice."

"So, you're a fugitive hunter?"

"Yes, primarily, at least for now. Each one of these renegades I follow is already indicted by a sitting Federal magistrate, and they're usually bail jumpers or prison escapees. The capture fee is not available to just anyone; it covers my expenses in chasing them."

"Isn't Judge Story thought to be pretty corrupt?"

"Yes, he does have that reputation, and he can hand down some harsh sentences. But I've never seen him be blatantly unjust."

"Well, how do you feel doing that? Doesn't it give you pause sometimes?"

"Yes, of course it does, Oskar. But if you think about it, would you want someone doing that job who didn't have reservations?"

"I never thought of it like that! You're right, Bobby, of course. But do you like it?"

"There's a lot of detective work involved, and that can be absolutely fascinating. Plus, you travel to lots of places you might never have gone to otherwise. So, you see a lot of the country, and you meet all sorts of interesting people; and they're not all crooks, of course!"

"So, what you're doing is sort of a cross between being a bounty hunter and a Pinkerton detective, is that right?"

"Yeah, maybe so. But I've worked with some of the 'Pinks,' and I didn't like it, or them, very much. I liked the Texas Rangers better. The Pinks have a reputation for results, for sure, but also a nasty habit of beating a confession out of a suspect, rather than finding the actual culprit."

"So, are you going to keep doing this?"

"Till something better comes along, I suppose. Maybe a cushy job like you've got with that Wells Fargo outfit will fall into my lap, like it did yours!"

"Maybe, big brother, you just never know."

By this time, the two young men were up in the drive of the Bethel house, and Oskar hopped out with a parting question. "You gonna be around for the reading of the will Tuesday?"

"Sure will! I wouldn't miss that."

"Good. I'll send Carmella right out."

That night was the loneliest for Angie since word had come that Robert W. Cunningham, her beloved Bobby, had definitely died at the Alamo, and no amount of hoping or wishing was going to return him to her side. It had been almost forty years since that first night she had gone to bed without a shred or faint glimmer of hope for his return, but on this night those old feelings came back as a flood.

After lowering Val's coffin into the ground, Bobby and Oskar had gone immediately to her, flanked her, and each given her an arm for support for the trek back up to the house. It was good they had done so, she thought as she lay alone in her now half-empty bed; otherwise, she believed she would have never made it.

Angie and Carmella had sat huddled together for a long time, commiserating in a heavy silence broken by occasional reminiscences or reflections.

It was not lost on Angie that her housekeeper was tragically in love with her husband; she'd actually known it for years. How could Carmella not be? She had lived in the same house with him, doing his laundry, cooking his meals, seeing to his children, and all the time loving him from afar by seeing how he treated his beloved wife. Half the women he'd ever met, or who had even seen him, were probably at least a little in love with him. Angie begrudged Carmella's feelings not one whit; she understood completely the loss that touched her so deeply as well.

Angie resolved that night, before her utter bone-deep exhaustion overtook her with the blessed shroud of sleep, that she would make sure that the woman who had become a true friend would be taken care of for the rest of her life.

◆

Oskar and Bobby drove Angie and Angelina downtown the next Tuesday morning to the law offices of Mayre B. Trezevant, for Val's will to be read. Although Oskar had drawn up and revised the will according to Val's wishes, he felt the reading should be done by his friend and occasional associate, for the sake of impartiality and decorum.

After they were all comfortably seated, Oskar spoke to his friend quietly. "Thank you for doing this for me, M. B. You may begin anytime you wish."

"It's my pleasure to do this service for you and your family, Oskar. Let's get started, shall we?

"For the record, the final will and testament of Valentine Marquis Dimand, hereby duly registered with the clerk of court, County of Shelby, at Memphis, Tennessee, is being read aloud by Mayre Beattie Trezevant, esquire, on this day of August 22, 1873. Present within earshot are widow Angie MacFee Cunningham-Dimand, daughter Angelina Dimand, stepson Robert Cunningham, and stepson Oskar Cunningham, esquire. Also present within earshot is law clerk Thaddeus Martin, recording."

"Now that the legalities are out of the way, let's begin."

M. B. Trezevant read the opening in a solid, firm voice. "I Valentine Marquis Dimand, being of sound mind, do upon occasion of my death make the following final bequests: First, to my beloved bride, Angie, I leave the Woodlawn house, grounds, and appurtenances contained therein or about, including (but not limited to) one hand-painted oil-on-canvas portrait of one Robert W. Cunningham.

"I also leave to her the entire sums yet payable by the Wells Fargo Company for the proceeds of the sale of the Dimand Freight Company, currently amounting to $416,000 dollars, to be administered and distributed by her as she sees fit.

"I leave to my dear daughter, Angelina, the sum of $150,000. I leave to my beloved stepson Robert Cunningham the sum of $150,000 and my prized horse, Vindicator, along with all my saddles and tack. I leave to my beloved stepson Oskar Cunningham the sum of $150,000."

Mayre Trezevant and Oskar explained the actual distribution of the funds, which consisted of accounts drawn up on the new Union and Planters Bank there in downtown Memphis, all of which was available to their immediate use by cash withdrawal or bank draft. Wire transfer by telegraph to another recognized banking institution such as Wells Fargo Bank was also available, usually with only one day required to complete.

After the family left the law offices downtown, they rode back toward the Woodlawn and Bethel houses in something of a state of shock, each one considering how much money they now had, compared to a single loaf of bread which could be bought for less than a dime or a month's wages at a good job, which could be as much as $30 to $40.

Angie was suddenly jolted out of her reverie by a pothole jarring the carriage, so she spoke after starting at the interruption. "My, that was a bump! You know, Bobby, I was glad to see that Val specifically left Vindicator to you, because I had been wondering what to do with him. He's gotten pretty old, so I don't know how much riding you'll be able to subject him to, but I guess your dad just wanted him to have time with you before he gets too old for anyone at all to ride him."

"Mama, I was thinking about him about a month ago, wondering what would become of him. I'd love to ride him for a while, around town when I get back, before I have to put him out to pasture. I have a friend with a ranch close to Pecos, Texas, who told me to bring him, and he'd be happy to board him for the rest of his days in exchange for breeding him. The Spanish Barb bloodlines are highly desirable for a good long-distance rider. So I told him yes, as long as I got my pick of any colts that came out of it!"

Bobby had another thought. "Mom, unless you're going to do something else with them, I'd also like to have some of Dad's clothes. I'll never be the man he was physically, but I'd love to be able to remember and honor him in that way, just by simply getting dressed. I know I'm not quite as tall as he was, but some things ought to fit, certainly his hats!"

Angie's reply was rather quick. "Honey, I can't think of a better thing to do with them. Oskar, would you also want some of them?"

"Well, Mom, someone'd have to cut them down a pretty good bit to fit me, so probably not. But some of his belts, ties, and other accessories would be great to have, if it's all right with Bobby."

"Sure, Oskar! We'll go through them together. I'm sure we can each find plenty."

Angelina had followed this discussion with interest. "Boys, if it's all right with you, Daddy had a couple of sets of containers, for shaving lotions and such, I think, and a set of hairbrushes I've admired since I was a little girl. Would it be all right if I had those to remember him by?"

"Whatever you want."

"Sure!"

Bobby finished the discussion with a question. "Mom, we've been sitting here dividing up Dad's things without regard for you. Is there anything specifically you'd like for a keepsake?"

"Oh, son! I have a thousand memories and more. That's all I need. But I'll find some small thing for myself, anyway."

◆

One of the first things Angie did was to hire a new cook and housekeeper for Carmella to train and assign duties. She explained to Carmella that she was now Angie's personal assistant to help her in her advancing age (which, of course, she had already been doing), at a new, higher salary, with living quarters provided right there in the house, just down the hall from Angie's bedroom. She checked with Oskar on the efficacy of the arrangement and the monetary maneuverings necessary to accomplish this, and he agreed totally and set up the appropriate funding requirements.

As far as money went, Angie had been working with the remnants of the gold and silver coins that Val had converted their holdings in the

Branch Union and Branch Planters Banks into, before those institutions' assets were seized at the beginning of the Federal occupation of Memphis. Her last count showed her with slightly less than $23,000 left in hard cash, which she had been trying to project forward to estimate at what age she would run out of money.

She now realized there was no need.

As the days slowly became normalized, and the pain of grief no longer trapped the family members in fog, the household of the Dimand-Cunningham family settled into a new "normal" rhythm. And Bobby Cunningham decided it was time to leave.

On a warm early-September morning with all his goodbyes said, and all his promises to keep in touch given, Bobby rode away from his tearstained mother and sister standing at the front door of the Woodlawn house. He rode past the Bethel house with a wave to Oskar, Ruthie, and the babies, who were all gathered on their wide front porch.

Vindicator seemed to want to move; Bobby kneed the big horse into a trot.

———————◆———————

All the way back into Arkansas and on across to Fort Smith, Bobby had time to reflect about the difference in his life after he had left Memphis so many years before. Whereas his younger brother, Oskar, now had a very pretty wife and two gorgeous babies, he had no such comforts to come home to.

To make no mistake about it, Bobby Cunningham had turned into a very handsome man, like his father, Robert W. had been. He had plenty of female companionship available but no marriageable prospects. Speaking of home, Oskar now held title to the Bethel house, large but snug; Bobby himself came home (when he was there) to a small clapboard house, two steps up from being a cabin.

But the thing that had been gnawing at his very guts for the last several months—and had really come to a head with Val's death and his own extended return to Memphis—was how close he had come to dying in a Cherokee courtroom in the Indian Territory. Dying alone and almost unnoticed, without any significant legacy to leave behind, just did not seem right, given the family and upbringing he'd had since he was born on an East Texas homestead. Val had left a rich legacy and heritage behind when he passed, and Bobby had begun to feel a pull to start looking toward his own, before time ran out.

It had to begin with Bobby thinking of more than himself and his immediate needs, he realized. He had a mother and a half sister and her little daughter who could use a man living right there with them and seeing to their needs. He also had a younger brother who was doing very well for himself but who also had his own set of mouths to feed and take care of. With all these considerations, Bobby began to feel a real pull to return to Memphis and settle down there.

Fort Smith had never had any particular allure for him. It was simply a conveniently central location from which to operate as the Colt firearms representative. He stayed on after the arrival of Judge William Story, mostly by inertia, not knowing he would someday work for the judge.

When the Texas Rangers Judge Story talked to were unanimous in their praise of Bobby Cunningham as a levelheaded, serious man with fine upbringing, the judge had decided he was an appropriate candidate for deputy United States marshal. Judge Story made it official in 1871, sending Bobby on apprehension duties with posses in the local area at first and, later, into the Indian Territory.

It was on one of these missions that Bobby had almost lost his life, with no trying on his part. In a crowded Cherokee tribal courtroom filled with armed participants and observers, tensions about mixed-race unions between Cherokee women and white men had erupted in a hail of gunfire. When the gun-smoke cleared and order was restored, one of the deputy US marshals, as many as six Cherokees, and at least four white men from the posse were mortally wounded.

Bobby had got off a couple of shots at an antagonist who was shooting at him. But mostly, he'd just stayed pinned down, as wild shots rang out from every corner of the packed courtroom and debris rained down on the yelling visitors.

The cries and screams of some of the innocent bystanders who were hurt would haunt him for years to come.

After the carnage from what was later called the "Goingsnake Massacre" was over, Bobby Cunningham truly felt lucky to be alive. He made it back to Fort Smith with the remnants of the posse and took stock of his position in life all along the way home. As he did so, by any assessment he came up short.

You see, it wasn't by any lack of courage on Bobby's part. He simply had this stubborn belief that, if he was going to give up his life, it ought to mean or be worth something.

Bobby had been taught by Val Dimand to be a dead shot with either rifle or pistol and was the near equal of him with either weapon. Bobby was not reluctant to return fire when he was being shot at. But to wound or perhaps kill a man or have it happen to him—Bobby was not willing to have happen until he understood the rationale for the fight. Fight he would, if he must, but he needed to know the reason.

Judge Story could send him out. It was his responsibility to get back alive; he took that seriously.

Bobby Cunningham stayed as a "peace officer" for another three years. Judge Story resigned under a cloud of malfeasance and was replaced by Judge Isaiah Parker, who became known later as the "Hanging Judge" for his harsh sentences. For both men, Bobby just did his job quietly and well, following where the evidence led and building solid cases against those wanted for misdeeds, and apprehension usually followed.

Still, he never forgot that courtroom and the lessons it taught.

———————◆———————

He had delivered Vindicator to his friend's ranch outside Pecos about a year earlier when he found himself on another horse cantering up the road from Little Rock toward Memphis. A whistle coming from his lips and a smile appearing on his face subtly informed him that, without overtly realizing or meaning to do so, he might just break out into a bout of happiness!

The sudden thoughts of his mom's face when she saw him in just a couple of days made his smile broader, and he kneed the horse into a slightly quicker gait.

Angie's reception for Bobby, her oldest, met his every expectation and then some. Sally, the new cook and housekeeper his mom had hired right after Val's funeral, cooked up a supper fit for royalty, and Bobby did his best to do it justice. Angie installed him in the upstairs bedroom all the way down the hall from hers. Clean, cool, and quiet with fresh linens everywhere, it offered comfort and privacy with its own outside entrance and nearby bath.

Bobby had been to first-rate hotels not so luxurious; his nights immediately took on a level of peace, which told him the certainty of one thing. He was home for sure.

Angie let Bobby know early on that the private entrance did, indeed, mean that he could bring a female friend over discreetly, but that advance notice he was doing so of an evening would be very much appreciated. She also reassured him that a dinner invitation to a companion was no real trouble to handle on short notice; all were welcome at their table.

Bobby, of course was pleased. As a man, he appreciated the privacy, discretion, and forethought, and he intended to not overstep and cause any distress to his mother or anyone else in the household.

Carmella had become Angie's full-time caregiving assistant during the time he had been away. That seemed to be working out well, with Carmella occasionally returning to the kitchen when Sally needed help or Angie had a special meal request. Carmella's caring assistance with bathing, dressing, and general companionship truly made Angie's life better.

By the time the fall weather turned crisp in the latter part of 1876, Bobby had been at the house about two months, and he was really feeling back at home. Angelina and Valentina were a warm part of the household, and Angelina seemed to be getting some of her lightness and humor back.

Valentina, now a young teenager, was totally reminiscent of Angelina at the same age. Tina was constantly with her mother and grandmother as they went about the house, making it into a comfortable family home and enjoying each other's company along the way.

When the three women of the house gathered in the kitchen with Sally and Carmella, conversation would fly, along with cornbread or biscuits in and out of the oven. Meals around the table at the Woodlawn house were made even livelier when Oskar, Ruthie, and the little ones were in attendance.

Lately, boys from school had taken to walking the pretty Valentina home after the classroom day was finished. Sometimes, Sally or Carmella would be in the kitchen with treats and lemonade. Frequently, Grandma Angie would be there to chat with Tina's young escorts, gently questioning each one about his background and home life.

Often, Tina would introduce her friends from school to her Uncle Bobby. As a man who had actually been in the West, he could impress them mightily with his tales of pursuing fleeing bail jumpers or prison escapees into the Indian Territory, apprehending them, and bringing them back under custody to face the federal magistrate in Fort Smith. Sometimes, he even showed them his deputy United States marshal's badge. Tina and her friends seemed to think it was all just so exciting.

After countless hours on dusty trails, bad food in endless small towns, or a surly renegade as your only company for days or weeks on end, well, home life such as he was now enjoying was tasting fine, indeed. Sprawled out on the divan in the main living room, Bobby was completely at ease. He was to use the carriage later on to pick up his date for the evening, a nice widowed lady friend of Ruthie's. They had met by chance at Goldsmith's on Main Street, where Bobby had gone to purchase some fragrances Angie had wanted.

The sales clerk was otherwise occupied, and Bobby simply asked the attractive lady standing nearby. "Is this sachet long-lasting? It smells marvelous!"

A smile as he held it toward her was his opening.

"I really don't understand all the variety of types of room fragrances available."

The lady sniffed daintily at the offered package and smiled again, looking Bobby directly in the eyes. "Well, this is a very nice one, and you simply replace it after it loses its aroma. This one here is a potpourri—mostly of rose petals I think; you simply pour as much as you want into a small bowl or dish to set out." She extended it toward Bobby to sniff, a smile on her face.

"Oh, that one is very nice, too! Why so many sizes of those bags of it?"

"Oh, a bag in one of the larger sizes can last you for months or do several rooms."

Bobby's reply included a gallant invitation. "Well, thanks for helping me understand this! I think I'll get a couple of the sachets, plus a smaller bag of the potpourri to start. And are you free for dinner this evening?"

"You are most welcome, and it so happens I am available for dinner. What did you have in mind?"

"Well, the Gayoso House Hotel next door has a very nice grill and restaurant. Would you like to meet there about seven? Or should I pick you up? I have a carriage just outside."

"Let's meet in the lobby at seven."

"Excellent! By the way, I'm Robert Cunningham."

"It is lovely to meet you, Robert. I'm Beverly Hotchkiss."

"The pleasure is mine, Miss Hotchkiss!"

"Please, call me Bev or Beverly, not Miss Hotchkiss!"

"And you can call me Bobby if you'd prefer; or Robert is fine. I'll see you at seven."

Paying for his purchases, Bobby walked out of Goldsmith's with a bounce in his step.

———————◆———————

At precisely seven that evening, Beverly Hotchkiss walked into the lobby of the Gayoso House Hotel. Bobby Cunningham was already waiting to meet her.

His attire was not remarkably different from what he'd been wearing that afternoon—a waistcoat over dressy trousers over riding boots and a loosely knotted cravat at his neck set off the pleated-front white shirt he was wearing. His long dress coat was draped loosely over the divan upon which he had, moments before, been seated.

For her part, Beverly was similarly attired in smart "dressy casual" fashion with a light long fabric scarf across her bare shoulders and a flouncy skirted dress suitable for any occasion. All that topped off a pair of leather shoes polished to a mirror-like sheen.

"My, don't you look lovely!" Bobby had stepped forward, extending both hands.

Taking both his hands in hers, Beverly's reply was quick. "Well, thank you, sir! It's kind of you to say so!"

"Are you hungry? I took the liberty of reserving a table so we could go right in. Or, if you'd prefer, we could look around for a little while before dinner, if you're not quite ready to eat yet."

"Oh, let's eat now and look later. I've heard you can go up high to balconies that overlook the river. I'd love to see that at night."

"Certainly, as you wish."

Bobby then motioned for the maître d'hôtel to assist; that functionary immediately began to glide over and greeted Bobby and Beverly with a broad smile.

"Welcome this evening for dinner, Mr. Cunningham and your very lovely guest."

"Hello again, Charles; delighted to be here!"

Ushered to their table, Bobby stood while Charles seated Beverly, and then he took his seat across from her.

After their orders were taken, conversation started with a comment from Beverly. "Well, Mr. Cunningham, it certainly seems you're known here!"

"Yes, I'm afraid that's so. I've been coming here occasionally since my half-sister got married here back near the beginning of the war, back in 1861. Did you know they quartered Union officers here at the hotel during the war and, after, during the occupation?"

"How fortunate for them, not having to live out of a tent!"

Bobby laughed heartily. "May I also say how absolutely lovely you are tonight? All the way down to your shoes, you are an absolute vision of feminine pulchritude! I've never seen ladies' shoes with such a shine; are they new?"

"Heavens, no! My husband taught me to polish them that way. Now, don't look so distressed; I'm a widow. My husband, God rest his soul, was a captain in the Federal cavalry and was, indeed, quartered here in the Gayoso House. He wrote to me of it, and Memphis in general, in such glowing terms that I took his recommendation to come, if I ever could, and see it for myself. I did, and I stayed!"

Somehow, during the delicious meal and further conversation that followed, Beverly's wrap had managed to slip down a little from her shoulders, revealing what Bobby observed as the beginnings of a very promising chest. As she leaned toward him during further conversation, Bobby was certain it was very, very interesting!

"So, you just up and moved to Memphis? Nothing to hold you back?"

"Not really. A few months after my husband, my four-year-old son died as well, so Cincinnati no longer held any particular allure."

Bobby's next words were said with true compassion, having seen death firsthand himself.

"I'm truly sorry for your losses. Was your husband taken in the war?"

"No, he made it all the way through, without so much as a scratch, only to come back home to me and then get killed by falling out of a tree and breaking his neck! At least, he didn't suffer I believe. My boy, Billy, died of yellow fever."

"My stepfather also died of yellow fever; it's a horrible death. You have my complete sympathy."

Something in Bobby's facial expression comforted Beverly tremendously, and she reached over to lay her hand atop his gently. She took a new path for their conversation. "I have a really good friend with the same last name as you."

"Really? And who might that be?"

"My friend is Ruthie Cunningham, and she is married to a fine man, an attorney, I believe, and she has two of the most delightful little ones."

"I know her well; her husband is my brother Oskar!"

"I must say, this must be fate—or something close to it!"

"What do you mean?"

"Ruthie told me she wanted very much for me to meet her brother-in-law. She said we'd be perfect for each other. You aren't by any chance a deputy US marshal, are you?"

"Guilty as charged! I'm deputized for the Western District of Arkansas, and I lived in Fort Smith until a little while ago. I've pretty much decided I'm staying in Memphis from now on to help take care of my mom and my half-sister. Now that my stepfather has passed on, I'll need to be the man of the house. Plus, I believe I've found, this very evening, a powerful reason to stay."

Beverly's blush was fleeting but sincere.

Their main courses had been finished for a while, so Bobby asked the question that had been burning in his mind for a while. "Dessert? Or would you like to see that balcony view of the river now?"

"Oh, let's go on up and see it now, if we can!"

As they left the table, Bobby offered his arm discreetly to Beverly, and she, just as discreetly, slid her arm into the crook of his, bringing her intoxicatingly close to him for a moment as they moved out of the dining room.

Many sets of eyes followed the gorgeous couple as they made their way back to the lobby, and onto the wide staircase that led upward toward the rooms.

After going up a couple of floors, Bobby paused on the landing. "It's a total of seven floors, I'm afraid. Do you need to stop for a moment to catch your breath?"

Beverly looked around after the question. Seeing no one, she stepped close to Bobby, and taking his face in both hands and standing on tiptoe, she kissed him passionately full on the lips.

Her reply was brief. "No, I just needed that!"

"Is that so?"

"I've wanted to do that since I first walked into the lobby, and I couldn't wait any longer."

"Well, before we go further, I took the liberty of booking a room for myself for tonight, in case our engagement went long into the evening. If I then needed to drive you home, I wouldn't have to disturb our household by coming in very late. I could simply come back here to stay the night. If you do not have to be back yourself for anyone or at any specific time, you are welcome to spend the night here with me."

"Ruthie was right when she said I really needed to meet you!"

"Seventh floor balcony then?"

"Lead the way."

Arm in arm, occasionally pausing to renew that delicious first kiss, they made it up to the seventh floor and started down the hallway.

Instead of going down to the public observation balcony down at the end of the hallway, Bobby stopped in front of the door of room 718 and inserted his key. Opening the door to the Regent Suite, he invited Beverly in. "The balcony is just over there, through those French doors. Or the bathroom is just there to your right, if you need it."

"Thank you, sir. I do. All that climbing, you know. I'll join you on the balcony in a moment."

As Bobby opened the balcony doors and let in the cool night air, he heard a delighted cry. "My goodness, a flush toilet! And running water, too! What luxury!"

As he stood on the balcony, with his hands on the rail and enjoying the view, moments later, he felt arms encircle his waist and another body draw impossibly close to his. The arms, however, were encased in fluffy cotton sleeves.

When he turned to look, he was met by Beverly's grinning face, straining up to kiss him once more. This time it was a full-on, open-mouthed affair, full of swirling tongues, pressing bodies, and roaming hands.

As they finally broke apart, Bobby was somewhat startled to see that the robe Beverly had found in the bathroom was now lying crumpled on the balcony floor, and she stepped forward and was now standing, as Bobby had been earlier, at the railing. Her hands were out on the rail, and her feet were slightly apart, her delicious derriere fully exposed to his view and her extremely comely breasts pendant. Her nipples stood out as firm projections into the cool night.

"This view is truly magnificent."

"It most certainly is!"

"I hope you don't think of me as totally scandalous, but this was the chance of a lifetime. I just couldn't pass it up! I could never have imagined the opportunity to do this."

Just as he was about to reply, a discreet knock at the door drew his attention. "Stay here and enjoy the moment for as long as you'd like. I'll be right back."

At the door to the suite as he opened it, a bellman rolled in a serving cart with a generous bowl of chopped ice with a large bottle of French champagne in the middle, already sweating rivulets, the droplets coursing down the bottle as it cooled. Two beautiful wine glasses stood on either side.

Rapidly scrawling his signature for the extra room charge, Bobby tipped the bellman five dollars and escorted him out, closing the door quietly but firmly behind him.

Whether the bellman had or had not noticed the strikingly attractive naked blonde's backside leaning on the balcony railing was left unsaid.

He most certainly had.

Bobby's reputation and respect with the hotel staff had just gone up several notches.

Rolling the champagne over closer to the bed, Bobby went back onto the balcony.

This time, it was Bobby's turn to encircle Beverly's waist.

"Just stand there and let me admire you."

He kissed her cheek and followed it in a series of kisses that descended to the fascinating nape of her neck and then continued down the center of her back.

At the beautiful divide between her delicious cheeks, Bobby dropped to his knees and spread them apart and then nestled his face between, his tongue beginning to lick wantonly.

He stayed there as her sharp gasps for air and fervid moans threatened to become loud enough to draw other guests to their balconies to see what was happening.

Because he could absolutely not help himself, he continued kissing down one leg and back up the other before turning her gently into his arms for a long-awaited, deeply-passionate kiss. Swooping her up easily and gently into his arms, he carried her to the side of the bed, laid her gently in, and followed with a question.

"The view just after sunrise is spectacular as well. Would you like to take it in, too?"

"Naked or clothed?"

"Your choice."

"Oh, I was hoping you would say that."

Chapter 15

HEADLONG FLIGHT

When the unseasonably warm winter; wet spring; and long, hot summer created ideal mosquito-producing conditions in 1878, Memphians were subjected to the worst epidemic of yellow fever yet seen in that ill-fated city. Still not knowing what brought the disease or how it spread, white residents fled the city in droves, in their haste sometimes leaving their houses wide open with possessions inside! Black residents, poorer or less able to travel (and often assumed to be immune), stayed and died right along with white citizens. After the epidemic had run its course, black citizens began to fill jobs vacated by whites, giving them an increased economic power that lasted for several decades.

1878

Bobby and Beverly were married six weeks after that memorable night downtown at the Gayoso House.

Beverly had been amazingly frank with Bobby from the start. From the time he first lovingly placed her on the bed in the hotel room, right up to the time they were ready and about to take their vows, she told Bobby exactly what she did and did not want out of her relationship.

On the side of the bed, she had told Bobby (who was still fully clothed) in a very serious voice, "Sweetheart, I'm a woman and not a girl, and I was married to a very virile and strong man for six years. I've had a baby. I love sex, so love my body all you want."

She continued as she rolled back onto the bed and stretched out before him. "I've had other men in the intervening years since my husband passed on, but you are the first I've had any real interest in, and I haven't even had you yet! So, don't feel like I'm a porcelain doll that will break; you don't have to always be 'kid-gloves' gentle with me. But do remember that slow and comfortable can be very nice for both of us, from time to time."

Bobby leaned over and kissed her very gently as she went on.

"You're a very, very handsome man, and I know you realize that, quite well indeed! You're probably used to getting any woman you set your eyes on. But if we're going to have a chance together, your roving eye needs to come to an end. If that can't be, and be completely honest here, just let me know, and we'll call it a night right here."

"Well! That was frank. You can't scare me off that easily, Beverly, my dear, I was, and have been, exactly the man you describe. My physical satisfaction was all I was looking to relieve; but in the last few years, I've begun to change. I've started to look to my future as a family man, and it sort of came to a head with my stepfather's death. I realized that I needed to start work on becoming the man I was meant to be. And then, magically, you showed up in my life! I'm looking to begin my future right here with you, if you're interested. There'll be no roving eye from me!"

"Then, why don't you get those very nice clothes off and climb into this very comfy bed with me?"

"My aim, fair lady, is to please you and only you."

Bobby began to strip his clothing while Beverly rolled over and laid up on one elbow, watching with keen interest. As he got his boots, trousers and undergarments off and stood before her naked, she couldn't help but whistle and comment. "My, my, my, my, my! If all those Johnny Rebs had had weapons like that, they wouldn't have lost! Please come in and make yourself comfortable."

The Gayoso House Hotel had been built in 1842 and remodeled in 1859. During both of those times, an eye toward guest comfort and quiet rest was paramount. Unfortunately, not as much was known about soundproofing as would come later.

It was sorely needed that night.

———————◆———————

The sky had lightened somewhat when Bobby began to feel the wet, wonderful tug of seeking lips on the tip of his already erect staff, and he looked through eyes still blurry from too much champagne and blistering sex, only to see changes in the density and texture of the shadows surrounding the bed. Rhythmic variations in those changes began to outline Beverly's head, bobbing up and down, while her mouth, so full of passion and apparent enjoyment, made soft slurping sounds as she moved. She had moved a hand up to the base of his shaft, and had grasped his stones and was delicately kneading them as her mouth continued its marvelous discourse.

Just as Bobby was about to tell her that the mounting pressure of a coming climax was soon to follow if she didn't stop (and he did not want her to stop!), Beverly spoke first. "Sweetheart, don't hold back. I want all you have in my mouth. I had your beautiful load inside me last night filling me up, and now I want to taste you and swallow your seed. I want to have you in every way I can think of, and every way you can think of, too!"

As Bobby's deep, extended groan announced the start of his release, Beverly began to suck with even more power and intensity. When he did climax, he felt like he had given her at least half a gallon.

He must have given her at least what she expected, as she rolled over on her back and swallowed and smacked her lips appreciatively. She used her fingers to wipe up every morsel of creamy effluent that had escaped her eager mouth and then licked and sucked them clean as she gazed lovingly up at Bobby.

"My goodness, but you are tasty. That was delicious, and so much of it. Sleep for a couple more hours, darling; rest and reload. I have some-thing else I want to try with you later."

Bobby didn't immediately feel as though he could go back to sleep. But with Beverly's plush body warmly snuggled next to him, her soft, ample breasts pressed against his back and her arm lovingly over his chest, Bobby drifted back off into a warm, pleasant slumber as the sky gradually lightened outside.

Sometime later, his drowsiness made him barely aware of her naked form headed for the bathroom. After a few minutes, she returned, and Bobby was treated to a marvelous view of her front side as she came back to the bed and climbed in.

Bobby's immediate desire was tempered by the urgent need to relieve his bladder in the toilet. "Pardon me, my dear. I must go take care of a very pressing need of my own. I'll be right back."

"Please, do. I'm ready to try something with you that I've been thinking about all night!"

To his significant relief in the bathroom, Bobby let loose a mighty stream and then, in a sudden wave of embarrassment, realized his mas-sive outpouring and mighty groan could probably be heard all the way to the lobby, if not Cleveland. With a chagrinned look on his face, he pulled the chain on the toilet, tried to tame his unruly hair (with very little success) while it was flushing and then turned and studied himself briefly in the mirror, before stepping back into the bedchamber.

As he walked toward the bed naked, Bobby's appendage couldn't help swinging back and forth, hitting first one thigh and then the other as he walked.

Beverly sat in the bed, naked herself, staring in obvious appreciation.

Bobby climbed back into the bed, casually noting it was now growing pretty light outside, and if she wished to do so with any pri-vacy or anonymity, Beverly ought to step onto the balcony soon for the early-morning view, if she still desired that particular pleasure. He said as much to her as she watched his naked form climb gracefully into the bed.

"Well, you incredibly sexy man, I'm desiring a new pleasure from you right now, so that view will just have to wait for later. Now, roll over on your side and let me get in front of you."

Bobby did as he was told, thinking casually, *"I could begin to like this being told what to do during sex!"*

Beverly came around the bed, treating Bobby to delightful jiggles in doing so. She then leaned forward, and after giving him a quite lascivious open-mouthed, tongue-filled kiss, she did the same for his now-stiffening manhood. She concentrated on the tip, with significant effect.

When her hand had detected a degree of hardness satisfactory for her purposes, Beverly took a small bottle from the bedside table and slid into bed, with her gorgeously-generous backside pressed firmly against Bobby's stiffness.

"I hope you'll like this. I love it and I've been thinking about doing it with you, all night long," Beverly moaned.

With that, she opened the small bottle and poured some into her hand; reaching back, she grasped Bobby's shaft and rubbed it with the cream, up and down, until her hand slid easily along it. She then reached between her cheeks and rubbed there, making soft moans as she did.

"Now, just relax. I'll do everything for you." She then returned her hand to Bobby's manhood, which was at full attention by this point, and guided into the cleft between the cheeks of her derriere; holding him firmly, she guided him in small circles around the hole located there, while she moaned further.

"No, lover. Just be still as you can. I'll handle this." Beverly's voice had a texture of pure lust just now.

She then proceeded to guide him into her hole, slowly at first and then she pressed herself back onto his staff, which quickly sank deep into her tight, exciting, forbidden hole.

"Ohhhh!"

Beverly's guttural moan was equaled by Bobby's.

She slowly slid herself off Bobby's length, almost to the tip, and held it there for moments.

"Aahh!"

Beverly's deep sigh carried the satisfaction of the physical sensations her body produced, as well as the emotional satisfactions from satisfying a deep-seated desire.

Bobby was having indescribable sensations himself. But aside from heavy breathing, he hardly made a sound.

It was obvious to him that Beverly was fulfilling her own need, and he was glad to let her have that for herself.

Her upper leg began shaking with her second thrust onto Bobby, which was even deeper, if that was possible. She held him inside her until he thought he was going to explode, and then she pulled out to the tip again and held it there for a deliciously long interval.

Her next sinking was more of an urgent plunge, completely submerging him inside her tight pressure. The leg shaking was now highly pronounced, as was the sharp intake of breath, followed by the most pronounced passionate sound yet. "Oh, Bobby, take all of me! Ohhh!"

Bobby was struggling mightily at this point not to lose his control. He wanted this marvelous woman to have all the pleasure she could get from using his body. For, make no mistake about it, Beverly was using Bobby's body.

Whether it was the luxurious surroundings or the length of time since she'd had a man or even just her admiration of Bobby himself, something had brought out a deeply held need in her, and he was determined to give her all she needed for the complete fulfillment of that craving.

After Beverly's next near extraction, her final push onto Bobby was so absolutely wanton that her sudden shout of orgasm caused him to finally lose his control and shoot his entire load deep into her, which caused her to again shout as the leg shakings now became closer to full body.

Her hand went out to Bobby as he tried to get close to her and bring her whatever comfort he could, pushing him back away from her as she continued to shake and moan.

He rolled over on his back and watched her in amazement and admiration as she, too, rolled onto her back. Spreading her legs and putting her knees up, she lifted herself slightly and put both her hands between her legs, one from the top and one from underneath. She began to rub herself as the leg-shaking continued and her moaning got louder. From time to time she brought a glistening hand, wet with Bobby's juices, up and looked lovingly at it before putting it in her mouth and sucking it dry.

Right when it seemed she might do physical harm to herself by continuing, she subsided, just lying there legs spread wide, with each of her beautiful nipples being pulled and stretched hard between two fingers from each of her still-moist hands.

She lay there, her face turned toward Bobby, looking at him as she fingered and nippled herself breathlessly into a semblance of calm. Her look was one of absolute pleasure and satisfaction.

Her next words were a surprise. "Well, if I'm going to enjoy that morning view of the river, I guess I'd better get out there. Come join me, when you can, if you'd like."

With that and a marvelous open-legged swing off the bed that left nothing to the imagination, she was gone in a flash out the balcony doors.

In an instant, she was there at the rail, hands apart gripping it and feet apart standing on the balcony floor. She stood there, looking down on the bustling panoramic view below, drinking it all in, her head with its tousled blonde hair swinging back and forth. She stood there, totally and unashamedly naked!

Bobby got up a few moments later, unable to miss the giant wet spot on the bed that marked the scene of their latest escapade. He grinned to himself as he thought of having to look any of the hotel staff in the eye on his next visit.

As Bobby stepped through the balcony doors a moment later, he couldn't help but admire the comely figure before him, unabashedly watching the river scape below. Her fantastic bottom glistened with residual moisture, and a small stream of discharged white overflow coursed its way down one of her thighs and just made it to her knee while he watched. Bobby thought it might be the most uninhibited and sexiest thing he'd ever seen.

The fellow guest three balconies over silently enjoying his morning cigar could not have agreed more.

After he'd spun her around and given her a good nipple-sucking and a passionate kiss, Beverly lovingly grasped his manhood and led him back through the balcony doors into the bedroom, where she also saw the wet area on the bed and put her hands to her face in mock horror.

"Whatever will they think of us?" she moaned mockingly.

"My reputation here will be ruined," Bobby replied drolly.

"I think it will only be enhanced," Beverly mocked.

They walked out of the hotel, arm in arm, at a little past nine that morning. They were redressed in the previous evening's clothes. They went directly to Bobby's carriage, brought up by the livery valet while Bobby signed for the hotel charges, and made their way to Beverly's rental abode off Poplar Avenue.

From there it was on to the Woodlawn house for Bobby. He figured he probably had some explaining to do. He also figured it was worth it.

◆

Bobby met Angelina at the door of the Woodlawn house as she was coming back in from walking down to the Bethel house and having coffee with Ruthie. While she had been there chatting with Oskar's wife, she absolutely cooed over how beautiful little Robert and Rose were getting. Together, they had made plans for lunch around the family dining table there at Woodlawn, she and Ruthie having several items for discussion with other members of the family. Angelina had spoken to her mom and Sally about a big family lunch before she had left for the Bethel house, and Sally was well underway with preparations for it.

Bobby and Angelina met at the door; he was about to open it.

Angelina spoke first. "My, you're dressy for this time of day, big brother. What's the occasion?"

"Out all night from a dinner engagement."

"Would it happen to be anyone I know?"

"Well, I don't know exactly, but Ruthie does."

"I was just down the street with her and the babies, and she didn't say anything about introducing you to anyone."

"That's because she didn't. I met her independently, before Ruthie could introduce us, so we met for dinner last night."

"Must have been some dinner!"

"Well, it was, and we talked for hours, it seemed. Then we went up on the balcony and saw the river at night. We found it very romantic."

"You think it's serious?"

"I sure hope so."

"Well, good for you, big brother! We all will talk more about it at family lunch later."

Angelina made a quick suggestion before they went through the front door. "Bobby, my sweet, you'll probably want to go upstairs quickly and change before everyone gathers around the table."

"Good idea, sis! Do you think there's time for me to bathe first?"

"Take time; it'll be worth it."

The house was open for the early-spring breezes, and Bobby was able to slip quietly up the stairs and down to his room. There, he put out clean clothes, stripped out of his evening outfit, and then wrapped a towel around himself. He then padded down the hall to the bath and began to fill the tub.

As Bobby sank himself slowly into the tub, he could feel the tiredness flowing from his bones. As he lay back with his arms over the sides, he looked down at his attachment lying there floating in the water. "Well, Mr. Willy, what have you gotten us into this time?"

After he lathered, scrubbed, and rinsed, Bobby stepped out of the tub to a fluffy towel and vigorously dried himself. He wrapped himself in the towel and then went the short distance to his room, where he changed into the clothes he had laid out earlier.

Neat, clean, and proper, Bobby went down the stairs to the table.

Angelina was sitting across the table from Ruthie, who was between her two babies, little Robert and Rose. After gently kissing his mother, Bobby took a seat next to Carmella, who was seated next to Angie at the head of the table.

Last to arrive at the luncheon was Oskar, who came in just after Bobby had sat himself. Oskar kissed Ruthie and sat on the other side of Robert, who was busy trying to see if the napkin ring would hold his tin soldiers. Rose was kicking the bottom of her booster seat and making up some sing-song little melody to go with it. Tina was sitting next to, and absolutely charmed by, her baby cousin and beamed at her.

As Sally began to bring in the dishes of food, Bobby couldn't help but compare this picture of family life to the emptiness he'd known for so many years in his own life.

After meeting Beverly, hope for this sort of future—for a family with children and grandchildren of his own—did not now seem to be so far-fetched.

As if on cue, Angelina said, "Ruthie, did you know Bobby's met someone new? He said she was a friend of yours. Tell her, Bobby."

Angie spoke next. "Yes, do tell us all, Bobby! Who is she?"

A chorus of agreement caused Bobby, normally a very quiet man, to yield to the pressure and address the whole table. "Her name is Beverly Hotchkiss, and she's awfully nice! She's extremely pretty, a widow, and she moved to Memphis from Cincinnati. We had dinner at the Gayoso House last night and talked for what seemed like hours. I took her upstairs to the seventh floor to the balcony view of the river, and she seemed to enjoy that very much. She really seems to love Memphis. I'd like you all to meet her, maybe here for dinner sometime."

Angie's reply was quick in coming. "Please do invite her, for as soon as she can make it. We are all, I'm sure, anxious to meet her."

Ruthie could not help putting in her glowing recommendation of Beverly. "Well Bobby, good for you! She is everything you described and more, and I had planned to introduce her to you at the earliest opportunity. But you've beaten me to it. How in the world did you do that?"

"Believe it or not, we met at Goldsmith's downtown, where I was looking for room fragrances for Mama. She helped me understand the differences between scent packaged in sachets or loosely packaged as potpourri in bags. Well, she was so helpful and so pretty, I went out on a limb and asked her to dinner! And she said yes. So the rest is, as they say, history."

After Bobby finished speaking, Carmella leaned toward him and whispered softly for Bobby's ears only, "Don't they have guest rooms on the seventh floor?"

"Yes, they do."

"Well, don't all those rooms have their own private balconies?"

"Yes, they do."

"And what time did you get in this morning?"

Good old Carmella didn't miss a thing. She hadn't since he was a little boy.

The dinner Bobby brought Beverly to was a roaring success, and the whole family was delighted with her. She held her own in conversation, and the two youngest members of the family were absolutely enthralled with her ability to entertain them.

In their subsequent times alone, both clothed and unclothed, they discussed many things—such as where they might live when they married; whether Bobby would or could continue as a marshal; and, of course, children and how many.

Unlike other times in his family, Bobby could not ask Beverly's father for her hand (he had been deceased for years, along with her mother), so he simply came out and asked her.

He wasn't surprised so much as relieved when she said yes. He really did not know what he would have done if her answer had gone the other way.

Their unclothed grappling continued unabated; if anything, they became more heated and adventurous. They both had the realization that, if they were to spend the rest of their lives together, they probably needed to get any questionable likes or dislikes out in the open before they became problems.

In one such discussion, while Bobby was lavishing her left nipple (he had just treated the right one to the same series of chewing, pulling, and kissing), Beverly asked a question rather casually. "What did you do for sex when you were out West? Aren't women pretty scarce out there?"

Bobby continued to rub her extremely moist crotch as he spoke. "Yes, my dear, they are. Most of the unmarried women (and a surprising number of the married ones, too!) are prostitutes. So, sex is available, if you are willing and able to pay for it."

"Did you ever do that? Pay for it, I mean?"

"Occasionally, I had to. As the old saying goes, 'There're only so many times you can flog your own horse,' and sometimes you need that company. It's not just about relieving the urge."

"I never thought of it that way. Does it really get lonely out there?"

"Sometimes you can ride for days on end without seeing another soul. Some of the men who spend most of their time out in the desert or the badlands can be so crazy from the sun, the weather, and the loneliness they're no longer fit for human company."

"What's it like to pay for it? Is it still good, even if you have to pay?"

"The thing you learn is that it's pretty impersonal. There's no love there, nor even like! It's a business transaction, nothing more. The physical feeling is the same, but it doesn't fulfill the need for companionship. It can leave you unsatisfied."

"I didn't know that. That doesn't make it sound too great."

"It's not the best. But except for the loneliness of your own hand, sometimes it's the best you can do."

Beverly seemed genuinely interested, even though she was breathing quite heavily due to Bobby's continued digital manipulation of her female regions, so Bobby decided the time was right to make his biggest confession. "I have always had certain standards, such as I would never approach a woman I knew to be married. This limited me severely, because unattached single women in the West are rarer than loose gold nuggets in Mississippi."

Beverly was close to climax now but managed to ask another question between gasps. "What about women who approached you, you handsome devil?"

"Women who approached me, I always asked if they were married; if they said yes, but they wanted me because their husband was gone or an abuser, I'd use my own discretion and act accordingly. Widows were the most likely attachments for me; they had a strong tendency to be very honest about what they liked and what they wanted from me. But prostitutes could give me one thing I desired that I never found much of in unattached women."

She was really close now but silently signaled him to continue.

"Well, and you can check with my mom on this, since I was in school, I've always enjoyed two girls at the same time. That's something prostitutes would do easily, especially if you were paying for the whole night with both of them. After I would finish and needed to rest, they had each other to kiss, lick, and rub while I watched. Let me tell you, two women can go at each other for a long time, and that could really get me up and ready to go again."

"Oohhh! Oooohhh!"

Beverly's cries of passion split the evening as she came.

After her shuddering body subsided and her frantic chest-heaving breathing returned to a more normal state, Beverly just lay there looking over thoughtfully at Bobby for quite a while before she spoke again.

Bobby was getting a little worried he might have crossed a line in telling her all this, but she had said she wanted frank honesty.

"Bobby, you sure know how to make a woman lose control. That was incredible. I came so hard in the part about two girls I thought I would wake up the whole house!"

Bobby continued to nip at the inner part of her thigh as he spoke. "I'm afraid you may have, my dear, but probably just Mom or Carmella."

"I forgot we were here at your house, darling, and I let myself get carried away. But while we're talking, and that feels really good by the way, what did you mean when you said I could ask your mom?"

"I meant just that! Mom saw me, at least a couple of times, with two girls at once having sex upstairs in the Bethel house where Oskar lives now. I don't think she knows that I know, but I saw her watch us having sex. She didn't say anything at the time or even later." Bobby paused midsentence to take a large and slow tongue passage up Beverly's glistening split, to her extreme pleasure, before he continued. "But I know for a fact that she saw us, and even watched for a while, before she snuck back down the stairs. She never even said a word, though. Mom keeps a lot of stuff to herself, though. But you could ask her; she'd probably tell you."

"Bobby, as exciting and interesting as your story about your sexual adventures in the West was, it did bring up a point I need and want to make."

Bobby completed another tongue slurp and then lifted his head from her crotch. "I'm all ears, my darling."

"You most certainly are not, you mountebank, you! Your ears are a very small part of your prowess.

"Bobby my love, what I want and need to tell you is that I too enjoy the touch of another woman in bed. After my husband died, a special friend I had at the time comforted me in my grief. Slowly and gently, she introduced me to the 'sisterhood of love' as she called it, and I was smitten. Since I left Cincinnati, I haven't had another woman, but your story of two women in bed with you gave me visions. If the opportunity comes along, don't hesitate to ask me, and I'll do the same for you."

Bobby's erection, semisoft only moments before, sprang to attention. With his still-glistening face inches above hers and his shaft plunging madly into her well-lubricated receptacle, they both climaxed quickly and collapsed into a tangled heap of arms and legs.

They finally separated and fell asleep.

That night (and more to follow) passed with the two lovers exploring each other in words and deeds before Bobby "popped the question."

The side entrance to the Woodlawn house came in handy, as did the private bath.

Carmella kept Angie up on everything she saw.

Angie was quite pleased.

———————◆———————

The Woodlawn house, like the Bethel house before it, had fitted screens on the windows. This allowed free air circulation for the outside air through the house, helping to keep it cool in all but the most sweltering days (of which Memphis, to this day, has plenty!), aided in no small part by the overhanging shade trees that surrounded the house.

They also kept the vast majority of bugs and flying insects outside, where they belonged.

When Val Dimand had commissioned the building of the Bethel house for his growing family almost thirty years before, window screens were an almost unheard-of luxury. By the time he had the Woodlawn house constructed, they were much more common, but still the vast majority of the homes in Memphis did not yet have them.

The *Aedes aegypti* mosquitos, thick swarms of them in the summer of 1878, had a bloodsucking field day.

Bobby and Beverly had only been married for three and a half weeks when the first yellow fever death struck the Greenlaw Acres neighborhood.

They had moved easily into the Woodlawn house with the rest of the Dimand-Cunningham family and were fully immersed in the everyday life of the family, both of them deliriously happy to be a part of such riches yet totally immersed with each other. The bustle and blather of family life was strangely pacific to Bobby, while it was stimulating and energizing to Beverly.

Tina, absolutely charmed and impressed by Beverly's sophistication and worldly humor, began to see her mother "come out of her shell" as Angelina too was delighted with this vibrant new family member. Shopping, cooking, sewing, and a hundred other things the women did together during that early summer (now that Tina was out of school) took on a new flavor with the addition of Beverly.

Angie could not have been more delighted with her eldest son's new bride (her pleas had been answered!). And she reveled in how well the rest of the family meshed around her. The noises coming from their room late at night bespoke of the possibility of more grandbabies to dandle and, judging by the frequency and intensity of those noises, maybe soon.

When Major General Adolphus Terry came back to Memphis after the war, his first order of business was to build a new home right next door to his old friend Val Dimand, right there on Bethel Avenue. He felt his wife of more than twenty years, who had waited patiently through campaigns and conflicts, wars and far-flung postings without complaint, deserved no less. The spacious single-story house with the four sturdy columns supporting the wide front porch and its ever-present swing, where the two would often share the evening breezes arm in arm, was their new sanctuary until General Terry was laid to rest after a major heart attack.

The widow Terry, already a great neighbor to the Dimand-Cunningham family, became a beloved neighbor to Oskar and Ruthie after they took over the Bethel house. And how she did adore baby Robert and little angel Rose!

Sweet Mabel Terry, the first to die in the Greenlaw Acres neighborhood, would not be nearly the last to suffer the harrowing, withering effects of the stalking killer.

When one of the Bastrop boys brought the news of how they'd found the Widow Terry, alone, jaundiced, and burning up with fever, Oskar began to fear for his family (particularly Ruthie and the babies) with yellow fever right next door!

Mabel Terry died horribly, along with another neighbor from down the street. Oskar helped all he could to ease her suffering, to no real avail. She was quickly embalmed and interred right next to her beloved husband.

Oskar then moved all his family down to the Woodlawn house two days later. He also had begun to work downtown at closing his immediate affairs—in case they had to flee Memphis as he had heard of others doing.

The decision to leave the Bethel house was fairly heart-wrenching, particularly for Ruthie, who had gotten used to being in her own home. She had been the "woman of the house" for the better part of ten years by now, and she was reluctant to uproot everyone and move to a household full of other people.

Still, she understood why Oskar was so concerned that he was even considering moving them. The first time she'd seen Oskar with a mask over his face when he came home from next door and then washing endlessly once he arrived—and even then holding himself apart from her and his children for twenty-four hours to see if he developed symptoms—she had known deep down how serious it was.

Rather than fleeing willy-nilly, Oskar and Bobby talked with the women of the expanded household about an organized and calm departure that would allow them to also make an orderly return when circumstances warranted.

Where to go was a fairly easy decision. None of the women besides Angie had much experience with anywhere but Memphis, and her Texas experience in a tiny hard-won settlement made her not want to start that over again. Bobby spoke glowingly of Arkansas in general and its opportunities, and Oskar noted that many Memphians were using the isolation of the Mississippi River to guide them into settling in Arkansas. With the abundance of farmland available, the proliferation and growth of towns nearby to Memphis, and the variety of other inducements, Arkansas became their destination.

Oskar also pointed out, to Angie in particular, that their fresh start would not be as a destitute bunch of refugees. If they saw something they liked, they should be able to buy. This seemed to calm Angie.

Beverly sat to the side and didn't insert herself. She already knew she could and would go where she wanted, and right now, that was wherever Bobby Cunningham went. If he went to Arkansas with his wonderful family, then it was Arkansas for her.

Bobby's original plan, anyway, was to go to Fort Smith and close out his affairs there and then return to Memphis to her, which was just fine with her. But if he needed to return to them in a new place in Arkansas, she'd be right there, waiting anxiously for him. And, if he asked her to follow him to somewhere else, she'd gladly do that, too.

From Baltimore to Zanzibar or even the Sahara Desert, Beverly would follow Bobby anywhere.

They buried young Rose Ellen nine days later.

One afternoon, Ruthie had had her out in the back among the trees playing in the grass but brought her in early.

"The mosquitos were just too bad out there. I've never seen them this thick!"

Oskar simply nodded.

Later that afternoon, Rose was fussy and didn't want to eat. By bedtime, she was chilled, so Ruthie wrapped her in a blanket and sat nervously beside her little bed as she finally went fitfully to sleep, and her mom fell asleep herself. In the morning, Ruthie awoke to a child burning with fever, and the worry almost paralyzed her.

She went down and had Sally soak some dish towels in clean, cool water; she then went up and tried mightily to bring Rose's fever down—with no success.

Oskar went downtown that morning to the telegraph office and to the Union and Planters Bank, stopped by his office for a few moments, and told his clerk what to do over the next few days and then to take some time off for himself (and get out of town if he could). Then he went back home to Ruthie's side.

Rose Ellen's skin had a decidedly yellowish cast. And her eyes, normally cerulean standing out in the white background, were now decidedly yellowish where the whites should have been.

Rose Ellen would not eat, no matter how Ruthie tried.

Oskar stayed with them, holding on to Ruthie through her (and his!) tears, and then he went down the stairs, through the kitchen, out the back door, and into the shop at the stables.

An hour later, Oskar had finished constructing the small, yet sturdy wooden box to hold Rose. As he brought it inside, he could barely see through his tears to find his way back to the kids' bedroom where Ruthie sat with the convulsing three-year-old and little Robert, whose eyes were wide with wonderment and sorrow.

Ruthie gathered together enough strength to ask a favor of Oskar. "Honey, could you take Robert downstairs and get someone to be with him? Then, if you could come right back, we can stay together with Rose Ellen till the end."

"Good idea. I'll get him right down there. And then I have a brief task to take care of in between, and I'll be right back after that."

Oskar scooped little Robert, who was now almost five, up into his arms and kissed him before he set him back down and spoke softly to his little boy. "Robert, we're going down the stairs to find Granny. Won't that be nice? You'll stay with her for a little while, and then Mommy and Daddy will be there as soon as we can."

"What about Rose Ellen, Daddy? Will she be there too?"

"Yes, son, we'll bring Rose with us when we come."

At this, Ruthie gave out a small cry and burst into tears. Oskar clenched ramrod straight to try to maintain his own control.

He reached down and gently took Robert's little hand and led him toward the stairs. As they went down the steps of the Woodlawn house, Oskar's eyes were so blurry with his tears he almost lost his footing at the bottom and stumbled a little.

Little Robert, not yet five years old, reached out a hand and tried to comfort his father. "It's all right, Daddy. I'll take care of you, because I love you, Daddy."

Oskar didn't know how he could see to get down to the main floor, but he somehow managed to get there.

Angie came to the entranceway and met them.

"Ruthie's with Rose Ellen, and she's real sick. Can Robert come in and stay with you folks for a while? I need to get back to them, but I also need Bobby. Can you get him, please?"

One look told Grandma Angie the story. She'd never seen Oskar cry this much before, so she took Robert in her arms and called out over her shoulder. "Bobby! Come quick! Angelina! Come quick!"

Bobby came running up and took a look at Oskar; he put his arm around his brother immediately. "What can I do to help you, little brother? What do you need?"

"Help me get back to Ruth and Rose. She's very sick."

"You want me to drive somewhere?"

"Please Bobby, that would be good." Oskar spoke in a choked voice. "I built a little box to bury Rose in, and I need to get back up to Ruth before Rose is gone, so I can help her when the time comes. Could you do something for me?"

"Anything, Oskar! Just tell me what you need!"

"Could you go on over to the freight yard and see if they have an overland freight wagon we can use for the move to Arkansas? If they have one they can spare for a little while, see if you can get them to deliver it, with a team and a tarp to cover the back after it's loaded, around to the back of the Woodlawn house. Could you do that for me, Bobby?"

"Sure. Glad to."

<hr />

The wagon was in the back drive at the Woodlawn house before Oskar and Ruthie came down a little while later.

Their tear-stained faces and the little wooden box Oskar carried in his arms told the whole story. So no conversations ensued after their arrival, just a chorus of hugs and tender kisses.

Grandma Angie sat on a settee with Tina beside her, looking stricken. Angie motioned Ruthie over to sit beside her, and Tina got up for Ruth to sit there as she walked over to begin helping.

It did not take as long to load the wagon as you might think.

The first order of business for Bobby, however, was to dig a hole to bury little Rose. With spade in hand, he walked out to the stand of trees where Val was laid to rest, picked out a lovely spot, and plunged the spade into the rich earth.

"Well, Dad, I never thought you'd have companionship out here this soon, but little Rose Ellen will keep you company till we get back. I don't know how long that will be, but we will be back."

After the hole was dug, small but deep, Bobby trudged, heart heavy, back up to the house, where loading the wagon was proceeding apace. "It's time to bury Rose, Oskar." Sadder words Bobby didn't think he had ever spoken.

As the family trooped down to the family plot area, with Oskar helping the devastated Ruth and Bobby carrying little Rose in her box, the rest of the family (including Carmella) followed. Beverly had taken the job of tending for little Robert, and they followed the rest.

When the box was lovingly placed inside and the hole was filled, Bobby was called upon to speak final words over the little body, thus interred.

"Lord, none of us knows or understands why you called this young one to you, but we trust the greatness of your wisdom. Keep her at your bosom is all we ask until we can be reunited. Heaven was made just a little more beautiful today, Lord. Amen."

A chorus of amens followed.

Bobby didn't know it would be the better part of fifty years before another Cunningham stood on the grounds of the Woodlawn House.

As the last spadeful of dirt covered little Rose Ellen Cunningham's tiny box, Ruthie collapsed into Oskar's arms. He swung her up with one arm underneath her back and the other underneath her knees.

Absolutely the saddest task he had ever had in his life was carrying his helplessly grief-stricken wife back into the Woodlawn House to lie forlorn and awaiting departure from yet another family home.

The wagon, the buggy, and the carriage left later that afternoon.

No joy at all accompanied that procession, and scant hope for a future.

Chapter 16

HOME IN ARKANSAS

Much of the history and economics and even, to an extent, the population of Arkansas is inextricably tied to Memphis. Indeed, if not actually from the Bluff City, almost any settler in Arkansas almost certainly passed through Memphis on the way westward across the Mighty Mississippi.

Grandma Angie sat on one of the long front porch benches next to her daughter Angelina, reminiscing about the trip over from Memphis with her and the travails embodied within that grim journey.

Having one of her rarer lucid days, her memory for the places and times involved in this conversation was sharp and clear. Her recall of the people's names involved in the story was remarkable, and Angelina could only marvel at her total recall.

The three conveyances that had left the Woodlawn house that afternoon had made the short trip down to the waterfront and up to the loading ramp of the SS *Natchez*, which was berthed there. The previous day, the riverboat had unloaded her cargo of cotton bales destined for the grading houses and the warehouses along Front Street.

With the on-deck and below-deck areas cleared of such a load, there was plenty of room for the loaded freight wagon, as well as the carriage and buggy, all that the Cunningham family had brought on board to be lashed down topside, while the horses were housed below decks. The family occupied several staterooms.

Angie correctly recalled that she, Bobby, and Oskar (with Beverly,

Ruthie, and little Robert), along with Angelina, Tina, and Carmella constituted the entire group making the westward journey into Arkansas.

The *Natchez* put them ashore at Caruthersville, Missouri. From there, it was only a little more than two days' travel overland to the homestead, outside the town of Jonesboro.

When the family first rolled up on the property, as Angie recalled, the similarities between it and the homestead she and Robert W. had had in Texas more than forty years before were striking. The house, long and low in the ranch style, was already far superior to the cabin she'd left behind back in 1836 to return to Memphis. But it was nowhere near the equal of the Woodlawn house she had just left, nor, truth to be told, even the Bethel house.

Still, with the rapidly flowing creek just outside the back door of the house, the barn and another outbuilding, and a fenced corral, it wasn't as if they were starting from scratch. A waterwheel, with its bearings and driveshaft nestled in a small building made from rounded stones (probably from the creek bed), promised to be able to at least give them an ample supply of water into the house without having to carry it from the creek in buckets.

Nowadays, a windmill graced the landscape. Erected during Bobby's extended visit back to Jonesboro after he and Beverly had set off for Fort Smith, it now pumped clear, clean water from a deep well.

Bobby, Oskar, and young Robert (who nowadays wanted to be called Bob) had spent three days constructing and erecting the tower and another day getting the drive to the ground and hooked up to a continuous pump.

Robert (or Bob) as a teenager had turned into a strapping young man, reminding Angie very much of Robert W. Cunningham, her first love and Bob's grandfather. She said as much to Angelina as she described the similarities and differences between the Arkansas homestead and the prairie homestead in Texas all those many years before.

Sometimes, Angelina felt like her mother remembered a little too much and was a little too frank in telling about it. This turned out to be one of those occasions.

"Oh, honey, we need a blacksmith shop here, right on the property. Back in Texas, we got most of the food we needed without growing it ourselves, just by trading items like hinges and horseshoes that Robert W. would make for the neighbors in exchange for food that they grew."

"Mama, nobody here knows how to blacksmith."

"Perhaps so, my dear, but Robert taught himself."

"Besides, the blacksmith shop was fun for me, too! I remember it like it was just yesterday, how I used to sneak in there when Bobby was working in his leather apron. Well, he didn't wear any shirt with it (it being so hot and all). So I could come right up behind him and put my arms around his waist and then let my hands travel south of that."

"Oh, Mama! You should be ashamed for telling a story like that. What would people think of you?"

"I don't really care, my dear. Those are very pleasant memories for an old woman to hold onto."

"Speaking of, my darling daughter, your Billy is gone for lo these many years. How are you doing at finding a suitable husband? You're not too old, you know."

"No progress at all to report, Mama, I'm sad to say."

"Just give it a little more time, dear and keep your eyes open."

"All right, Mama, I will."

◆

Bobby and Beverly Cunningham, as displaced newlyweds, had left the Jonesboro area for Fort Smith about a week after the extended family got to the homestead and began to settle in.

It was a fortunate set of circumstances indeed that had let the family do this. Oskar had gotten word that the entire 140-acre parcel, including the house and all improvements, was available for quick purchase, as the previous owners wanted to head west and needed cash to do so.

He jumped at the chance, withdrew the money after negotiating a remarkable price, and completed the sale by viewing the location himself and paying "cash on the barrelhead" right then and there. Therefore, when other Memphians began to flee yellow fever in abject haste, Oskar and his family (all nine of them!) had made an orderly, prepared withdrawal in the face of such a devastating menace. This preparedness and order served all of them well in the coming weeks; months; and, indeed, even years.

The very day that Bobby and Beverly drove the buggy into Fort Smith, dusty and weary from the road and ready to close out Bobby's affairs in that burg and get on with married life was the day that James Diggs was finally brought in. This was significant for Bobby, as he had been in on several pursuits of Diggs, ever since Diggs had been indicted for the murder of Texas cattleman J. C. Gould back in 1873.

Finally in Judge Parker's courtroom, Diggs's fate was almost a foregone conclusion. Known far and wide as "the Hanging Judge," Parker frequently lived up to his notoriety by using the gallows he had had erected right next to the courthouse often enough to be guaranteed to draw a good-sized crowd to town on the day of the execution.

Bobby wryly thought that such entertainments showed off the basest bloodlust in people but were always counted on for a draw for hotels and saloons. That meant he and his bride had better find accommodations quickly before the word got out.

Bobby's deputizing as a US marshal was still valid, so he was unchallenged at the courthouse. Making his way to the cell where Diggs was being held, he finally was able to lay eyes on the man he had once been in pursuit of.

Bobby had left Beverly to enjoy a nice tub bath in the upstairs room of the Imperial Hotel on Crawford Avenue in downtown. He calculated that, having seen his fugitive, he'd better get back to the hotel and see what sort of marital duties his bride had dreamed up for him after her luxuriating soak.

His only hope, having secured lodging at this, the best hotel in town (according to his prior experience) was that the accommodations would keep her "in the mood" till his return. Nowhere near as sumptuous as the Gayoso House in Memphis, it would simply have to do.

Bobby needn't have worried. By her estimate several pounds of dirt lighter and randy as hell from sitting so close to her handsome husband for days over road bumps, Beverly was ready when he got back for some fireworks to begin.

Smelling wonderfully fresh, his bride began to prepare a nice, cool bath for Bobby. Easing him into the tub, she lathered and rinsed him, all the while lasciviously touching and kissing him in the most erotic manners she could come up with, many of which were pretty darned carnal, indeed.

By the time she had washed and rinsed his hair (twice) and had treated him to a different breast nipple for each time, Bobby was ready to step out of the tub a brand-new man!

Instead of going to the bed, where Bobby's bone-deep tiredness might make him fall into sleep too early, Beverly grasped his manhood and led him, instead, to the table. Her beautiful blonde bush parting to briefly reveal the pink gash hidden underneath, she hopped up and centered her delicious bottom onto the table and spread her legs. Putting her feet up on the table and with her knees spread wide apart, she began to stroke Bobby with one hand and herself with the other. The ripe air didn't have a breeze to stir it, and the darkened room was still.

After he had gotten a good look for at least two minutes, she spoke to Bobby in a low, husky voice. "You take over and rub yourself now, sweetheart. I'm going to need both my hands for this next part."

With that, Bobby did as he was told and watched, his amazement and erection growing as he did.

What Beverly had in mind, it seemed, was to see if the copious amount of lubricant flowing from her as she rubbed furiously at her aforementioned slit was enough to allow lubrication of her other hole to the point that two (or even three!) fingers would be able to treat that puckered little sphincter to the same furious plunging her vaginal hole now enjoyed.

From the moisture that was flying off her as she exorcised these tensions from her body, she was well on her way. She truly did need both hands, and the spectacle stiffened Bobby's manhood to a consistency of rugged steel. A light sheen of perspiration enveloped both of them in a soft glow in the muted light.

Just when he thought he was going to explode, Beverly replaced his hand with one of hers, after dipping it into her ever-present hand lotion, and rubbing his impressive erection's tip with it, she spoke again.

"Now, see if you can get that beautiful shaft in my bottom, and then go all the way in. If you can go all the way in, just hold very still with it completely inside me."

She barely croaked out the next words. "I want to move against you and make myself come! Please! Go in as deep as you can, and hold it there... Oh Yes!"

Bobby, trying to be the good husband, did as he was instructed. He was then treated to the absolutely raunchy vision of his beautiful blonde wife, her eyes alternately tightly closed and then staring straight into his in wanton lust and absolute abandon.

As she ground herself onto his shaft with powerful writhing, her moans and groans became lower in pitch by the moment, matching the intensity and frequency of her hip flexing.

Bobby was certain he had never seen anything like this, nor felt it either! He simply hoped he could hold his discharge until after she had had her complete emission and release.

Her wail told him he had made it as she shuddered and pressed hard against him; two hard and deep thrusts into her allowed him to release his whole load deep into her forbidden hole.

Overcome with desire and barely able to stand, Bobby knelt quickly between her legs and licked her slit, sometimes firmly and other times gently, as she held his head rigidly in place, moaning all the while.

Both lovers collapsed on the bed afterward and fell into a satisfied sleep.

The pangs of hunger awoke them in time to go and get supper. Just down the street, a nice dinner satisfied them both and sent them back and to bed, full and ready for an evening of lovemaking and sleep.

It was a good night.

The next day, Bobby took Beverly to his gunsmith shop, and she sat there and assisted him where she could to assemble and crate up his tools, parts, and equipment. Not intending to remain in Fort Smith beyond this trip, he had not yet decided where, or even if, he would reopen as a gunsmith. They could, with significant difficulty, transport all they had packed in the buggy, but it would be easier to ship by Wells Fargo Express, once they had decided where it needed to be shipped. The express agent said they could leave it with them for up to a month before they had to inform them of the shipping destination, so they did.

After a light lunch, they visited a couple of Bobby's in-town accounts, where Bobby introduced Beverly and explained that his family had moved from Memphis to northeast Arkansas and that they would be closing the Fort Smith shop and joining his family in Jonesboro.

While his customers were disappointed to hear of his departure, they were delighted with Beverly and considered Bobby fortunate indeed to have bagged such a beauty.

Afterward, they went to the courthouse, where Bobby introduced her to Judge Parker, who did his best to be charming. He also informed Bobby that his marshal's credentials would remain valid. He would be listed as "on long-term furlough," so he would be able to serve when and where he could.

A quick stop at the Western Union office to telegraph Oskar about their return to Jonesboro, and the happy lovebirds made their way back to the hotel, with time to rest before supper.

Bobby opened the window and drew the curtains shut before stripping off his shirt. Naked to the waist, he lay back on the bed and shut his eyes for a moment. A light breeze ruffled his chest hair as he relaxed and gazed at his bride.

Two hours later, his eyes snapped open. He looked over and saw his beautiful wife sitting in the stuffed chair, naked and rubbing herself languidly, and staring over at him. "Hello, sleepyhead! I had been sitting here looking at you for more than an hour when I got the idea to strip and do this to myself. It's very, very pleasant, and you can sure think of some erotic things to do while you're sitting here. And that's exactly the position I find myself in now."

Bobby looked down to his waist at the growing lump in his trousers and then back over at Beverly. Her grin easily matched his.

Supper was late that evening.

Oskar was amazed at how much more the house had become a home to them, after their first two weeks there.

Ruthie had really gotten busy on their bedroom after they had unloaded the wagon, and now it was a retreat for the two of them at night. Their bedroom was directly off the main living room, and the kitchen and dining room were behind the living room. It wasn't the Bethel House, but it was becoming home.

Grandma Angie and Carmella shared one of the two remaining bedrooms, and Angelina and Tina shared the other. Each opened with its own door into the living room, and they were separated by a hallway leading to a door that led outside to the outhouse.

For now, Robert spent his nights on the sofa in the living room.

Obviously, the living arrangements as they existed were not perfect, but everyone was pitching in and making do.

They had left Memphis in the middle of a major epidemic with nine people, and they hadn't lost anyone on the trip, although it had been touch and go with Carmella for a couple of days.

The reliable old (she was now over sixty but hadn't lost a step) cook and house servant had had a touch of fever for two days, and everyone feared the worst. The morning they got off the *Natchez*, she was at her lowest. She lay across the back seat of the carriage for the start of the overland part of the journey to Jonesboro, but her fever broke by noon.

By nightfall, good old Carmella was right as rain, and everyone breathed a sigh of relief. A couple of days of taking it a little bit easy let the treasured servant get "back up to speed," and she was ready to begin her duties in the new house.

The house had been built with one main fireplace in the living room and a smaller one, primarily for cooking, in the kitchen. One of the first things Oskar did was to order in a good cast-iron range and stove, and run the vent pipe out through the back wall and up the back side of the house to jut above the roofline.

Because everyone was sleeping on pallets on the floor after they arrived, a priority for Oskar was to order new mattresses for each bed in the house with all new bed frames. Since they could bring very little furniture with them as they fled Memphis, these purchases (and many others) were necessary to turn the bare house into a home.

What they *were* able to bring, in far greater quantity than most refugees, were clothes, bedding, and other cherished personal items such as books and keepsakes. This wise apportionment and allocation of space in the wagon meant a great deal to the displaced family. The new house became a home much quicker because of the things they had brought with them from Memphis.

The portrait of Robert W. Cunningham was one of these vital things. Carefully wrapped in blankets and firmly fitted into the overall wagonload, it made the trip without damage or incident.

With the whole family gathered 'round, Oskar lifted the painting gently up on the mantel and set it in place. "Welcome to your new home, Papa! I hope you find happiness here."

Because the family had had to leave so much furniture and other items behind in their two houses, Oskar had taken the time to establish tenancy for both the Bethel and Woodlawn houses before they left.

The freight yard kept on paying benefits for the Cunningham family, as Bob Allen, still the foreman of the yard under Wells Fargo's ownership, moved his wife and eight children into the spacious home. The cost to him was merely to see to the upkeep and management of the property and grounds until the Cunninghams could return.

Phil Reesthaus, who had been one of Val Dimand's pallbearers, moved into the Bethel house with his brand-new bride. Maintenance and caretaking of the property were also his only costs.

All this preparation prior to the family's departure was done after much consultation with Bobby and Angie. Bobby was able to give his brother excellent advice about what life in semirural Arkansas was going to be like, as well as essentials (like tools!) that the family would need right away and, thus, had to carry with them away from Memphis.

Having had to do it once before, it was Angie who stressed the importance of clothes, cookware, and eating utensils, as well as keepsakes in order for the family to establish a *home* as soon as possible. She told Oskar how it was Val who had taught her that valuable lesson when he'd brought her and the boys up out of Texas after Robert W. had died at the Alamo.

Angie had looked up as she remembered Val's words from long before. "If you can't easily replace it in Memphis, carry it with you!"

The family had used up two very busy days of packing essentials into bundles safe for travel in a wagon over potentially rough terrain; these bundles needed to be able to be easily carried by one person. And so the wagon load had thus been established, even before the wagon got there.

After the wagon came, loading had gone swiftly, partly because it was well prepared and partly because of the haste to put Rose Ellen to her grave and flee the awful curse that had claimed her young, unfulfilled life. It was a tough day.

The wagon had been a sort of lifeboat for their family. Along with the carriage (which held four, but in a pinch could hold six) and buggy (which held, pinch or no, only two), the wagon made many trips over the coming weeks to the rail station in the tiny but growing town of Jonesboro.

A fire had devastated the Main Street commercial portion of the town only a few months before. It had also destroyed (for the second or third time!) the courthouse as well. All had been rebuilt or was in the process of being rebuilt.

Several times, as he was picking up things like the stove, mattresses, and other furniture he'd ordered, Oskar was approached about carrying other loads away from the rail depot for hire. Oskar didn't need the money, but he did it anyway. He figured this was a way to get to know people who lived and worked there, as well as getting a look at ventures he could get into to help provide for the future of the family. Even at this early stage of life in Arkansas, he didn't feel cut out to be a farmer.

He planned to hang out his shingle as a lawyer, but he had to wait until the state of Arkansas certified his credentials, allowing him to practice law in their state.

Meanwhile, as he carried one of several loads of lumber away from the railhead to construction sites in town, the thought hit him. *A local sawmill could provide all their needs for decades!*

Crowley's Ridge, where the town was located, was in the Boston Mountains portion of the Ozarks and there was plenty of timber available in the well-forested region. Hunting was good, too. Land was cleared of its timber for crops.

Farmers, in clearing more land for crops, could raise cash by selling the logs they cut down. Thinking of his already installed water wheel turning endlessly in the creek, he wondered if he could somehow connect it to a saw blade big enough to cut logs into building lumber.

Oskar did not know, but he knew where he could find out. Always having run to bookishness, Oskar nevertheless wasn't scared to work with his hands when it was necessary or when he wanted to. Val had encouraged this in both boys, teaching them what he knew about many different kinds of work and also teaching them to ride and shoot. Really shoot. It was needed soon after.

The Cunningham house was only three miles from town, along a dirt road heading northward toward the town of Paragould. Trouble came down that dusty road one day. A band of ruffians out of Ripley County, Missouri, had come over that road after having run roughshod through Paragould with the idea of doing the same in Jonesboro. They had stopped a couple of times before then for water and rest at the vacant house that now they found was full of Cunninghams. Their surprise was palpably apparent when they rode into the yard and found the house occupied.

Oskar stepped confidently onto the front porch, a Walker Colt at his side. "Hello, friends! What brings you here? You need water, take all you need from the trough over there before you move along."

The ostensible leader of the pack of ruffians sneered back at Oskar. "Who's calling for us to go anywhere?"

"I'm Oskar Cunningham, and I bought this farm about a month ago."

"Well, that's just too bad for you!" He drew his pistol and shot at Oskar but missed.

The homeowner fired back and did not miss, hitting the man directly through the breastbone, causing dust to fly from his shirt and him to fall backward out of the saddle, dead as he hit the ground.

"Why you—"

Whatever the next words were from the miscreant who yelled out, they were drowned out by the sound of a shot from the house, as "Yelling Fella" fell to the ground clutching his right shoulder and writhing and cursing in agony.

At this, several of the Missouri outlaws began firing at Oskar, who went down in a hail of gunfire and lay still on the front porch, bleeding visibly from at least one wound. At first the only sounds were his moans and kicks on the wall.

The scream that followed was itself followed by a hail of gunfire from the house. Angie and Angelina, both firing Winchester Model 73 rifles that Bobby had provided and then taught all the women how to use, began a volley into the outlaws that made them dive for cover. You could hear the levers working rapidly.

Angie took the 73 that she was shooting back from Ruthie, who had reloaded it, just as Angelina had emptied her fifteen-shot magazine and, thus, handed hers to Ruthie for a reload.

During the ensuing silence, Angie yelled out the open window she was firing through. "You boys had better know I shot and killed my first two outlaws back in 1836, and I haven't forgot how!"

One of the outlaws yelled forth. "You sure talk tough, for an old woman!"

A new voice cut through the air. "You boys come on ahead if you're that brave. We've got a year's supply of cartridges, and we could just as well use them up on you and then buy more. I used to shoot varmints and Kiowas down in Texas, but I guess you'll do! Now, come on and have at it", she snarled.

Just then, a buggy with a crazed and lathered horse in headlong gallop came crashing into the yard. A wild-eyed man with a Walker Colt in each hand leapt out and ran toward the startled outlaws, firing offhandedly into their midst and leaving two of them with bloody holes between their eyes and the backs of their heads blown wide open. His face was a hideous mask of rage and indignity.

As another man raised his pistol, Bobby Cunningham shouted, "You fool!" and treated him to the same fate. He stumbled backwards, his head half-missing.

His shout could be heard all over the yard, and through the house as well. "Surrender! Now!

"I'm United States Marshal Cunningham and you are all under arrest. Throw your guns into the dirt and line up over there by the water trough, and you can live. If one of you starts fightin' again, I'll just have to kill you all, and I'll be totally justified. The posse is coming hard just behind me, so make your choice now—surrender or die in the dirt." The looks on their faces ranged a great deal.

One by one, the Missouri ruffians tossed away their arms and went over to the trough. Two men needed help to get over there and collapsed on the ground afterward. All the fight had gone completely out of them as they got to the tank.

Of the twelve outlaws who had ridden so violently into the yard, six were left standing, two were down wounded, and four were decidedly dead, dead, dead. The wounded men occasionally moaned softly.

Bobby called out once again, this time toward the house. "You all can come on out now, but keep these boys covered with those rifles."

Angie, Angelina, and Ruthie came out onto the front porch, where Angie went straight to Oskar's side and knelt after handing her rifle to Ruthie, who immediately pointed it at the outlaws, murder sullenly glaring from her eyes.

"He's alive, thank the Lord!" Angie's voice carried hope.

Carmella came out from the house with flinty eyes and took Ruthie's place with the rifle.

"Go see to your wonderful husband. I can take care of these polecats if I need to!" With that she stepped down the front steps into the yard, stopping just a few yards away and cocking the lever, causing a new round to be chambered.

At this distance, they all knew instantly that she could not miss.

Bobby stepped quickly to the porch and looked at the tearstained faces of Ruth and Angie.

"Where is he hit?"

Angie answered. "One in the shoulder that's still in there and one low on the side, with an exit out the back. I don't think that one is serious, but he's lost some blood, and he might go into shock."

Bob appeared in the doorway, looking toward his father with great concern.

"Bob, help your mom get him into the living room and on the couch. Then go and get me all the pieces of rope from the moving bundles and bring them out here. Good lad!" A gust of wind swept across the yard, accenting his words.

With that, Bobby turned his back and marched across the yard. His heart screamed for him to stay there and help his brother. But his mind told him that what could be done, for now, was already being done, and this was a dangerous crowd to turn your back on for very long. The ruffians glared back sullenly.

Angelina and Carmella had not moved during the two minutes or so that he'd been at the porch, and Carmella was looking like she was subconsciously just begging for one of the varmints to actually make a move.

Just then, Bob Haskins from up the road toward town and three of his boys rode up in a cloud of dust with their rifles in hand. "What can we do to help?"

"I need to get these bastards tied up and then get in to see after Oskar. They shot him, and he's pretty bad off."

"How bad?"

"Don't know yet, but bad enough he might not live."

Haskins immediately turned to his youngest son. "Phillip, go get Doc Mars. You'll probably need to go into the saloon if he's not in his office. Tell him Oskar Cunningham's been shot and come as quickly as he can."

"Yes, sir, Pa!" With that, young Phillip wheeled his horse and galloped off toward town, leaving flying gravel and dust in his wake.

"Now, Mr. Haskins, if you and your boys will keep these rats covered, I'll tie them up and explain to them the consequences of their actions this day."

Young Bob went right along with his Uncle Bobby behind the row of outlaws, where he paused long enough at each one to rapidly but efficiently tie their wrists together. After he'd done the fifth outlaw and was beginning the sixth, he at last began to speak. "You fellas may have thought you were tough, but today you were stupid. You shot a man on his own front porch, and if he dies, that's murder."

"It wasn't us that shot him, but Harry over there. And he's dead where that fella, your brother, shot him," harshly replied one of the men. "We didn't have nothin' to do with it."

"Always a jailhouse legal expert in the bunch, isn't there?"

Bobby sat the six non-wounded ruffians on the ground as he continued. "Bob, why don't you go into the house and see how your dad is and see what else you can do to help out, like maybe getting Tina to start boiling some water. And Mr. Haskins, if you want to send your boys into the house, they won't have to hear what I have to say, seeing as how it probably will not be fit for young ears."

"Aw, we're old enough, Pa."

"You two get on in the house, now. Marshal Cunningham is trying to be a gentleman, so let him. No more back talk!"

"Boys, if you want to guard the prisoners while I get things ready to take them into town, you can do that. I'll come get you when the time comes."

"Yes, sir! You can count on us, sir."

Excited, the boys ran toward the house.

Bobby began to quietly explain what the lawbreakers had done and how they would be tried by a judge sitting in Arkansas. The crimes of murder and attempted murder, assault, and other (as yet unnamed crimes) were all committed in that state. But in addition, they had crossed state lines in order to commit those crimes, and that could be a federal offense, which could land them in front of Federal Judge Isaiah Parker, known as the "Hanging Judge."

"My first inclination was to take you into town to the local sheriff, but, what the hell? After I've gone to the trouble to get all of you into the wagon, might as well head to Fort Smith. I just got back from there today, and my wife will probably be mad as hell if I go back this soon. But I know you boys just can't wait to meet him, especially if my brother doesn't make it. My wife enjoyed meeting him. Judge Parker is a friend of mine, and I'm one of his marshals."

Bobby continued, growing more vituperative the longer he spoke. "If my brother survives, Judge Parker may not hang all of you. He may decide life in prison is appropriate punishment for you. I know Judge Parker to be tough but unceasingly fair. One thing I know is, no matter what judge you stand before, or what your sentence is, you are finished with this homestead and in Craighead County. I've gotten a good look at all of you, and if I ever see any of you again, I'll make sure you see the bottom of a freshly dug hole!

"You scum better sit there and think long and hard about what I've said, because I've chased better men than you by a long shot, all the way to California before I finally got them. And don't think I won't follow any of you filthy bastards that far, either!"

Bobby neglected out of forbearance to tell them the story of getting in a gun battle with that fugitive and ending his life right there on the boarding ramp at the pier in San Francisco, as he was trying to escape on a ship bound for the Far East.

Bobby did end with one more thought before he went into the house and sent Mr. Haskins's sons out to guard the prisoners. "My brother, who you have gravely wounded, is an attorney. If he survives to the point of being able, I'm certain he will draw up a whole list of charges to prefer against you, and I will happily bring those before any judge in the state."

His last words came out somewhere between a hiss and a shout. "You absolute pieces of horse dung are not even worthy to be mixed with the real thing, and I'll make sure you rue this day!"

Bobby went into the house, and the Haskins boys came out along with young Bob to guard the prisoners. The silence was broken only by the wind.

Inside, Bobby found Oskar, pale but conscious, with his side wound (which had bled most profusely) bandaged and no longer bleeding. Ruthie held a clean compress on his shoulder, awaiting the doctor's arrival.

Tina had begun to boil water over the kitchen fire when Bob had told her to do so. Therefore, everything in the house was ready for the doctor's appearance, which was a scant five minutes later.

Those five minutes could have seemed like an eternity to Oskar. The whole incident, from the time Oskar had first stepped onto the front porch with a peaceful greeting to the time when Doc Mars began to examine his shoulder, had not taken forty-five minutes.

———————◆———————

When Bobby drove the freight wagon later that afternoon into town loaded with live outlaws to deliver to Sheriff Barnes, it was quickly made clear to him that there wasn't enough room at the town jail to hold all that bunch. But Barnes quietly told Bobby he'd take over from there and deliver the gang to Little Rock, into Judge Henry Clay Caldwell's care, as soon as he could round up four to six extra men as guards.

"You've had enough with these rats for today, although you'll probably have to testify before Judge Caldwell at some point. But right now, I know you want to get back to the house to see about Oskar. I heard from Doc Mars that he's OK and, except for some blood loss and a sore shoulder from getting the bullet out, he'll be fine. That's great news. Give him my best! I know you folks are new to the area, but he's already made a lot of friends. I suspect you did today as well."

"Thanks for saying that, Matt. But, for the record, I wish this whole day hadn't happened. I'm for sure going back to the house to see about my brother. But first, I'd better go over to Claire's rooming house, clean up a bit, and tell my wife what happened."

"Yeah, I heard you got married. I haven't met her yet. So if you'd like, please bring her around sometime and introduce me to her."

"Will do, Matt. And listen, if you hear of a place to live that we might rent or buy, I'd love to get us something more permanent as quickly as I can."

"I'll keep my eye out for you, Bobby, and see what I can do. By the way, would you mind if I borrow your freight wagon for the trip to Little Rock? Those scum are already loaded, and I'd hate to delay for having to find something else suitable to do the job."

"Naw, Matt, that's fine. Sorry I didn't offer in the first place. Anything you can do to get this Missouri trash outta here—the quicker, the better—I like it. Just return it empty is all I ask!"

With that, Bobby walked down to Claire's. To say that Beverly was glad to see him would have been a mammoth understatement; to say that she was highly peeved would also have been. You could almost smell her anxiety in the small room.

They worked everything out after Bobby had a much-needed bath. Clothes were not involved at that point.

Later, they rode livery rented horses out to Oskar's and found Angie applying the same nursing skills she'd shown Val almost forty years earlier, taking good care of her youngest son and helping to instill confidence into the rest of the household with her quiet, calm, but firm assurance.

This was the Angie of old, and it was wonderful for all to see her lucid, vital, and needed again, especially for her children. Bobby felt he could cry at this.

Oskar managed to squeeze Bobby's hand affectionately with his left (non-wounded) arm, while croaking out a single word. "Thanks!"

Bobby looked at Ruthie, who had not left his side, affectionately as he replied. "What are brothers for if not that? We'll be back tomorrow to check on you folks and help any way we can. Is there anything we can bring from town as we come?"

A chorus of simple "No" followed.

Bobby had just one more thing on his mind. "Bob, tomorrow

morning early, can you drive the buggy into town to Claire's rooming house and pick me up?"

Bobby would have liked to take Beverly back in the buggy, but it seemed wiser to return the livery horses that night and let young Bob pick him up with the buggy the next morning, so they could spend a quiet night together.

The two lovers, so newly married and suddenly uprooted from Memphis, spent the night together in married bliss, but it wasn't necessarily quiet.

Healing, adjusting to a new home, and growing as a family started the next day.

Chapter 17

IT WAS IN THE BLOOD

Ever since B. B. (Blues Boy) King walked into the lobby of their studios in downtown Memphis in 1948 and up to the top floor where radio station WDIA broadcast to the Negro population of the city, "Thangs just ain't been the same here in our town—Memphis Town."

1890–1910

By the last days of the nineteenth century, the Cunningham family had undergone significant changes, but ties to their earliest days remained as strong as ever.

Grandma Angie passed away in the hard winter of 1887 at the fine old age of either eighty-two or eighty-four. They weren't really sure which because she had not been completely sure what year she'd arrived, record keeping on the frontier being what it was back then when she was born.

She died peacefully in her sleep.

Carmella had died earlier in the spring of that same year, shooing away a raccoon that had gotten into the kitchen and was rummaging for food. She took out after the varmint with a coal scuttle from the stove, and ran headlong into the side wall of the house, knocking herself completely unconscious.

After a time, Angelina found her and, with Bob's help, got her to the living room couch. Tina rushed to town and brought back old Doc Mars, but to no avail.

Carmella, the beloved servant and companion to Angie, never woke up.

Bobby and Beverly clung to each other during good times and bad and aged together so gracefully they were easily the handsomest couple in town, well into their fifties. They were also easily the most amatory couple in town. But, perhaps because of their age or other factors (or perhaps out of just pure ill fortune), the two lovers, out of no lack of trying, remained childless.

Bobby had been approached several times about becoming the county sheriff after Matt Barnes had been killed chasing down out-of-town drunkards who had shot up the saloon, cowardly wounding a woman in the process. Matt had bravely charged out after them as they fled, dying for his troubles.

Bobby turned down each offer as it came, preferring to stay a deputy U.S. marshal instead. He enjoyed the occasional travel to as-yet-unseen places, especially when it allowed him to take his beloved Beverly with him.

These days, his marshal's service was primarily investigative in nature, rather than in direct pursuit of fugitives, though he still had the occasional tangle with a miscreant. He kept his gun skills top-notch over the years with his practice.

Long before, Bobby's stepfather Val Dimand had taught him to shoot. Val's stance and manner were those of the classic pistoleer or duelist. A sideways stance, presenting the smallest target to your opponent and the pistol cocked and ready for firing, the arm fully extended with careful aim, was the method Bobby had been taught by Val, and it was the method he still used.

The "quick draw" method of gunfighting, which had grown in popularity following its inception after the Civil War, relied on being able to get off the first shot, rather than accuracy with that shot. Generally attributed to a shotgun-toting gunfighter from Tennessee named Cullen

Baker, who escaped into Arkansas and then Texas, the quick draw method for pistol fighting he had developed was fairly reliable in getting off the first shot but not in putting away your opponent.

Generally, the first shot from a quick draw fighter could come somewhere near the other fighter. Sometimes, it would actually strike him, usually in a nonlethal manner but thereby exposing him to the generally far more accurate and deadly fire from the classic pistoleer.

The classic method was slower but more lethal.

Bobby knew that for sure, for he had survived several such battles. Bobby had stuck with his Walker Colts, even though the big gun had several drawbacks.

Its biggest advantage went hand in hand with its biggest disadvantage. Properly loaded, the Walker was the most powerful handgun made. With a 60-grain load of powder and a .44 caliber ball in each of its six chambers, the powerful handgun could easily pierce a wooden wall and lethally strike an outlaw hiding behind it. Blasting apart brick structures was also possible.

Hand pouring the chamber's powder and then loading the hand-molded ball and pressing the load down into the chamber with the Walker's built-in ramrod was needed for each of the pistol's six chambers in the revolving cylinder. This meant spending several minutes just in loading the six chambers, at best. Putting a percussion cap on each of the six firing nipples was what completed the process.

Meanwhile, a shooter using one of the newer Colt or Smith & Wesson cartridge revolvers could simply open up the cylinder, replace the spent cartridges with new factory-made bullets, and put a fully loaded weapon back into action in less than a minute.

Bobby still carried the Walker-model Colt revolvers as a matter of course. But he had had some experience with the newer single-action, cartridge-firing Colt Army model 1873, which would become commonly known as the "Peacemaker," and he liked them a lot.

Bobby would always reload spent chambers in his Walkers as soon as he could, so that, if he found himself in a fight, he had twelve accurate shots before he was out of ammo. That was usually more than enough. Lately though, he had been toying with the idea of converting the Walkers to fire the Colt .45 caliber cartridges. He had actually done this, with parts supplied from Colt, to Model 1860 army revolvers, and he thought he might do the same for Walkers or Dragoons.

Meanwhile, Beverly and Bobby had found a place in town big enough for their needs, and he was able to buy it at a good price for cash.

One important thing had changed about Bobby; he no longer spent money as soon as he got it. He now was using Val's financial model from long ago, where his living expenses took up no more than half of what he made, and the other half went into savings.

He set up his gunsmithing operation in Jonesboro to have something to do when he was in town. He didn't really need the money. Bobby already had enough in the bank to last both him and Beverly the rest of their lives.

Meanwhile, out at the main homestead where the largest portion of the remaining family lived, Oskar had, over the years, built up a progressive, modernized abode for the Cunningham family. He'd added two more bedrooms and a bathroom onto the existing house and had put indoor plumbing into the kitchen and baths, with running water from the deep well fed by a pump driven off the windmill.

He'd also built a smaller, two-bedroom house for visitors, with an eye toward it being Bob's place when he married.

But the biggest change at the homestead had nothing to do with the house or family. There was far more land than the family really needed, and Oskar *really* didn't want to be a farmer. So, when—after they'd moved in comfortably—he'd been approached by Wyman Parks, who had the adjoining farm and wanted to expand, he'd been happy to oblige. Oskar worked out a deal with the veteran farmer to use a hundred acres; for ten years, Parks would give Oskar 20 percent of the revenues from crops grown from those acres. And at the end of the ten years, he could renew the agreement if he wanted, or let the land pass back into Oskar's control. Oskar had calculated that this arrangement would pay the entire cost of the homestead and all of its subsequent improvements, even before the first ten years were up.

Oskar also got in the deal that he would retain all the cut timber removed from the acreage for planting crops. In this manner, he had free access to the raw materials for building a new, larger house a few years down the road, which had been his plan all along.

In his master plan for the Jonesboro homestead to be self-sufficient in terms of revenue, one element had still been missing. Oskar had been fascinated with sawmills since he was a little boy.

The first sawmill on the property was run by the waterwheel in the creek through a step-up/step-down belt-and-pulley system, turning a rotary steel saw blade almost five feet in diameter. This was adequate for making some types of lumber from some of the softer woods such as yellow pine. But the system had trouble delivering enough power for the blade to cut many of the hardwoods the Ozarks had in abundance.

Still, it was a start. As Oskar and Bob (who was indispensable to the project) learned more and more about what it would take for a local mill to be able to keep up with the area's demands, new methods, equipment, and fixtures were brought into play over the succeeding decade, changing the face of the homestead and the family's fortunes in the process.

Oskar and Bob, both together and independently, made several trips to places like Pittsburgh and St. Louis to look at machinery and techniques involved in a modern sawmill. A steam-powered "donkey" engine was one of their first additions. This allowed the raw logs to simply be rolled onto the conveyor rollers from the wagons they were brought in on and then pulled along by the donkey engine up to the saw platform for the first shaping cuts. This greatly increased speed and safety in bringing the logs to where they were to be cut, as well as cutting down on the manpower needed for that dangerous job.

Over the following years, a dedicated steam engine, using coal for fuel (for powering the main saw blade and cutoff blades), had been added to produce sized lumber for construction. Drying racks and sheds were added to allow the mill-cut lumber to age against warping. Stockpiles of salable lumber meant that the mill could, many times, accommodate unforeseen orders.

This whole operation turned into a significant employment opportunity over the years for residents of the small town of Jonesboro, wanting to grow beyond its current status. The rebuilding and subsequent expansion of downtown completely absorbed the capability of the first mill operation and its water-driven blade.

Fortune had provided Oskar and Bobby in the fall of 1881 with a man with plenty of sawmill experience.

He'd been right up the road all along!

Tatum Haskins, Bob Haskins's eldest son, had been working in various sawmills just outside Pittsburgh, Pennsylvania, for almost twenty years, when his father's health caused him to move back home to the farm.

"Tat" Haskins was in McCurdy's dry goods store one afternoon when Bob Cunningham came in, after bringing in a load of lumber for one of the buildings going up down the street. The two chatted affably about many things, especially their families. Tat seemed fascinated with Bob's Grandma Angie, and her frontier days in Texas before coming to Memphis. He hoped to talk with her, he told Bob.

When Bob casually mentioned the sawmill they had operating on the homestead and the expansion plans they had for it, Tat mentioned he had some experience in that area and, if they needed help as they proceeded, he was right up the road.

Bob extended the invitation to come and visit and meet his father, Oskar.

A couple of weeks later, Oskar and Bob were working hard on a stuck pulley on the "shift-up/shift-down" speed selector they had fashioned for the saw blade coupling to the waterwheel shaft. Tat came riding up from down the road; saw the two men straining mightily; and hopped down, stripped off his shirt, and began to throw his weight into the problem. The pulley finally broke free from the extra pressure applied, much to the relief of the other two men.

As Oskar invited Tat to sit and enjoy a cool dipper of water with them and "catch your breath whilst we catch ours," you could see the strained muscles in his arms beginning to twitch from his efforts.

"You sure came along at just the right time. My son and I were just about to run out of steam!"

"My pleasure to be of help, sir."

"Please, call me Oskar."

"Thanks, Oskar. Bob and I were talking at McCurdy's a couple of weeks ago about your sawmill project. And since I was riding by into town today, I thought I'd like to see the place he described."

"Thanks again for jumping in to help."

"You folks have all the elements you need here to build a fine big mill if you're of a mind to. You have flowing water, plenty of space for the cutting platform and a building around it, along with drying sheds, and you could build a good long conveyor for the logs to come in on."

"Bob told me you had some sawmill experience."

"Yes, sir ... uh, Oskar! I spent almost twenty years working in one or another mill outside of Pittsburg, until my dad got sick. Then I decided to come back home and help out around there."

"How is your dad?"

"He's fine, but he gave Doc Mars and all of us a scare about two months ago. So, when Mom sent me the telegram about it, I came home to stay. I'm glad I did. I just love it here!"

Oskar asked a question that would help shape the family for another generation.

"Are you looking for a job?"

◆

At the same time Oskar was asking Tat that question, Angelina had been looking out the side window of the house toward the wheelhouse at the handsome stranger sitting there talking to her Uncle Oskar and cousin Bob.

"Mom! Over here at the window! Who's that fella?"

Angie came over and stood beside her daughter, looking out with her. "My, he's pretty, isn't he? If I was thirty years younger, I'd go and see for myself."

"Mama!"

As they spoke, Tat stood up to his full height and began to put his shirt back on, his chest and torso rippling with mature muscles. As he donned his shirt, not knowing he was being watched, he turned himself in profile to his unseen watchers, presenting his lean frame and muscular arms to their view, as he approached his horse and swung up into the saddle.

A stirring erupted in Angelina's lower regions that had not been there in quite a while. And no matter how she tried to quell it, it would not subside.

Angie had gone back over to the living room sofa, and Tina was still off in town. So, Angelina did something she had not done in ages; she went to her room and latched the door.

After hiking her dress up to her waist, along with her thin undergarments, she lay back across her bed and put her feet up, her knees apart. Her fingers reached down to her mound, and spreading her folds gently apart, Angelina began to rub her yearning into submission, slowly at first, but gaining in intensity and speed.

As the new images of Tat Haskins, which had been seared into her mind, replayed themselves in her fantasy, Angelina brought herself into a scalding climax that pointed out vividly to her what she had been lacking for years.

Rolling and shuddering silently on the bed and biting her lip the whole time to keep quiet, she waited for the tremors to subside a bit before standing. Smoothing her clothes and checking her appearance in the mirror, she went down the hall to the back bathroom.

After freshening up a little, she headed back to the living room.

Her mom was still sitting there.

"Tina home yet?"

"No, sweetie. But I don't think it will be long. You look a little flushed, though, dear. Are you feeling all right?"

"Mama, I'm fine. I was just in the bathroom."

"Well, he *was* mighty pretty!"

Good old Mama Angie; she never missed a thing!

Angelina was forty-four that summer; Tat was forty-two.

———————◆———————

After Oskar had hired Tat, things really shifted into high gear around the fledgling mill, as new equipment was ordered and installed, more men were hired as workers, and the whole operation took off. With his years of experience in many areas of sawmill operations, Tat could advise Oskar and Bob on exactly what tools and techniques were needed for commercial success (fifty thousand board feet per day capability, to start). This was important to Oskar for three significant reasons, besides the revenue the mill would generate for the family.

First, Oskar had wanted, from day one, to be able to "hang out his shingle" to practice law again. To that end, he had gotten himself certified to do so with the state. Second, Bob wanted to go off to school and study architecture. He'd read from Oskar's encyclopedias since he was a boy and had personally seen two houses, four buildings, and a bridge being built. The love of creating things was strong in Bob, and Oskar wanted for him to be able to "spread his wings and fly." Third, Oskar was looking to be married again.

After losing his beloved Ruthie to pneumonia in the brutally hard winter of 1888, he had not been in a rush to be remarried. They had clung to each other through thick and thin, through even the unbearable tragedy of losing a young child, and Oskar had felt her loss keenly. Though still saddened by the memory of putting Ruthie into her grave there on the homestead, lately Oskar had been hoping the Lord might allow him to father more sons, even at his advancing age, so he began to cast about in the area for a suitable helpmate and partner.

Recently, in August 1894, Oskar Cunningham had met a nice woman named Henrietta Parsons in town. Slender and lively, where his beloved Ruthie had been plush and calm, Henrietta had talked with Oskar after he had made a speech at the town hall meeting. What started out as an earnest conversation about the future buildings going up there in downtown, morphed gradually into a conversation about her future and morphed again into an examination of their futures together.

More than thirty years his junior, Henrietta nonetheless found Oskar almost intoxicatingly interesting to be around. His urbanity and smooth, easy style, coupled with his almost encyclopedic knowledge of every subject she could bring into a conversation, infatuated her.

Oskar was not infatuated with Henrietta for her knowledge or charm. At almost sixty years of age, he knew he had a brief time left in which to father some new sons—if the Lord allowed it at all. Fortunately for him, courtships between widowers and prospective new brides did not customarily last more than a few days, at most.

When he spoke of marrying Henrietta to Bob, his son's reply was simple. "Gee, Dad, I was wondering why you hadn't done something sooner!"

Angelina's reply was even simpler. "Good for you, Uncle Oskar!"

In a small civil ceremony officiated by Reverend Teasdale of the First Baptist Church and presided by the Honorable Phillip D. McCulloch, the congressman representing Craighead County, Oskar and Henrietta were married.

They began their lives together that night as man and wife. Oskar, who had not had the touch of a woman since Ruthie died, and Henrietta, who was not a blushing virgin but someone who thoroughly enjoyed the touch of a man, came together that first night and established a pattern that was to last and satisfy them for more than twenty years.

Oskar stripped and got under the covers, while Henrietta finished getting ready in the bath. When Henrietta entered their bedchamber and closed the door, he told her to drop the bathrobe and stand before the bed, so he could look at her.

She did as she was told, and Oskar admired his new young bride methodically, starting with her long lean legs (amply rounded but firm) and moving up through her extremely enticing crotch with its tuft of reddish hair. His enchanted eyes then assessed her gently curved belly (only very slightly protuberant), flowing up into her graceful rib cage and then on to her softly pendant breasts. These were each topped with broad and deep reddish-brown areolae with sizeable "hatbox-shaped" nipples in their centers, begging (it seemed) to be gently kissed, sucked, and chewed, in that order. Oskar looked forward to doing just that!

Atop her lovely shoulders flowing into firm arms, sat her head with its comely face, featuring somewhat full and pouty lips, as well as a straight nose and startlingly green eyes. That lovely head and face were topped off with a mass of auburn curls.

All in all, Oskar quickly decided, he had caught quite a catch. "My goodness! You are lovely!"

Henrietta's reply was direct. "Thank you very much! And if you'll peel back those covers, I'll see how you are."

Oskar did as she directed, peeling back the covers to expose his supine nude form.

Henrietta drank Oskar in with those striking green eyes. What she saw was a sixty-year-old man, lean but not skinny (work-hardened and toned by daily physical work around the homestead), with a head of blond hair with a slight orange tint that he'd inherited from his mother, graying only slightly.

She could not help but notice, above lean hips and buttocks, a generously long shaft protruding from a tuft of the same orange-blond hair. Judging by its length and rigidity (with no touch yet from her!), it was her assessment that she was about to be explored deeply and well.

"Well, my dear, do I pass your initial inspection?"

"Indeed you do."

"Remember, I'm what is considered an 'old man,' but I'll try to give you what you want and need."

"Thank you, sir; I will try to do likewise."

"Well, how do you want to start?"

"Like this!" With that brief rejoinder, Henrietta climbed into the bed, got beside Oskar on her knees, and bent over at her waist with her smooth bottom facing him. She immediately took his manhood in her hand and stroked it gently but firmly, up and down, up and down.

It responded most appropriately.

This period of attention to his protuberance was shortly followed by her bending lower at the waist and putting her lips over his shaft head in an open-mouthed circumference of his tip and subsequently by a sliding up and down of her incredibly soft and moist mouth. Delightful feelings coursed through Oskar.

This, coupled with the deliciously complete view of the valley between her buttocks, just inches from his face, forced Oskar's rigidity to reach epic proportions. He almost felt like he was sixteen again, up in the attic on Bethel.

Oskar reached over into the slit between her large lips there and began to caress her bud. He gently spread her smaller lips and continued to manipulate her until her lubricant began to flow, and she began to make soft moans.

"You've done this before!"

"Well, I *was* married for a long time."

Oskar was noticing all the while how her darker red vaginal and anal skin stood out in such contrast to her otherwise alabaster skin tone.

His thoughts were interrupted by Henrietta's question. "Well. You're certainly ready, and I am, too. Is there any way you particularly like?"

"I believe in giving my lady first choice. What's your absolute favorite?"

"Me on top."

"Take me that way then."

"Oh, goody."

Henrietta was explored deeply and well indeed that night.

She and Oskar both fell asleep afterward, she still lying on top of him.

Sometime later, Henrietta awoke enough to go over across the room and turn off the lantern to darken the room. Making her way back naked across to the side of the bed, she climbed back in next to her new husband. She gave him a butterfly-soft kiss on the shoulder and gently put her arm across his bare chest.

Oskar had once been so used to the warmth of a female body next to his that he did not awaken, and the two slept blissfully content till morning. A single tear of happiness rolled down Henrietta's cheek before sleep took over.

Thirty-five years of marriage would come and go by so fast.

New sons did not happen immediately, but Oskar was persistent in trying with Henrietta, who thoroughly enjoyed the efforts.

After more than five years of wedded bliss, Chester "Chet" Cunningham was born in 1900 and his brother Melvin "Mel" followed in 1904.

The boys grew up around the sawmill and were bright, lively sprites in a world of wood. Their education was both scholarly and practical, and they shone.

By 1895, Oskar's long-awaited law practice was well-established in downtown Jonesboro, and he handled cases large and small with equal parts urbanity and aplomb.

He had represented the Saint Louis and Southwestern ("Cottonbelt") Railway in a dispute over right-of-way and successfully defended the county decision by Judge Riddick about it, all the way to the Arkansas Supreme Court.

He'd also defended farmers in foreclosure and represented in-town citizens wanting to halt rampant growth, to make sure all new buildings were solidly built, and generally had made sure he was available to the downtrodden, in spite of their ability to pay.

Oskar could walk down the street in downtown and receive a hearty greeting from everyone he met along the way. Respected and well-liked, he was a fixture in downtown Jonesboro. It was well known he would not stand for women to be mistreated, nor the poor to be ignored or run roughshod over. A man of principle, Oskar truly strove to make the lives of the people who lived there better, if he could. Hardly anyone could not name someone he'd helped or bailed.

Henrietta also became a fixture in downtown. Many days about noon, she could be seen strolling to Oskar's law offices with a picnic basket, full of a tasty lunch for the two of them. After they had enjoyed the prandial interlude, if no one was in the outer office and after sending his clerk out to his own lunch, Oskar would lock the outer doors to the law offices and hang the "Be Back in a Little While" sign in the front window. Entering his office and closing the door, he and Henrietta would engage in scandalous, half-naked (sometimes totally naked!) sex acts that belied their ages and the number of years they had been married.

Meanwhile, Bobby Cunningham continued as a deputy US marshal and still occasionally traveled around the country, mostly by rail these days. On longer trips, to California, for example, he would bring Beverly and would enjoy the comforts of a Pullman sleeping car while on the rails and fine hotels when in big cities. She really enjoyed not having to be apart from her rugged, handsome mate, any more than was absolutely necessary. He kept her safe as they went.

As a Marshal, Bobby still went armed everywhere, now carrying a pair of Model 1873 Army ("Peacemaker") Colts, chambered to fire the Colt .45 pistol round, in tooled-leather holsters on a matching tooled-leather gunbelt, with loops to carry extra cartridges. Suave and urbane in his dress and manner, with his beautiful and stylish wife at his side, Bobby was a welcome presence, indeed, in Jonesboro. Having such a man in their midst lent security to one and all, no doubt.

The growing town appreciated the Cunningham brothers for what they brought to the community in terms of stability, vision, and ambition for their adopted home. Their civic endeavors helped to make Jonesboro the lovely place to live it became over the following decades. The ensuing years also allowed both men to age gracefully and well.

There was even talk and then a movement to have Oskar Cunningham, esquire, serve as county judge.

By 1884, the Cunningham brothers no longer had much to do with the mill. Tat Haskins had turned that operation into a steady revenue producer for the family. He was a tireless, productive worker. His ideas and innovations in products and techniques kept the mill profitable, even in lean times.

By getting the Cottonbelt Railway to agree to put in a siding for the mill, Oskar and Tat enabled the operation to be able to ship anywhere in the country. Special wagons were constructed to move lumber onto boxcars or flatcars in preassembled loads, made to a size standardized to fit regular railway cars. This greatly sped up the loading process over pitching and stacking the lumber by hand on a car "one piece at a time."

By being on the Cunninghams' place every day from before the steam whistle blew to call workers till it blew again to announce quitting time, Tat Haskins was under Angelina's watchful eye constantly.

For the first month he had been there, she manufactured excuses to come within his range of view and even managed to say a polite, "Hello!" or, "Good Morning!" a few times, sorrowfully, to no great avail!

Angelina at forty-four was the picture of her mother at that age—in other words, a true beauty. So why wasn't Tat picking up on all her signals?

Angie had suggested to her daughter one day that maybe she needed to be more direct in her approach. "Honey, sometimes men just can't see the signs. Val used to tell me all the time, 'I'm not a mind reader,' so I learned to tell him when I wanted his attention about something."

"What would you have me do, Mama, strip off naked and run out and jump into his arms?"

Angie chuckled deeply. "That does sound like fun, doesn't it? I'll be darned if I wouldn't like to try that myself! But no, I don't think you need to go that far, at least not at first. I think asking him to share a nice picnic basket you just happened to bring out should do the trick."

The next day Angelina spent the morning preparing fried chicken, green beans, and mashed potatoes with gravy to fill a generous picnic basket, along with some bottles of sarsaparilla she had gotten in town the previous week. While the food was still warm, and just before the whistle blew for lunch, Angelina marched up to Tat with the picnic basket over her arm.

"Hello, Tat, I'm Angelina. And I'd like you to share this picnic lunch with me in the shade of that tree over there, if you would, please."

Tat looked at her as if someone had just hit him between the eyes with a piece of his own lumber and stammered out an answer. "Ye-yes, ma'am, if that's your pleasure, ma'am!"

"Good. Please come over and help me spread the blanket, so I can lay out the food, and we'll eat."

Tat carried the picnic basket for her as they ambled over to the oak's shade next to the house. Angelina spread the blanket she'd brought to form a nice place for them to enjoy the shelter from the sun. Lounging there, they chatted as they ate. Tat complimented her on the victuals— hot food at the midday repast was a rare treat, he told her.

The sarsaparillas were a hit. Tat told her he'd heard of them and had been wanting to try one but didn't want to go into the saloon to get one, seeing as how he didn't drink. She told him of their availability now in the general store, right near the candy.

They chatted the time away after they finished the food. It was a delightful time getting to know each other, but all too soon the whistle blew to call the workers back. Frantically, Angelina searched for the right thing to say.

Angelina, no longer worrying about being too forward, spoke quickly as the handsome man got up easily to his feet and prepared to leave. "Tat, this was very nice. And I'd love to do it, or something like it, again soon."

"Yes, ma'am. This was really pleasant, and your food was terrific!"

"Well, you could call on me some evening, and we could go into town and take in the sights or some such thing."

"I can do that, and I'd like that, too."

"Well then just pick an evening."

"Would this Friday evening about six thirty be convenient for you?"

"Sir, you have yourself a date."

Friday evening came and went splendidly. When Tat Haskins dropped Angelina off at its end, their kiss on the front porch before she went in was not their first of the evening, but it was warm with the promise of much more to come.

After a courtship that was incendiary in its intensity, the two were married.

Tatum Paul Haskins wed Angelina (Estes) Dimand at her family home on April 8, 1882. Attendees and witnesses to this nuptial were her mother Angie MacFee (Cunningham) Dimand, her half-brothers Bobby and Oskar Cunningham, and her daughter Valentina Estes and nephew Bob Cunningham. Also there were Bob and Clara Haskins and Tat's four brothers, Aaron, Jeremiah, Ezekiel, and Phillip. A lively mingling broke forth with participation by all in the merriment.

Reverend Teasdale from First Baptist Church in town officiated. A full house enjoyed the couple's bliss before they departed on their honeymoon by rail to Denver and the Rocky Mountains. Tat had happened to mention to Bobby Cunningham Angelina's desire to one day see the Rockies up close and that he was of a mind that their honeymoon was an excellent time.

Marshal Cunningham agreed strongly with Tat. He recounted many of his good times there and listed some places to stay while there, as well as some fine places to eat and some extraordinary sights to see.

The Denver hotels received a telegram from Marshal Cunningham, informing them that Mr. and Mrs. Tatum Haskins would be attending their facility, and that he, as a longtime customer, would deeply appreciate them being shown every courtesy on their honeymoon. The telegrams went out five days before the nuptials.

The couple was treated like royalty wherever they went.

Coming home to the Cunningham house, Tat and Angelina moved into the smaller two-bedroom house, and Tina returned to the main house to Angelina's room.

Bob kept his old room.

Bobby Cunningham died of a heart attack in February 1900; Beverly passed less than a year later. Most people said it was from grief and loneliness from losing her treasured husband. Reverend Teasdale even spoke of their love in a sermon.

The veteran marshal had lived long enough to see his nephew Bob (who adored his Uncle Bobby) go off to college and see his nephew Chet be born. Holding baby Chester in his arms was one of the last things Bobby Cunningham did on this earth. Holding his beloved Beverly was another.

Holding his brother's hand was the last.

Bobby was not quite sixty-three when he went, and Oskar, the little baby boy who he had splashed merrily in the creek behind the Texas prairie cabin, would outlive his older brother by a little more than twenty-five years.

Reeling with grief at the suddenness, Oskar nonetheless mustered enough fortitude to have Bobby's body prepared and laid in a fine casket and he scheduled a service for him at the courthouse. The entire town, it seemed, turned out to see their beloved marshal off.

From the courthouse, a black-lacquered hearse drove the coffin to the train station, where Bobby would make the fairly short trip to Memphis. Oskar had decided to bury his brother beside the man they had called Dad for so many years, so the back lawn of the Woodlawn house would be his final resting place.

Oscar had telegraphed Bob Allen's son Raymond, now caretaker of the house after Bob's passing a few years earlier, to make arrangements for a place to be dug, a headstone carver to be contacted to speak to Oskar while he was there, and sundry other things as they might arise.

Henrietta and Beverly would be coming along to help support, leaving baby Chester in Tina and Doc Lambert's care while they were gone.

When they got there, everything was ready. The hired hearse brought Bobby to the little grove at the back lot and delivered him to the freshly dug grave.

Surprisingly, Raymond had been able to find old Brother Jack Tichenor, who had spoken over Val Dimand almost thirty years earlier. Still at Seventh Street Baptist Church but now retired as pastor, Brother Jack had really moved Bob Allen, who had always remembered the grace with which the Baptist preacher had delivered his words the day of Val's funeral. He had spoken of it to his children many times. Raymond set out to see if Brother Jack could be found. And if he remembered Val, would he be willing to do the same for his stepson Bobby?

He could and he gladly would.

Oskar, Henrietta, Beverly, Raymond Allen and his brother Wallace, and Brother Jack Tichenor, along with the hired funeral home workers, were the only ones there to see Bobby Cunningham laid to his final rest. Raymond's hired funeral attendants lowered the casket into the grave after Brother Jack spoke.

As they were beginning to fill in the grave, Oskar went over to Val's tombstone and patted it fondly. "Well, it's taken me nearly thirty years to do it, Dad. But I've brought you a little more company."

He then went and patted the beautiful spot where Rose Ellen was buried. "Hello, sweetheart, I've brought your Uncle Bobby to be with you."

Oskar spoke with the stonemason about headstones for both Bobby and Rose Ellen, drawing sketches and writing out what each was to say and then paying him upfront for them and their placement.

That having been completed, he spoke with Raymond, thanking him profusely and explaining the continuation of his caretaker duties. Then he had the hired carriage driver pass by the Bethel house to show Henrietta and Beverly where he'd been raised. Now almost sixty years old, the house and grounds still looked good, even since Phil's death.

From there, it was downtown to the train station to get back. His cherished brother now gone, Oskar's heart was as heavy as it had ever been. With his beloved brother Bobby laid to his rest, Oskar faced the daunting idea of being the new patriarch of the Cunningham clan.

Chapter 18

ONE BY ONE: BACK TO MEMPHIS

For decades Memphis was, at the same time, spoken of as both the "cleanest city in the United States" and "the murder capital of the USA!"

1915–1925

By 1915, Bob Cunningham had felt the strong tug to return to the city he barely remembered. Finished with his architectural studies at Arkansas Industrial University (renamed to its present "University of Arkansas" in 1899), Bob had come home to Jonesboro from Fayetteville in spring 1896, with a fresh degree and a ton of ambition. That drive had become frustrated and thwarted in Jonesboro by the lack of need and desire for local architects, and for the last five years or so, Bob had been seeking outlets for his creativity and finding few locally.

He'd consequently spent much of his time during those years in making improvements on the family homestead, as his father Oskar had been immersed in his judgeship. During this time on the homestead and around the mill, Bob got to be with his little brothers, Chet and Mel, both of whom he loved deeply.

Bob had grown up having to be older than he was, with family responsibilities since he was eight years old. So, it was refreshing indeed to be around his younger brothers, who didn't have a care in the world.

Valentina, with her husband and two children, had elected to move back into the Woodlawn house. Raymond Allen had telegraphed Oskar and reported they were no longer going to be able to be caretakers of the property, as they were moving to San Diego. Rather than lease out the property, as the family had done rather successfully with the Bethel house just down the street, Oskar felt it was fitting for a member of the extended Cunningham family to take up residence there again.

Valentina had been twenty-six when she'd met a young sawmill worker by the name of Mark Barnes, the eldest son of the former town marshal, Matt Barnes. Stricken at first sight of the burly young man, shirtless with the sheen of a light perspiration causing his distinct musculature to stand out even more than normal as he lifted logs onto the conveyor rollers, she thought of Hercules and some of the other heroes from ancient Greece. As she watched him work, the lower regions of her body began to feel warm and moist, and she even thought she felt a slight tingle.

His decidedly handsome face, with its slim aquiline nose and firm jaw, was overset by diamond-blue eyes under bushy brows. The massive shock of blonde hair topping his head instantly made her want to run her fingers through it and, truth to be told, head south from there. She longed to drink in his aroma and feel his flesh on hers.

She'd had to deal with boys and *their* desires since she was fourteen, and she'd become accomplished at satisfying their needs temporarily, without sacrificing her dignity and virtue. It was always her choice how an encounter went. All the young men knew her one uncle was a lawyer, and that her other uncle was a US marshal, and they knew how both of them could shoot.

With Mark, after their very first buggy ride, sitting so close together she couldn't avoid touching him every now and again, Tina found his massive body irresistible under the shade of a spreading sycamore and allowed him to please her as a woman. When it became obvious the affair was casual to neither one of them, wedding plans started to be discussed.

Mark Barnes and Valentina (Estes) Dimand were married in front of his mother and grandmother and her extended family at the Cunningham house and went off to honeymoon in Memphis at the Gayoso, Valentina having heard so much about it from her Uncle Bobby and Beverly, his wife.

During their magical three days in Memphis, Mark took Valentina by the Woodlawn and Bethel houses at her request. Having grown up for the most part in Jonesboro, on the limited salary of the town marshal to feed and house the family, Mark was really impressed, particularly with the size and abundance of the Woodlawn house.

The idea of actually living there someday seemed very remote to Mark, but he had fallen in love with Memphis as a whole. The lumber industry was enjoying a boom in Memphis; more and more sawmills were opening in the area, and Memphis began to bill itself as "the hardwood capital of the world." Therefore, Mark Barnes was fairly certain that, with all his experience, he should be able to find a good job somewhere in town, should they move there someday.

Someday had to wait several years for the birth of their first two children, the rambunctious Billy (named for her father) and his willing follower Matt (named for Mark's father). But as they grew, the Barnes family rapidly needed more space.

When it became necessary for Mark and Tina to travel to Memphis and take up permanent residence in the Woodlawn house, it was done with Oskar Cunningham's complete blessing. Although he and his half-sister had been together since she was a toddler, and he would miss her daughter Tina intensely, he also welcomed the opportunity to reestablish the Cunningham family's presence in his beloved Memphis.

Oskar Cunningham felt a strong affinity for his father, Robert W., and the old portrait of him that still sat on the living room mantel in the Jonesboro house, revered and cherished by the entire family. But Robert Cunningham had died at the Alamo while Oskar was still a baby.

It was Val Dimand, as father, who had guided and molded Oskar's life, and as such and as the man who had brought the three Cunninghams to Memphis in 1836 to begin that new life, Memphis held a strong sentimental tug for Oskar.

At nearly eighty years of age, Oskar realized that, though Robert W. Cunningham's blood coursed through his veins, Val Dimand's deeds and words had shaped the very fabric of his life. He could not count the times when faced with an important choice or decision, he had turned to something he had learned from Val, and he thanked the Lord for it.

Oskar had come to peace with the fact that, given his responsibilities as a judge there in Arkansas and his advancing age, it was highly unlikely he would return to Memphis, except in a box destined for the dirt. To that end, and given his marriage to Henrietta and the birth of his new sons, Oskar had worked on the family fortunes and their distributions.

The sawmill was doing quite well. The homestead had greatly increased in value with the new house Bob had designed and had built on the property. All of their investments had significantly enlarged the family "nest egg," so that every member of the extended family could be well taken care of.

To that end, he'd worked on his will to name his son Bob, as the eldest, as executor of his estate at Oskar's demise and funded immediate-draw accounts at the Union Planters Bank downtown for each member of Tina and Mark's family as they went to Memphis. As Bob got ready to leave, Oskar funded an account for him, so he could continue his studies while in Memphis without working or having to even look for a job. All these accounts in no way diminished any person's inheritance. Rather, this was "walking-around money," to ensure no one had to "go broke" at any time.

As an attorney, Oscar had seen the power old money gave to a family. Money that stayed with and within a family through generations and grew through those generations, through good management and wise investing, could be counted on in times of crisis. Oskar intended this should be true for his family and made provisions for new members of the youngest generation, as yet unborn.

When Bob got to the Woodlawn house in the summer of 1915 and moved in with Tina and Mark, he knew he had left there many years before. He had been less than five at that time, and those memories weren't strong; there was plenty of room in his mind and heart to add new ones.

Bob, with Mark to help him, made several significant improvements in the Woodlawn house, which had suffered from normal wear and tear over the years. Plus, the city of Memphis was now pumping water to homes. Good, fresh, artesian-well water in almost unlimited quantities was being piped directly to houses and businesses, making indoor bathing and toilet facilities cheaper and more accessible to citizens than ever before.

The first flush toilets in the United States had appeared in a Boston hotel in 1828. Almost a novelty at that point, by 1850 a plantation home in northern Mississippi just below Memphis had been built with them, and they were beginning to be more commonplace throughout the mid-south. Even the Bethel house had been built with indoor toilets and plumbing designed in, although it was some years before they were installed. But it was the free-flowing running water available for sinks and bathtubs that did the trick. No longer was a hand pump needed in a bathroom to supply the water necessary to meet such needs; rather, free-running water for the tubs, sinks, and toilets was available right there at each at the turn of a handle.

At the Woodlawn House, the porcelain-covered cast-iron claw-foot tubs got faucets added above the rims, and the drains were connected to a city sewer line, along with the sinks and toilets.

The flush toilets were all new, replacing units installed earlier; those had drawn their flush water from a reservoir (refilled from the hand pump in the bathroom), whereas the new units were directly connected to the city water and refilled their tanks automatically.

Hot water for washing and bathing came from an innovative system that Bob designed and built that heated water with a kerosene heater unit that turned on only when the water temperature in the tank dropped below a certain level and off again when it rose again to the desired heat. This hot water was stored in a tank until delivered to the bathrooms by turning on a hot water faucet on a bathtub or sink.

The original hot water tank was made of copper by a local boiler plant and was then well insulated. But the system wasn't perfect, especially the length of time it took for actual hot water to reach the far ends of the house. Later improvements to the system helped, but real progress came when commercially available units could be independently located near each bathroom and the kitchen and laundry areas to solve that problem.

Meanwhile, as Bob was gaining knowledge in equipping new, more modern houses, he was also studying innovations in larger commercial buildings being built in downtown Memphis. Things such as escalators and elevators, as well as large kitchens with dishwashing and cooking equipment on a large scale, meant structural support technologies were required to erect multistory homes or buildings with steel and concrete instead of wood. After having worked some on the buildings for the new Eastern Arkansas Agricultural and Industrial College (now Arkansas State University) in Jonesboro, Bob had seen some things in Memphis he wished he'd known of before he'd worked on those buildings. But they could be retrofitted, if desired.

To further study and scratch this new itch to learn modern and developing building practices and innovation, he took trips to New York City and Chicago to study there with architectural firms based in those cities, as well as simply walking into prominent hotels and office buildings, just to see their architectural designs and contributions.

On a similar trip to Washington, DC, he was in the lobby of the Willard Hotel, enjoying its furnishings and ornate fittings when an absolute goddess of a woman in her mid-thirties, he supposed, came up to him and asked if she could share the settee he was occupying.

"My pleasure, Miss!" Bob managed to croak out as he stood and gestured for her to sit, which she did most pleasantly to his view. "Robert Oskar Cunningham at your service, Miss."

"Evelyn Jane Estes at yours, Robert!"

"You are not, by any chance, from St. Louis are you, Miss Estes?"

"No, but I do have family there. And it is, or rather was, Mrs. Estes, Mr. Cunningham. My husband died several years ago. Please call me Evelyn, rather than Mrs. Estes."

"Well, it is certainly a pleasure to meet you, Evelyn. Was your late husband from St. Louis, then?"

"He was, indeed, Robert. Or may I call you Bob?"

"You most certainly may; I actually prefer it to Robert or Bobby. The reason I ask about the Estes name is that my aunt Angelina was married to Billy Estes right before the War Between the States and then moved to Texas to ranch with him, but he died suddenly."

Her reply was cheerful and bright. "I thought it might be something like that! Billy was my husband Arthur's stepbrother, about fifteen years older! Arthur was born to Robert Estes and his new wife Lois about 1875. Captain Estes spoke well of all of you, right up till the day he died. He loved your family," she said.

"Well, I'm certainly pleased to make your acquaintance, Evelyn! What brings you to the Willard?"

"Oh, I often come here of an afternoon, just to see who I might meet. I spotted you. You looked like you'd be quite interesting. I came over to chat. I hope you don't think that's too forward of me. Whatever brings you to the Willard, Bob?"

"Well, Evelyn, nothing terribly dashing or even important. I'm simply on a tour of cities, studying the architecture of various homes and buildings for ideas. I'm an architect, you see, and I'd like to bring some improvements home to Memphis with me."

"Well, that certainly completes the circle. Arthur said many times his father had spoken glowingly of Memphis and of his wish someday to return there. He had a good friend there; his name was something like Hal?"

"You're speaking of my sort of step-uncle, *Val* Dimand, who was my Aunt Angelina's natural father. He married her mom, Angie, after her first husband died at the Alamo, and Angelina was born to them a couple of years after."

"Wasn't he a famous gunfighter?"

"Yes, he had a reputation for being deadly accurate in a gun battle. He was ready for trouble if it came, but he never went looking for it. At least, that's what I've been told. I haven't seen him in a long time, as he died of yellow fever when I was quite young."

"Do you live in Memphis now?"

"Yes, right now I'm staying at the family home with Valentina, Angelina's daughter, and her husband Mark and their kids. The rest of the family has been living in Jonesboro, Arkansas, since we all left Memphis during the yellow fever epidemic, back in 1878. I might need to go back there someday, because my dad's there and he's getting old. But I really love Memphis, and I'd love to stay there forever."

"Do you know a hotel in Memphis called the Gayoso or something like it?"

"The Gayoso House, down at the Mississippi River. It burned down in 1899 but was rebuilt and reopened a few years later.

"My uncle Bobby and his wife Beverly spoke glowingly of it and their times there and strenuously suggested taking the view of the Mississippi waterfront and river at the first light of morning. They said it was not to be missed, especially as many of the rooms there had private balconies that opened right on that view. They also said the luxury there was unmatched anywhere in the city. And they were the ones to know, since they had stayed in fine hotels from New York to San Francisco."

"Oh Bob, I do love a fine hotel with posh amenities! We're in one now, and I wonder if you'd like to join me in enjoying as many of those as we can, starting with dinner! Or, do you have somewhere else you need to be?"

"Nowhere else at all."

"Wonderful, then. Let's eat and then find out what's next."

Over the course of a fine meal, Evelyn let Bob know that Arthur had left her in fine financial shape, and therefore, she could travel about the country as she pleased and pursue what or who interested her at any moment.

Bob let her know of his plans to have his own architectural firm, whether it was in Memphis or, of necessity, Jonesboro. He described the life on the homestead in terms of peaceful, almost idyllic charms, and Evelyn seemed mesmerized. In fact, she seemed to hang on every word Bob uttered.

He was under no illusions about his appearance. A man edging into middle age, he still had a trim waist with no bulge at all; his hair was still a dark, lustrous brown with just a hint of graying at his temples; and a fine smile, with a neatly trimmed beard and moustache to frame it, underpinned flashing dark eyes.

Bob had enjoyed the company of a number of very attractive women in his life, starting with Maryanne Parks (whose father Wyman had leased a hundred acres of land from Bob's father Oskar) in the loft of their barn while the two men talked. The look Maryanne (who was almost three years older than him) had on her face as she began to remove his shirt and overalls was the same look he was seeing on Evelyn's face right there at the dinner table.

Evelyn had a way of jutting out her tongue after an amusing remark or innuendo, which reminded him in that instant of Maryanne's tongue plunging and swirling into his mouth as she stripped him nude.

He wondered if her impression of him naked (if that was where this was all leading) would be the same as Maryanne's had been.

◆

The shock on her face when she first saw his erection was replaced by a low, mischievous grin as she thought about what it made her want to do.

"If I'm going to take all that, and I sure want to, you're going to have to get me wet and ready, where I need." To that end, Maryanne had laid back on the blanket and, totally naked by this time, spread her legs wide apart with her knees up, giving startled seventeen-year-old Bob his first-ever view of a female displayed in wanton abandon. As she began to rub herself slowly in the pink slit beneath a tuft of brunette hair, she motioned for Bob to get to his knees.

"Rub yourself, too, but don't come!"

Bob did as he was told as he stared, totally mesmerized by what he was seeing.

Her next words were a wonder to him, but he complied as best he knew how. "I need to be really wet to take all of you, so stop rubbing yourself and lick me right here." She touched where she intended for him to start.

Bob dove into his assignment with abandon and came up for air and further instruction and encouragement periodically, until Maryanne gave him a new instruction.

"Let me turn over now."

As she turned over with her generous bottom in the air and her delightful pancake breasts smashed flat against the blanket, Bob got a new view. Her glistening slit, well-lubricated with his saliva and her juices, now was topped to his view by a small, fringed opening which she tapped with a finger. "Get me wet here, too, please!"

Surprised, Bob bent right to the assigned task with equal gusto, wondering what he was going to do with all this.

His questioning was short-lived.

His throbbing member seemed about to explode when she pointed again at the opening at the top of her slit and whispered hoarsely to Bob. "Put it in there, but don't come inside me."

Since it was his first time, young Bob Cunningham had no frame of reference for the exquisite feelings derived from sinking his massive shaft deep into Maryanne's slobberingly wet canal; he could assure anyone within earshot that he was deeply satisfied by the physical experience, but it wasn't until an unstoppable force began to well up inside him that he cried out slightly. "Oh … Oh … Ooohhh!"

Maryanne whispered quickly, "Be quiet and pull completely out of me, now!"

Bob immediately did as he was told and witnessed a white geyser shoot from his shaft, flood the valley between her cheeks, and start dripping down onto the blanket under her body, now glistening from perspiration.

She was shuddering.

So was he.

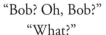

"Bob? Oh, Bob?"

"What?"

"I'm right here, Bob! Where did *you* go?"

"I'm so very sorry, Evelyn! I was lost in thought, and I just drifted away to an old memory. You just reminded me powerfully of someone from long ago; please accept my deepest apology."

"I was thinking maybe you had lost interest in me. You are interested in me, aren't you?"

"I most certainly am! You triggered that memory in me, and I'll tell you the whole story sometime, if you let me do the same things to you."

"Oooh, that sounds erotic, and promising. Sometime?"

"Sometime, when you're ready."

"How will I know when I'm ready?"

"When you're ready, you'll know."

"Confidence! I love it. Will I need to change for this tale?"

"You are, right now, maybe a little overdressed, my dear."

"Should we retire from dinner to my room to continue this discussion?"

"Is it secluded and quiet? It would be nice to continue in a place where we won't have to compete with all this hustle and bustle."

"Yes it is, and that would be nice."

"Lead the way, my beauty,"

Evelyn's room was on the third floor, and by the time they had reached the third floor landing, they had already kissed and rubbed each other several times. As she handed him her room key at the door and he opened it for her, she prepared to step past him into the dim room. Inside, after Bob had closed and latched the door, she turned and presented her back to him.

Bob took the cue and, while lavishing her exposed neck and shoulders with kisses soft and slow, he undid the fastenings on the back of her dress.

As her dress and her undergarment slid to the floor, Bob's kisses followed them down her back. Pausing briefly to admire where her delicious cheeks flowed delightfully into the tops of her plush thighs, he spread them ever so slightly and gave her a mischievous little lick before continuing on down her sculpted leg toward her foot.

With a couple of quick steps forward to clear the pile of her clothes on the floor, Evelyn made a quick, sassy turn. With one hand on her hip and the other making a "how's this, mister?" gesture to Bob, she presented her full naked self brazenly to his obvious approval.

"Well, Robert," she slowly drawled with a wide grin, "I think it's about time you told me a bedtime story—a nice, juicy one, if you please."

"You're certainly dressed for it now, I must say."

"You're not, so fix that and quick. I want a good look at what I'm about to get into—or, rather, what's about to get into me." She grinned even wider and then put her hands over her mouth in mock horror at what she had said.

Bob was quick on the uptake. "If your ladyship wishes, then I shall make it so."

Turning his back to her, he laid his jacket across the high-backed wing chair, and followed it with his pleated-front shirt. Stripped to the waist, he turned back toward Evelyn. "Is this what you had in mind? Or do you want even more?"

"I want to see it all, if you please, sir."

Turning again to the chair, Bob slipped off one shoe and then the other. As he placed them under the chair he began to unfasten his trousers.

As he slid his trousers down, Evelyn feasted her eyes on the sight of his trim waist flowing into his firm, slim buttocks, and he treated her to a quick glance at his exposed crack as he bent forward to step out of them.

Evelyn was mesmerized most of all by the amount of male append-age dangling between his legs.

Bob turned back toward Evelyn and stood there as she had, stark naked with a hand on one hip and making a "how's this?" gesture with the other.

Evelyn responded most appropriately with a surprisingly long and low whistle. "Mister, I knew you had potential, but oh my! Come and tell me a story, right now."

With that, Evelyn whirled and ran to the bed (treating Bob to a delightful view of her bottom in action) and jumped up on it, lying there on one elbow with one knee in the air and making a 'come-hither' gesture with her free hand.

Her femaleness being so completely exposed hastened his steps.

She begged for the story that had drawn his attention away from her at dinner, and after several feigned attempts at embarrassment, he told it.

As he spoke of Maryanne's words and actions, Evelyn would act them out. She asked Bob for explicit details in what she was to touch or say next as the story progressed.

Evelyn even had Bob rub himself as Maryanne had done. And he complied while watching her rub herself, furiously at first, and then slowly and liquidly while staring him in the eyes, producing her own liquid.

When Bob told her it was time to turn over with her butt in the air, Evelyn buried her chest into the covers and turned her face to the side as she followed his directions.

"I can't see you as well this way, love."

"As long as you can feel, you'll know how this part goes."

"Oooh!"

He continued.

"And then Maryanne had me lick her up and down her slit to try to make her as wet as possible. And she made sure I understood that I was to lick her everywhere by touching herself here."

Evelyn felt Bob's touch on her puckered little anus and shivered as if she had touched something electric.

She reached back with one hand. "Like this?"

"Exactly!"

With that, Bob did his best to emulate that long-ago memory. His best must have been pretty good, for, as if on cue, Evelyn re-issued Maryanne's command from his youth. "Put it in now, but don't come inside me!"

Bob's stallion-like thrusts deep into her had Evelyn rocking back and forth in moments.

"Ahh … Eee ... Ooh … Ooohhh!" She screamed her climax as things came to a head for Bob.

When he exploded onto her small hole, his white flood poured down between her cheeks, flooding her already sopping valley with his effluent and causing it to steadily drip onto the covers.

Evelyn rolled over onto her back and stuck one hand down to her molten crotch and began languidly rubbing Bob's juices into herself as she pulled, stretched, and twisted each nipple in turn with the other hand. At one point, with her eyes and mouth tightly shut, she began to bounce up and down on the bed furiously rubbing herself. Suddenly releasing her grip on her crotch, she lay there shaking as she stretched out both her nipples to unimaginable heights before releasing them.

When the shaking from her second orgasm subsided, Evelyn's attention to her nipples continued calmly as she looked at Bob with soft eyes and spoke. "That was some story, Bob. How old were the two of you when it happened?"

"I was seventeen and she was nineteen. The only difference (besides our ages now) between what we just did in this hotel room bed and what Maryanne and I did long ago is that we're not in a hayloft and your father isn't just outside the barn below, so we didn't have to be quiet."

"I certainly wasn't quiet!"

Evelyn had another thought. "Sweetheart, after we rest quietly and then you're ready, I want you to touch me there again and get me ready for that magnificent spear of yours to go inside me there. And next time, I want that flood of yours inside me, right in there."

To make sure Bob knew exactly where she was talking about, Evelyn rolled over on her side, spread her cheeks, and touched herself so he could see.

Bob understood.

———————◆———————

Washington was followed by St. Louis, where Evelyn visited the remaining Estes family and then on to Memphis. When they got to the city,

Bob had them stay the first night at the Gayoso, since their arrival from the train station was so late. Evelyn had wanted to stay there some while they were in Memphis, anyway.

Bob used the hotel operator to phone the Woodlawn house the next morning. Mark Barnes was the one who answered the telephone. After explaining why they hadn't come straight to the house with their late arrival, Bob told Mark about Washington and meeting Evelyn Estes, who had joined him in traveling to Memphis.

"I'd really like for everyone to meet her, Mark, especially Valentina. She and Evelyn have something in common."

"Both of you come for supper tonight then. I'll ask Tina when she gets back from the markets just to make sure it's okay. Should only be about a half hour or so. She has both Billy and Matt with her, and that's about all they, or she for that matter, can stand!"

"I'll call you back in a while to make sure."

"Great! I'll expect your call."

After Mark hung up, Bob called the front desk and inquired whether their checkout could be postponed until 3:00 p.m.

Having thus arranged a late checkout, Bob hung the little stamped-brass "Please Don't Disturb" sign on the outside of the room's door, shut it firmly, and set the latch.

He went into the bath and found Evelyn luxuriating in the tub.

"Did someone come in? I thought I heard the door."

"No, it was just me putting the do-not-disturb sign on the door, so no one will bother us for the next couple of hours."

The look on Evelyn's face was faux scandalized. "Whatever will we do with that time?"

"Got room for one more in there? We can talk about it while we soak."

"Yes, I do, but I cannot promise I won't take advantage of you while you're in here."

"That's all any fella could hope for."

As he stepped over the tub wall his appendage hung close to her face and she reached forward and seized it with her hand, guiding it into her mouth. A considerable portion of its length disappeared inside that orifice as she slurped and sucked greedily.

Bob had to just stand there and take such treatment like the man he was, he figured.

"I was sort of thinking on maybe using that for something else a little bit later."

Evelyn's next words were spoken around his hardening shaft, coming out muffled. "Involving me?"

"If you could join me, that would be great."

"What did you have in mind there, big boy?"

By this time Bob was fully in the tub, sitting between her legs. An interesting development of this arrangement was that the head and the first couple of inches of his now fully erect rod were sticking out insistently above the waterline, much to Evelyn's delight.

She got to her knees and reached down to her crotch. Rubbing herself gently, she transferred some of her lubricant to his *glans* area just below the head, repeating the process twice more and then beginning to rub him there gently with her thumb.

She knew from prior experience that this was extremely stimulating to a man, and particularly Bob, as it could make him produce huge quantities of cum in short order, with very little effort on her part. She also found the process quite stimulating visually for her.

However, that was not the desired outcome for this particular time; a mere stimulation was all that was desired by her at this point. So, she had to be careful not to stimulate him to the point of orgasm but, rather, to induce maximum rigidity in him for other activity, as yet unspecified.

As an practiced widow with a strong affinity for men in general, her vast experience led her to an artful mastery of the task at hand, to the point that, after she pulled the drain plug on the tub and the two of them stepped out, she was able to lead him to the bed by his fiercely erect pole and position him by hand, just so.

She laid out, legs spread wide, and he climbed on top of her and began to move the head of his shaft around at the top of her slit and then up and down, moistening it, before he sank it into her casually open hole. As he inserted himself deeper and deeper into her, his flashing dark brown eyes searched hers for any clues he was in too deep. Seeing none, and hearing nothing but moans of absolute pleasure from her, he continued to thrust himself slowly into her until he reached the point he began to slide in and out, almost to the tip before going in again, so slowly that, to an observer (if there had been one), his motion would have been almost imperceptible.

It was in the middle of this torturously exquisite pleasure that Evelyn chose to speak, slowly, through labored breathing. "Are you close to coming yet?"

Bob's reply was also hampered by forced breath. "Yeah, darling, I am! Why do you ask?"

"Well, sweetheart, and I know this is a little over the edge in eroticism. But could you pull out and shoot your load all over my chest and belly and maybe even my neck?"

"Sure thing!"

Two more quick thrusts from Bob to the full extent of his manly protrusion, and he groaned mightily. Holding his purple-tipped shaft firmly in his left hand, he guided the gushing torrent emanating from it to land on her delicate neck, on each nipple in turn, and on her belly with a diminutive reservoir forming in her navel and with even a small amount available to garnish her flaming-pink slit!

"My goodness! That was a big one, and really hot, too."

After she rubbed his outpourings into her valley and then smeared the rest into covering her belly and breasts, she did the same for her neck before she stuck her fingers into her mouth, noisily and greedily sucking them dry.

As she returned her hand to her crotch to continue her manipulations there, she again had a positioning command for Bob.

"Honey, please straddle me on your knees up here by my mouth so I can love on you a little more, before I tell you the absolutely scandalous thought I had while you were plunging that sword of yours into my scabbard."

Once again, Bob did as he was bidden, his now dangling flaccid member hanging deliciously close to Evelyn's voracious mouth. She did what he had hoped she would do, reaching up slightly and stretching it downward by hand before encircling it with her wanton orifice and its wet, tongue-swirling tunnel of delight.

"Honey, that is marvelous. Don't stop, except to tell me this 'scandalous' idea of yours, please."

She stopped long enough to speak. "Well sweetie, I just thought how, normally, I would go back into the bathtub to wash myself before we went out for supper. But what if, instead of doing that, I just let it dry right where it is and then put my clothes on over it? That way, you'd know all night long what you did for me and that I still had you on me! Our little secret, so to speak."

By this point her words came haltingly as her one hand was joined at her crotch by her other one and she began to writhe on the bed and moan.

Her mouth was once again full of Bob and stayed that way through her flailings, which gave him some very wild tuggings and pullings from her insistent oral grip.

When Bob could manage to speak during Evelyn's "oral death grip" on him, his words surprised both of them a little bit. "Honey, if that's what will keep you 'tingly' all evening, I'm all for it. A little perfume should help us be the only ones who know, I hope."

Bob brought up another subject. "When I spoke to Valentina's husband, Mark Barnes, this morning, he invited us to supper. I live there at the Woodlawn house, so it will probably be OK if you move into the room next to mine for some weeks or more. The house is spacious, and there're plenty of bathrooms close by, so we can easily be with each other as much as we want without destroying their sense of propriety. Does that sound OK to you?"

Evelyn let go to speak. "It certainly does, love, as long as it means I'm close to you. I can sneak a couple of doors down a hallway to get to you without losing my composure."

"Well, I'll call back to the house and see about tonight and whether

316 | *J.M. Hopkins*

you're to stay with us there. You go ahead and get dressed up for supper while I do that."

As she was dressing, Bob had the hotel operator connect him to the Woodlawn house. When he had Valentina herself on the line, she was quick to assure him that supper at six thirty with Evelyn was fine, and of course she was welcome to stay as long as she liked in the room across from Bob's, next to the bath. They could use the side entrance to come and go as they liked without disturbing.

Valentina did have one request for Bob over the phone, however. After looking around carefully to see who might be within earshot, and seeing no one, she spoke carefully but seriously. "Look Bob, I know you're both adults with no commitments to anyone else, and I know you've been staying in hotel rooms together till now. That's all fine with me, and I for one am happy to see you find companionship and, perhaps, even love. But could you both, while you're under this roof, do your very best to see that I don't have to answer uncomfortable questions about why Evelyn is in your room at night or what those noises in the dark were about? What the two of you do together in private is no concern of mine, as long as it doesn't affect the boys, so could I ask those simple things of you and Evelyn?"

Bob's reply was quick. "Certainly you can ask that; I'd be shocked if you didn't. Evelyn and I had already talked about this, and if we find that we can't maintain proper decorum, then it's back to the hotel with us."

"Wonderful! We'll all see you folks at half past six then."

As Bob hung up the phone, he thought about it for a moment and then called the front desk. "We're the Cunningham/Estes party in room 704, and we'll indeed be checking out promptly at three. Could I ask if we could have our bags held there at the front desk and a carriage for hire summoned to meet us at the front desk at five-thirty? We'd like to do a little shopping at Goldsmith's next door before we leave downtown, if that is all arrangeable for you.

"It is? Excellent! Thank you very much. Goodbye."

Bob looked over to find Evelyn's eyes appraising him with a profound look of admiration. "You'll do, Mr. Cunningham! You'll do, quite nicely."

After a quick checkout from the hotel (with a generous tip for all parties involved), Bob took his paramour to a little café next to Goldsmith's for a delicious light snack to tide them over till supper (after all, they *had* been quite active, up to that point). And then they went to the big department store and shopped. Evelyn purchased a light stole for her bare shoulders in case it turned cool of the evening, as well as a purse-friendly size of a very light but beautifully fragrant misting eau de parfum to carry in her clutch.

Bob got very close to her at several points and detected no unpleasant aromas emanating from her to mark the afternoon's activities. Still, he was happy when she ducked into a ladies' powder room to "freshen up" for the ride out to the Woodlawn house and came out with a distinct but not overpowering floral fragrance. This was from lightly misting her bare skin, as well as the stole, now draped loosely and comfortably over her shoulders.

The livery carriage standing in front of the hotel already had their bags aboard as they arrived at the valet stand. A healthy tip to that gentleman, and then the two were seated comfortably in the ornate vehicle and ready to depart.

"Always a pleasure to have a Cunningham in our house, sir. Come back and stay with us anytime, and you as well, milady."

Bob answered the valet's cheery farewell with a quick toss of his hand in salute, and they were off.

Evelyn's eyes glowed with soft admiration as she snuggled up closer to her robust, handsome, and most gallant man.

The driver was quite familiar with the Woodlawn house and needed no additional directions, so they proceeded apace and were there knocking on the front door in under fifteen minutes.

Mark and Valentina both met them at the front door and fawned over them all the way through the front foyer and into the living room. Their driver brought all their bags into the foyer and set them down at the base of one of the staircases, receiving a handsome tip from Bob for his troubles.

Billy and Matt were sitting quietly at the dinner table, set and ready in the dining room, just off the living room. As the adults moved into the living room, Mark motioned to the boys that they too should enter the living room. As they did, Mark instructed Billy to take "Uncle" Bob's bags up to his room and Matt to take Miss Evelyn's to the room across the hall from Bob's. A couple of trips for each lad, and the job was done, so they joined the rest of the group at the table.

Mark, as head of the household, was seated at the head, with Tina to his right and Evelyn next to her. Billy was seated to Mark's left, with Matt just beyond his brother, and Bob beyond him. Thus, Bob ended up almost directly across from Evelyn.

Throughout the evening's tasty, if less than gourmet, supper, the two were roundly occupied by the conversation aimed at them by the other participants in the supper. The boys were delighted to have their Uncle Bob back at the house, because they both adored him and were mesmerized in his presence. The myriad of things he showed them engendered a host of questions, most of which he answered by demonstrating principles of physics and science in general. History, Latin, and literature also became important learning foci for the boys.

Meanwhile, Valentina and Evelyn got on like they had known each other since grade school, chatting about this and that as they pleased. Evelyn was stricken by the massive but undeniably handsome Mark, presiding over the feast with beaming pride. She said as much to Tina, leaning over to her and presenting these views as though they were some great secret to be kept in confidence.

"That's some man you have there, Tina!"

"I can say the same for you, and I've known him since I was a baby!"

Tina kept leaning very close to Evelyn, whispering in her ear as she pointed out some pertinent thing about Bob, whom she had lived with since she was a toddler. Indeed, she knew Bob very well, including details of his physique, especially the things Maryanne Parks had told her about that fateful encounter the two of them had had together. The two women looked like schoolgirls, they were so close and chummy.

For his part in all this, Mark surveyed the suppertime repast and its participants with a combination of love and genuine satisfaction. Little did he know what awaited him in the marital bedchambers when supper was finished and the boys were sent to bed. As he and Valentina watched the striking pair of lovers climb the western staircase to the second floor, to ostensibly go to their separate rooms, they each independently noticed the plush movement of Evelyn's derriere beneath her skirts, setting each of them to thoughts of what would go on between the two before very much time had passed.

Neither said anything to the other about those thoughts.

Valentina could hardly walk to their bedchamber on the other side of the house because of the intensifying fire in her loins. It had started when first she leaned in toward Evelyn and smelled her lovely fragrance. But as the evening went along and she repeated the move, she became aware it wasn't simply the delightful floral fragrance Evelyn was wearing but, rather, something more. It was a very subtle undertone of aroma that, each time she caught a whiff of it, she wanted to put her head on Evelyn's neck and drink it in so deeply she could feel it down to her toes. The feeling passed by her crotch along the way there. She burned with imagination for what those two could be doing to each other, even right now.

Her hand dropped to Mark's tight, sturdy waist as she encircled it and held herself close to his muscular chest, walking a little more clumsily because of it, but relishing the closeness until they could go in and latch the door and she could ravish her man thoroughly. She and Mark had so few of these undisturbed nights together, what with the boys being so active at all hours, that she wanted this one to be something he would cherish.

The other randy couple was busily taking up where they had left off earlier, Bob with his head buried between his beauty's legs and she trying to be as silent as possible during the waves of pleasure he was creating with his tongue. He had already wiped clean her earlier musk (which had so intoxicated Valentina) with his trusty tongue, and now it felt as if he were trying to lick her navel from the inside. As her juices ran rampant, she prepared to receive his plunging staff and its marvelous outpouring.

Across the house, as Tina undid Mark's trouser fastenings and stripped off his shirt, she was delighted to see that his manhood, though not as long as she knew Bob's to be, was extended to its fully ample length and swollen to its amazingly thick girth and already oozing a little lubricant from the tip.

Letting him lie comfortably on his back with his thick appendage jutting forcefully upward, Tina straddled her husband, treating him to an absolutely stimulating view as she did. Rubbing herself as she prepared her loins to receive him, she settled her profoundly moist love canal over his shaft, relaxed, and sank herself down with a sharp intake of breath. Riding his amazing trunk in impassioned abandon as she struggled mightily to not scream with delight, Angelina knew this night would be very special indeed.

A little later that very evening, Robert Oskar Cunningham and Angelina Louise Barnes were each conceived, practically within minutes of each other.

Young Billy and Matt, having consumed a hearty supper each and sated as well by lots of conversation, slept soundly through the noises of passion coming from both ends of the Woodlawn house that night.

Chapter 19

THE END OF AN ERA

(Clarence) Saunders was a bit of an iconoclast. For the store's (the first "Piggly Wiggly") opening ceremonies, Saunders promised to hold a "beauty contest" that he advertised in local newspapers. "At the door Saunders shook their hands and gave to their children flowers and balloons," Freeman writes. "Newspaper reporters posing as contest judges awarded five and ten dollar gold coins to every woman, while the supply lasted. A brass band serenaded the visitors in the lobby."

—Mike Freeman for the Tennessee Historical
Quarterly/Tennessee Historical Society

1925–1929

Valentina and Evelyn had had fun being pregnant together. They'd shopped; planned; exchanged dreams and desires for the future; and, in short, became fast friends for life. They shared continual reflective dismay over the changes to their bodies, although Tina had already been through this successfully twice before and was able to coach her slightly older but inexperienced maternity mate through the entire nine-month process.

Evelyn and Bob had gotten married about three weeks after that memorable first night in the Woodlawn house, and the wedding was held there. All the family in residence attended, as did several friends and neighbors.

As a widow with no prior ties to the Bluff City, Evelyn had no family there, sadly.

Bob had called the Jonesboro homestead (they had a phone there now!) and informed the family of his impending nuptials, causing delight to run rampant through that entire household. Tat and Angelina, along with Bob's younger brothers Chet and Mel (the latter of whom was just about to go off to Eastern Arkansas College) represented the Jonesboro elements of the family.

Unfortunately, at almost ninety-one years of age, Oskar Cunningham was reckoned to not be up to the journey but sent his congratulations via the others.

He had a full-time nurse to help care for him, and these days (having retired from the bench in 1920), he stayed at the house constantly, occasionally spending long restful lounges on the front porch in his favorite chair just watching the sawmill operate and reflecting on his almost fifty years there in Arkansas.

There had certainly been some changes and accomplishments along the way.

Bob and Evelyn would be traveling back to Jonesboro with Tat, Angelina, and Mel. Bob wanted to visit his father and introduce his new bride to Oskar, and Chet would be staying on in Memphis to begin work on a grand new residence being built over on Central Avenue.

◆

Bob Cunningham had been back to Jonesboro in 1922 for a working visit with his father. Using the newly opened Harahan Bridge over the Mississippi, rail traffic between Memphis and any point in Arkansas (and, indeed, anywhere in the West!) was greatly improved. And this had expanded freight shipments by rail into Memphis; this included shipments of lumber from the C&H (Cunningham and Haskins) Lumber Company into customers there, primarily the E. L. Bruce hardwood operation. Bruce had moved its headquarters and much of its manufacturing operations to Memphis from Arkansas the previous year, and business for the sawmill was improving daily.

Bob had been appointed to be executor of the Cunningham family's fortunes when the time came that Oskar would pass. As that time drew nearer, more and more often, he was called back to lend advice or be updated to changes in those fortunes.

The trip to Jonesboro in 1925 with his new bride was no exception. Happy as Oskar was to see his oldest son finally begin to be setting down roots (no one knew Evelyn was pregnant yet, not even Evelyn), Oskar still had things he wanted to discuss with Bob, such as passing on the control of the mill completely to Angelina as part of her inheritance. That item of business (which Bob heartily agreed with), was joined by a number of others to be discussed, as the old judge worked through what he expected to be the final version of his will.

Chet had also been back and forth from Memphis several times during this span of years, having bought a 1920 Ford TT truck for his carpentry work, which had been steadily increasing in quantity and revenue.

Lately, there had been rumors that Chet might have met someone romantically, and Bob was happy for his kid brother, even though the relationship was in the very early stages.

For the last several months, Chet had been a finish carpenter on the giant house going up for Clarence Saunders, out on Central Avenue. Saunders had invented a thing he called a "supermarket," which he named Piggly Wiggly and which was wildly popular. It turned out to be so well-liked, in fact, that by now there were at least nine stores in Memphis.

What made the invention so successful was that customers no longer had to wait for a clerk to assemble their order from bulk materials, weighing dry goods and counting out items. Now, all shoppers had to do was select products from shelves full of prepackaged, ready-to-buy items and then proceed to the clerk to pay for their purchase. The supermarket even provided handbaskets to put your selections into for convenient carrying.

The women of the Woodlawn house loved going to the Piggly Wiggly. The novelty of self-shopping made each trip to the store a social occasion—at least until they got so large with pregnancy that they had to forego their weekly visits.

The babies were born a little more than a day apart, little cherub Angelina Louise Barnes on a Wednesday at three in the afternoon and bouncy little Robert Oskar Cunningham on Friday at one o'clock in the morning.

Over the next couple of months, life changed, once again, for the men of the house. The things they had learned to live with during pregnancy were replaced with a whole new set of needs and demands.

For Mark, these were things he'd been through twice before. So, he was invaluable in helping Bob, a first-timer, cope with the awakenings at night, the sleep deprivation, and the other requirements of being a new father.

Bob learned quickly and well.

The final journey home to Memphis came for Oskar a little after his ninety-first birthday. The once laughing little toddler, content to have his big brother, Bobby, splash him incessantly in the creek flowing by their Texas prairie cabin had excelled in school subjects (including Latin). He'd graduated from college as the first in his family to do so and had successfully read for and practiced law. As a family leader, he'd shepherded his family to Arkansas, away from yellow fever. The sawmill he'd begun, from an interest formed when he was a little boy, was still earning a major income for his family, and he had sat on the bench as county judge for almost twenty years.

Now, he was gone.

By any measure, it had been a full life, well-lived.

Oskar came to rest at Woodlawn right by his older brother, Bobby, who he had cherished and looked up to for all of his days and for all of his accomplishments.

Robert W. Cunningham lay somewhere beneath the courtyard soil of the crumbling old Texas mission known as the Alamo, and his beloved bride Angie lay beneath the Arkansas soil at the Jonesboro homestead. Their two wonderful sons lay side by side at last there in Memphis, along with their devoted stepfather, Val Dimand.

Oskar was at last reunited with his lost little girl, Rose Ellen, there in that beautiful setting at Woodlawn.

Bob, Chet, and Melvin Cunningham stood up tall as they finished the ceremony. Like the prior generation of Cunninghams just finished, their generation was destined to go their separate ways, meeting up when they could and also being apart when they must. A whole new chapter in the Cunningham family story would shortly begin to unfold.

AUTHOR'S NOTES

The Bethel House was inspired by the house in which I spent most of my boyhood. At the time our family moved in (about 1957, or so) it was reputed to be over 100 years old. We lived there until the summer of 1965 (I believe; no one is left alive to ask!), and it stood for at least another fifteen or twenty years. Its construction is much as I have described the house at 686 Bethel to be, to the best of my memory. Being a kid at the time, with no interest whatever in architecture, my description will not be 100% accurate, but hopefully, close enough to give the flavor of the old house to the reader.

By the time I lived there, fireplaces were covered up with cast-iron fronts to block chimney drafts, and the attic was a spooky, "off-limits-to-kids" mystery, as was the sometimes flooded basement. Between gaps in the worn-away floorboards in my room, as a kid I could see down into the basement just well enough to discern that I really didn't want to go down there anyway.

The attic, however, was a different story. Mom and Dad would not let any of us kids (I had two brothers and one sister) go up into the attic, because it was "dangerous", perhaps because of the dormer windows at each end causing vertigo in my Mom. She was so highly afraid of any harm from falling out for any of us kids that the door was kept locked, and so we never got to see the view I have described in the book as "so magnificent".

Everything else - the oak, the uphill drive, the fence, the out-buildings, the garden, and the orchard - where I spent many happy childhood days up in a tree alongside my little brother – they were all there as I described them, with a hundred years of "wear and tear" on them.

686 Bethel was a wonderfully-shabby home to grow up in!

Robert W. Cunningham's parents did settle (with the rest of their family) sometime in the late 1820s or early-to-mid 1830s in Arkansas.

Dallas grew mightily from the "dusty, one-horse cow-town" that Val Dimand and Bobby Cunningham experienced in 1863. It went through many "tearing-down-and-rebuilding" cycles along the way. The Val Dimand tomahawk mark was still there in the Imperial bar top in Dallas when the old saloon/hotel was torn down in 1908.

The "Walker" model Colt revolver was reckoned to be the most powerful handgun ever made, until the introduction of the .357 "Magnum" revolver in 1938.

Angelina (Estes/Dimand) Haskins sold the sawmill to a Jonesboro lumber conglomerate during the Depression years before World War II, adding to the Cunningham/Dimand family fortunes, then she and Tat moved back to Memphis, moving in for a short while with Valentina and Mark into the Woodlawn House. Angelina lived until 1937 (almost 100 years old); Tat had passed in 1935 at 98.

The Barnes family moved from the Woodlawn House after World War II; the old painting of Robert W. Cunningham was lost or stolen during the move; it was never found and has not been seen since.

Oskar's son Bob flourished as an architect who, with his wife Evelyn, moved back to Memphis and they clung lovingly to one another there where he had been born; he died peacefully at home in 1960. Evelyn passed in a rest home in 1970.

Because the new owners of the Cunningham family property in Jonesboro when it was sold in 1977 did not intend to keep care of the family gravesites on the homestead, Dix Cunningham had the remains of Angie and Ruthie disinterred and transferred to the family plot in Shady Grove Cemetery in Memphis. There they joined their beloved, nestled around the empty grave for Robert W. Cunningham, his magnificent stone marker in the center of monuments for Bobby and Oskar, Val and Angie, Beverly, Ruthie and Henrietta, and little Rose Ellen. Bob, Evelyn, Angelina and Tat came to reside there, as well. That one cemetery section chronicles more than one hundred years of history of a single family nestled in shady rest. More graves would be added in future years.

Printed in the USA
CPSIA information can be obtained
at www.ICGtesting.com
LVHW092053240823
756176LV00030B/1399/J